The Signature

The Signature

DANIEL R. McARTHUR

RESOURCE *Publications* • Eugene, Oregon

THE SIGNATURE

All Scripture quotations, unless otherwise indicated, are taken from the Holy Bible, New International Version®, NIV®. Copyright ©1973, 1978, 1984, 2011 by Biblica, Inc.™ Used by permission of Zondervan. All rights reserved worldwide. www.zondervan.com The "NIV" and "New International Version" are trademarks registered in the United States Patent and Trademark Office by Biblica, Inc.™

"As We Gather" by Dan and Theresa McArthur Copyright © 1987 Dan and Theresa McArthur All rights reserved. Used by permission

"Into Your Presence" by Dan and Theresa McArthur Copyright © 1997 Dan and Theresa McArthur All Rights reserved. Used by Permission

The Signature is a work of fiction. Names, characters, places, and incidents either are the product of the author's imagination or are used fictionally. Any resemblance to actual persons, living or dead, events or locales is entirely coincidental.

Resource Publications
An Imprint of Wipf and Stock Publishers
199 W. 8th Ave., Suite 3
Eugene, OR 97401

www.wipfandstock.com

PAPERBACK ISBN: 978-1-7252-5445-9
HARDCOVER ISBN: 978-1-7252-5446-6
EBOOK ISBN: 978-1-7252-5447-3

Manufactured in the U.S.A. 01/23/20

This book is dedicated to my wonderful wife,
Theresa McArthur, who without her encouragement
I might have never finished this book.

Contents

Acknowledgements   ix

Introduction   xi

1   Encounter   1

2   Fleeing   21

3   Adventure   33

4   Promises   51

5   Betrayal   66

6   Explosion   83

7   New Life   98

8   New Essence   111

9   New Existence   124

10   Retaliation   139

11   Homecoming   148

12   Prayer   168

13   Resolution   189

14   Truth   196

15   Reunion   211

16   Restoration   221

Epilogue: One Year Later   239

Acknowledgements

THERE ARE SOME PEOPLE whom I want to give praise and thanks to. First off, my wife, who did so much of the original editing taking off the rough edges and smoothing out my writing. Also for her ideas that helped form some of the story. Thank-you to my children, Shonda Mangabhai, Lisha Fine, Robby McArthur, Charis Barrins and Andy McArthur, whom I sent copies of the book to as I wrote it so I could receive their thoughts.

I want to also thank my mom, Barbara McArthur, who sowed a love of books into my life. Mom read all the time and encouraged me and my brothers to read. I'm glad she did. It has made my life a much larger place to live in.

There were others who helped with editing at different times. Gwynneth Wannell, former principal of the Teacher Training Centre in Gweru, Zimbabwe; Juliyah Cruywagen, a good friend in South Africa who spent lots of time reading my manuscript and correcting where it was needed; Barbara Warren founder and president of Blue Mountain Editorial Services who kindly donated her professional editing.

Thanks also to so many others like Pastors Chinyoka, Mpofu Sr. and Jr., Hlambelo, Michael, Joule, Sibanda, Kamupandi, Khuleya, and Dziwedziwe. These men, along with their wives, have taught me so much about cultures and beliefs in Africa.

The world is such a big place with so many different cultures, but the one thing that draws us all together is Jesus Christ, the son of God. If it wasn't for him, I wouldn't even know these people. He brought us all together and I'm thankful for it. Thank you Lord for loving all of us in such a special way.

Introduction

IN 2008 I WAS on furlough visiting a new church in Joliet, Illinois. On that Sunday Morning I woke up and remembered the amazing dream I had dreamed. As I told the dream to my wife I commented that it would make a great story thinking maybe she could write it. I wrote down the dream that morning and then, as often happen, got busy with life. A few months later, realizing my wife wasn't going to write the story, I got my laptop out and started writing. I would write in my spare time so it took several years to finish that first rough draft. I loved seeing the characters come to life. I would talk about them to my family as if they were real. After many edits and rewrites the book was finally finished and eleven years later Wipf and Stock Publishers agreed to publish my book. I was elated.

A lot of exciting things happened during the writing of this book. There are many miracles written into the story, some of the miracles I had seen in my ministry but others were inspired by the Holy Spirit and my imagination. As time passed, though, my wife and I began to experience the reality of some of the miracles that I had written about in the story. As my wife and I prayed for a drunk lady, she became instantly sober. An elderly gentleman who complained of his legs hurting when he walked, was instantly healed and he had no more pain. The evidence of God's power in healing and miracles is a testimony to the world of his great love.

The story takes place in Zimbabwe, and Zambia, Africa. I lived with my wife, Theresa, and five children in Zimbabwe for twenty–eight years as a missionary. My ministry wasn't just in Zimbabwe. During my years of service I traveled to Zambia, Botswana, South Africa, and Mozambique ministering to the people there as well.

Many of the fictional towns, locations and people in the story derive their names from real places in Southern Africa but they may not share the actual geographical or time frame placement. For example, the story speaks of a fictional big game park between Kafue and Lusaka and there is no NGO named MAWFA.

People ask me why I have given English names to the African people in my story. Many African countries were colonized by Great Britain. Therefore, many African men and women have English names in Zimbabwe and Zambia such as Mary, Martha, Alfred and Alex. Their last names, though, are always African like Mpofu, Dube, Sibanda and Tembo.

Both Zimbabwe and Zambia are beautiful countries. Religion is very serious amongst the people groups of both countries and on Sunday mornings it's always a joy to see people all dressed up, Bibles in hand, heading to church.

A few years ago the president of Zambia declared Zambia to be a Christian nation. Even with a declaration such as this there are still many who do not know Jesus and what he has done for them. As you read this book, remember to pray for the people of Africa.

1

Encounter

"Hans, I need you to make a run to Harare." Director, Charles Lizer, had his head down looking at some papers on his desk. He glanced up at Hans, "There are four new recruits coming this afternoon, I need you to go and welcome them."

He handed Hans a folder and started shuffling papers on his desk, Hans knew he was dismissed. As he walked out he looked at the papers in the folder. One was the requisition needed for a vehicle and fuel, the other was the information on the new recruits and the time of their arrival. Looking at his watch, he realized he had to hustle to get to Harare on time.

As Hans walked out Charles and his secretary watched him. They saw the children run away from him to hide behind trees and bushes. With a sigh Charles said, "He loves people so much, it's such a shame so many of the Africans fear him because of his size."

"How tall is he sir?" asked his secretary.

"His medical record said he was six feet eight inches tall, and with all those muscles his shoulders are almost as wide as the doorway."

The secretary thought for a moment then replied, "I think his swarthy complexion and longer black hair also make him look a little like a pirate."

"Yes, that hair," the director said, shaking his head. "He's cut it some, but it's still a little long.

I know he joined the NGO because of his desire to help others. I wish people would accept him."

"Don't worry, sir, I'm sure they will in time."

Hans had been in Zimbabwe for just six months working for MAWFA, an acronym for Medicine And Water For All, a non–governmental organization from the Netherlands. It was just what he wanted. He'd been the foreman for a construction company in Holland and was, he thought, recruited to help run a crew, but so far all he'd done was drive the director around to meetings and pick up new recruits. He'd thought he would be a part of the crew that went out to the rural areas digging wells and building clinics. Something that would make a difference in people's lives.

"Hi Jorge, I need a big vehicle to go and pick up four new recruits. Two women and two men plus all their luggage."

"Well you better take the Land Cruiser, it will be a little more comfortable for those rookies, plus you'll have enough room for all the junk they brought with them that they'll not be able to use out here in the bush," Jorge quipped.

"Is it full of fuel? I need to get going. With all the rain the road's like a washboard now. It'll probably take me six hours just to get to the Karoi–Harare road. Then another couple hours to get to the airport. I'll be pushing it to get there before they land."

Although in a hurry, Hans added an extra few minutes to his trip by taking a detour in order to help an elderly neighbor woman transport her two goats to her house. He hoped that the vehicle would air out before he picked up the four new recruits, but if it didn't, that was okay too, since they were going to have to get used to new smells once they arrived.

When he finally got to the tarred road it was only two more hours to Harare. He stopped at Ander's petrol station for fuel and a cold Coke.

"What's new with you, Chris?"

"Well, not much. I told you that my wife and kids went to South Africa, didn't I?" Chris, the owner of the petrol station, spoke with the happy English/Zimbabwe accent that endeared them to so many people.

"No, I don't think you did. The violence was just too much, hey?"

"Not so much the violence. It's pretty quiet in our area. The violence seems to only break out in the rural areas. The problem is traveling and the shortages in the shops. I went out yesterday to buy some milk and there wasn't any in town. I also needed bread and I had to buy it from a guy on the street. He came over to my car with the bread in a box all covered up. I handed him the money, he shoved the bread in my car, then turned and quickly walked away. I felt like I was buying drugs or something. It's just become too hard for Katie."

"Wow! I hadn't realized things were getting that bad."

"You probably wouldn't hear way out where you are and you probably send someone to buy food for everyone in the compound each week."

"That's true. I only go to town when I'm picking someone up or taking someone to the airport."

The conversation continued for some minutes centered on the situation in the country. Soon Hans was back on the road again traveling through Karoi and headed for Harare to the airport.

Hans arrived just as the plane was landing and right away was able to recognize the four he was to pick up. It was winter in the Netherlands and summer in Zimbabwe; they were the very white, pale–looking creatures. He grinned as he looked at them.

Then he saw her. As she disembarked from the plane, a wisp of her long blond hair blew in her face. She was wearing a white dress and he thought she looked like an angel. He had never seen anyone so beautiful.

Once the four had been cleared through customs, he went over and introduced himself.

Trying not to stare at the pretty girl, he shook his head to clear it.

"Hi, I'm Hans Grundey here to pick you up and take you to the MAW-FA compound. Welcome to Zimbabwe."

"Hi, I'm Ingrid Van Devander, this is Corrie Filer, Willem Dreijer, and Gerrit Nagel."

Hans shook hands with all of them but didn't really notice the other three, nor did he catch their names. He only had eyes for Ingrid, this angel in white. He led the way to the car and opened the back. Picking up the suitcases that were on the ground beside her, he loaded them in the car, the whole time trying to watch her every move without obviously appearing to stare. Shutting the back of the car, he hurried over to open the door for Ingrid. The four all stood there looking a little perplexed.

Willem asked, "Would you like all of our suitcases in there?"

Embarrassment flooded over Hans when he realized that he only loaded Ingrid's suitcases and none of the others.

"Sorry, I wasn't thinking," he mumbled as he opened the back again and placed the remainder of the luggage in.

The other three all glanced at Ingrid, who just smiled.

Hans didn't remember what he said or any of the conversation on the return trip. He didn't even notice the hot dusty road as they traveled. All he could think about was her. He knew he was in love.

Ingrid Van Devander had dreamed of being a nurse even as a child. When one of her childhood friends got hurt she was the first on the scene to see what she could do to help. Small in stature, she made up for it in her tenacity. There was nothing that Ingrid wouldn't do to help people. One day while visiting the local Rotary Club she saw pictures of children in Africa that needed help. She was only a junior at university at the time, but she knew this is where she wanted to go and work. It took seven years but now here she was in Zimbabwe.

"It's so warm here. When we left it was snowing. Look I'm still carrying my coat." She patted her coat that was still on her lap then handed it back. "Here, Willem, could you put this back with our things? Thank you."

Hans looked over at Ingrid and smiled, "The weather here is nice all the time. The winters can get a little cold, but even the cold here warms up with the sun."

With the windows rolled down Ingrid's hair was getting blown so she reached in her purse and pulled out a hair band, quickly wrapping her hair in a ponytail. "That's better. I guess short hair would be more suitable here."

"I don't know about that, but I do know that the African children will love your hair. They don't very often see blond hair, so you will be a novelty."

Hans and Ingrid talked almost the entire way to the compound. The other three, feeling the jetlag, fell asleep in the back seat.

When they arrived back at the compound it was late. "Well, I guess we better see where you need to go. Wait here while I find someone who can help us."

Ingrid, in a slightly dazed state, looked around. The last hour she too had succumbed to sleep. "It's so dark here. I really can't see anything much, can any of you?"

"No," came the reply from the back seat. Corrie opened her door. "I really need to stretch my legs. Do you think it's safe to get out?" She turned and dangled her legs out the door.

"I don't know. Hans just walked out. Do you think there are lions around?"

Never had someone turned, pulled her legs in, and shut the door as fast as Corrie did. "I think I'll wait to stretch until he gets back."

Just then Hans came from around the corner. Motioning to them to get out of the car he said, "They've decided to put you up in the teacher's house by the school. There's no one there right now, so it will just be the four of you. If everyone would grab their bags, I've got a couple guys here to help also, we can just walk there."

"Is it safe?" Corrie wasn't going to go traipsing around if there were lions anywhere.

"Yes, it's perfectly safe here. I'll walk in front, then if there are any snakes they will hear me coming and take off."

"Snakes?" both girls said in unison as all four of them looked down at the ground.

Hans smiled, "Don't worry, we haven't had any snake bite problems since yesterday."

Ingrid reached over and playfully slapped Hans on the shoulder. She knew he was joking with them. "Don't do that, Corrie has had a hard time really wanting to come to Africa, don't scare her off."

"I'm just joking Corrie. There's not a lot of snakes around because too many people live here and it's true that most of the snakes are more afraid of you. Since they live on the ground, they can feel the vibration of our walking so they take off and get out of the way."

"Well okay, but you go first and I'll stomp as loud as I can just to make sure they don't come back after you walk by."

The teacher's house was a small rectangular house with regular windows and a small front porch. Hans opened the unlocked door, reached in and flipped on the lights. They were greeted with a fairly large room with five doors, two on each side and one in the rear. There was a couch and chair in the room but nothing else.

"This is the common living room." Walking to the first door on the right Hans opened it and flipped on the light. Nothing happened. "I guess the bulb has blown out. Ishmail could you go and get another globe? Wait, let's check and see if the others need one too."

Ishmail, Willem, Garret and Hans all opened the other doors to see if the lights worked. "Okay Ishmail it looks like we need two light globes." Reaching in his pocket Hans took out a set of keys, "This one opens the door and this one opens the cupboard. *Ndatenda*, thank you." Turning back to the four newcomers, "These are your bedrooms for tonight. Tomorrow you'll be assigned a house to live in, since you are single you'll probably share a house, men in one and women in the other. Some of the women are coming to make the beds. The sheets are clean, but from the hospital so may be stained. They should be here soon."

Hans walked over to the back door. "This is your kitchen. I know you don't have any food yet. The main kitchen is preparing food for you now. You'll get to eat the staple diet of Zimbabwe, *sadza* and chicken with a side of relish. We'll also have tea things brought in for the morning. They drink a lot of tea here. This country was a British colony and that tradition has stuck. The driver will go into town tomorrow to buy groceries for you. I know you don't have any money yet, so the company will foot your bill this time. I need you to make up a grocery list tonight so that we can give it to the driver. Do you have any paper?"

Ingrid spoke up, "Yes, I have paper. Should we do that now?"

"It's probably best that you do it now since you're still awake and if you have any questions about what you can get I can answer them."

Ingrid dug into her carry-on bag and pulled out a small notebook. She had two pens and gave one to the men along with a piece of paper.

"Remember, you're in a third world country so there are some things you can't get. There are no microwave popcorn, or frozen dinners. Most of what you have to cook will be from scratch. The driver will go to the grocery store, the vegetable market, the butchery and the bread store. I've also given him a list of items like candles, matches, soap, laundry soap, toilet paper and other items that you will need that you might not think of. All you have to do is write down what food stuff you will need. Don't forget desserts. If you want cookies or chocolate put it down. They don't have the same brands as us and it taste different, but you will get used to it."

They all started talking about what they would want and making a list. Garret hadn't spoken much since he arrived in Zimbabwe, "Uh, what is this sadzy stuff you're going to feed us?"

"*Sadza* is the main food that the Africans eat. It's a very thick corn meal mush that is served with either meat or vegetables. The normal African family will eat this two times a day at least, sometimes three. To an African if they haven't eaten *sadza*, they haven't eaten. Try it, it's really good. Even if you don't like the *sadza*, you'll love the chicken that they cook with it. It's rural chicken so it's lean and very tasty. The relish is usually a mixture of tomatoes and onions cooked in oil. Sometimes they will use a green vegetable called covo or rape."

"Well, I'll try it, I'm famished."

The others all nodded in agreement. They had stopped at Chris's petrol station in Karoi for fuel and had a Coke and some chips, but it wasn't enough and they were all hungry now.

"Choose a room and put your bags in, supper will be here soon." Ishmail arrived at that moment and they got the light bulbs changed. Each room had a bed and night table next to it.

"This will be fine Hans," Ingrid said as she came out of her room. "I don't know if I'm more tired or hungry. Here's our list, I hope it's everything we need."

"I'll look them over and make sure you have enough. Once you get used to having someone go to the store for you it will be easier." Hans replied glancing at the list.

"Here's the food now, come on out and have a seat."

The four of them sat on the couch and chair. Someone had brought a wooden chair for Hans to sit on.

One of the women had a large red plastic bowl and a pitcher. She went over to Hans and he held his hands over the bowl as she poured water. "Here, you must wash your hands before you eat. Someone will always come with water to wash with first." He shook the water off his hands as she handed him a towel to dry with. Next she went to Willem then Garret. After they had washed she went to Ingrid and last Corrie.

Hans explained, "Everything is done in a specific way. They had me wash first and they will serve me first because I am the oldest here." As he was talking other women started handing out plates of food and true to what Hans was saying he received food first.

"This is done out of respect."

Confused Ingrid queried, "But I'm older than either Willem or Garret and they washed their hands before me, and look they are being served already."

"Yes, this is the way things are done here. The men are served first, but did you notice that you washed before Corrie? They respected you because you are older than Corrie."

"This doesn't seem right. I don't know if I like it."

"Women's lib hasn't made it very far here especially in a rural area like this. Did you notice that when they held the water and bowl and when they served us they got on their knees to do it? It's part of their tradition and as an NGO we are not here to change their traditions, but to help in other ways."

"But what if their traditions are wrong?"

"There are missionaries with the church that can address that. Our job is to drill boreholes and start clinics. Don't worry, you'll get used to all of the things that are done here."

Garret again spoke up. "Uh I hate to be a bother, but how are we supposed to eat the food, they didn't bring any utensils to eat with."

"Like this." Hans reached into his *sadza* and took a small amount, rolled it in a ball, dipped it in the relish and popped it in his mouth. "You eat with the utensils that you were born with." Smiling he watched as each one reached in and started eating.

"Why this is very good. I don't know if it's because I'm so hungry or not, but I really like *sadza*." Ingrid took a piece of chicken and ate it, "Wow, this chicken is really good. It's moist and full of flavor."

All agreed and finished their supper in quick order. "It's also a tradition to wash after you eat, mainly to get the bits of *sadza* off that is stuck to your hands." Hans went over to where the plastic bowl was. There was already water in it and placed his hands in the water to wash. He rubbed and rubbed to remove the *sadza*. Then took the towel and dried. "You are expected to wash in the same water if it gets too dirty we will change it, but for the most part you'll have to use dirty water to wash." Nodding toward the kitchen he said, "Afterwards you can wash with soap in the sink."

After they had all finished their meal Hans left to allow them to sleep. As he stretched out in his own bed he again thought of Ingrid. "I think I'll marry you," he said to the darkness.

The next morning the four newcomers were greeted by the head of the NGO, Charles Lizer. "I guess the first thing we need to do is get you all settled in your houses." Pointing to a map of the compound he continued, "We have singles houses that will allow two of you to share a house. It's easier since there are two men and two women who came this time. I live with my family here," he said pointing to the map. "Hans lives next door to me here. He has his own house because of his status with the NGO. Right now he's my right–hand man, but we're making changes and soon he will be the one in charge of a crew that will travel throughout the country, starting and building clinics and drilling boreholes. We are setting up three crews with someone in charge of each. The leaders will answer to me and their crew will answer to them. I don't know right now if any of you will be on his crew, we are still putting them together." Charles rambled on about the work that they would do and how the crews would work.

"One of the most important details that you will need to know is about Jason Deke. He's a bandit that is running around the country side trying to change the government. I don't know if he's a good guy or a bad guy at this stage. He's keeping the government in check right now. A lot of the local people are calling him Robin Hood. He is taking from the government and giving to the people but he's also taking some things from the people and it's causing problems. You'll find out soon that the government control all prices and owns many companies. So he takes from them or destroys them. The problem is that he has no way to supply the need that he has taken away."

Charles looked at each one of the newcomers, "Even though our embassy is watching the situation you are not allowed to go out of the compound unless you are on a work detail or with the people who know what to do. If things get too bad the embassy will get us out. It's only a handful of men that are with Deke, but rebels breed rebels and before long there will be others here causing problems. So stay close."

Hans was in the room during this talk to the newcomers. It was a surprise to him to find out that soon he would be in charge of his own crew. He hadn't realized that the boss had been grooming him for this position. He spoke up now, "I met a few of these rebels. I was in one of the work areas where we were setting up a clinic. They came rushing in with two injured men. We treated them as best we could and they left. They were very nice to us, but like Mr. Lizer said, people are drawn to someone like Deke and there will be some people who are mean and nasty. Stay with your groups."

As Hans spoke Ingrid couldn't help noticing his dark wavy hair. It's a little long, she thought to herself, but with those broad shoulders it doesn't look too bad.

Hans had not gone unnoticed by Ingrid. When she walked out of the plane he was the first person that she saw mainly because he stood a head taller than everyone else, but she also thought he was a very handsome man. On the ride to the compound he was so easy to talk to. She was glad that the others had allowed her to sit up front with him.

Her thoughts were in a whirl, he seems to like me, does he? Oh, what was Mr. Lizer saying? Break time, oh good I could use a break.

As Ingrid got up from her chair Corrie whispered to her, "Ingrid, I have to go to the bathroom do you know where it is?"

"No I don't have any idea, I have to go too. I'll go find out."

Just then Charles Lizer announced, "Oh the facilities are out back of this building, they are Blair toilets, or outhouses, whatever you want to call them. The design was made by a man named Blair that came up with a way that the flies don't bother you. It's a unique construction and it's what we build in the rural areas. They are simple to make . . ."

As Charles rambled on the girls who needed a break walked on out and around back.

This is going to be an exciting time I think. What do you think of Hans? He's huge isn't he? Reminds me of a Neanderthal or something like that. Maybe he's really a giant, you know like in Jack and the Beanstalk."

"Corrie, don't talk like that. He's a very nice man and he seems to be very knowledgeable about everything that goes on here. I hope that I get on his crew. I think he will get more done than most."

"Oh, do I detect a little bit of Cupid working here?" Corrie had that knowing glimmer in her eye. "He does have a very handsome face."

Ingrid looked over at Corrie with a little apprehension. "Yes he is very handsome."

"Don't worry Ingrid, I'm not interested in Hans. He's all yours."

They had arrived at the facilities by this time. It was a long thin building, shorter than the building they had just come from. Each end had a doorway with some writing on the side, but it was in the Shona language. They knew it said Men and Women, but since neither of the girls knew Shona they weren't sure which door they should go in. An African man was walking by at that moment. He pointed to the door on the right, "*Vakadzi*, Woman. This is the side you want." then walked on to where he was going.

"Well that is a very good thing to know." Both of them laughed but also felt a little apprehension of learning a new language.

When the girls got back the director was just finishing up. "Sorry, I know we are supposed to be on break. Go ahead and take a fifteen minutes break."

Willem and Garrit got up and went over to the girls.

"Boy I didn't think he was ever going to stop about the toilets." Garret was stretching his arms in the air. "I wonder if we had walked out like you girls if he would have carried on talking?"

"Don't talk so loud Garrit, someone might hear you." Willem whispered. "If you'll excuse me I need to go inspect those Blair toilets that he was talking about."

Hans had gotten up and went over to where the coffee was. He picked up two cups and filled them. Not knowing what Ingrid would like he left his cup on the table and carried the coffee, sugar and cream over to her. "Here you are Ingrid, I didn't know how you like it so I brought everything."

"Why thank you Hans. I like one sugar and just a tiny bit of cream." She went ahead and put the sugar and cream in while Hans held her cup. Taking her cup she took a sip. "Now that's just what I needed."

Hans started walking to return the condiments and pick up his coffee and Ingrid followed. "Where is your home in Holland, Hans?"

"I'm from Venlo in the Limburg province. I grew up and lived there until I came to work for MAWFA."

"Well, that explains your last name. It's German isn't it?"

"Yes, my family left during World War II to get away from Hitler. My grandfather could see that it was not going to go well in Germany. I still have some family there but don't really know them."

"I've never been to Venlo, isn't that funny, it's only around 150 kilometers from my home, but I've never been there, and now we meet here in Zimbabwe, Africa. I think Corrie's family is from around there though."

"Hmmm, I've never heard of any Filer's around where I lived." Hans was thinking, Wow! She lived so close, but he had never had any occasion to meet her. "I could be wrong." Ingrid was glad to find out that Corrie wasn't from the same area. It seemed like people from the Netherlands like to stick by people from their areas. "I'm from Deventer in the Overijssel province. My ancestors started the town but used a different spelling. If you ever owned a Burgers bicycle, it came from Deventer. In fact my uncle was the manager there."

"I did own a Burgers bike," was Hans surprised reply, "it was a really good bike. I think it's still at my parents' house hung up somewhere in a barn or garage. I used to ride that bike everywhere."

"Well there you go. We're almost related." Both laughed at the joke.

Mr. Lizer was calling everyone back to their seats. When Ingrid got back to her chair Corrie mischievously asked, "How did it go? Are you engaged yet?"

"Hush Corrie, He'll hear you."

The meeting went on all day. Whatever else Mr. Charles Lizer the director of MAWFA did was nothing compared to his ability to talk. The four newcomers got the entire history of the NGO plus a lot of other information that they would never use. Toward the end of the meeting he did make a statement that made Ingrid's heart fly. "The four of you will be starting tomorrow to get to know the people and how we work here. Hans will be in charge. I am not going to send you out to any new zones yet. I know that some of you are trained in specialized areas, but you will be doing other types of jobs first. I want to see how you work together and your strengths and weaknesses. I've given Hans a list of things that need to be done around the compound so you will report to him at 7:00 tomorrow morning for assignments."

There were some groans when he announced the time.

"Don't be put off with the early time. You'll find that here in Zimbabwe you have twelve hours of daylight and twelve hours of night. The sun comes up around 6:00 am and most people are already up and have their day going. So 7:00 is a late start. Please have a nice evening and a good sleep tonight and we'll see you tomorrow. Oh yes, wear old clothes tomorrow. You'll probably get dirty."

With that Mr. Lizer picked up his papers and left the room. "Okay now what do we do with the rest of the evening?" Willem wanted to know.

Hans spoke up, "There's not a lot to do here. Behind your house there's a basketball court, but it's only a half court. A lot of times the guys will play a game after they get off work. You'll learn that with it getting dark at 6:00 pm most people work, go home, eat supper, spend time with their families and then sleep. There is a beer hall in the settlement just outside of the compound. We drove by it coming in. They don't have electricity so the beer is warm and unless you buy something else from the take away shop there's nothing to eat there."

"That sounds good. Anybody want to go out for a drink?"

"Do they have anything more to drink than beer?" Corrie asked, "I don't like beer."

"It's either warm beer or warm coke. Nothing else out here." Hans really didn't want the newcomers to start off by spending all their time at the local beer hall so he added, "The driver got back with your groceries about twenty minutes ago. I think he left everything in the back of the truck for you to sort through and pick up what you ordered. You may want to do that first and then have supper before you think about going anywhere else."

He knew that if he could get them into their houses and get a hot meal into them, along with the jet lag, they would be too tired to do anything else. He really wanted them to be fresh for the morning.

The four followed Hans to the truck and started shuffling through the boxes to find what they had asked for from town. Hans watched as they picked through the boxes and bags and noticed Ingrid glance over at him more than once. He thought to himself, "If only . . ."

The next morning they were all up early and at Hans's house to get the work started. Mr. Lizer had told Hans that none of them were to work in the capacity of what they were trained to do. He really wanted to see if they were flexible. Charles had been running NGO's for twenty years and knew if a person wasn't flexible, they wouldn't last long in this type of work. Just because you were trained as a nurse didn't mean that you wouldn't be called on to fix a bicycle or paint a building.

Hans had work for them to do in three different areas of the compound. Most of it wouldn't take more than five or six hours, but they didn't have to work a full eight hour day, they just needed to get the job done that they were assigned. He knew what each of them were trained to do and what the NGO had hired them for, but per Mr. Lizer's instructions he had Willem and Corrie, who were trained in business and office work, go out with a group who were repairing the borehole and building a new wood–burning hot water heater. Garrit, who was a certified electrician was sent to the clinic to help out in whatever they needed help with. Ingrid, who had been a nurse for eight years already, was assigned to follow Hans around the compound doing different jobs, from the bearings in a bicycle wheel of one of the employees to welding a new tailpipe on one of the vehicles.

Ingrid was glad how the jobs were split up. She was also quite taken at how the people took to Hans. Although some of the children ran when they saw him coming most of the people greeted him warmly. It was also nice that he knew some of the Shona language. He was even able to joke around with some of the men in their own language.

They were both on their backs under a sink fixing a leak when Ingrid said, "I'm a little worried about the language. I can't even understand people when they're speaking English to me. Their accents are so strong."

"You'll get used to it. At first when I arrived I couldn't understand people at all, but after a time your ears get accustomed to the accent and you'll pick up some of the language." Hans looked over at her, "That's really one of the most important things you need to do, learn some of the language."

Hans arm was wet and Ingrid sat up and got him a towel to dry it. "Thank you, it is a little wet where we're working, you have some smudges on your forehead too." He handed her the towel back so she could wipe it off. "When I first came, the children and women used to run from me because of my size. I really love children and had dreams that I would be able to hold and play with them, but they were scared of me. Even the men were apprehensive of me at first. So to try and change that I worked hard at learning some of the language, I'm not real good, but I get by." "You sound like you know a lot to me." Ingrid had only managed to smear the smudge more. Hans thought it was cute.

"There that should do it." Hans pulled himself out of the cupboard and sat up with his knees bent and his arms leaning on them. Holding a wrench he looked down at his massive hands, "I really wanted to be friends with the African people, but my size really did scare them."

Ingrid could see that this memory hurt him. "It looks like they like you now."

"Like I said, I started learning the language. It's funny, I thought I was doing well and then I would speak in Shona to the people and they would laugh. I was told they weren't laughing at me really, but just that I was learning their language. It really endeared me to them. Now only some of the children run from me."

Ingrid had started cleaning up where they had been working and Hans joined in. "I did notice some of the smaller ones hiding behind their mother's skirts as we have been walking around the compound."

Hans looked up and grinned, "Yes and I'll win their hearts someday." They walked out of the house and back into the sunshine. Ingrid's hair gleamed in the sun. "Now with you it will be different. The people will flock to you. Blond hair is a rarity around here. The children and some of the men and women will want to touch it. Don't be afraid. It's just that your hair is so different from theirs."

Hans was contemplative for a minute, "After some of the children started coming to me, I would pick them up and a lot of times they would just rub my arm. They were just amazed at the hair on my arm."

As she worked with Hans and got to know him better, Ingrid found that he was the sweetest, gentlest man she had ever met. It seemed with every new assignment they would always end up in the same group. She didn't know if it was because Hans worked it that way, or if it was just fate. After a few months she started to depend on him. When she needed something he was always there for her. If her car broke down, it would be Hans who would come to fix it.

In the months that followed, Hans was given a crew to oversee. Since Ingrid had arrived it seemed that they were always together. Her house was just above Hans's so she had to walk by it every day and Hans was always waiting for her ready to walk with her wherever she was going.

"Hans?" The director needed to talk to him, "I've noticed you giving a lot of attention to the new nurse, Ingrid. I want to put her on your team, but I don't want her to be a distraction to you. Will she be?"

"No, not at all, she would be a great asset to my team." Hans was excited about this. "I do like her, but I will make sure she doesn't interfere with my work and I won't interfere with her work either. She's not afraid to get her hands dirty and she loves to help people. Just yesterday I was repairing that old borehole pump up at Sanyati and as I was pulling the old greasy pipe out it slipped. She was right there and took hold of it getting herself filthy. If she hadn't grabbed it, it would have fallen back down and I wouldn't have been able to pull it back out. She doesn't just do what she's told to do, she thinks and does what is needed to be done."

Hans felt he needed to really talk her up so that he could keep her on his team. "She's already started learning the language and is doing very well. She can greet people and is starting to understand what people are saying to her. She loves the people and even spends time just visiting them."

Hans was going to go on talking, but Mr. Lizer spoke up. "Okay, okay, I'll put her on your team, but if I see a problem, I'll move her to another team faster than a rabbit running from a dog." Mumbling to himself he said, "Learning the language and loving the people aren't reasons to put her on your team."

Mr. Lizer was looking at a paper on his desk but Hans could see he was contemplating things. "I'm going to keep Corrie and Garrit here at the compound. Corrie is very good in the office and I'm going to have Garrit replace you as a driver. He's quiet and I could use some peace and quiet."

"I think he's quiet around you because he's afraid of you."

"Afraid of me?" He looked up feigning surprise. "Good, that's the way it should be." both he and Hans smiled about that. "You need to know though, she only signed up for a one year stint. She's already been here six weeks so she only has ten and a half months left."

Hans didn't know that, "I thought everyone signed up for two years?"

"Normally that's true, but when we hire a nurse with the experience and training that she has our government won't allow them to be away from home for that long. She is single and can move anywhere she wants too. Socialized medicine needs people like her and there are few of them left."

"But we need her here." Hans blurted out. He didn't want her to leave so quickly.

"Don't worry, if she decides to stay she can apply for an extension or she could even quit her job as a nurse at home. Of course if she does that she wouldn't be allowed to work for us. I am hoping to get her to stay for at least three years with us though. We can probably work it out."

Hans was relieved. He now knew that he was going to have to work harder at winning her heart.

Hans's new crew consisted of himself, Willem, and Ingrid, plus two more Zimbabwean nurses, and five Zimbabwean men to help in the construction work. They were given three trucks, two of which were loaded with cement to form bricks and build the clinics. The other one had the roofing, the wood to build the trusses, nails, all the pipes for the borehole and all the tools they would need to build, construct, repair, and live their lives out in the bush for extended periods of time.

Along with the trucks they were given a Land Rover. Three men drove the trucks and two of them had passengers. The women, Hans, and Willem hit the road together in the Land Rover which was packed with their food and luggage and tied on top were four tents. Two for the men, one for the ladies, and a smaller one for Hans which served as his quarters as well as an office.

Behind the vehicle they towed a borehole rig. The tall derrick would fold in three pieces and made for a very compact rig. It was run by a large diesel engine which also doubled as a generator. Even though they would be in the bush they were allowed some comforts. They had lights, a small refrigerator, and stove. Willem had brought a small television and VCR with a few video tapes for them to watch.

Their first assignment was a small village near Mlibizi where the mighty Zambezi River flows to form the beginning of Lake Kariba.

"Here we are, welcome to your home for the next couple of months." Hans said as they all got out of the vehicles and stretched.

"Yeah, here we are, but where is here?" Willem wanted to know.

Denford spoke up being the local historian in the group. "We're on the Zambezi River and it does have crocodiles so be careful. There's some nice fish in the river too, Bream and Tigerfish. You're welcome to fish if you want, but make sure you take someone else along with you to watch for crocs."

"We're also at the mouth of Lake Kariba. It's the largest man–made lake ever built. It was built between Zimbabwe and Zambia in 1958 to 1963. At that time these two countries were part of the Federation of Rhodesia and Nyasaland. They were known as Northern and Southern Rhodesia and Nyasaland is now Malawi."

"I remember reading about that in school." Willem said, "the federation didn't last long did it?"

"No it only lasted for ten years. It ended when Northern Rhodesia, which is now Zambia, received their independence from the United Kingdom in 1963."

"So they spent all that money to build the lake together and then split up when it was finished?" Ingrid asked.

"Yes, but both countries have an agreement that they share the lake."

"I hate to stop this history lesson" Hans said, "but we need to get started setting things up as soon as possible, that flat tire on the trailer slowed us up and it will be dark in a couple hours. Let's get the tents set up and the generator where we want it. I need to go see the chief and let him know we're here." Looking at one of the African men Hans spoke for everyone to hear, "Denford, since you have done this before you'll be in charge of getting everything set up."

They needed the Land Rover since it had all the equipment in it that needed set up so Hans took one of the trucks to visit the chief. Everyone pitched in and the camp was set up in no time.

That night after they had eaten a good meal of *sadza* and stew Hans called everyone together. "Alright there are some things we will need to do first before we can begin any other work. We'll need to build a small pond of cement, probably five feet squared. There's no running water until we get the borehole done and we'll need water to drink, wash with and make bricks with before that can be accomplished. The river is close so we bring it with buckets. I've talked to the chief and he is sending some young men who have nothing else to do to help with that and any other work we might need them for. We should be able to get that built by tomorrow and filled quickly. Tendai has boiled water already for drinking and there is some hot water in buckets if anyone wants to bath."

Hans fell into his role as leader with ease. He was glad to finally be doing what he came to Zimbabwe to do. "You nurses will be expected to help with all the work not just the medical side, I think Mr. Lizer has already informed you of that." The women nodded in agreement.

Hans looked around at his crew. "We're going to be here for quite some time, we need to get along together. If you have any problem with someone else, come talk to me or Miss Ingrid. She will be in charge of the nurses and the clinic."

He focused his attention on the men, "That means you men will take orders from her while the clinic is being built. She knows how she wants things done and what it will look like. If you argue with her it is the same as arguing with me and I want to give you a heads up . . . don't argue with me." He spoke each of the last four words slowly and with finality so that everyone knew he meant what he said.

"We'll start at sunrise tomorrow. You're free to do what you want until then. You can bath tonight or in the morning. I don't know when the young men from the chief will get here, but I expect you to be ready to start work on time."

The days and weeks that followed went fairly well. There were some minor hiccups, but that was to be expected. The small pool was built and not only was it used by the crew, but also by some of the smaller animals that roamed those parts. The drill rig was set up and from early morning until sunset each day the incessant pounding was heard in the area. No one complained though because they knew it was going to bring fresh clean water to the village.

With the help of some local young men the clinic was built in no time and Ingrid, Rumbidzai, and Kudzai started the medical side of MAWFA. Rumbidzai had been assigned to this location by the government and would be running the clinic when they finished, so Ingrid allowed her to be in charge of things as much as possible which freed her up to spend more time with Hans over at the drilling rig.

There wasn't much to do at the rig once it was set up and drilling. The machine did all the work. Every once and a while they would have to adjust something or other, but it pretty much just continued to work. So the men did other chores around, helping wherever they needed help in the village. This was a policy of the NGO, they wanted to be on good terms with the chief in case they needed to do anything else in one of his areas.

One day Ingrid had been working for several hours in the clinic when a man came in needing help. Rumbidzai and Kudzai had gone out on a call to a nearby village in the Land Rover and she didn't expect them back until supper time. She had learned a lot of the language in the time she had been in the country, especially now that she was in a rural setting and there were some who didn't speak any English. Greeting the man in Shona, she asked how she could help him.

"I'm not feeling well." was the man's short reply. Ingrid noticed that he was jittery and his eyes were bloodshot.

"Where are you not feeling well?" Ingrid tried to pry information out of the man.

"My mouth is dry, I have the shakes, look." He extended his hand and she could see it visibly shaking. "I need some medicine."

She knew right off what his problem was, he was a drug addict. There was no way he was going to get any drugs from her. "I can see what's wrong with you and I won't give you anything." She turned to go and felt his clammy hand grab her around the wrist.

"You will do as I say." He spoke in a guttural voice and she knew he meant business. Letting out a scream she swung her other arm at him. He ducked just in time for her to miss. Pulling out a large knife he put it to Ingrid's throat.

"Get me what I want."

Scared but undaunted by the knife Ingrid struggled shouting, "No!"

Right then the door flew open and a giant of a man came charging in. Hans didn't stop at the doorway but let the momentum that he had carry him right toward the assailant and Ingrid. Just as he got close he grabbed the startled man's arm and twisted. They heard the bones snap as the man screamed and dropped the knife. The would be thief started to run, but Hans held on to him. Others came running to see what all the excitement was about.

When Ingrid saw that the man's arm was broken she set it and put it in a cast with Hans watching in case the man decided to try anything else. She always felt so safe with Hans around. Ingrid didn't know what she would have done if Hans had not been there that day.

From that time on their relationship was more than platonic. They were now a couple and spent more time together than ever.

That's when they found their spot. They had been out on a walk looking at the many different species of birds in the area.

"Look over there" Hans spoke quietly so the birds wouldn't hear his voice, "right there on that tree limb by the edge of the water."

"Oh Hans, it's two Fish Eagles, they're so beautiful."

"Now that's something I've never seen before. They are majestic birds, aren't they? Let's see if we can get closer." They quietly walked through the bush getting closer to the water. Hans was watching the birds and also keeping an eye out for crocs.

"Oh, I can't see them anymore. There's too many trees and leaves."

"I've got my machete I can cut some down."

"No, you'll make too much noise. We're by the water maybe we can just move them out of the way."

In front of them was a big Callistemon tree known locally as the Bottle Brush tree because the red cylindrical flower resemble a traditional bottle brush. It was such a picturesque place with the weeping evergreen branches hanging down swaying in the breeze. Ducking under the leaves of the tree, Hans and Ingrid saw that on the side by the river the branches of the tree opened up and they could see the rushing water and Zambia across from them.

Ingrid whispered, "Look, there they are."

Hans had been overcome by the beauty of the place under the tree and was looking lovingly at Ingrid when she spoke. He followed her pointing hand and not fifty feet away were the two Fish Eagles. He could have thrown a rock and hit them. As they were watching the male bird dove into the water and before they could say anything, came back out with a fish in his beak.

Hans gasped, "Did you see that?" Forgetting to keep his voice down, the two birds lazily flew off.

Ingrid leaned back into Hans, "This place is so beautiful."

Wrapping his arms around her they just stood and watched the beautiful panoramic view of the river from this secluded spot. Looking around he saw that they were closed in on every side except in front. It was as if someone had built this place, but he knew no one had, it was all natural.

"Wait here, I saw a log just a little ways back, I'll go get it and roll it here so we can have a bench to sit on."

They spent the rest of that day under the tree watching birds and the sunset over the Zambezi. This became their favorite place and anytime they were in this area they would go and find their spot again.

Several months later they had to go back to repair the borehole pump and Ingrid needed to restock the medicine. When they weren't busy they always found time to visit their spot.

One evening they were sitting on their log under the tree, the air was cool and the sun was setting.

"I really love it here. I wish I could stay forever," Ingrid whispered.

"Forever is a long time," replied Hans.

"No, not really, not if you are with someone you really care about and everything is right, then forever really isn't long at all," she replied.

That's when he knew it was time. Hans had bought the ring in Harare on one of his trips. He had been carrying it around with him for months. He had been holding her, keeping her warm, but quickly releasing his embrace, he stood up. She wasn't happy that he got up and let the cold in.

Then he got on one knee and said, "Ingrid will you become my wife and stay with me forever?"

"Yes, yes! I will! Oh, Hans I will marry you and live with you forever," Ingrid replied as she threw her arms around his neck.

From that time on, the hideaway under the Bottle Brush tree was the most beautiful place in the world for her.

The next week they went to Harare to get the marriage license. They had hoped to be married that weekend, but the laws of Zimbabwe stated that after obtaining the marriage license the engagement had to be announced and submitted to the newspapers so if anyone had good reason to object to the marriage they would have time to come forward and explain their issue.

Hans and Ingrid put the proper notice in the local paper and had another paper printed up to post at the compound for all to see. The two weeks seemed like two years to them, but they got through it and had their wedding on the twenty-first of May. It was a very simple wedding with just a few of their closest friends in attendance. Everyone present knew this was meant to be and could see from the couple's faces they were each totally gone over the other.

Hans and Ingrid honeymooned at Lake Kariba on a rented private houseboat. It was a wonderful time. The houseboat was completely staffed with a captain and a cook, so the two of them had no responsibilities. They relaxed during the day in the hot tub on deck or with a good book. Late in the afternoon the captain would dock for the night along an island or by the shore and the next few hours were spent either fishing or game hunting in the dingy. Nights were filled with passion and desire. The couple had not a care in the world. Life was theirs to live. Love was theirs to make as though they were the first to have ever done so.

2

Fleeing

"*Nyandanura*, come here!" Simon Sibanda shouted out the open door, "Where is that girl," He shouted even louder, "*Nyandanura*!" Frustrated he called out to his wife in the hut next door, "Martha, where is that daughter of yours?"

Martha, lying in her bed called back to him in a weak voice, "She's getting ready for church, what do you want? I'll get it."

"No, you stay where you are." He spoke with a softer voice to his wife, but it still had that harsh tone. In anger he shouted a third time, "*Nyandanura*! Come here now."

"Here I am father, I was getting dressed." Standing in the doorway was a very attractive eighteen year old girl. She was wearing a plain flower printed dress, the nicest one she owned and the one she saved to wear to church. She was brushing her wet hair and was barefoot.

Simon reached over to her and slapped her on the face. "You come when I call, do you hear me. You almost made your mother get off her sick bed. Do you want to kill her? I need you to go to the shop and buy me a beer. Here's the money," He looked up at her with a menacing stare, "and don't lose it."

"But father it's almost time for church and I still have to help Mai Kuru get Belinda and Promise washed and dressed."

"Don't talk back to me." Simon raised his hand ready to strike her again.

Quickly she grabbed the money from his outstretched hand and bolted from the doorway. "I'll hurry father." She ran down the path to the main road and all the way to the store.

Her real name was Chipo, but her father called her *Nyandanura* which meant "to be put in disorder." She hated the name, but there was nothing she could do to change it. Her father had told her when he found out her mother was pregnant it put his life in chaos. First because he had never told Martha he already had two wives and second because of Martha's father.

The thought hurt her and as she approached the store she let out a little whimper. James Malunga, the owner of the store was sitting on the steps reading a newspaper. When he heard a noise he looked up and saw Chipo coming, he stood up and walked into his store. He reached the shelf where he kept the beer, grabbed a two liter bottle that looked like a barrel and set it on the counter as she entered. He knew she was there to buy her father a Scud, the locally brewed beer, it was the only reason she ever came to his store.

"Good morning Chipo, you're going to be late for church." Although he was as old as her father and a good friend of Simon's he was always friendly to her. In fact he was friendly to all the girls who came in especially the pretty ones and Chipo was the prettiest. His eyes roamed over her body and his thoughts were far from anything to do with church.

"Good morning Mr. Malunga, yes, I am. I still have to get some of the little ones ready." She knew he was looking her over, all the girls hated going into his shop because of his lewd looks and comments. She handed over the money and reached up to take the scud. The plastic lid popped off and some of the beer spilled on her hand. "Ahhh. This stuff stinks, how can anyone drink it?"

"It taste good, you should try some." He always joked with her about drinking, he pictured her drunk and the fun he could have with her in the back room.

She grabbed the lid and put it back on. She'd have to wash her hands when she got to the water pump just before her home. She wouldn't want her father to think she was drinking any of it.

When she got back to the house her father wasn't there. She placed the container on the table by his chair and went next door to her mother's rondoval.

Chipo Sibanda lived with her mother, Martha, her father, Simon, her fifteen brothers and sisters and two other "mothers" in the rural area of *Silobela*. Her father, who was much older than her mother, had three wives, Martha being the youngest of the three. Martha was considered the "young mother" to the children belonging to the other two wives.

There were nine rondovals, round thatch roofed huts, on their property and one larger rectangular house all surrounded by a crudely made fence. The rectangular house was for her father. It had two rooms, a bedroom and a living room. It was the only house that was made with proper brick blocks, framed windows and a store bought door. The rondovals were constructed of poles and mud *dagga* with triangular shaped holes in the walls that served as windows.

The largest rondoval was the kitchen. The floor was constructed with a bowl shaped dip in the center where the cooking fire burned, providing a warm shelter on cool winter nights. The inside thatch was blackened from the smoke and various herbs and onions hung from the rafters. A built in bench circled the inside wall on either side of the door. Similarly constructed cubbyholes on the wall opposite the door served as cupboards for dishes and utensils. Seven smaller rondovals served as bedrooms; one for each of the wives, two for the boys and two for the girls and babies. The smallest rondaval was the storage room filled with produce and grain. Fields and pasture land surrounded the fenced in area with the nearest neighbor about half a mile down the road.

"*Ko, ko, ko,* mommy" Chipo called out, in the African tradition, at the doorway of her mother's hut.

"Come in Chipo." Her mother responded in a very weak voice. Her two brothers who were also her mother's children, were sitting by their mother. Simba who was fourteen and wanted so much to be a man and Dumisani who was eleven and couldn't understand why his mother was so sick. Chipo had thirteen older and younger siblings from her other "mothers" whose ages ranged from two to twenty two.

Both the boys looked up as Chipo entered the room. "Hi Simba, hi Dumi, how are you this morning?"

"We're doing well and how about you?" Simba answered for both of them.

Chipo could see the look of fear in his eyes and knew that her mother must be having a bad day. "It's time for church so you boys head on out, I'll catch up." As the boys walked out she looked over at her mother, "How are you today mommy?"

She walked over to where her mother was lying on a mat on the floor and touched her hand with her finger.

"I'm doing alright Chipo." Martha had been sick for just over two months and was very weak and frail. The worst part was Chipo knew her father was doing nothing to help her.

Although Martha was from a strong Christian background and her grandfather, Alex Dube, was a pastor, Simon had a strong belief in spirit worship. He was afraid that her sickness was due to something she had done to offend the ancestors or because of a curse someone had put on her. He had taken her to the clinic but they could find nothing wrong. So he took her to the witchdoctor. This witchdoctor confirmed Simon's suspicion that there was a curse and so he would have nothing to do with her for fear of the curse coming against him.

"Is there anything I can get you?" Chipo was worried for her mother, but really had no idea what she could do to help her.

"Chipo, I want you to know that I love you. I know that life has been rough for you. I want you to know that it is all my fault."

"No mother, it's not your fault at all, if it's anyone's fault it's mine."

"No Chipo, you have not done anything wrong. You are my beautiful daughter and I know that you will do a lot of good things. God has blessed you with a very pretty face and you can do anything you want if you put your mind to it. I just wish I could be there to see all that happen."

"Mother, don't talk like that. You'll get better I know it."

"I've been sick for so long, I am weak." Her mother paused to catch her breath, "I don't think I'll be around much longer. Promise me you'll look after Simba and Dumi."

"Mommy, don't say that." Chipo was crying now, "I don't want you to die. I still need you to look after me."

"I'm so sorry Chipo, I wish I could change things, but I can't. You know I named you Chipo because you are my gift from God, my precious gift. I have always looked at you as my gift, remember that." As she spoke her voice kept getting softer.

Chipo was on her knees with her arms around her mother, sobbing. "Oh Mother, I love you, you can't go." Her head was under her mother's chin and she could hear her heartbeat faint as it was.

Martha reached up and took Chipo by the shoulders. Lifting her head she spoke in a louder more firm voice, "Okay enough of that. It's time for church and you are late. Go wash your face and get to church." She reached under the pillow and took out a piece of paper. "Please deliver this to the pastor for me."

Chipo saw the determine look on her mother's face and knew she needed to go. She took the paper, washed her face and walked the two kilometers to church.

They were serving communion when she arrived so she sat down and joined in the service. The pastor preached a message but Chipo didn't really hear a word of it, all she could think about was her mother. At the end of the service she was shaking hands with all the people, greeting each one. When she shook hands with the pastor she handed him the paper. He started unfolding it and asked, "How is your mother doing?"

"Oh pastor," she wailed, "she is so sick." She fell into his arms just as he got the paper open. Looking down at her he felt such compassion. He knew what Chipo and her brothers were going through. They had such a hard life with their father being the angry man that he was. He patted her on the back and by then his wife had come over and put her arms around Chipo. He glanced at the letter and read, "Please could you deliver this to Alex Dube" He didn't mean to pry, but his eyes saw the first line. "Dear Father, I am so sorry for the disappointment I have been in your life . . ." He knew Martha was dying and this was a final letter to her father.

When Chipo arrived home that afternoon her father was drunk. "Chipo get over here." He stumbled after her swatting at her. "Get my lunch, I'm hungry."

Chipo ran to the kitchen where her other two "mothers" were. They were much more quiet than usual. "Father told me to get his food." The older of the two handed Chipo a plate already dished up. This was strange and Chipo looked quizzically at her. It looked like she had been crying. Then she looked at her other "mother" and she too had been crying. Something was wrong.

Just then Simon shouted out in a drunken slur, "Chipo, bring me my food."

She thought, "What? He just called me Chipo, he never calls me that." When she got to her father it looked like he too had been crying. Something was wrong. 'Her mother!' She tossed the plate on the table spilling half of the food and ran to her mother's hut. Inside lay her mother, but now she was wrapped from head to foot in a blanket. "Noooo!" She shouted and fell on the floor.

Her father had followed her in. In an unprecedented move he reached down and placed his hand on Chipo's shoulder. Still drunk but quiet he said through sobs of his own, "She's gone. I loved her so much but now she's gone." Simon raised his hand from her shoulder and walked out. Shutting the door to his own house he was not seen the rest of the day.

In a daze Chipo walked through the next several days. The burial was held right there in the yard of their home. She stood with her two brothers on either side and the rest of her brothers and sisters all around her. Simon sat in a chair being consoled by beer. Her other mothers stood behind the children and as they lowered the body in the ground started to sing an old hymn. Friends and relatives from all around came for her funeral.

The village was full of people who knew and loved Martha. Simon allowed Pastor Alex Dube and his wife Mary to come to the funeral. They hadn't spoken to each other since just after Chipo was born. Alex wanted to mend things between them, but Simon would have nothing to do with this "man of God." His anger became worse and he stayed drunk for days after the funeral.

"I've got to get out of here." She confided to her best friend Tatenda, whom she called Tata. They had been sitting under a tree looking at some magazines in the heat of the day.

"What are you talking about? Where would you go?"

"Tata, I'm serious, I can't take anymore. Ever since my mother died my father has been mean. He beats me for every little thing, even if it's not my fault. If some of my "brothers" are late for school he beats me. What's worse is if they get bad marks at school, for some reason it's my fault, I'm the one who gets in trouble. Tata my life is unbearable! I've got to find a way to leave."

Tata thought about it, "What would you do Chipo, you don't have much education. I know you did okay in school, but you would need a job."

"I know, and it would have to be a good job, one that paid well. My dad did it when he was young. I've heard him tell the story hundreds of times. He ran away from here and got a job in Harare. He even bought a car, he's still one of the only people around here who has a car. If he can do it I can too."

"Yes, I've heard the story too. I've also heard that what he did wasn't exactly a good job. I heard he sold drugs and was wanted by the police at one time."

"I don't know about that, but I know that I could really make something out of myself if I could get out of this place."

Tata glanced down at the magazine. She raised her head up and said excitedly, "I know, I know Chipo, look you could become a model like these girls. You're just as pretty as they are and you are prettier than some of them. Look at this one, she's not near as pretty as you."

Chipo looked at the magazine, she looked close at it. "I've never really noticed what the models looked like before. Do you really think I'm as pretty as they are?"

"Oh come on Chipo, you could ask any of the boys and they would tell you that you are really pretty."

Chipo's mind started wandering, thinking of how romantic it would be to be a model. Then she started giggling. "But look at that one, I could never wear so little clothes as she is."

"Oh, I don't know . . . " Tata took hold of the dress Chipo was wearing and pulled it tight around her waist while hiking it up above her knees. "You've definitely got the body for it. Look at your small waist and you've got great looking legs. Turn around."

Chipo turned and Tata gathered the dress in the front this time to see what it looked like from the back. "Yes, you would look really sexy in that two piece bathing suit that model is wearing. In fact you look better from the back than she does."

Right then two boys from the school walked by, "Whoa, look at that will you?" they both whistled.

Chipo brushed Tata's hands away, "Oh quit it. You're embarrassing me."

"Chipo, you've got what it takes to be a model. If you could get to Harare, you could get a job with Meikles department store or maybe Woolworth and be a model."

"Do you really think so?"

"I know so."

Chipo sat back down flipping the pages of the magazine looking at the models. "I could do this couldn't I?" She thought out loud.

"The only other thing to do is to marry Temba. Then you will have your own house and he would take care of you."

"Temba, are you kidding? I wouldn't marry him."

"Why not, he's good looking."

"That may be, but I don't want to marry someone, especially someone from the rural area. If I do that I would be just like every other girl here. My life would be the same as it is now, only I would be beaten by my husband instead of my father."

"Oh come on not all guys beat their wives."

"Well, it's all I've ever seen in my family."

"Chipo, you've got to understand not every family is as dysfunctional as yours. I would love to marry Temba, but when I'm with you all he does is look at you. It's like I'm not even there. I would like to marry him and have 5 or 6 children. We would live together in a house and have two more houses for our children and a big beautiful kitchen. We would have cattle, chickens and a donkey or two to pull our scotch cart. I dream of it all the time."

"Would you like to be alone with your thoughts? I didn't know you thought about Temba that way. I'm sure he likes you. I've seen him look at you checking you out. I guess it's more important than ever for me to leave so you and Temba can get together and start having all those babies."

"Don't you want to get married?"

Chipo thought about it for a minute, "I don't know. Not right now, I want to live my life. I want to have adventure." She stopped talking and dreamily said, "I think I'll marry a white boy."

"What, what are you talking about?"

"Have you ever seen the missionaries. They are always so happy. You can see that they love each other and I know that Mr. Perry is nice to Mrs. Perry. I want to marry a man like that. So I figure if I married a white man he would be good to me like Mr. Perry is to his wife. Plus white people don't have more than one wife. I would never want to marry a man with more than one wife. I want more than my mother had."

That night after everyone had gone to bed Chipo made a decision. She would leave *Silobela* and go to Harare to find the kind of life she wanted in the world of modeling.

She didn't tell anyone what she was going to do, not even Tata, she didn't want her to have to lie or worse tell people where she was or what she was doing. She figured once she got a good job and was making some money she would write to them and let them know where she was and what a good life she now had.

"Now how can I do this?" She stayed up late that night hatching a plan. "I have to be able to leave without anyone suspecting what I'm up to. I can't just go out to the road and catch the bus, there are too many relatives around. Someone would see me and tell father."

"Somehow I have to get out of this area and then get a bus to Harare. I have some money saved that mother gave me, I wonder how much it is." Very quietly reaching under her mat she pulled out a purse and counted her money. "Okay that's enough to get me to Harare. I'll have to get a job quick though, it isn't enough to live on. I'm sure I'll get a job with one of the stores. Maybe they have houses for their models." As her mind wandered about all that could happen, she fell asleep.

The next day, after her siblings had gone on to school and the younger ones had been fed and were playing nearby she sat down under a tree. Her mind was in a whirl trying to find out how best she could get away. She would have to have a real good excuse to be allowed to go anywhere. Her father never sent her to the store, except Mr. Malunga's shop to buy beer, he always sent the boys in the donkey cart to Crossroads. If she could only get to the Crossroads where the shops and buses are she could catch a bus to Harare.

Tata came over and sat down heavily on the ground. "My dad wants me to go to the college over in Malisa to learn to cook. I don't want to do that, I want to marry Temba."

Chipo's eyes got big, that's it, that's how she could do it. "Don't worry I'm sure they won't let you in the college. You have to be smart to go there."

Tata looked up and saw Chipo with that mischievous grin and knew her friend was teasing her.

The next morning Chipo was up early, got all her chores done and walked to the college in the next village. Entering the administration office she was met by her uncle. She had forgotten that her father's young brother worked at the school.

"May I have an application form?" Chipo asked after the proper greetings were finished.

"Chipo, do you have your father's permission to apply to the college?"

"No, not yet." Chipo was a little flustered at her uncle's question but recovered very well. "I . . . I knew that I must first have the form so my father will see that I am serious."

"Okay, here's the form, you have to do it in triplicate, that means three copies, and you have to bring your school results. Do you have them?"

"No I don't," Chipo feigned ignorance, "where do I get them from?"

"You'll have to go to Kwekwe to the regional office of education. It will cost $10.00 and they will give you a certified copy of your grades and your "O" level results."

"I'll have to talk to my father about that, can he go and do it or do I have to?"

He can do it, but then he will need your birth certificate and national ID, plus a letter from me. It would be so much easier if you go."

Chipo was elated. This was exactly what she needed. She knew if she made it to Kwekwe she could get a bus to Harare. Kwekwe was a big town and there wouldn't be anyone there she knew.

After returning home Chipo got her pen out and started filling out the form. Her father saw her working on something, but didn't question her. That evening she cooked his favorite meal the way that he liked it.

Her mother had always made a chicken dish that was his favorite and Chipo had helped her mother many times. While her mother was sick it was Chipo who had prepared her father's food without his knowledge. Simon always thought his first wife, Amanda, had prepared it especially for him. Chipo took special care to make it the same way that her mom did and he loved it. After supper she brought him a bottle of beer that she had put in a bucket of water to keep cool. He was quite surprised and pleased that his daughter had done that for him. The meal reminded him of Martha and the beer put him in a relaxed state.

While he was still drinking his beer, she came to him, "Father I went over to the college at Malisa today and got an application. I filled it out and need your signature. There's also a list of things I need to be accepted."

"What? Why do you want to go to college?"

"They have a course on catering and culinary. I want to learn how to cook and make better meals for you and the family. They also teach what herbs and vegetables I would need to grow so that I would have the right ingredients. I would learn how to bake as well, cakes and scones. "

"Yes, maybe this is a good idea." Simon was thinking of the cakes and scones. "Then you would be able to make a good meal like your older mother made for me tonight. Okay, I'll sign the form."

After he signed the paper, Chipo remained where she was.

"Well, what else do you need?" Simon asked gruffly.

"I will have to go to Kwekwe to get last year's exam results. See, look on the list uncle gave to me, it says that you could go for me but would need my birth certificate and national ID."

"No, I don't want to go, you'll have to go?"

"I could leave on the early bus tomorrow and be back before dark. Sipho can get the children ready for school and the younger ones dressed and fed. She isn't in school now so she would have time."

Simon grunted his response as he reached over to a tin setting on the table by his chair.

"Here's the money you will need to get to Kwekwe and back. I suppose you will need some money for food too." It was a comment rather than a question.

"No, Father, I will prepare some food to take with me."

Quickly leaving her father's house Chipo returned to her own hut and began packing for her journey. Her sisters asked what she was doing and Chipo explained that she was going to Kwekwe to get her school results, appeasing their curiosity.

"Sipho, I'm leaving on the early bus so you will have to take care of the children in the morning," Chipo said taking advantage of the conversation.

"That's okay. I've been bored every day anyway since school finished," Sipho said agreeing with the plan.

That night before bed, Chipo took a bath and got ready for her trip the next morning. She laid out her best dress and even got some of her mother's stockings to wear. The next morning she was up early to catch the bus. Since she didn't own much in the way of clothes, Chipo was able to pack all her belongings into her school book–satchel, planning on buying new clothes when she got her job. If anyone saw her they would figure she just had her food and money in her school case. No one would think anything of it.

As Chipo was getting on the bus she met her aunt and uncle, "Hi Auntie and Uncle, how are you?"

"We are fine Chipo, we're just coming back from a trip to Kadoma. We saw your cousin and her new baby, he is so cute. Where are you going?"

"I'm on my way to Kwekwe to get my school results. I'm planning on starting college next term." Chipo was thankful for her ruse knowing very well that her aunt would head directly to her home to quiz her father about Chipo's business in Kwekwe.

The trip was an adventure for Chipo. She had only traveled outside of *Silobela* one other time with her mother. That time they went to Gweru, a much bigger city than Kwekwe.

She had never seen such tall buildings Chipo reminisced. The tallest one was the Standard Bank Building; it was four floors high. Chipo got to eat in a restaurant, The Dutch Oven, and after lunch she and her mother walked over to Creamy Inn and had an ice cream cone. She had never tasted anything so wonderful in her life. It was cold, sweet and rich. There were people everywhere and so many cars. In *Silobela* there were very few cars. Occasionally a car would drive by their home, but most of the time there were only donkey carts and the two buses that came by every day. In Gweru though, there were many cars parked along the street and even more driving down the road. You had to be very careful about crossing the road and Chipo was a bit frightened by the fast moving cars. She was only a little girl of eleven then. Now she was eighteen and much wiser.

The bus ride to Kwekwe took three hours, but it was still early, only 9:00 am when she arrived. Chipo saw none of her relatives on the bus and she didn't see anyone she knew at the bus terminal. She was safe. She looked at all the buses and read the sign on the front of each bus telling where they were going. She found several buses going to Harare, so she chose the newest looking bus for her trip. She knew that the older buses sometimes broke down on the way. A newer bus would get her to her destination quicker.

Chipo was told the bus for Harare didn't leave for another hour but she boarded the bus anyway and waited so that she would have her seat. Two or three times the conductor got on the bus and looked at her as if wondering why she was on the bus so early. The bus was scheduled to leave in an hour, but in reality, true to African form, it wouldn't leave for two hours. As the time drew nearer eleven, more and more people crowded onto the bus. She was glad that she had stayed and saved her window seat where she could watch all the activity around her. Vendors crowded around the bus selling fruits and Cokes to the passengers. They weren't allowed to enter the bus, so they hawked their goods through the open windows.

Chipo watched as the men loaded big fifty kilogram bags of maize onto the top of the bus. One man was on the roof of the bus and there were two others on the ground. The two would take hold of a bag by the corners and swing it back and forth until they got enough momentum, then they would toss it up to the roof. The man on the roof would put his arms out and stop the bag in the air right above where he wanted it to land on the roof, the bag would drop with a loud bang. Inside the bus it was a very loud noise and startled Chipo the first time it happened. One person had bought a couch and the men tied a rope to it and hauled it up on top as well. Another man had brought two goats that he wanted to take to Harare. The man argued with the conductor for a while about how much the charge would be to transport these animals. The conductor wanted to charge as much as it cost for a person, but the passenger with the goats refused to pay that much. They finally agreed on a price. The two men who had loaded the bags of maize wrestled the first goat into a large burlap bag so that only his neck and head were sticking out. Then they hauled the goat up onto the roof and repeated the process with the other goat. The goats were neighing and protesting the whole time. Once they got them up on the roof they tied them down so they wouldn't fall off.

After everything was loaded the bus started on its journey. As it started pulling out toward the road, people were frantically buying their last minute items for the trip. There were men and women, boys and girls running alongside the bus trying to make that last sale. Chipo thought it was funny and was a little frightened by how close the people would get to the bus. She was afraid that someone would slip and fall and be crushed under the wheels. She was also amazed that so many people wanted to go to Harare. There were several buses and it looked to her that all of them were full. It would be a good four hour trip unless the driver decided to make an unscheduled supper stop along the way. As the bus pulled out on the road, Chipo felt scared and excited all at the same time. She had begun the most daring and frightful journey of her life.

3

Adventure

NINETEEN YEAR OLD ETHAN Benham could hardly contain his excitement. He couldn't wait for the plane to land. He had finished school in England and his graduation gift from his parents was a trip to Zimbabwe. They had told him that he could travel anywhere in the world and stay for a month but when he got back he had very important decisions to make. As the eldest son of a titled family, Ethan would someday be Lord Benham, an Earl with all the responsibilities that come with title and wealth. Ethan was the son of Sir John and Lady Barbara of Argyll. He had a brother, younger by two years, named Sean who was very jealous of his brother's adventure. His parents assured him that when the time came he too could take a trip.

Ethan had heard of Zimbabwe for many years. One of his best friends at school was from Zimbabwe. Ethan thought that Nigel had such a funny accent. It wasn't British and it wasn't Scottish. It had its own distinct Zimbabwean sound which Ethan found very charming in an African, earthy sort of way.

Standing just over six feet tall with brown hair and green eyes that sparkled when he smiled, Ethan was quite the attraction to most girls his age. He was very athletic and played on the school's soccer and cricket teams. When he was younger he played a bit of rugby, but one day while playing a simple game of 'touch' rugby he somehow managed to break his collarbone. His mom decided that rugby wasn't the game for her young son and she did everything she could to get him interested in soccer instead. That was okay with Ethan. He enjoyed sports, but his main objective was to just have fun.

The plane had been descending for the last twenty minutes and he knew he would soon be on Zimbabwean soil. Peering out the window, he could see land below him through the break in the clouds. It was still winter in England but since Zimbabwe is south of the equator it would be summertime. He couldn't wait to get out in the fresh sunshine and enjoy the weather that he had heard was better than anyplace on earth. The seatbelt light came on and he made sure his was fastened. Now looking out the window, Ethan could make out roads and cars. His excitement escalated as the plane descended. As they touched down and taxied to the terminal, people began standing up and retrieving their carry-on luggage out of the overhead compartments. Ethan got up and did the same. They had been standing for about ten minutes when the captain's voice came over the intercom.

"Ladies and gentlemen, this is the captain. The crew seems to be having problems connecting the passenger boarding bridge to the airplane, but hopefully that will be taken care of shortly and then we will be able to disembark."

Another ten minutes went by and the intercom buzzed to life one more time. "This is the captain speaking again. It seems the boarding bridge is still not in place. Please can you all turn and face the back of the aircraft. We will be disembarking at the rear using the attached steps. Sorry for the inconvenience."

Everyone turned and the line started filing out the rear of the plane.

It was a beautiful day, not hot like you would imagine Africa should be, but pleasantly warm, no humidity and a lot of sunshine. Ethan took a deep breath of the fresh African air. He had his camera in hand and took a quick shot of the airplane wanting to remember this journey forever. The passengers walked down the steps and along the asphalt for a short distance. Then they climbed back up some steps into the boarding bridge that they should have entered originally. The crowd quickly filed into the terminal and lined up in front of several immigration counters in the expansive room. The airport was fairly new and had a new shine to it, but in an old fashioned sort of way. He went to the line marked for visitors and proceeded to the counter where he handed his passport to the immigration officer. Since he was of a titled family he carried a diplomatic passport. The immigration officer was surprised. There had been no word that a diplomat was coming. He hurriedly called his supervisor over and they looked at the passport together. The supervisor didn't know what to do either. They hadn't received any instructions about this arrival. Normally, if an important visitor was scheduled to arrive, advance notice would be given. There would be a lot of fanfare with an African dance troupe in the entryway singing and dancing to African drums. The two immigration officers discussed what to do for a few minutes and then the supervisor decided to simply stamp the young man's passport and let him go on through.

The entire conversation had been in the Shona language and Ethan had no clue they were in such a quandary about him. He loved hearing the rolling sounds of the African tongue even though he didn't understand it in the least.

Once past the immigration counters Ethan proceeded to the luggage carousels, all in one expansive room. He joined the other passengers waiting for their luggage. The belt started moving and suitcases of all different shapes and sizes began their circular course. He found it strange that some pieces were taped up all over like a mummy. One that struck him as being very curious was a large bag that looked like it was made out of some type of plastic material, like an oversized grocery bag with a zipper. As it passed beyond Ethan, a large African woman stepped forward to retrieve it, hefting it off the conveyer belt and onto her head in one fluid motion. Ethan watched in amazement as she walked away with the heavy bag perched on her head as if it belonged there. Soon Ethan's bags appeared and circled to where he stood. Quickly retrieving his bags, he preceded toward the front of the building unsure where to go next. Seeing an African man and woman in uniform he stopped to ask for help.

"Pardon me, but I'm not sure where to go from here."

"Let me see your passport," the man replied unceremoniously.

Opening the passport, the man looked from it to Ethan and then back again. Handing the passport to his co-worker he quickly replied, "Right this way, sir."

The woman had a similar response. As she returned the diplomatic passport the two of them lifted Ethan's luggage onto a nearby cart and together took him to the front of the line marked 'green route'.

The officer there quickly ushered Ethan through as well. He walked through the doorway into the airport entrance area and immediately saw a man with a sign bearing his name.

"I'm Ethan Benham," he said approaching the man.

"Hello sir, I'm Andrew your driver. Is this all of your luggage?" Andrew was a small man, but took charge of the cart with Ethan's luggage on it. "The car is right over here sir."

"Please Andrew you don't have to call me sir."

"I'm sorry sir, I do. You are an important man in your country and I must give you the respect you deserve." Andrew pushed the cart with ease as they exited the building.

"Wow! It is so beautiful here. I just can't get over it. The air is so clean and it's such a warm day."

"Yes sir, Zimbabwe is a beautiful country."

"Look at all the flowering trees and even palm trees."

Andrew knew this type, he had been driving for the embassy for fifteen years. There were some who could care less about the country and then there were those like Ethan who really appreciated it. He smiled and said, "Zimbabwe has some of the most beautiful flowers and trees on the planet and I'm glad to hear that you like it sir."

"I do Andrew, everything is so green and there are colors everywhere."

By that time they had arrived at the car and Andrew was busy loading it. "I'll be taking you to the Monomatapa Hotel right in the city center. I know you'll love it. It will take a few minutes to get there though. Would you like a Coke or something to eat before we leave?"

"No, they gave me Cokes and food on the plane." Ethan replied. "I really want to see the sights anyway. Is it possible to take the long way there? You know, drive around a bit, see the sights and a bit of Harare. I want to get a feel for the city."

"That is indeed possible. I'm at your disposal, sir."

They drove down tree-lined streets toward the city center. There was a beautiful park next to a tall building. "That is Freedom Square, named after independence for those who died during the struggle."

"I read about the war for independence in a book from the library. It was written by a lady whose father had been prime minister at one time."

"It must have been by Judy Todd then. Her father, Sir Garfield Todd was a great man who did a lot of very good things for the African people. He was put in prison for the things he did by the last government."

Ethan could see by the way that Andrew spat out 'the last government' that he had a distinct distaste for it. "It's amazing how clean everything is. There's no paper or bottles laying around anywhere." Even in his beloved London, it wasn't this clean.

"No, sir, we try to keep the city clean. Since labor is cheap there are plenty of people who work for the city and all they do is clean."

They drove around for forty-five minutes and saw many sights. The driver pointed out the parliament building, the reserve bank, and the courthouse where the Supreme Court met. Ethan was interested to see a Barclays Bank and a few other familiar names and logos from back home in England. Even the post boxes were just like at home.

As they sat at an intersection an oncoming bus caught Ethan's attention. "Look at that, how do they get all that stuff up there. I can see a mattress, a big wardrobe, and look there's a crate of chickens. When I first saw it I thought it was a double decker bus like we have in London, then the mattress swayed a bit and I noticed it was stuff."

"We call those chicken buses. That's how most of us in Zimbabwe travel." Changing the subject Andrew commented, "If you look in front to your right you can see your hotel."

Looking above the trees to where Andrew was pointing, Ethan could see a very tall building in a crescent shape.

When Ethan arrived at his hotel he was even more impressed. The hotel was a beautiful building, very tall and new looking. It overlooked a picturesque park with grass, trees and a swimming pool. Ethan checked in while Andrew brought in his suitcases and waited to carry them to his room. Ethan was given a room key and told where the elevators were.

"Would you like me to put your clothes in the drawers, sir?" Andrew asked as they entered Ethan's room.

"No, I'll put them away myself later. I want to get out of these clothes and go jump in that pool. It's such a nice day and it will help me to unwind from the trip."

"Yes sir. I have been assigned to help you in any way that you want. I have been given a room in the worker's quarters here and am on call twenty-four hours a day. If you need me, all you have to do is call the front desk and they will direct your call to me. If you need to go somewhere by car just call and I'll pull the car around front for you."

"Okay, that's great. If I need you I'll let you know. I won't be needing your services any time soon, so you may go for now."

"Thank you, sir. Good day," Andrew said as he let himself out the door.

Alone at last and abandoning all reserve, Ethan ran toward his bed, jumped and landed on his back. He couldn't believe his luck. Here he was in a great hotel, in a country that he had heard so much about and completely alone. No nagging parents, no pesky little brother, and no rules. Ethan had plans. He was glad the embassy had sent a car and someone to help him around, but some of what he planned he would do on his own. He wanted to enjoy this holiday. At the moment, the pool was his number one priority. Then he planned on sleeping for a couple of hours to shake off his jet lag. After that he would figure out what to do next.

Peering out the window he could see the entire downtown area from his room fourteen stories up. It really was an amazing city. The tall buildings and city streets were lined throughout with flowering trees. From his vantage point the city looked like a fantasy land and he was eager to explore it and beyond. He had a month all to himself and he planned to see everything Zimbabwe had to offer.

He hurriedly got out of his clothes and into his swimsuit. Donning the hotel robe, Ethan went back down to the main floor and out the door to the pool. There were just a few people in the pool when he got there. The water was fantastic. It was just what he needed after the long flight.

"This place would be perfect if only there were a few girls in their bikinis lounging around," he thought to himself. There were none at the moment. Maybe later.

After several laps around the pool he climbed out wanting to enjoy the sunshine and get a little tan. Choosing one of the many colorful chaise lounges, he leaned back and closed his eyes thinking, "This is the life." He could just fall asleep right where he was but the problem was his pale skin from a long English winter would burn to a crisp. At that moment a waiter interrupted his thoughts.

"Would you care for something to drink, sir?"

Ethan thought a Coke would be nice, but asked the man what they had.

"I can bring you anything from the bar. Whatever is your pleasure?"

Ethan sat up immediately, "Anything?"

"Yes, sir, anything."

"What do you have?"

"We have several different brands of beer, imported and local, most any type of mixed drink and of course any soft drink that you would care to have."

"I'll have a whisky sour," was his rather detached reply but inwardly he couldn't believe his luck.

"Yes, sir, would you like anything from the kitchen? We have twenty-four hour service."

All Ethan had eaten since the day before was airplane food and that could hardly be called food at all.

"Yes, I would like a steak and some chips if you have it."

"We have rump, T-bone, sirloin or fillet."

"I'll have fillet."

"Yes sir, how would you like it cooked?"

"I'll have it medium, just pink in the middle," Ethan replied, shying away from rare meat in a third world country.

"Yes, sir, pink in the middle."

"Sounds good. Thanks."

Ethan was amazed. He had just ordered his drink, offered by the waiter, and he wasn't even twenty-one. Back home he would have had to have a fake ID to get away with that. He found out later that the legal drinking age in Zimbabwe is eighteen. What a break.

His drink came a moment later and he leaned back in his chair enjoying his whisky sour. It tasted so good and he soon felt very relaxed. Closing his eyes Ethan opted for a quick nap knowing that when his food was brought out they would have to wake him up thus avoiding any sunburn. He set the empty glass on the grass next to him and promptly fell asleep. It seemed like seconds, but it was actually fifteen minutes and the waiter was back with his food. It smelled delicious. He got up and went to the table to eat. After being in the sun the shade really felt good. He hoped that he wasn't too red, but if he was he knew that by the next day he would be brown. He ate his food and debated whether or not to go back out in the sun to tan his back a bit. At the moment his quiet room and bed seemed more appealing so after finishing his food he returned to his room. Disregarding the air conditioner he opened the window to the pleasant breeze. He shut his curtains to keep the bright sunlight out, pulled off his swimsuit, fell on his bed and was asleep within two minutes.

While Ethan was arriving in Harare, Chipo was on her trip from Kwekwe which was long and boring. Except for a drunk man trying to get on the bus at a restroom break nothing else happened. The bus arrived in the center of the city just a little before three o'clock. Leaving the bus she decided to walk around and see where she should stay. With the money that her father had given her plus what she had put aside Chipo had almost one hundred dollars in her pocket and to her that was a large amount of money. In *Silobela* there had been times where she would go a month without ever seeing a cent, now she had money and knew she could live like a queen.

She had never seen so many cars, people, and big buildings in all of her life. The cars were flying past her as she stood on a corner wanting to cross. She didn't know when she should go. They had lights that changed from green to yellow to red. She had seen a couple of those in Gweru when she was a girl, but never so many. Almost every street had them. She was just getting ready to step off the curb when someone shouted and a hand grabbed her arm pulling her back to the sidewalk just as a car careened around the corner right where she was standing.

"Hey, you better watch out. That car almost hit you."

Chipo had fallen on the sidewalk and dropped her school satchel. Looking up she saw a young African man probably in his mid-twenties and a woman carrying a baby on her back.

Embarrassed, she reached over for her bag and started standing up, "Thank you sir, I think you saved my life."

"You have to be careful here in Harare. There are cars everywhere and some of the drivers aren't very good." The man said as he helped her up.

He had been speaking in Shona, the language of the largest tribe in Zimbabwe. Chipo, being Ndebele only spoke a little Shona, but understood what the man had said.

"Are you alright? Are you hurt?" Hearing her own language Chipo looked over to the woman with the baby.

"Yes, I'm alright, I'm so sorry for causing so much trouble." Chipo started to cry.

"Now, now, it's okay. You've just come from the rural area haven't you?" It was more a statement than a question.

"Yes, from *Silobela*. How did you know I just arrived?"

"I can tell by the way you look, your clothes and even your hair style say that you are from the rural area."

Looking around Chipo could tell what the lady was saying. Women in the city had very nice dresses on and their hair was longer and combed different. She could tell that some of them were wearing wigs because of the different color hair they had. "This is my first time to Harare, my name is Chipo Sibanda"

Chipo had noticed that no one else had paid any attention to what had happened to her. A few people looked at her when she was on the ground, but no one else stopped but this kind couple.

"My name is Shamiso and this is my husband Alfred." The light had changed and the three of them were able to walk across the road together. "You must be very careful here in the City Chipo. There are some people who would take advantage of you. Don't let anyone carry your bag or they might just run off with it. There are people who prey on young girls who just arrive in the city from the rural area. They steal from them and even worse . . . " Shamiso let the last part of the sentence go unsaid, but Chipo knew what she meant.

"Where in *Silobela* do you come from?"

"I'm from *Siyezi*, do you know *Silobela*?"

"I'm from Zhombe so yes I do know a little about *Silobela*. My husband and I now are working in Kadoma, he's a pastor and we are in Harare attending a pastor's summit."

"Oh, I go to the Church of Christ. What church are you with?"

"How about that we are also with the Church of Christ. We know pastor Alex Dube from *Silobela* do you know him?"

"Yes, he is my grandfather. My late mother, Martha, was his daughter."

Alfred and Shamiso looked at each other knowingly. "Yes we knew your mother years ago. I was so sorry that she passed away." Shamiso had such a look of tenderness in her eyes. She placed her hand on Chipo's shoulder. "What are you doing here in Harare?"

"I'm looking for a job. I'm going to be a model." She spoke it out as if she already were. "Right now I'm looking for a place to stay. Do you know of any place?"

"We're staying at the Bible college and that's where we usually stay when we're in Harare. I know there are some nice accommodations in many places in Harare. If you go across Simora Machel avenue about five blocks you'll find Baines avenue. There are several motels and accommodation places on that street. It's expensive do you have enough money?"

"Oh yes, I have plenty." Chipo spoke with such assurance that neither Shamiso or Alfred doubted her. They felt if her father had allowed her to come to Harare to get a job then he probably would have given her enough money to live on until she was settled.

Alfred spoke up for the first time since they met, this time speaking fluently in Ndebele. "Please be careful. You're a young attractive girl and some will try to take advantage of you. Can we pray for you?"

Chipo was taken back by this, she had never heard anyone ask to pray for her before. "Yes you can pray for me." She thought he meant that he would pray for her during his prayer time, but he reached over and took her hand in one of his and his wife's in the other, bowing his head he prayed, "Lord, thank you for bringing us in contact with Chipo. We know that it was you who has put this appointment together. It's a divine appointment. Father I ask you to watch over her and protect her. Lead her, guide her, move in her life. We know that no one can snatch us out of your hand, so Father, keep Chipo in the palm of your hand. In Jesus name, amen."

Chipo had never prayed in public like this before and was a little apprehensive about it. "Thank you. I've never had anyone pray for me like that before."

"Chipo we will continue to pray for you." Shamiso was holding both of her hands and smiling at her. Nodding toward a building she said, "This is where we need to go. Here's the phone number of the college if you have any problems. Please call and ask for us, I don't know what we would be able to do, but we would do everything that we could to help you if you needed it."

"Thank you again," Chipo had never received such kindness before and these people were strangers to her. "Where was this place that had accommodations?"

Alfred pointed across the main road and explained again. "You can get to Blaine on any of these streets that are going north, but I know there is a couple places on the corner of Fourth Street."

"Okay, goodbye. It was nice getting to know you." As they parted Chipo was happily thinking to herself, 'If this is the way people are in Harare I'm really going to like it here."

She had noticed while walking with Alfred and Shamiso that they would cross the street when the little box with the lighted drawing of a person walking turned on. She waited by the curb, this time not so close, and when the light changed she crossed with the crowd. She kept walking north toward the street that the nice couple had told her about.

When she arrived at the next block she saw a very tall building with a sign that said The Monomatapa Hotel. It looked like a very nice place to stay, so she walked over toward it.

The building was so pretty to look at. There were trees and flowers all around it. A driveway looped around to the front door and a man stood there in a uniform opening the door for people coming and going. She noticed how friendly he was, smiling at the people. Boldly she strolled up to the door. The friendly man had just closed the door behind some people who had arrived and was just getting ready to open it for her when he looked at her. His smile vanished and he had a stern look on his face. "What are you doing here?" he demanded.

Her boldness disappeared, "I . . . I need a room to stay in."

"Do you have any money?" His fingers were still on the door, but he wasn't about to let a vagrant in his hotel. Then again, if she did have money she was a customer and he needed to treat her that way.

"Ye . . . Yes, I have money." Chipo wasn't sure if she should stay here now or not. She had never seen a person change from being so happy to being this grumpy before, it frightened her.

As soon as he heard that she had money he was all smiles again. Opening the door he said, "Right this way madam."

Chipo looked at the man as if he were a lion ready to pounce and scurried past him. There was a long desk in the front with a man and a lady working. The ceilings were high and the whole place looked like a palace to Chipo. She walked up to the desk thinking she would talk to the lady instead of the man, but right when she got up front the phone rang and the lady answered it. The man looked very busy and Chipo didn't know if she should bother him.

After a few minutes he looked up and saw her standing there. "May I help you Ma'am?"

"Yes, I would like a room. How much does one cost?"

"A single room for one night is $119.00. How many nights would you be staying?"

"That much?" Chipo was startled, "I don't have that much. Don't you have anything cheaper?"

Looking at Chipo he then realized that she was just a girl from the rural area, "No we don't have any cheaper rooms."

"Could you direct me to a more affordable hotel then please?"

"How much are you wanting to spend?"

"I only have $93 and I don't know how long I would need a place to stay."

"The only place I can think of is the Seven Miles Hotel, they charge by the week and I think it's only $50 or $60. You can try there."

"Is it near here?"

The man was getting more annoyed by the second. He didn't want to have to deal with this girl. "It's on the other side of town, off Airport road. Now, if you'll excuse me I'm busy."

Chipo turned to go and saw a young white man walking out the door. She could see that he wasn't much older than herself, but the doorman smiled at him and another man opened the door of a car for him. "Why did he get better service than her? What's wrong with me?" Chipo slowly opened the door for herself and walked out the door.

When Ethan awoke it was dark in his room. Oh no, I slept the rest of the day away. Then a breeze blew through and lifted the heavy curtains away from his window. Although the sun was getting lower in the sky, there was still plenty of day left. After showering, Ethan put on his blue suit, planning on going to the embassy to let them know he was here. That was not what he particularly wanted to do; he would rather have gone back to the pool and work on his tan. But duty won out over pleasure. The tan would have to wait until tomorrow. At least the errand would allow him to see more of the city. He called the front desk and had them call for his car.

Entering the lobby he noticed a girl at the front desk. She was an African, dressed in a very simple dress, but her face was beautiful and she had a figure to match. He overheard her talking to the man at the desk as he passed by. The man was telling her the cost of a room and Ethan heard her reply as she calculated the cost against what was in her purse, the first far exceeding the second.

"Could you direct me to a more affordable hotel?" the girl asked of the man at the reception.

Since he was just walking through the lobby he didn't get to hear much more except something about the Seven Miles Hotel. Exiting the hotel he found his man was waiting with the car door open for him.

"Thank you Andrew. We need to go to the embassy," Ethan instructed as he climbed into the back seat. As Andrew took his place behind the steering wheel, Ethan saw the girl from the lobby exiting the hotel. He also noticed that his driver looked her direction as well. He thought about the conversation that the girl had with the man at the front desk and felt that the man had been rather impatient and had talked down to her.

" Andrew, wait just a minute. Let's offer the lady a ride," Ethan said to the driver. "Do you need a lift?" Ethan asked the girl after he lowered his window.

The girl shyly lowered her eyes. She said something in the African language and the driver replied to her.

"What are you saying?" Ethan asked the driver.

"She says that she needs a lift, but she doesn't know you. Sir, she is a girl from the rural area and has just come to Harare. You probably don't want her in your car."

"No, I think it would be fine if we gave her a lift. Offer her a ride. It's okay."

Ethan had a double motive for offering the girl a ride. Firstly he thought she was one of the most beautiful girls he had ever seen and hoped they could become friends. Exploring Harare with her as his guide would be great. Secondly, if they drove her to the place where she was going to stay then Ethan would know where to find her again.

Ethan's driver offered the girl a lift and she reluctantly took it. Ethan opened the door for her and invited her to climb in.

"Andrew, do you know where the Seven Miles Hotel is?"

"Yes sir, but it is a little way out. We have to go back toward the airport to get to it."

"That's okay." Ethan then turned to the girl, "What's your name?"

"My name is Chipo Sibanda."

"Hi Chipo, I'm very glad to meet you. My name is Ethan. I just flew into Harare today. I'm from London and you are the first Zimbabwean that I have met, well, besides my driver. Tell me about yourself."

"Really there's not much to say. I just got off the bus from Kwekwe and I am here in Harare to find a job as a model."

"Oh, you're a model. What modeling school did you go to?"

"I didn't go to school for modeling. I didn't even know there were schools for modeling."

"Well, I really don't know about all that, but I can see that you definitely have what it takes to be a model. When I saw you in the lobby, I was hoping that you would check in so that we might get to know each other better."

Chipo blushed at his comments, but his remarks made her all the more determined to see her plans through to the finish.

Ethan was thinking to himself that this was the prettiest girl he had ever seen and the prospect of spending time with her made his Zimbabwe holiday even more appealing. His only objection to her appearance was her clothes. They left a lot to be desired. He could imagine her in a beautiful flowing gown, or even better, a nice pair of jeans with a scoop necked top. She would be the envy of any girl.

The conversation continued as they rode through the city and Chipo became more relaxed. She'd never met anyone from the UK before and was anxious to know all about him, but she felt too shy to ask as many questions as he was asking her.

"We should have dinner together sometime," Ethan said hopefully.

Chipo didn't know what to say to that. No boy had ever asked to eat a meal with her. "I will have to let you know. First I must find a job," she replied with a shy smile.

"It won't take you long at all to find a job," was Ethan's earnest reply.

As they drove along Ethan was aware that the scenery was changing block by block as they moved away from the city center. The nice gardens and manicured lawns were disappearing and in their place he saw more litter and dirt. The buildings and houses appeared old and more run down. Soon they were driving through a residential area where there were very small houses, one after another, spaced so close together that a borrowed cup of sugar could be passed from one neighbor to another without even going outside. Well, maybe not quite that close, but almost. There were people walking everywhere, even in the road. Ethan felt the urge to quickly lock all the car doors but felt that would offend his guest.

Soon they were in a less crowded area and pulling in to the Seven Miles Hotel. Ethan was surprised. After seeing the luxurious Monomatapa he was shocked to see this hotel. It looked run down and a bit squalid. There were men congregated in front of the building, drinking from big brown containers. He presumed they contained beer. It didn't look like a very nice place for a single young girl to stay.

Chipo got out of the car and took her suitcase. "Thank you so much for the lift. I would have never found the place without your help."

"That's okay, don't mention it. I was glad that I could help. Are you sure you want to stay here?"

"The man at the other hotel said this was where I would be able to find a place I could afford, so I guess I don't have much choice."

Turning to the driver Chipo spoke in Ndebele, "Thank you very much for driving me here. I really appreciate it. I have walked long distances before but I don't think I could have walked this far." She smiled at him and shook his hand.

"Is this place safe for her?" Ethan asked the driver as she walked away.

Andrew shrugged his shoulders and said that she would probably be okay. Ethan didn't like it at all. How could such a beautiful young girl stay in a dump like this? He was just thinking that he should run in and drag her out when she returned with another girl walking beside her.

"This is my relative, Peggy," Chipo said, introducing the girl with her. "I was surprised to find her working at this hotel."

Climbing from the car, Ethan extended his hand to the young woman.

Chipo went on to explain that she wouldn't be staying in this hotel, but at her cousin's house. Ethan was relieved. "Peggy, may I have your address please, and a phone number. I'd like to keep in touch. I'd also love it if the two of you would join me for a swim tomorrow. I'm staying at the Monomatapa."

"I'm afraid I have to work all day tomorrow," Peggy explained. "But I'm off on Friday. Will that be ok?"

Ethan was a bit disappointed because it was still early in the week and Friday was a long way off. "Sure, that will be great," he responded, covering his disappointment with a quick smile. He gave the girls his room number and instructed them that when they arrived they should just ask at the front desk to call up to his room and he would meet them downstairs in the lobby.

He said goodbye, got in the car and they drove off. As the car headed back towards town, Ethan felt very pleased with himself. Here he was, only six hours in the country, and already he had met two girls and had a date. Ethan's gloating was interrupted when he noticed the driver's look in the rearview mirror.

"What's the matter, did I do something wrong?"

The driver looked again at Ethan and said, "Sir, if I may be so bold, those girls aren't the type of girls that you want to hang around with. The one lives here in Harare but the area she lives in is not a very nice one. She is just a common girl and isn't the sort for you. If she knew who you were she would do everything she could to get her clutches in you to get as much money from you as possible. She would even try to get you to take her back to England when you go. The other girl is a simple rural girl. Yes, she is very pretty, but she doesn't even know what it's like to live in the city. The reason she didn't give you an answer about going out to eat with you is because she didn't understand. In the rural areas most women are not much better than slaves. She probably works the fields and cooks the food. When she serves the food to her father he probably doesn't even notice her. I'm sure he never thanks her. She probably didn't even understand what you meant when you asked her to dinner. She might even think you want her to cook for you. Sir, these are just not people who are in the same class as you."

Ethan was taken back by what the driver said. He was very attracted to Chipo and would have liked to spend some time with her.

"I don't think that they will show up on Friday for your invitation for a swim," continued Andrew. "Most likely, neither one of them swim and the rural girl probably doesn't even own a bathing suit. I wouldn't hold my breath for them to show up. Plus, it would cost them a lot to get a bus to come all the way into town."

The driver continued talking but Ethan put it all out of his mind. He was thinking of Chipo and how she carried herself. In his way of thinking he couldn't see any difference between her and a lot of girls he went to school with. She spoke very good English and seemed to be well educated. He didn't understand why the driver had such a low opinion of her. He hoped that they would come to the hotel on Friday for a swim. He would buy Chipo a swimsuit if she needed one. He had seen them for sale in the gift shop when he went out to the pool earlier that day. As he gazed out of the car window, he soon spied the Union Jack flying in the breeze and knew that they were at the embassy.

Chipo was stunned. She had just been feeling sorry for herself and thought everyone in Harare must be rude and now here was a nice boy that was willing to give her a ride, and a very nice looking boy at that.

At the Seven Miles Hotel Peggy still had to finish her shift at work. She told Chipo that she could stay in the lobby and wait until she was off at 4:00, only half an hour away. Chipo took a seat close by so she and Peggy were able to talk. The motel itself wasn't a very busy place. Peggy got called into the bar occasionally to run the cash register, getting change or taking the money and putting it in a safe. Only once during the half hour did someone come in for a room, and that man only wanted a room for a couple hours. Chipo didn't understand why you would want a room for only two hours.

She and Peggy talked about family and *Silobela*. Their mothers were cousins and Peggy knew all about how Chipo's father had tricked her mother into marriage.

"So what brings you to Harare?" Peggy asked.

Chipo decided to tell Peggy the truth and explained what she wanted to do.

"Well, you certainly have the looks to be a model but you do realize that modeling is a hard business to get into," was Peggy's all knowing reply. "I won't tell anyone that you're here, not even my mother. Your secret is safe with me."

Peggy had left *Silobela* several years ago to find work in Harare as well. Her father had passed away and the family needed someone to work. She was the oldest and so it was decided that she would find work in the city. She first went to Kwekwe, but there was nothing for her there. She then came to Harare and found this job at the Seven Miles Hotel. The money wasn't bad, but she spent most of it on her own living expense. There was always a little though, for her to send home to her mother. After living in the city for so long she said she would never return to the rural area.

"I'm so glad I found you Peggy. I was getting a little frightened walking around the city and then the way people treated me at the Monomatapa Hotel. It was like I was a second class citizen." Chipo was glad to have someone that she could talk to, someone that understood, especially about her father.

They talked a while about the family then the conversation turned to other things, "So who was that young man that brought you to the Seven Miles?"

"Oh, he was a guy that I met at the Monomatapa Hotel in town. He had heard me talking to the desk clerk and knew that I couldn't afford a room there so he offered to drive me to the Seven Miles."

"Well he seemed very nice and nice to look at too. What was his name?"

"Ethan, he said it was Ethan."

"Ethan what?"

"I don't know, he didn't tell me his surname. He said he just flew in this morning from London and was new to Zimbabwe."

"Well, he must be fairly well off if he is staying at the Monomatapa. It's a very expensive hotel. Whatever made you think you could afford it?"

"I didn't know what it would cost. I just thought it looked like a nice place to stay," Chipo replied.

Chipo was thoughtful for a moment. "He was rather handsome though, wasn't he? His eyes were amazing. So green. Oh well, we'll probably never see him again."

"Hey, he invited us to go swimming on Friday. We could show up and see if he really meant for us to come. I think he was interested in you. You're a very pretty girl, Chipo. I noticed several guys around here looking at you. Do you know how to swim?"

"Yes, mom taught all of us how to swim. You remember we lived near the dam. It was only ten kilometers away from our house, and she was afraid that one of us might go into the water on a hot day and drown, so she made sure we knew how to swim. She even had a book that she got from the missionary that taught us what to do if we needed to revive someone who had drowned. She made me read it myself and then she made me read it to my brothers. Then she made me read it again to her. We practiced on one another until we were tired of doing it, but even today I can remember everything."

"Well then, I guess on Friday we should go in to town for a swim."

"I do have one problem. I don't have a swimsuit. At home we wore our underwear or nothing at all. We were young and it didn't matter. I don't think I can get away with that at the Monomatapa," Chipo said with an awkward laugh.

"Don't worry, we'll find you a swimsuit somewhere."

Ethan had finished his business at the embassy and got back to the hotel around 5:00pm. It was still warm outside, not as warm as the afternoon, but warm enough for a swim. He got into his swimsuit and went to the pool. There were more people there this time, several young people, guys and girls. It looked like they were having a party of some kind. He dove in the pool and swam several laps. When he got out, the same waiter that had served him in the afternoon was there at his side asking if he wanted anything to drink. He ordered a beer and sat down on one of the lounges watching the other young people playing in the pool. One of the guys, a tall, thin, white boy with shaggy blond hair came over and sat next to him. He ordered a beer and started up a conversation.

"Hi, my name is Steve."

"Hi Steve, I'm Ethan." They both stretched out their hands to shake.

"I've not seen you here before, did you just arrive?"

"Yes, I flew in from London this morning. I'll be staying for a month. Are all of you staying here?"

"No, we all live here in Harare, the manager is a friend of my fathers and he allows us to come and swim sometimes. So you'll be here a month. That's great, you'll have to let me and the gang show you around."

Ethan couldn't believe his luck, now he had a new friend that knew his way around Harare. "That would be great. I've got a few trips around the country planned, but I'd love to have some people to talk to and do things with."

"Hey I know, would you like to come to a *braai* on Friday night?"

"What's a *braai*?" Ethan asked.

"Oh, it's an Afrikaans word. Means to cook. Maybe you call it a bar-b-que or a cook out."

"Okay, yeah."

"A bunch of the university kids are home at the moment and one of the girls is hosting the get together on her parent's farm," Steve continued. "I'm sure you'd be welcome. After eating we'll probably dance for a while and then when it gets dark we'll go bunny bashing."

"Bunny bashing! What in the world is that?"

"You've never been bunny bashing? Ahh, it's great fun, Zimbabwe style. We get in a couple of Land Rovers and drive around the farm looking for rabbits. When we spot one we shine the headlights and flashlights at them and they freeze. Then we get in a circle and walk closer to the rabbit until we are right up to it, or until it runs. Whoever is closest to it kicks it and then we keep on kicking it until we kill it."

"That's morbid, my friend," Ethan said. "Doesn't sound like much fun to me."

"Oh don't worry, we never get to the rabbit, and if we did the girls would never let us kick it. One time some guys did get to the rabbit and kicked it. The girls yelled and started chasing and kicking them. The fun part is driving around, looking for rabbits, if you get what I mean. We'll probably swim if the weather stays nice. If you want to go, give me a call."

The waiter had just brought the bill for the drink and Steve asked for a pen. Tearing a corner off the bill, Steve wrote his phone number on it.

"Don't call me too early in the morning. I plan on getting as much sleep as I can during the holiday," Steve said as he handed the paper to Ethan.

Turning to his friends, Steve called out, "Hey guys, this is Ethan; he's going to come to the party with us on Friday."

Ethan was pleased and a bit surprised when Steve's declaration was met with "Yeah! Great! Glad to meet you Ethan. See you at the party." Ethan just smiled and waved at the crowd of kids smiling over at him. It was a very mixed group of kids, most were white, several appeared to be of Indian race and a few black skinned kids, but not as dark as others he'd seen. He assumed they must be of a mixed race.

Later that night Ethan lay in bed thinking about the day. He had already made some friends and it was only the first day of his African adventure. His holiday was off to a good start.

4

Promises

Ethan was having the time of his life! All week long the same kids that he had met that first afternoon came for a swim and he would join them. Steve introduced him to several of the guys and they included him in their plans each night, frequenting different bars, going to parties and enjoying the night life in the city. He would stay up most of the night and then sleep late in the mornings, sometimes into the afternoon. He was really looking forward to the *braai* planned for Friday.

As he felt more comfortable around his new friends he began to ask questions about the cultural differences he was seeing. He found out that there were several different races in Zimbabwe; White, Black, Indian, and Colored. Ethan was quite shocked when he first heard someone use the word "Colored." Where he came from that was considered very offensive. But here it seemed to be the acceptable term used for the mixed race. Most of them were what he would call Black in England, but in Zimbabwe he had learned that people differentiate between the Black African and someone of mixed race. All his new "colored" friends seemed very happy, almost proud to wear that distinction. With this group of kids no one really paid any attention to the difference in color, they were all just friends. Ethan felt very comfortable with them, especially Steve and a few of the girls.

Ring! Ring! Ethan cracked open one eye. "What is that?" he asked himself. Then waking a little more he realized it was the phone. Looking at the clock he saw that it was not yet 11:00 so he knew it wasn't Steve calling. Steve never got up before 11:00. Reaching over he answered the phone. "Hello? Can I help you?" He was still a little groggy.

"Good morning sir, this is the front desk. You have some visitors here. Would you like me to send them up?"

'Visitors, now who could that be?' "Who is it?"

"Well sir, I don't know their names, but it's two young ladies."

Ethan perked up. It must be a couple of the girls he had been hanging around in the evening. "Uh, no don't send them up." Looking around at his messy room, "I'll come down there."

"Yes sir, I'll let them know."

The phone hung up with a click. Ethan quickly grabbed the clothes that were strewn about on the floor and straightened the covers on his bed. Walking by the couch he grabbed the empty plate and glass from last night's supper and put them in the sink. That looked better, he guessed they could have come up.

Going into the bathroom he looked in the mirror, his hair was sticking up all over the place. Turning on the water he stuck his head under the tap, grabbing the towel he quickly rubbed his hair then ran a brush through it. Well, it's an improvement. He quickly brushed his teeth and threw on some clothes.

As he walked out of his door he looked back at his room, "not the cleanest, but if they want to come up I guess it's presentable."

When he arrived at the lobby, to his surprise, he found Chipo and Peggy standing there with bags in hand. It had been five days and his invitation for the girls to come and swim had slipped his mind, but he was pleased to see them.

Chipo was dressed in a pull over top and a pair of jeans. "Hi Ethan, we're here." She was a little worried because of the surprised look on his face. She wasn't sure if he really wanted them there.

"Hi Chipo and Peggy, you came. I wasn't sure if you would or not."

"I hope it's okay, the invitation is still open isn't it?"

"Yes, by all means. Why don't you come on up to my room so you can change into your swim wear." He saw that they had towels and their suits in the bag that they carried.

Peggy spoke up, "Alright. I've always wanted to see what the rooms here look like."

Chipo felt a bit shy about going to his room and was about to decline the offer when she heard Peggy agreeing with the plan and saw her following Ethan in that direction. There was nothing to do but to follow them.

Ethan soon stopped at a door and pressed a button. The door slid open and there was a tiny room before them. Ethan and Peggy walked in and again Chipo followed. The doors slid shut once more. As Ethan pressed another button in a long row of buttons on the wall, it dawned on Chipo that the tiny room was actually an elevator. She'd read about them and at the moment was very thankful for the many hours she had spent with her nose in a book. The elevator started upwards with a jerk and Chipo nervously grabbed hold of Peggy's arm hoping that Ethan wouldn't notice her anxiety. Peggy laid a hand on her shoulder and reassured Chipo with a look of humor on her face.

"This is your first time in an elevator, hey?" Peggy asked Chipo in their African language so that Ethan wouldn't understand. Chipo gave an affirmative nod and squeezed Peggy's arm a bit tighter as she noticed Ethan looking her direction.

From the moment he'd met the girls in the lobby, Ethan had been struggling to keep his eyes off Chipo. He had been struck again by her beauty. He would catch himself staring at her and then felt self–conscious and would try his best to stop. When the elevator jolted he immediately saw how frightened she was. He'd known people who had a fear of elevators, but never this serious.

Stopping at the fourteenth floor the doors opened and Chipo exited as quickly as she could. She looked around confused because the hallway looked like the same one they had walked down before they had gotten in that contraption. Again she found herself following behind like a lost puppy. They finally stopped at one of the many doors and Ethan used his key to open it. Ethan and Peggy walked in, but Chipo remained in the hallway.

"Come on in, Chipo," Peggy implored.

"It's not another elevator is it?" Chipo quizzed her cousin apprehensively.

"No, no, this is his room."

Chipo peered in and saw chairs, a table and a bed. She blushed at the thought of being in that room with a strange boy.

"It's ok, Chipo. Come on in."

Still feeling a bit unsure, Chipo gingerly took a step in and Peggy shut the door behind her. Even though Chipo and Peggy were speaking in their native tongue, Ethan was pretty sure what was being said gaining a clue from the occasional English word thrown in like "elevator" and "bedroom." He had to turn his face to keep from laughing. It was amazing to him to think that this beautiful, intelligent girl was so naïve to things that he just took for granted. It only caused him to want to get to know her better. It would be fun and interesting to explore Zimbabwe with her at his side.

Ethan quickly remembered his manners, "Would you like something to drink?"

Opening the fridge the girls saw that he had Cokes, orange juice or water. "I would like a Coke please." Chipo responded.

"Make that two."

Ethan thought it was too early for Coke, but then they probably were up earlier than he was. "Please sit down while I get some glasses."

Sitting down Chipo looked around the room. "This is such a beautiful room, the rug covers the whole floor."

Ethan brought the drinks over and sat down on the couch next to Chipo. "Yes, have you never seen wall to wall carpet before?"

"No is that what this is?" Chipo was embarrassed, she was out of her comfort zone in this big place. "Peggy I think you could fit your whole house in this room."

"It is a big room, but I don't think my house would quite fit here." Turning to Ethan to change the subject she stated, "Were you surprised that we came for a swim?"

"Yes, I really was. After I left you my driver started talking and he said you wouldn't come. He said it was too far for you and not to hold my breath."

"We talked about it and decided to take you up on the offer," Peggy replied. "Both of us know how to swim and it's been really hot these last few weeks," shrugging her shoulders she said, "it sounded like a good idea."

"Well, I'm glad you're here. Just give me a moment and I'll get into my swimsuit."

Ethan hurried into the bathroom to change and the girls looked at each other.

"I guess we need to get changed also," Chipo said. "I suppose we better wait to use the bathroom. Are you sure I look okay in this bathing suit? I feel like I'm not wearing anything when I have it on."

"You look fine." was Peggy's quick reply. "In fact, I'm sure that your "boyfriend" will really like you in it."

"Peggy! Don't say things like that. I've never had a boyfriend in my life and besides I really don't think he likes me that way. Anyway, my father would have a fit if I brought home a white boyfriend."

The girls both laughed at that. Chipo's laugh was more forced though. She could not imagine what her father would do if she brought any white man to their home, much less a white boyfriend. Chipo got up from the couch and walked over to the window. She could still hear her father talking about the war and how he was tortured and mistreated by the *Makiwas*, the white man. "Don't ever trust a *Makiwa*!" He would spit out the words with bitterness.

"Oh! Look how high up we are. I didn't know we had gone so high. We weren't in the elevator very long."

About that time Ethan came out wearing his swimsuit and the girls went in to change into theirs.

Ethan finished his Coke thinking about Chipo and how different she looked today. Her new look was much better than the old one. She looked nice! He had no doubt that she would make a good model, even internationally. He heard them talking and laughing in the bathroom and was curious to know what they were saying, not understanding a word of their language. He wished his friends were already here for an afternoon swim. Then he could introduce them around and maybe the girls would feel more at ease. Just then the door opened and the girls stepped out. Chipo was wearing a nice conservative navy blue one–piece suit, one that his mother would approve of, but on Chipo it looked great.

"Wow!" Ethan exclaimed and remained speechless for a brief second. "Okay, let's go swim." Ethan grabbed his towel from the back of the chair and they started down the hallway.

"Are we going to use the uh . . . the . . ."

"The elevator?" asked Ethan filling in the elusive word.

"Yes, the elevator. I'm not sure I like it. Is it safe?"

Peggy replied to that one, "Yes it's very safe. Since we are on the four-teenth floor we would be too tired to swim if we walked all the way down."

"Okay, I'll try it again, if you're sure it won't fall all the way down."

"It's been working all day and for many days before this. I'm sure it will be fine."

As Peggy was talking, Chipo turned and saw a brief half–smile on Ethan's face and then had to smile at herself. She realized that she was over-reacting and so she quickly dropped the subject.

The three of them walked to the elevator, Chipo pushing aside her fears and walking with more confidence than she felt. The elevator brought them quickly down to the lobby and Chipo was very glad to get out of the little room. They went outside and after laying aside their towels, got into the pool. Chipo had never swum in a pool before. She had only swum in the river or dam. This water was crystal clear. She could see all the way to the bottom. They spent the rest of the morning and into the afternoon swimming and had a great time. When it was time for lunch they ate at the poolside. The girls were a bit anxious about the cost until they realized that Ethan was paying for the whole thing.

After lunch Ethan decided that he should stay out of the sun for a while, still careful of his pale skin. He sat on a chaise lounge in the shade of an umbrella and watched the girls swim. Chipo was a fast swimmer and could beat Peggy in a race every time. She held his rapt attention. Even when he closed his eyes he couldn't get her out of his mind. Maybe he was falling in love with this African girl. "No," he thought, "There's no way that I could explain this girl to my family." When it came to love and especially marriage, Ethan's parents believe their son needed to marry someone from "a good family with a good name." Ethan quickly laid aside all of these qualms. He thought Chipo was pretty and he liked looking at her and being with her, nothing more.

After a while Ethan got back in the pool and the fun antics were better than ever as the trio relaxed in each other's company. Peggy couldn't help but notice the looks that Ethan was giving Chipo. She also noticed the looks that Chipo was returning his direction. Beginning to feel like a third wheel, Peggy decided to try a little experiment wondering if they would even notice if she was absent. So when neither one was looking she slipped out of the water and went to the ladies room. She made sure that she stayed out for over ten minutes and when she got back they were out of the pool, sitting by each other on one chaise lounge talking away. As she came up to them Chipo said, "Oh hi. Why, you're not even wet, when did you get out of the pool?"

So much for being missed.

Chipo continued, "Ethan and I were just talking and he needed to get out of the sun again, so we sat down."

"Yes, I see that you are sitting down," Peggy replied as she observed the close proximity of the two. "I left the pool for thirteen minutes and you didn't even miss me." Peggy gave a sly smile to the pair. "Maybe you would like it better if I were to leave you two alone?" Chipo and Ethan exchanged a look. Both were thinking she was right, but kept their thoughts to themselves.

"No, don't be silly, we're just talking and having a nice time. Why would we want you to leave?" Chipo replied. "By the way, Ethan has invited us to a *braai* tonight hosted by some of his friends. It sounds like fun. Can we go?"

"I don't know. Who are these kids?"

"They're just some kids home from university on school break. They invited me to come and I think it would be alright if you come too," Ethan replied.

"Well, I don't know," replied Peggy cautiously. "Maybe things are different where you are from, but here . . . well, I just wonder if they would really want us to join them."

Reading between the lines Ethan sensed what Peggy wasn't saying.

"Oh I don't think that will be a problem. This group is a very mixed group of kids. They all seem to get along and have a great time together. I'll tell you what, the kids are meeting here and traveling out to the farm together. You can hang around and I'll introduce you. I'll bet they'll invite you right away."

"Well, I guess we can hang around a little while. If it doesn't work out we can always get a taxi and go back home."

"If it doesn't work out I'll stay behind with you and drive you home myself."

Both Peggy and Chipo were satisfied with that plan.

"Okay, when will they be here?" Peggy quickly replied.

"Around 4:30 or 5:00. That's just a few hours away and I would really love for you to stay." Although Ethan had been speaking mostly to Peggy, he directed this last remark to Chipo.

Feeling sufficiently waterlogged they decided to go back to Ethan's room.

"They have a VCR player in the room and they rent movies in the lobby. Why don't you girls go on up and get changed and I'll look for a good movie to watch." He handed the key to Chipo.

"That sounds like fun," Peggy replied. "Chipo you're really in for a treat." Then Peggy turned to Ethan. "Now don't go and get one of those shoot them up, blow them up movies. Get a nice one that we'll all enjoy."

"Don't worry, I know the perfect movie, it's called "While You Were Sleeping" with Sandra Bullock and Bill Pullman. You girls will love it."

Peggy and Chipo returned to the room and were changed by the time Ethan got there. "Here it is, Peggy. Can you get it ready while I change? I also ordered some popcorn which they are going to bring up to us in a few minutes."

"I'll have it all ready when you come out," Peggy replied as she took the video from Ethan's outstretched hand.

Chipo watched and wondered about the black box that Peggy put in the machine. Peggy tried to explain that it was like a cassette tape but with pictures. She could see from Chipo's expression that understanding was slow in coming.

"Just wait. You'll figure it out when we watch the movie." Peggy continued to set things up and used the remote control to turn the TV on. Then she noticed that the room was wired with surround sound. Turning the volume up to the max, Peggy pressed 'play'. The 5.1 Dolby surround exploded from the THX screen. Chipo jumped with a start and looked around the room wide eyed and frightened. Peggy laughed and turned the sound down. She pointed to the speakers and tried once more to educate her cousin concerning the modern world of technology. Chipo had to laugh at herself as understanding sunk in. She sat down on the couch and watched in awe while the previews played. The pictures moved so fast and the sound was all around her. There had been occasions back home when the missionary played movies using a reel to reel projector and a white sheet hung from the clothes line as the screen. There was one little speaker and unless you sat real close to it the sound was very hard to hear.

"This is going to be exciting!" declared Chipo.

At that moment a knock at the door announced the arrival of the pop-corn. Chipo had eaten popcorn before but never as nice as this, drizzled with butter and salt. It tasted so good. Ethan emerged from the bathroom, dressed and with his hair combed neatly in place. He shut the curtain and turned the lights down low to provide a better theater effect then took a seat beside Chipo. Peggy squeezed in on the other end of the sofa and pressed 'play'. At one tender scene in the film Peggy glance over at her cousin beside her and noticed that the TV screen was not the only place where romance was being played out. Ethan and Chipo were snuggled close, Ethan's arm across Chipo's shoulders, the two sharing the bowl of popcorn. Peggy smiled to herself and wondered if her sweet cousin was ready for such a romantic adventure.

Chipo had experienced her share of attention from boys. When she was in school there were many boys who tried very hard to get her atten-tion. Some were even bold enough to try to get alone with her. She quickly learned their tricks, though, and she always managed to avoid that situation. There were a couple of boys who were very persistent, but she had no inter-est in them and was not shy to let them know. But with Ethan it wasn't the same. He made her feel . . . different. He was not like any boy she had ever known.

"Well, Steve should be here with some of the kids," Ethan remarked as the movie ended. "We better go down and see them." Ethan rose to his feet pulling Chipo to hers as well. Peggy joined them and noticed that Ethan and Chipo continued to hold hands. They went back down to the pool and found that most of the kids were there.

"Hi everyone." Ethan called out. Many answered his greeting and some of the boys, noticing the new girls, came over to shake hands.

"This is Chipo and Peggy. I met them the first day I arrived."

Steve, being the leader that he was, spoke up first and surprising Ethan he spoke in Shona, "Hi Chipo and Peggy, it's very good to meet you. Where do you live?"

"Hi Steve, it's good to meet you too. I live in Chitungwiza, Chipo is my cousin who has just arrived in Harare and is living with me."

"That's Harare's gain." Steve decided he better speak in English so ev-eryone could follow the conversation. Only some of the kids spoke Shona. "We're having a *braai* tonight out on a farm, do you want to come?"

"Yes, we'd love to come." Peggy knew her cousin really wanted to stay and spend more time with Ethan. She also knew that after they left, they would probably never see him again. "Ethan mentioned that you were hav-ing a *braai*. We don't have anything to bring though."

"That's okay, there'll be plenty of food. Just bring yourselves."

A little later Chipo and Peggy went to the lady's room and Steve found his chance to talk to his friend alone.

"Where did you find these girls? That Chipo is hot. I can't believe it. You are here for less than a week and already you're into someone."

"Yeah, she is pretty, isn't she? We met here at the hotel the day I arrived. I had invited them to come for a swim today and . . . here they are."

"Well, you're a pretty fast worker, man. I saw you holding her hand. Have you kissed her yet?"

"No I haven't kissed her yet. But I am looking forward to it," Ethan replied with a grin.

"You know, I could never get away with what you're doing," Steve continued.

"What do you mean?" queried Ethan

"You getting it on with a black girl. Man, I could never get away with that, although there have been a couple of girls I wouldn't have minded trying. But if I did, wow, my parents would have a fit."

Ethan didn't reply, but his thoughts wandered to his own parents. He was real thankful they were nowhere near.

In the ladies room Peggy took the opportunity to quiz her cousin.

"So, Chipo, what's going on with you and Ethan?"

"Oh Peggy, isn't he the most handsome man you've ever seen? And to think out of all those girls out there he likes me."

"I know you like him. I could tell it from the start and I knew he liked you. I think it's great, but I also want you to be careful. He is only here for a month and then he goes back to England."

"Maybe he won't go back to England. Maybe he could stay here and we could . . . "

"Chipo, listen to yourself. You've only just met this guy and already you're making plans!? What's gotten into you?"

"I just think he's wonderful and I think I could live with him forever."

Realizing talk was no good at this point, Peggy let it drop. "We better get out with the rest of them so we don't get left behind."

"Ethan would never leave me behind, I'm sure of it."

Joining the rest Chipo found Ethan and together they got seats in the back of a Land Rover. The ride out to the farm, as the sun sank low in the sky, was enjoyable with lots of laughter, joking, and lighthearted conversation. Ethan sat there holding Chipo's hand and yearned to kiss her.

"Ethan, do you think . . . " Chipo lost all train of thought as she turned her head toward Ethan and found him very close, their lips almost touching. Startled, Chipo quickly turned her face forward again, feeling shy but also tingling all over with anticipation. Ethan blushed as well sensing her shyness and hoped no one noticed in the fading light. Longing for a private moment, Ethan looked forward to the evening's event knowing one way or another he would get alone with Chipo.

Arriving at the farm the group was met by their hostess, Bridgette, and her parents, Tommy, and Valda Botha. The meat was already cooking on the *braai*, smelling wonderful and making mouths water.

"Who's hungry?" Tommy called and didn't have to ask a second time as the crowd of kids enthusiastically grabbed plates and formed a line. As Ethan approached the hot *braai* loaded with meat he saw sizzling steaks and some kind of sausage.

"Those are called *Boerewors*, which is an Afrikaans word meaning 'farmer's sausage'," Steve explained, standing next to Ethan, as they piled their plates high with the good food. Forking one, Ethan took a quick bite.

"Mm . . . um. They look like Italian sausages, but, wow, they don't taste like them," Ethan commented as he forked another *Boerewors* and put it on his plate.

"This is called *sadza*," Steve said pointing to a huge pot filled with white stuff that looked like thick mashed potatoes. "It's the staple diet of most Zimbabweans. It's made from mealie–meal, or corn meal as you would call it. Try some." Ethan held his plate as Steve dropped a heaping spoonful onto it. "If you want to get the full effect, you need to eat *sadza* with your hands, African style," Steve added with a grin.

"Here, take some relish too," Chipo said as she ladled a soupy substance made from tomatoes and onions next to the *sadza*. "You eat it with the *sadza*."

After finding seats together, Ethan took a bite of *sadza* as the others looked on.

"So, did you say this *sadza* stuff is the staple diet here?" Ethan asked.

"Yeah, it is," Steve replied.

"Most Africans eat it every day," Chipo added.

"Well, it's ok," Ethan replied, "but I wouldn't want to eat it every day."

Once the meal was finished and the bowls on the table were empty, having been scraped clean by the gang of teenage boys, several of the kids opted for a quick swim in the farm reservoir. The green water wasn't very appealing so Ethan and Chipo chose not to swim. Instead, they went off by themselves for a walk in the garden, resplendent in gorgeous blooms and lined pathways throughout the yard around the old stone farmhouse. Once out of sight of the other kids, Ethan turned to face Chipo. Drawing her close, Ethan gently kissed Chipo and she responded the way he had hoped she would. The first kiss was followed by another and another till they finally came up for air. Looking into each other's eyes, Ethan was the first to speak.

"Chipo, the first time I saw you standing at the desk in the lobby I knew that we should be together."

"I was frightened of you at first. I don't know any white boys and I didn't know what you were like. But I liked what I saw, especially in that blue suit you were wearing."

"I'm glad you came to swim. Wow! This has been a remarkable day . . . a remarkable week. I didn't even know you last week and now . . . "

Chipo lowered her eyes feeling shy and giddy at the same time.

"I want to see you as much as possible. Do you think Peggy will bring you over every day?"

"I don't know. You'll have to ask her. I don't know my way around Harare, so I'm not sure if I could make the trip by myself or not. I'll make sure I pay attention to which bus we take next time so that I can come alone if Peggy is working."

"Good. I want to see you every day. You can come over and swim and we could watch movies all day long. We can explore the city together."

"That sounds great. I'm really glad I met you, Ethan. I like you a lot."

"I feel the same."

They kissed once more and then heard Steve and Peggy calling their names. Retracing their steps they made their way back to where all the kids were.

Later, on the way back to the hotel, Chipo snuggled up to Ethan and put her head on his shoulder. After just a few minutes she was asleep. When they arrived at the hotel, she was awakened as everyone piled out of the vehicle.

"Why don't we have a cup of tea in my room before you head out," Ethan invited after saying their goodbyes to the rest of the gang.

"I don't think so. It's rather late and we need to get home," Peggy responded before Chipo could reply. Not wanting to go their separate ways just yet, Ethan and Chipo joined forces to persuade Peggy to change her mind. Without too much effort the two succeeded and after ordering the tea from the phone in the lobby, the threesome made their way to the fourteenth floor. The tea arrived a short time later and they sat on the couch and talked, Ethan eager to know more about Zimbabwe from two qualified teachers. Before they knew it, it was 2:00am. Peggy was a bit distraught when she realized how late it was.

"There won't be any busses running this late. I doubt we'll even be able to find a taxi."

"Well, why don't the two of you just stay the night here? You can have the bed and I'll take the couch," Ethan offered.

"We haven't got a change of clothes or . . . anything," Peggy said feeling a bit wary of the idea.

"I have some T-shirts that you can use as night gowns. They will be quite big on both of you and I will be a perfect gentleman. You'll see."

Peggy was still a bit wary, but the idea of staying was more appealing than walking all the way home or spending the night on the streets. She soon agreed to the plan. Besides she could tell she was outnumbered.

Taking the proffered shirts from Ethan, the girls made their way to the bathroom to change. When they came out Ethan had already pulled the covers down so they could get right into bed. Once they were tucked in, Ethan leaned over and gave Chipo a quick kiss.

"Good night. I'll see you both in the morning."

After turning off the light, Ethan went into the bathroom to change into his pajamas and then found the couch. He lay there thinking about the day and about Chipo. As sleep found him his thoughts turned to dreams.

The next morning they slept in until almost 11:00.

"Oh, my. We need to get going. I have to be at work by 2:00," Peggy said as she headed toward the bathroom.

She returned after a few short minutes to find her cousin still in bed.

"Ethan wants me to stay for the day," Chipo said. "and I really want to stay." she added with a pleading look that matched the one on Ethan's face.

"What will you do about clothes?" Peggy asked feeling a little anxious for her cousin.

"Don't worry, I'll buy her some new clothes at the department store," Ethan quickly replied. "She can wear what she has to shop in and I'll get her what she needs."

"Are you sure this is what you want to do Chipo?"

"Yes, I'm sure. Just tell me what bus to take and I'll be home before dark."

"Or better yet," declared Ethan, "give us your address and I'll get my driver to drop her off."

"Okay, if this is what you want. Give me a piece of paper," Peggy said with a shrug. After writing the address, Peggy grabbed her things and headed for the door.

"Bye you two. I'll see you tonight, Chipo."

Ethan and Chipo said their good-byes as Peggy exited, leaving the two of them alone in the room.

Ethan approached Chipo hoping to get a kiss, but Chipo was quick to the defense.

"Now Ethan, you said you would be a perfect gentleman, and perfect gentlemen don't kiss a girl before she is dressed and has brushed her teeth." She quickly slipped out of his arms and into the bathroom.

Ethan was disappointed, but he knew he had the whole day to spend with her. He planned for the two of them to get out and do something, hoping to avoid Steve and the kids at the pool in the afternoon. So after ordering some tea and scones for "breakfast," he called his driver and asked him what daytime activities he could recommend. Andrew quickly ran down a list of interesting sites in Harare.

"Well, let's see. There's the Lion Park or Snake Park just outside of town, or you might enjoy going to Mazoe estates to see where the oranges are grown. There's a casino at the Mazoe Hotel and they have a real nice restaurant."

Ethan agreed to the latter of the choices and told Andrew to be ready in an hour. Forty-five minutes later Chipo came out of the bathroom. Her hair was all washed and combed and she had changed into her clothes. He told her what the plan was and went into the bathroom to get ready too.

When Ethan and Chipo came down, the driver was surprised to see Chipo with his young charge.

As they climbed into the car, Ethan immediately told him that their first stop would be a department-store in order to purchase the needed new clothes for Chipo, which only confirmed Andrew's suspicions about the girl.

They shopped for two hours and Ethan bought Chipo four new outfits. He had only planned to buy her one, but she looked so pretty in the other three that he had to buy them also. When the driver saw all the packages he just rolled his eyes and decided he needed to talk to this young man.

"Now I only need to find a place where I can change," Chipo said as they put the packages in the car. Andrew knew of a public rest area that had clean bathrooms and they were quickly on their way. While she was changing the driver decided it was a good time to speak to Ethan.

"Sir, if I may be so bold."

"Yes, what is it?"

"Well sir, you have only just arrived in our country and . . . well, Sir . . . there are some people in my country . . . when they see someone like you, a foreigner, they try to take him for all he has. Now I don't want to speak bad of the lady but . . ."

Ethan quickly interrupted. "Then you'd better not. I really like this girl and I won't have you saying anything bad about her. She's a nice girl and I just felt like buying her some clothes. They really didn't cost very much at all when calculated at the exchange rate. So just keep your comments to yourself!" Ethan was angry. Andrew had no right to say those things about Chipo.

"And you better treat her like a lady or I'll have your job," Ethan continued.

"Yes Sir, sorry Sir, I didn't mean anything by it."

Andrew walked to his side of the car and turned away. Jobs were hard to find in Zimbabwe and he couldn't afford to lose this one.

At that moment Chipo came out wearing Ethan's favorite of the outfits they'd bought. It was a deep purple sundress with straps just wide enough to be modest and the length just short enough to be fashionable. It flowed around her small frame as she moved towards them and Ethan noticed how the dazzling colors made her soft skin look smoother than ever. Ethan thought she looked just like she'd stepped out of the pages of one of those teen girl's magazines. He opened the door for her and she got in.

"Right, to Mazoe Estates, Andrew," Ethan spoke cheerfully. "Let's get some food first, Andrew, at the nicest restaurant in Mazoe. We missed lunch and I'm famished."

The young couple enjoyed the late lunch and the remainder of the afternoon was pleasant as they visited the simple attractions in Mazoe.

The trip back from Mazoe was relaxed and enjoyable. Chipo talked about her family and Ethan told her of his.

"I'm sure my family would love you," Ethan said casually.

By the time they got back to the hotel it was getting late.

"Chipo, why don't you stay for supper and then we'll drive you home afterwards," Ethan said as they entered the lobby.

"Thanks Ethan, but I can't. I need to get home to Peggy."

"Just call her and let her know we are going to eat and you'll be back later," Ethan pleaded.

"Okay, I guess I can do that."

Chipo called Peggy and told her. Peggy sounded a little skeptical about it, but what could she do. She wasn't Chipo's boss. Chipo was old enough to make decisions on her own.

Ethan ordered room service for them and they ate at the table in his room. Afterwards they sat close together on the couch. They were finally alone with no one to interrupt and pretty soon one thing led to another. Chipo ended up staying the night again but this time Ethan's T-shirt was not required.

The next morning over breakfast, the two talked about the days ahead. Ethan wasn't shy to express his desire for her to remain with him at the hotel during his stay. Chipo was easily persuaded and they decided that while Peggy was at work they would go get her things. Later they would call Peggy to tell her.

The month flew by. The couple traveled all over Zimbabwe even going to the big game park together. Chipo had never seen big game like this before. She was elated when the elephants passed right by their land cruiser on the way to a water hole. They saw all but one of the big five, lions, elephants, buffalo, and rhino. The only one of the five they didn't see was the leopard.

Nights were filled with romance. Living in a tree house, they could hear the animals roaring in the night just beyond the camp's fenced enclosure, causing them to hold one another all the more. Neither one of them thought of the prospect of their love making having any long term consequences. "Family planning" was far from their thoughts.

Ethan was overjoyed. He was so glad he'd found Chipo. He knew they were soul mates and he hoped they would spend the rest of their lives together. He wasn't sure how, but he hoped to take Chipo back to England with him to marry her. Neither one had thought through how they would live. Ethan was well off financially, or at least his family was, and that lifestyle was something he just took for granted. He naively assumed that nothing would change, even if he married. Having to work to support a wife never even entered his thoughts.

5

Betrayal

"Ethan, please don't go." Chipo wailed.

"Chipo I'm not leaving yet, I still have three days to go."

"I know, but that will go by very quickly. I don't want you to leave me," she said through her sobs.

Ethan didn't know what to do. They had fallen so deeply in love during the month that Ethan had proposed to Chipo and wanted her to go back to England with him. When he had first suggested this Chipo was elated, but then she remembered she had no passport.

The two went to the passport office to try and expedite a passport or emergency travel documents, but without a birth certificate, that was impossible. They declared her birth certificate "lost" knowing her father would never release it and started the procedure to obtain a new one. That in itself would take two weeks. Wanting to move the process along as quickly as possible, the couple got the paperwork from the passport office and filled as much of it out as possible hoping that just maybe the birth certificate could be obtained sooner. In the end they were informed the application process for a new passport would take six weeks. So the two lovers were looking at two months apart from each other. They hadn't been apart a single day in the last three weeks and the separation seemed unbearable.

The day came when Ethan had to leave. It was a very sad trip to the airport. Chipo cried the whole way and Ethan didn't know what to say to comfort her. At the airport they clung to one another for as long as they could. The final boarding call was announced and Ethan pulled himself away.

"I'll phone you as soon as I get home," Ethan promised as he turned to go.

"Ethan . . . " The cry in her voice wrenched his heart and he turned back and drew her into his arms once more. Their kisses were salty, mixed with the tears.

Ethan turned once again, determined to just keep walking.

Chipo stood in the viewing area until Ethan's plane was in the sky and then turned to go. Andrew stood waiting by the car having been ordered to drive Chipo back to her cousin's house. Chipo climbed into the car and Andrew carried out his duty without saying a single word. Chipo sat quietly in the back seat holding a picture of herself with Ethan. Steve had taken the picture and as a farewell gift had printed and framed two copies, one for Ethan, the other for Chipo. Heavy thoughts assailed her. What was she to do now? Her modeling plans had gone out the window with Ethan's invitation for her to join him in the UK. All she had left to do was wait.

When she arrived home, Peggy stood waiting for her. Peggy's heart wrenched at the sight of her broken hearted cousin. Embracing her, Chipo's tears flowed once more.

The day Ethan arrived home was a dreary winter day. He missed the warm Zimbabwe sun all the more. The whole family had come to the airport for his arrival and he ran to them, hugged his mother and shook hands with his father and brother. It was good to be home in spite of the emotions gnawing away at his insides. The journey home was good as his family bombarded him with one question after another and Ethan excitedly told them of all the sites and animals he'd seen. Not knowing quite how to broach the subject, Ethan left out any details concerning Chipo. Being face to face with his family, his planned speech and explanations somehow eluded him.

It was evening and supper was ready when they arrived home, the family enjoyed the meal together.

"Well, you certainly got a nice tan, Ethan. You're so dark," Lady Barbara commented between bites.

"Hey, I'm still pale compared to most people in Zimbabwe," was Ethan's reply much to everyone's amusement.

Once dinner was finished Ethan politely excused himself. "If you don't mind, I think I'll head for bed. I feel really worn out."

"Of course, dear," Barbara said as Ethan rose to leave.

Up in his room he opened his suitcase. Right on top was his framed photo from Steve, he stood looking longingly at it, don't worry my love, I'll do everything in my power to get you here as soon as I can. He spoke to no one, but meant every word.

He had just finished bathing, donned his pajamas and was climbing into bed when there was a knock at the door.

"Who's there?"

"It's me." His mother's voice came from the other side of the door. "May I come in?"

Ethan was a bit surprised and puzzled at this since his mother had not tucked him into bed for many years.

"Sure, Mother, come on in."

"Ethan, you seem different than you were when you left," Barbara began as she sat at the foot of his four poster bed.

"Yes, mother, I guess I am different. You don't travel that far from home and not change at least a little. Zimbabwe is such a wonderful place. And mother," Ethan stuttered a little, "I . . . m–m . . . met a . . . a . . . girl there."

"Oh, so that's it. What is she like?"

"She is the most beautiful girl that you have ever seen. Mother, I think I am in love. I want to marry her. I wanted to buy her a ticket and would have, but she didn't have her passport so she couldn't come with me."

"Wow, this seems serious. Do you have a picture of her?"

"Yes, right here on my table," Ethan said as he hopped out of bed, and picked up the picture. "I know you'll like her, mother. She's so wonderful, look."

Ethan handed the picture to his mother. She flinched when she saw the girl but didn't express any of her true feelings.

"My, she is very pretty. It's no wonder you liked her."

Lady Barbara hesitated a moment but then continued, "You know, I saw Lisa yesterday and she was asking when you would be back."

Ethan's thoughts drifted to his girlfriend from his school days. They had broken up several months before. Ethan didn't want to talk about Lisa; he wanted to talk about Chipo.

"Her name is Chipo," Ethan said a bit emphatically as he gazed at her face in the photo. "I told her that I would call her when I arrived home. Is it okay if I call her?"

"We'll have to ask your father. It's awful late tonight, why don't we talk to your father tomorrow and see what he says."

"Ok, thanks mom." He was too tired to argue at the moment. "I probably wouldn't remember what we talked about anyhow. Besides, it's late and it must be close to midnight in Harare. I guess I can wait until morning to call her," Ethan paused a moment then continued. "I can't wait for you and father to meet her."

Lady Barbara smiled a response as if not knowing what to say and then rose to her feet.

"Okay, well, I'm glad you're home. We'll talk to your father tomorrow. Have a good sleep." Lady Barbara kissed her son on the head and Ethan gave his mother an awkward hug, unaccustomed to such behavior. Drawing the duvet up under his chin, Ethan thought of Chipo and let sleep come, hoping his dreams would take him back to her arms.

The next morning Ethan woke up around five o'clock. He was the only one up and so he wandered down to the lounge. He decided that he would call Chipo right then since it was a good time of day to reach her. He carefully dialed the long number, but there was no answer on the other end. Assuming she had gone to the market he hung up planning to try again later.

He had been up for about an hour when he heard his parent's voices coming from the kitchen. He started to go in there when he realized that they were talking about him.

"What do you mean he fell in love with an African girl?" asked his father, his voice slightly raised.

"He's met this African girl and says that he is in love and wants to marry her. Oh John, I just don't know what we should do."

"I'll tell you what we will do; we'll talk to the boy and explain to him that he can't just marry any girl. He has to marry right. The girl has to be of the right social class, just as he is. What was he thinking? I'm sure it was just a fling and he'll get over it soon enough."

"Yes, I hope so. I never dreamed this would happen. I would have never agreed to him going all the way to Africa if I had known."

Lady Barbara paused briefly and then continued. "I saw Lisa the other day and she asked after him."

"Now, Lisa is the type of girl that he needs. She comes from a good family and we know them. Maybe we should invite her over to supper tonight, help them to get reacquainted again."

"Mmm, yes, that's a good idea. But we need to be careful of the timing. Tonight may be too soon. "

Ethan was stunned. What was he hearing? His parents were against Chipo already and they hadn't even met her. What was he going to do? Should he just go back to Zimbabwe? No, that wouldn't work. What would he do there to earn a living? He decided that he wouldn't say anything to his parents just yet till he could think things through. He quietly reversed his steps and then approached the kitchen again, this time so he would be heard. As he entered the room he greeted them normally.

Later that day his father approached him and asked if they could have "a bit of a talk." Knowing what was coming, Ethan braced himself as he took a seat in front of his father's polished desk.

"Son, your mother told me about this girl in Zimbabwe that you met. You need to understand that as our oldest son you have a burden to bear that your brother does not. Someday you will become Lord Benham and will have a lot of responsibilities. You will be in charge of all our estate and also have political duties. With all the obligations you will need a wife that will be able to accomplish these things along side you, a wife that knows our culture and how we do things. Do you understand what I am saying?"

"Yes father, I understand, but I really love Chipo and I want to marry her."

"Listen Ethan, I know that's how you feel now, but you are very young and I can't let you throw you life away. You had a fling. She's thousands of miles away now, just leave it at that. You had a great time in Zimbabwe. You experienced a lot of new things . . . had a girlfriend . . . sowed your wild oats."

Ethan cringed at his father's trite expression.

Lord Benham continued. "Your mother and I allowed you this trip so that when you got back you would settle down, get to your studies and grow into your role in this family. You don't have time for a wife right now. You have university and that's a lot of work, plus you will be starting on your political career. Ethan, you are not your own. You are part of a titled family."

He paused a moment sensing his approach was not getting through. "I know that you are serious about this girl, but let's give it some time and see what happens. How's that sound?" Ethan's father was a very persuasive man; he had always been that way. Ethan bolstered his resistance. He knew he loved Chipo and so time would not change anything. Having no other plan at the moment, Ethan chose to go along with his father's plan or at least make his father think he was going along with it. He had time. Everything would work out. When the time came for him to marry he knew Chipo would be the one, but with college before him, waiting a while was not a bad idea. Chipo didn't even have her passport yet so nothing could happen right away anyhow. He was sure she would understand.

"Okay father, I'll give it some time. I know that I have a lot to do, so I'll wait."

Lord Benham was quite surprised by Ethan's reply. He thought that he would have more resistance, but he was glad Ethan understood.

Later, alone in his room, Ethan decided that he would write to Chipo and let her know that his parents weren't exactly happy with the plan and explain that their plans would have to wait for a while. He labored over the letter for quite some time and was finally satisfied with the final results. He quietly made his way to the foyer and tucked his letter in with the other letters to be mailed out, oblivious to the presence of his mother looking on from the landing above.

Ethan proceeded outside for a walk and Lady Barbara took advantage of the chance to investigate her son's business, suspecting what she would find. The letter bearing the Zimbabwe address was easy to spot. Lady Barbara removed it from the pile and quietly made her way to her office. Wrestling with her options, she finally hid the letter in a drawer.

The letter never got mailed.

"Peggy, why hasn't he called? He said he would call as soon as he arrived. I waited up all night waiting for his call and every day since."

"Chipo, I hate to be the one to tell you, but he's probably forgotten all about you. Boys are like that. Once they get what they want they seem to just disappear." Peggy's words only added to Chipo's growing doubts. Depression settled upon her until Chipo didn't know what to do.

"What should I do?"

"Just forget about him. Chipo, you're young and beautiful, you'll find another man."

"I don't want another man, I want Ethan." Chipo's replied through sobs. "I love him Peggy, I miss him. It's been almost a month now since he left. And . . . and another thing, I, I, think I'm pregnant."

"Oh no Chipo." Peggy reached out toward Chipo, "Are you sure?"

"No I'm not sure, but I've been feeling sick and it's been over a month since . . . " Chipo let her words just hang in the air.

"Chipo, we need to find out. They have home pregnancy test at the pharmacy, let's go buy one. Then we'll know for sure." Peggy looked like it was the end of the world for Chipo and in a way it was. Peggy knew that no man would want her if she was pregnant or even after she had a baby. In their culture she was damaged material.

"Peggy, don't be sad for me. I was frightened at first, but then I realized that it's Ethan's baby and I'm glad that I am having his baby. I know that once he finds out he'll send for me. I have my birth certificate and I've already applied for my passport, so all I need is for him to send for me."

Peggy, being the more world wise, knew this probably wasn't going to happen, but wanted to make her cousin happy. "I'm sure that will come to pass. Why don't you write a letter to him and tell him. I'll run to the store and buy the test and we can know for sure if you are pregnant."

"Thank you so much Peggy," Chipo stood up and hugged her cousin, "for being such a good friend."

"There's paper in the drawer, write to Ethan. I'll be right back." Peggy walked out the door shaking her head knowing that writing Ethan would be futile.

"I'm back Chipo." Peggy had only been gone for about ten minutes. "Here's the test."

Chipo, sitting at the table, reached out and took the small package. "This is it? How does it work?"

Peggy explained how the test worked and Chipo looked at her incredulously, "You're kidding?"

"No, that's what you have to do."

"How is that going to tell me if I'm pregnant?"

"Well I'm not a doctor so I don't know how, but I know it does work. Go on, go do it."

A minute later there was a scream from the bathroom. "Peggy, I'm pregnant. I really am. I'm going to have Ethan's baby." Chipo was overjoyed.

Peggy wasn't quite as excited, "You are welcome to stay here, Chipo, until the baby is born. By then hopefully you will have figured out what you are going to do," Peggy offered.

"I know he will send for me, don't worry. I'm going to run to the post office and mail this letter. Oh Peggy, I'm so happy."

When Chipo's letter arrived at the Benham house, Lady Barbara was first to see it. After wrestling with her conscience for a few brief moments, Lady Barbara opened her son's letter, thankful in the end that she had. Resolve rose in her heart to keep the contents of the letter a secret not just from Ethan, but his father as well. They must never know of this girl's claim. Never! A fire was roaring in the fireplace so she simply walked over to it and dropped the letter into the flames.

Not knowing of his baby growing in Chipo's womb. Ethan couldn't understand why she never replied to his letter. Didn't she love him? Had she just been using him to get to England? Had Andrew been right about her? Maybe she wasn't the right girl for him after all.

Lady Benham sensed that the time was right for the proposed visit from Lisa, so she made the supper invitation for the following evening. Ethan enjoyed the visit. They talked late into the evening, mostly about Ethan's trip to Africa, excluding any details concerning Chipo.

"I wish I could have gone with you, Ethan. We would have had a great time together."

"I wish you could have gone too." Ethan said it and meant it. Lisa was a very lovely girl. They had dated for two years and only broke up because he spent a lot of his time playing soccer and she was a bit jealous. She kept nagging him about quitting the team, so he finally broke up with her. All that seemed quite trivial now.

Soon Ethan was off to university and Lisa just happened to be going to the same school. They had several classes together and before long the two were seeing a lot of each other. Ethan's mother and father were glad and very relieved when they learned of this development. In spite of it all, Ethan continued to think of Chipo, still not understanding why she had never written back, feeling betrayed and rejected.

In Zimbabwe, Chipo's emotions ranged from anger to deep sorrow. Not aware that Ethan had not even received her letter, Chipo could only assume that he never really loved her and had forgotten all about her. She felt used. Her feelings for him had been real. He must have been just leading her on. Peggy agreed with that point and told her to forget him. But that was not possible since she was pregnant with his baby. She couldn't go back home; her father would beat her, first for getting pregnant and then again when he learned that the father was a white man. Depression's grip grew tighter and tighter till Chipo withdrew into her grief, never even leaving the house.

Peggy's concern deepened until she decided that she needed to get word to Chipo's family about her situation. Peggy contacted her own mother so that she could break the news to Chipo's father.

Just two months before the baby was due, Chipo's father came to Harare. He arrived at Peggy's house already in a rage and his greeting to his daughter was to spit in her face.

Terrified, Chipo crouched by a chair as her father ranted and raved about what she had done. "You deceived me when you snuck away like a slithering snake and now look at you. What is the matter with you?" The accusation was followed with a swift slap to her face.

Chipo could only be thankful that he didn't know the father of her baby was a white man or his anger would have been even more brutal.

During the war of independence in Zimbabwe her father had been abducted by some young white men. She had heard the stories as she grew up. They treated him like an animal, beating him and mistreating him for two weeks before an officer found them. It turned out that the young white soldiers had been separated from their platoon and where just wandering around the bush when they found Simon. The officer made them release Simon, but did nothing to help him. He was cut and bruised with broken ribs and a broken leg. They just left him there. Before, he wasn't even interested in the war, but after his wounds healed he joined up and tried to kill as many white men as he could. His hatred for the white man was deep.

"Get up!" he shouted, "Get your things and go out to the car. You're going home with me." He stormed out of the house and Chipo had no recourse but to obey. She quickly packed her clothes and then, looking at the table by her bed, spotted the picture of Ethan. Picking up the bag she left the it where it was and walked out.

The trip home was long and draining. Chipo sat huddled in the back seat of the car, her father didn't say a word the whole way. Immediately upon arriving home, Simon sent her to her room. After just a few minutes, Amanda, the younger of Simon's two remaining wives came into the small hut. Chipo knew she had been sent by her father. Her greeting was clipped and unfeeling and then she began with the questions.

"Who is the boy that got you this way? Is he going to marry you?"

Chipo tried to remain calm as she explained that the father of her baby had left Zimbabwe and was never coming back.

"But he must pay us damages even if he is not going to marry you."

Again Chipo tried to explain the situation but she could see she was getting nowhere. The mother asked when she was due and Chipo told her.

"That is two months away so you can still work in the fields," was her curt response and then she left the room.

Chipo's thoughts drifted back. She had such big plans when she escaped to the city, but they failed. Now she was back with no money, nor any prospect of getting any. She didn't know what she was going to do when the baby came, or what her father would do. He was capable of anything, even killing the baby. Chipo was frightened, not just for her baby, but for herself as well.

Soon after Chipo's return something new started happening. Some people moved into the area and had set up a compound in her village. They were digging Blair toilets and pitching tents. All the villagers came around to watch the activity wondering who they were and what they were doing there, "Was it a church group starting a new church? Did the chief know about this, someone should go tell him." The people had a lot of questions.

Just then the chief and his headmen came over to where the newcomers were setting up their camp. Quieting the people he stood on a large rock and spoke, "I have allowed this group of people to come in and drill boreholes for us." He made it sound as though it was all his idea. "They will be here for quite some time. There will be five boreholes drilled in our village."

With that there was a shout of approval. The people were elated.

"Not only will we get new boreholes, but they are also going to build a clinic right here where they are camping."

Again, cheers rose from the crowd.

"They have brought nurses and the large tent near the big acacia tree will be a temporary clinic until the permanent one is built. They are also asking for our help in building the structure. So any of you who have nothing to do will help them." He said this not as a request, but as a command. "If any of you need medical attention you are welcome to come to the clinic starting tomorrow."

Some of the young men had already drawn nearer the site and were standing watching when Hans and Ingrid drove up. Hans stepped from the car and the young men who were near ran away. Some of the women and children audibly screamed and hid behind trees and bushes.

Hans lowered his head and shook it wishing people would know that he cared for them and would never hurt them.

Walking up to the chief, he stood by him. The chief, being a man of small stature, was still standing on the rock and Hans was as tall as him standing on the ground.

"This is Mr. Grundey." He pronounced it Groon deee. "He is the man in charge of this operation. If you need anything go to him."

The people were listening, but were thinking they would not go to him.

Right then a pretty blond headed lady walked up. The children all watched her, afraid that the giant would eat her up.

"This is Mrs. Grundey, she will be in charge of the clinic. You must go to her for any medical help."

People were surprised that this small, pretty lady was the wife of the giant. Many who weren't sure about him thought maybe he wasn't as bad as they first thought.

After the chief finished many people lingered to watch the newcomers set up. Many continued to run when Hans came around, but some of the young men realized he was just a big man and talked with him. Several of them even offered to help with construction.

When time allowed it, Chipo would join the many others who were permanent spectators at the NGO work site. Curiosity was the drawing card, many just wanted to get a glimpse of the giant who did the work of three men.

"Chipo," Her father had come up to her while she was cooking food. "I want you to go to the clinic so you can be examined by the nurse." Simon had not gone near the place since they arrived because of his hatred for the white man. After doing her chores Chipo went over to where the activity was. She had only seen the men who were building the clinic and drilling the boreholes before this trip. As she walked toward the tent she saw a good number of young men she had known from school who had nothing better to do.

Walking into the tent that posed as the clinic she was surprised at the kindness and efficiency she was met with. Although there were a lot of people in the tent waiting to be seen, everything was organized. The fair, blond nurse was quick and efficient and within two hours it was Chipo's turn to see her.

"Now, I'm guessing you are here for me to check you over before you have this baby," the nursing sister said with a smile. "Do you know when you are due?"

"Yes, I went to a clinic in Harare when I was first pregnant and they said that I am due November thirteenth. I . . . " Chipo paused, not knowing how to explain her situation. "I returned to my village a month ago and haven't been to a clinic since. My father told me to come and see you."

"Your father?" Ingrid looked up surprised that she still lived at home and not with her husband. "And where is the father of the baby?"

"He moved back to England," was all that Chipo said about Ethan.

Ingrid proceeded with the examination talking all the while, making Chipo feel at ease.

"Well, I agree with your due date," Ingrid said when she had finished. "Our team will finish at this site soon and then we will move to the next site but we will be in the area for the next six months. So when the time comes, if you need me, just send word. I'll come."

"Thank you," Chipo replied with a smile.

"You are a very lucky lady. My husband and I have wanted a baby for a long time and it just hasn't happened. My husband is the one called Hans," Ingrid said with a smile. "Now, you take care of yourself and that baby."

Chipo left the clinic feeling better than she had in a long while. It was nice to know someone else cared about her baby.

That evening in the kitchen rondoval, Chipo talked about her visit to the clinic with her two mothers and her sisters.

"You know the big man named Hans? The one married to the small blond nurse at the clinic," Chipo shared to the amusement of the ladies in the room. Anytime anyone talked about these two being married, people smiled. "She told me they are not able to have children."

Chipo's announcement was met with clucking tongues and shaking heads. What could be worse than a married woman not being able to bear children? The women in the room knew the serious consequences for a woman in that predicament. It was a very bad omen and many women were "sent away" because of that very thing.

The borehole was finished within a week's time and the team, with their tents and all their equipment moved on to the next location. Two weeks later Chipo had her baby. Her labor began in the afternoon and the two older mothers stayed with Chipo till the baby was delivered late that night. It was a baby boy.

When her father saw the fair skinned child he was in an outrage. "What is happening? How could you bring this mixed child into my home? Get out of my sight."

Simon wouldn't even look at the child a second time. He ranted about the baby to his wives for hours until he finally fell into a brooding silence.

He drank heavily that night and early the next morning he went quietly into Chipo's room. Chipo and the baby were sleeping. Being careful not to waken either the baby or the mother, Simon picked the baby up and left the hut carrying the child. He walked ten kilometers to the new location of the NGO team. When he arrived with the baby he went straight to the clinic looking for the small blond nurse that had been in their village.

"Good morning," Ingrid turned to greet this man as he entered surprised to have a patient before clinic hours opened. "I'm sorry the clinic isn't open yet." She saw the bundle in his arms and headed closer to him thinking there must be something wrong with his baby.

"Here, I want you to have this baby," Simon blurted as he held out the small, sleeping bundle. "The mother of the child was my daughter but she died in childbirth. You can see he is not of full African descent. He is light skinned and cannot stay with my family. Your husband is very dark and this child looks like he could be your baby. So I am giving him to you. Please take him and give him a good home. If you don't want him give him to someone else. I don't want him in my home."

Ingrid was speechless. She knew that this must be the baby of the young girl she examined and that there was no father that would lay claim to him.

She took the baby in her arms and looked into his tiny face. What a beautiful face. Her heart was torn. How could anyone not fall in love with such a beautiful baby.

She had lived in Africa long enough to know what this man meant. If she didn't take the baby he would kill it. Directing him to a chair, she asked the man to wait. Quickly going to where she knew Hans would be working, she quietly drew him aside and told him what the man had said to her as she stood gazing into the face of the baby in her arms.

Hans looked at the little bundle in her arms and knew that his wife loved this baby already. He moved the blanket away from the baby's face and peered down at the little one. The baby's arm came loose when he moved the blanket and a tiny hand grabbed hold of Hans's finger. Choking back tears he said, "Honey, if you want this baby we can keep it."

Returning to the clinic tent together, they joined the man for tea prepared by the clinic staff.

"What is your name, sir?" Hans began.

"I am Simon Sibanda," came the reply.

"Simon," Hans continued, "We will take this baby on one condition. You can never have any more to do with him. He will belong to us and you can have no claim on him."

"Agreed." Simon rose and shook hands with the huge man before him. "I don't want to have anything to do with this mixed child anyway." Simon turned and walked away never looking back.

Carrying the precious bundle, Ingrid moved into Hans embrace, tears streaming down her cheeks.

"Hans, I can't believe it. We have a baby. He is ours, to love, to keep!"

Upon awakening, Chipo found her baby gone and was instantly in a panic. Where was he? She quickly ran to see if one of the other mothers or girls had him. The only ones anywhere to be found were her two older mothers and neither of them had the baby. But where was her father? Fear gripped her heart when she realized he was gone as well. In his ranting he had threatened to kill the baby. Had he made good on his threat? At that moment her father entered the gate . . . alone.

"Where is my baby?" She hurled the accusing question as she ran toward him.

Turning toward her with a cold expressionless face he replied. "I took him away. He is safe now. I have removed the disgrace you brought to our family." Without any further comment he walked on into his house and called for his second wife to bring some food.

Chipo was stunned. She ran out of the compound hoping to follow her father's tracks, but they were obliterated with so many other footprints. She searched the bush most of the morning thinking her father may have dumped the baby in a secluded place but her search was in vain.

She cried ceaselessly for hours and soon she was exhausted. A deep hatred and anger rose in her toward her father and she determined to leave him, but this time not without him knowing it.

Returning home she found her older mothers alone in the compound and her father sleeping off the liquor in his house. Chipo banged loudly on her father's door.

When Simon opened the door Chipo vented all her anger and hatred. "What did you do? He was my baby, not yours. I hate you! I will never talk to you as long as I live," Chipo screamed as she cursed her heartless father.

Before Simon could even have a chance to retort, Chipo stormed off the porch and ran to her room. She quickly packed her bag and walked out of the gate never to return again.

She didn't know what she would do. She had no plan except to get away from her father. Chipo walked aimlessly and finally ended up at her grandparent's home. Finding them together in their living area she told them all that had happened. She vented her frustration and when she was done talking she broke down and cried again. Her grandmother was sitting next to her and she pulled Chipo into her arms and just held her as Chipo sobbed.

"Shhh, my girl. It's ok. Everything will be ok." Not knowing what else to say, Mary remained silent, praying as she held her precious granddaughter.

After a few minutes Alex rose to his feet and left the compound, returning late that evening. Chipo never really knew for sure what he did, but she assumed he had gone to see her father.

"The baby is safe. He is with people who will take good care of him. Your father told them you are dead." That was his only explanation to Chipo's questions.

Exhausted and emotionally spent, Chipo finally fell asleep with her head on her grandmother's lap.

The next morning, still dazed and in no condition to make any decisions, Chipo left her grandfather's home and made her way to Crossroads. After selling her clothes, all but the first outfit that Ethan had bought her, she had enough money to get to Harare and to buy food for a few days. The one thing that was clear in her mind was this; if her father told those people she was dead, she would be dead to her father. She determined never to return home. Going to Peggy's house in the city was out of the question as well. Blind rage pressed her forward.

When Chipo arrived in Harare she had no place to stay, so she slept in the streets. After four days she ran out of money and became very hungry. She didn't have a job and she needed to eat, so in her desperation Chipo sold her body for the price of a meal.

With Chipo gone, Simon's scheming just naturally went to the next level. In her absence he would convince people that she and the baby had both died shortly after childbirth. Simon had no problem persuading his wives to go along with the scheme. In his home he was master and he knew that his wives would never reveal the truth. Only the three of them had been

at home that morning when Chipo found the baby gone and then again
when she returned after searching for the child. Simon plotted a way to fake
Chipo's death. Going to his grain shed he took bags of grain and laid them in
Chipo's bed, then covered them with a sheet so they appeared to be a body.

"No one is to go into that hut. I will take care of everything." he commanded. Simon knew that his order would be obeyed.

After instructing his wives to tell people that Chipo had died along
with the baby he left to go buy a coffin large enough for two bodies, mother,
and child.

When he got back the mourning women had already started to gather.
They wanted to come in and clean the body for burial, but Simon wouldn't
let them.

"She is my daughter. I will take care of it. I need only the help of my
wives."

With basin and towel in hand, the two ladies led the way into the small
hut with Simon following behind carrying the coffin. He laid the bags of
grain into the coffin, carefully distributing the weigh. When a sufficient
amount of time had passed for the washing of the body, Simon closed the
lid of the coffin hammering the nails into place. Then the three emerged
from the hut to the sound of wailing from the growing crowd of mourners.
Simon, playing the part of a mourning father well, tearfully asked some of
the men who had gathered to come and carry the coffin to his house. He
then ordered some of the older boys to start digging the hole for the burial.

"Are we going to wait for the pastor to come to officiate over the burial,"
Alice asked as they made their way toward the main house.

"No. We will bury her ourselves in the traditional way," Simon quickly
replied.

The mourning women, seated on the floor around the coffin, began
singing burial hymns. All of the furniture had been taken outside and placed
under a tree for the men to sit on. Even the curtains had been removed from
the windows in the traditional custom of mourning. Comfort for the living
was laid aside in the time of mourning in order to accommodate the spirit
of the deceased. As Simon joined the men seated under the tree, the group
rose together to shake his hand and give him their condolences.

"When did Chipo die?" The question came from one of the older men.

"It must have been early this morning. I had gone in to check on the
mother and child and found them dead," Simon lied. "I stayed in the hut with
her body weeping and mourning for the loss of my daughter and grandson,"
he continued. "When I was able to get up and walk I went to my house and
got a sheet to cover the bodies. I went to get the coffin by myself as an act of
my mourning," he concluded tearfully to demonstrate how much he cared

for his daughter and to establish his fabricated story, believing that Chipo would never return. Now he would bury her and be done with her.

Many people had gathered for the burial. After a few hours Simon decided it was time to have the service. Entering the house, he announced that they would bury her now.

The women wanted him to open the coffin so they could see her one last time, but he refused stating that they needed to get her body in the ground before it became too dark. The men carried the coffin outside to the grave-site. They lowered the casket into the ground and started filling in the hole. The family was first to shovel dirt into the grave and then friends were allowed to. They had put sticks in each of the corners of the grave in order to mark the boundaries of the grave as well as to allow the spirits of the dead to leave the grave.

When all was done and the gaping hole was now a mound of dirt above the grave, they pulled the sticks out. Taking a plastic tea cup that had belonged to Chipo, they punched a hole in it with a pick and placed it on the grave. This was done to bring comfort to the spirit of the deceased by providing a familiar item to have with them always. The item had to be damaged so that no one would be tempted to take it, stealing from the dead. Finally they had a time for the family and friends to say a few words about Chipo and then the mourners returned to the house to share a meal.

Before passing through the gate into the compound each person paused to wash their hands in a large metal laundry tub. Medicinal leaves and plants had been placed in the water in order to wash off any spirit that might have clung onto them at the grave-site. The men gathered under the trees again and the women proceeded to sit on the floor in the house. They ate *sadza* and goat meat. The women sang and the men drank beer. This went on all night long and in the morning people returned to their homes.

On the walk back to their homes certain ones commented that they had seen Chipo the day before, walking around searching for something.

"I even greeted her, but she did not reply," one woman added with a tremor in her voice.

"Yes," another woman agreed. "She had a strange look in her eyes."

They shuddered and knew that they must have seen Chipo's ghost wandering around looking for her dead child.

A few days later Peggy got word that Chipo had died in childbirth. She was saddened with the news. Thinking of Ethan, she sat down and wrote a letter to him telling him all that she knew of Chipo's death and the death of his son. She dropped the letter in the post box and then boarded a bus headed for home to pay her respects to the family.

A week later Ethan received the letter telling of Chipo's death.

"She was pregnant with my baby," he exclaimed to himself. "I killed her." The tears flowed till he could weep no more.

He didn't go to classes for the remainder of the week and Lisa wondered what was up. Going to his apartment she found him drunk and unshaven. She had never seen him like this before.

"It's my fault, it's my fault." His slurred words made no sense.

"What is your fault?"

"I killed her." Still not understanding at all, Lisa consoled him as best she could. After getting him sober and cleaned up she took him to get some food and then pressed him for an explanation.

His response was to hand her a letter. After reading its contents, understanding began to dawn. By nature, Lisa was a very caring person, the type who needed someone who needed her. At the moment, Ethan desperately needed someone and Lisa was very happy to step into that role. She was a good listener and was there for him during this dark time. She was able to get him to go to his classes and get on with life.

When Ethan finally came out of his stupor, he was glad she was there. The two of them spent many days and nights together after that and within a few months announced their engagement. Ethan's mother and father were elated. They never heard about what happened with the African girl, they were just happy that he had made a good choice. A year and a half later Ethan and Lisa were married. Ethan had grown to love Lisa and knew she was the bride for him, but he never forgot his first love.

6

Explosion

HANS AND INGRID WERE happier than they had ever been in their lives. They had longed for a child for so long. They had gone to doctors in Harare, but couldn't find anything wrong. Now, all of the sudden, they had a baby boy of their own.

"What should we name it?" Hans asked.

"Hans he's a boy not an it, and I think we should name him after you. Hans Grundey Junior."

A big grin broke out on Hans face. "Hans Grundey Junior, I like it. But if we name him after me when you are mad at him and yell out 'Hans Grundey you get in here' I'll think I'm in trouble. Why don't we give him a second name that we can call him by?"

"That's a good idea. My father and brother both had the same name and it was hard when my mother called to one of them, they both answered." Ingrid thought for a moment. "I think we should give him a Shona name. The Africans always give meaning to the names they give their children."

"That's a good idea, what name?"

"I remember meeting a little boy named Nyasha and always like that name. I don't know what it means though."

"I've got a dictionary in the car. I know I've heard that name too, but I don't know what it means either." Hans went over to their Land Rover, opened the door and pulled out a big red book. It had to have been three inches thick. Opening it to the N's he said, "Here it is. Nyasha a noun meaning grace, compassion. A strong feeling of sympathy and sadness for the suffering or unfortunate. That's a great meaning. We both have a strong feeling of compassion for the African people." Looking at the baby Hans said, "Hi, Hans Nyasha Grundey, it's really good to meet you."

"Look Hans, he smiled." Ingrid drew him closer and buried her face in the blanket he was wrapped in. "I love you little Nyasha." After a few seconds she looked up at Hans, "We need to take him to our special place. It's where everything that ever happened that was good happened to me."

"Okay, we'll head out there for the weekend." Ingrid just looked up at Hans with a big grin on her face.

"First I think we need to figure out how to make him our own. You're not allowed to adopt babies from Zimbabwe, so we'll have to figure out how to go about adopting him."

"That man who brought him to us made mention that because of our coloring he already looks a bit like us. He's not very dark, in fact, look." Ingrid put the baby next to Hans's arm. "See, with your tan you're even a little darker than he is. I can get the papers saying that he was born to us pretty easy. I am a nurse you know. Then all we have to do is get his Zimbabwe birth certificate and take it and him to the embassy. Remember that's what the Borg's did after little Pieter was born."

"Yes, that's true, we can get everything we need. I think we'll have to get someone else's signature on the papers besides yours though."

"I know that. We can get Elsa to sign them. I'm sure she would do that for us. It's not like we're doing anything bad. If we hadn't taken this baby from that man he probably would have dumped him somewhere and left him to die." Ingrid looked down at Nyasha feeling the grief that only a mother can feel. "We couldn't have ever let that happen to you could we Nyasha?"

"Uh, I don't think he's going to answer you." Hans smiled, "I'm game if you are. The worse they could do to us is throw us out of the country. Maybe make us pay a fine. It's not our fault that we were given a baby."

They found out there were two things they needed to prove to their embassy that he was their child. The Zimbabwe birth certificate showing them as parents, which was no problem for them at all. The other issue was they had to bring the child to the embassy so the consul could personally see him.

"I'm scared Hans, what if they don't believe Nyasha is ours?"

"Don't worry," He looked down at the little baby Ingrid was holding, "I'm sure it will be okay." Hans put on a brave front, but deep inside he too was scared.

There was a guard at the entrance of the embassy who asked to see their passports. "What about the baby's passport?"

"That's what we're doing here to get all of that done."

"Oh okay go on in."

Inside they had to go through a metal detector. Hans hated these things. It seemed that no matter what he did it always beeped on him. Walking through, sure enough it beeped.

"Sir could you step over here?" Was the command from the guard.

Knowing the drill he stood facing the guard and lifted his arms up. The guard waved a metal detecting wand over him and waved him on through. They walked on through the next set of doors and found people sitting in chairs and even more standing. There was a line at one window so they got in it. After forty minutes they finally reached the window.

"Hi, my name is Hans Grundey this is my wife Ingrid. We need to get the paperwork done to get our baby's birth certificate and passport."

The man at the window looked up and was startled to see how big Hans was. "Okay you need to fill out this paper and then the consul will call you."

He handed Hans some papers and they walked over to a counter to fill them out. After they were done they waited. They waited and waited.

"This is ridiculous. I'm going to go find out what's happening."

"Honey be nice to them."

"I will."

Walking right up to the window Hans called out. "Hi, excuse me. We've been waiting a long time for the consul to come out to us. Is there a problem?"

The man in the window looked up exasperated. "Sir, there's a lot of people here, what is it you need?" Seeing Hans again he remembered what he wanted. "Oh yes, you have the baby." He looked at his watch. "She should be here in just a couple minutes. Give me your papers and I'll make sure she sees you first."

"Well thank you very much."

"It's okay, I have three children and I wouldn't want to have to wait in this crowd with them very long. We'll call you soon."

Hans nodded his head and walked back to Ingrid.

"Well what happened? You didn't get him angry did you?"

"No as a matter of fact he was very nice and took our papers so that the consul would see us first."

Just then they heard their name being called. "Grundey, Hans and Ingrid Grundey." A man was calling from a doorway.

"Yes, here we are."

As they walked toward the door the man said, "Go to counter three." And with that he walked back inside the offices.

Going to window three they were glad to see no one in line there. They walked right up to the window. The man who called their name came to the window and sat down. "Let's see what have we got here. Hmmm, a baby needing his birth certificate and passport." He looked up and smiled at Hans and Ingrid. Glancing at the bundle in Ingrid's arm she thought he wanted to see Nyasha but as she started to unwrap him the man looked away.

Looking again at the papers the man said, "It looks like everything is in order here for the birth certificate. Let me call the consul so she can see him." He stood up and walked to the back room.

Just a few seconds later a harried woman emerged from the same door the man had just gone into. She sat down behind the window and looked at the papers. "Hans and Ingrid Grundey." She looked up and saw Hans and Ingrid nodding. "And Hans Nyasha Grundey." Again she looked up. Ingrid started to unwrap him but again, before she had a chance, the consul's head was looking down at the papers. "Alright, it looks like everything is okay here." She took a rubber stamp and stamped the paperwork. "It will take a few minutes to make the certificate, while we're doing that you can go over to the payment window and make your payment for his passport. The passport will take three days though so you'll have to come back for that."

She stood up to leave and Hans asked, "Do all of us have to come back?"

"No just one of you. Make sure you have your passport and another photo ID with you. They won't let you in without your passport and we won't give you his without a second photo ID." With that said she left.

Hans and Ingrid just looked at each other and grinned. Hans felt a load had been taken off his shoulders.

Walking over to the payment window Ingrid whispered, "I'm glad that is done."

Whispering back Hans agreed, "Me too."

After leaving the embassy and since they were in Harare they decided a celebration was in store so they splurged and went to the Chinese restaurant in town.

A month later, war broke out in Zimbabwe. With the heightened risk, especially for the women, the overseeing office restricted travel, scheduling projects far away from the "hot spots" throughout the country. That suited the Grundeys just fine. They were happy to live and work in the compound where they had first met giving them time to enjoy family life without having to live out of a tent. Hans travelled more without Ingrid, occasionally to nearby villages to do drilling, sometimes for a week at a time, but never longer than that.

One day Hans arrived home with an amazing story to tell. The team had been in a village drilling a borehole when suddenly a group of armed men came in. They were a fierce looking group and very mixed, some white, some black. Hans said that the men came in fast with their guns up and told everyone to stay still. It turned out that they were mercenaries assisting the government in the fight against the rebel forces. They said that they were looking for rebels reportedly in the area. Only after searching the compound and finding no dissidents did they release the staff to move about again, telling them not to worry.

A little later, while the soldiers were renewing their water supply, Hans got the chance to talk to the leader of the group, a man named Keith, and found out that he was from Australia. Hans learned from the Australian that the rebels were on the move and proving to be a more elusive enemy than had been expected. Many of the locals were sympathetic to the cause of the rebels, assisting their resistance. During their conversation Keith half-jokingly asked Hans if he would like to join them.

"You look like a man built for action," was his line of persuasion.

"I have a wife and a child to look after," Hans replied.

"Well if ever you want to join just look me up."

The mercenaries and the work crew ate together and after supper the soldiers left.

"It was like they were there and then all of a sudden they were gone," was Hans's observation as he told the story to Ingrid. "We could find no trace of them at all. Even their shoe tracks in the sand were gone."

Hans had no idea how they did it. The team jokingly pondered the idea that the soldiers had been an illusion, but seriously, they knew the day had been all too real.

Ingrid was glad Hans was safe. When Hans described how the soldiers appeared out of nowhere with no warning it made Ingrid feel very nervous. The couple talked long into the night about the situation in the country.

"I think we are safe here in the compound," Hans gently assured her. "The embassy is keeping an eye on things. I'm sure they will pull us out if they feel it is no longer safe."

Seven months had passed and there had been many changes in MAWFA. Hans was now in charge of several crews and had personally helped put in five boreholes and clinics. They were always busy, but they enjoyed their job. There had been no other chance encounters with the mercenaries or even the rebels. It seemed as if things had quieted down a little. Because of this Hans and Ingrid signed a contract for a five year term working in Zimbabwe.

It was Friday and the work load was light that day. The day before they had finished putting the hand pump on the well they had been drilling and the clinic was all setup with medicine and government nurses in place. All they had to do today was clean up camp and head for the compound. The drill was already hitched to the truck so there wasn't much cleanup to do.

After the crews were assigned their jobs, Ingrid walked over to where Hans was working on a bicycle for one of the villagers. "Hans, instead of going straight home let's stop at our spot and have a picnic. I have some steaks that need to be eaten, the ice has pretty much all melted in the cooler and I don't think they will keep on the four hour trip back to the compound. Our spot is on the way and it will be right about lunch time when we get there. Please can we do that?"

"That sounds great my love. We've been working very hard these last three weeks and I could really use a break. Since Nyasha is seven months old he will love our spot now. He can crawl around and find bugs and chungalolos, we'll just have to watch him by the water."

"Yes we have been working hard." Ingrid wanted to make sure Hans realized he wasn't the only one who had been busy. "Plus when we get back to the compound you'll have meetings to go to and as soon as we drive in people will flock to you for help. You'll get so busy with them you'll forget Nyasha and me."

He looked over at his son, "I definitely don't want to be one of those dads who work so much he never sees his kids."

Nyasha was playing in the dirt oblivious to the conversation around him. They had a girl who watched him while they were working, but all she did was keep him out of the way. He had been crawling around near the new water pump and was covered with mud from head to toe. "Before we go anywhere it looks like you will have to clean up your son." Hans was smiling as he spoke.

"Oh, my son, is he only my son when he is dirty? I thought he was our son." Ingrid feigned anger, but in reality she was smiling also. They always argued about whose son he was when it was time to clean him up.

The cleanup that day went quickly and they were on their way back home. Hans had told the other drivers to go on ahead because they were going to make a stop.

When they'd arrived at their special place, Ingrid dug out a blanket and placed it on the ground for a tablecloth and Hans brought out all of the other things for the picnic. He started cooking the steaks on their small gas grill that they always had with them. Nyasha was crawling all over the ground getting himself good and dirty. Ingrid was busy chasing him around under the tree keeping him away from the river. After the meat was cooked they got out the salad and plates and started to eat. It had been a great idea to stop and have a picnic, Hans was glad Ingrid suggested it.

Once lunch was finished, Nyasha started getting fussy and needed a good nap so they decided to head for home. In the car Ingrid fed the baby his bottle and he had begun to fall asleep.

She was still holding him leaning back in the seat with her eyes closed when suddenly the earth exploded! The noise was deafening ripping through the interior of the car causing her scream to melt into the air. The explosion rocked the car and flipped it off the road and into the Zambezi River. Being very deep, the car quickly started to sink all the way to the bottom.

Hans saw Ingrid swim out of the window with the baby and he for some reason reached behind the seat to grab his tool belt. The belt caught on something so he bent over the seat to see what it was. He tugged and tugged, but it just wouldn't come lose. The car was sinking deeper and he needed to get out, so finally he let go and swam for the surface.

"I'm alive!" thought Hans, as he broke through the surface of the river gasping the fresh air. His lungs were burning from the lack of oxygen. Taking a deep breath he looked toward the bank expecting to see Ingrid and Nyasha climbing out of the water onto dry ground.

"Ingrid!" He called out, but there was no reply. Treading water he frantically looked around, "Where are you?"

His voice sounded muffled and his ears were ringing. Again he called, louder this time, "Ingrid! Ingrid, answer me! Where are you?" He shouted over and over again, but all he heard was the sound of the water flowing along the banks. There was an eerie silence all around him, no birds singing and the incessant chattering of the monkeys had stopped, stunned into silence by the magnitude of the explosion.

"This can't be happening, Ingrid, where are you?" He swam to shore and pulled himself up on the bank. Standing up he called again, "Ingrid! Ingrid!" There was no answer. He scanned the water and the far shore. There were leaves blowing in the wind and the ripples of water on the river but no sign of his wife and son.

The sulfuric smell of the land mine that had flipped their vehicle into the river was still in the air, as was a trace of haze over the land. He couldn't even see the Land Rover. It had sunk deep within the folds of the mighty Zambezi river.

Hans was getting frantic now. The current was swift so he ran further down along the shore hoping to find his wife and baby. He looked up and down calling all the while, first running one way then the other. He scanned the far shore, the Zambia side of the river, but he could not see them anywhere. If they had made it to the other shore, he thought, surely I could spot them from here.

Hours later, after endless searching, Hans knew in his heart they were gone. He fell on his knees hard on the ground, "Why! Why!" came the gut-wrenching, desperate cry of a man who had lost everything he had loved.

He took one last look in the fading light of the African sunset, hung his head and gave way to despair. Slowly he stood and mindlessly started walking down the lonely road toward the compound where he lived. The pain in his heart was so heavy, he didn't know if he would even make it to his house. As he trudged home, his thoughts were on everything he had lost.

Now they were gone. His precious wife and beautiful child were gone. What was he going to do? Hans was standing in the doorway of his house looking in. He didn't remember arriving at the compound let alone unlocking the door of his house. He couldn't even remember walking the ten or fifteen kilometers it took to get home.

Staring straight ahead he walked into his house, sat down at their breakfast table and lit a candle. At first all was quiet, then Hans started weeping, quickly the quietness was broken with loud and sorrowful gasps. His shoulders shook as the sobbing racked his body. Hans was not a man of great emotion, but this time he allowed his feelings to flow freely. After a long time the weeping started subsiding and Hans started thinking and talking to himself.

"What could I have done? Why didn't I come home with everyone else? Why did we go on a picnic? If we had followed the rest of the crew they would still be alive." He spoke loudly through his sobs.

"I know who did this." Slamming his fist down on the table, "It was that Deke and his men. They're the only ones who have set any land mines."

Hans was starting to seethe with anger. "They took my family. They took my family!" He kept getting louder and louder as the anger grew within him. "They can't get away with this. Not this time. I'll make sure of it."

Hans was shouting now, he jumped up from the chair and shoved the table with all his strength. As it slid and tipped, the salt and pepper shaker along with the lit candle flew across the room and fell onto the floor. Hans stood up and yelled at the top of his voice, "They can't get away with this, I'll kill them all!" followed by a scream that was filled with all the pain and agony he felt in the deepest part of his being that echoed throughout the village.

Consumed with anger and blinded with revenge, he ran out of his house and away from the compound. He knew what he was going to do. He would join the mercenaries that were fighting against these murdering rebels. He would get them, he would find out who it was that set that mine and then he would destroy him, slowly, with a lot of pain.

The house caught fire and burned to the ground that night. Hans could see the flames in the distance but he didn't care. He had nothing to go back to.

The villagers never thought of him again as the kind man that helped so many of them. Fear gripped their hearts that night. Superstition, tradition and experience dictated that tragedies always struck in groups of three. To remain silent was the only way to keep the attention of the spirits away from oneself. So no one would speak of what they saw or heard, not even when questioned by the authorities or the NGO staff. The official reports read "assumed dead."

It was dark when Ingrid woke up. "Where am I? What happened?" The thoughts ran quickly through her mind. "Where is Nyasha?" Then she became aware that he was right beside her, in her arms. Alarm gripped her for a brief moment as she feared he was dead. Quickly checking for his pulse, she was relieved to see he was peacefully asleep. Her head was hurting and in the darkness she was confused. "Where is Hans . . . what is going on?" Then, she remembered. "The explosion!"

"What happened?" Her mind was still cloudy and her head hurt more than it had ever hurt before. She reached up and touched her scalp feeling a huge bump on her head. It hurt to the touch.

Then she remembered. As she broke through the water, she turned to see if Hans had surfaced and as she turned a log hit her in the head. The blow knocked her semi-unconscious but there were images that were growing in her mind. It was dark now so she knew she had been that way for hours.

Through the haze in her mind Ingrid remembered holding on to the log that hit her and made sure little Nyasha's head was above water. The log was moving fast down river and heading toward the Zambia shore. When land was near she let go of the log and holding the baby up swam as hard as she could trying to reach the edge. Crawling on her hands and knees still holding her child, she collapsed in a sandy place beyond the tree line. Nyasha, seeing his mother lying there, crawled into her arms and quickly fell asleep.

"But where am I? Where is Hans?" She had a horrible feeling in the pit of her stomach. What had happened to Hans? She started calling his name, she called it over and over, but there was no answer. She knew he would never leave her alone, not out here in the middle of nowhere. Where was he?

She called again, but there was still no answer. Her head was throbbing and she didn't know what to do.

She closed her eyes and putting her arms across her knees she started to cry. She knew he must have drowned in the river. Now what was she going to do? The Zambezi was the border between Zimbabwe and Zambia and she was on the Zambian side. As grief settled upon her, Ingrid was ready to give in to despair. Then she heard Nyasha. It was just a whimper, but it was enough. She knew she had to live for him. She went over to her baby and picked him up, cuddling him close to her breast.

"There, there little one, don't cry. We'll somehow find out where we are and then . . . then . . . , I don't know what."

When Hans left the village that night he had only one objective in his mind. He would find the mercenaries and join them. He was angry and he wanted revenge.

He walked off into the night and although he knew the mercenaries must be a long way away by now, he planned to search until he found them. All through the night he thought of his beloved wife and child as he walked. All the next day he walked until finally he got to the tarred road heading toward the town of Karoi. He caught a lift with the first car that came along. The driver quizzed Hans about who he was and what he was doing. Hans gave a quick and plausible explanation.

"I'm with the borehole construction team. My vehicle broke down a few kilometers back and I need to get to town to contact headquarters so they can send a mechanic."

The explanation satisfied the man's curiosity. When they got to town, Hans thanked the man and asked to be dropped in the center of town. From there he proceeded to Ander's petrol station. Finding Chris alone in his office, Hans explained that he needed a car to get to Gokwe.

"Well, my old pickup is running pretty well for a change, you can use that," Chris replied handing Hans a set of keys. "How are Ingrid and the baby?"

A brief stricken look crossed Hans's face but he quickly replied "They're fine." Crossing to the truck, Hans climbed in and left. Chris thought it was strange that he didn't stay and talk a little. Hans was always talkative, wanting to find out what was going on in the world. He was also puzzled as to what happened to the Land Rover Hans usually drove. Certain that his questions would be answered upon Hans's return, Chris got busy with the day's work and soon forgot all about it.

After driving five hours, Hans arrived at the village where the previous borehole had been drilled, the same place where the team had met up with the mercenary group. Hoping that someone would know where to find them, he started asking around. That night Hans camped just outside the village. While he was cooking his supper over the open fire, the Australian leader, Keith, suddenly appeared.

"I heard you were looking for me."

"Yes. You asked me if I wanted to join up with you before. Does that offer still stand?"

"Why, what has changed?" asked Keith, "When I asked you before you weren't at all interested, you wanted to spend all your time with your family."

"That was when I had a family. They killed them. A land mine. The rebels killed them. And if it were possible for me to kill every one of them . . . " Hans chocked back his tears. Keith knew that vengeance was a great motivator in war. He had seen something in Hans the first time he met him and now that he was angry and ready to kill, he knew that Hans would make a great soldier and a valuable addition to his team.

"Alright, come with me. I'll show you where our camp is and introduce you to the men. Let's go."

Leaving both the fire and the food, Hans and Keith walked on through the bush for about four kilometers and finally came into a clearing. As they got to the other side of the clearing, the camp was suddenly before them, hidden in a shallow area, unseen, until they were right upon it. Their camp along that clearing would have been unseen even in the daytime. The men had a fire going, banked, and hidden so well you didn't even know that it was there unless you were next to it. Keith introduced Hans around. There were eleven men including Keith and now Hans made it a complete dozen. They ate and talked quietly into the night and then slept. A guard remained on duty all night long. Being new to the group and still needing to prove himself, Hans was omitted from guard duty. He sensed right away that it would take time to prove that he was really one of them.

In the morning Keith took Hans to the clearing and set up a target. He needed to know if Hans could shoot a gun. First he gave Hans a pistol. Hans fired all the rounds in the handgun, hitting the target, but not very accurately.

"When I get done with you you'll be able to put a dollar coin over the shots."

Next he gave Hans a rifle, a weapon that Hans was more familiar with. He used to go hunting with his dad years ago. This time his shots were grouped together, well aimed, finding their mark.

"Well, I guess we have a sniper here," Keith exclaimed. "Do you think you can do the same with a human target?"

"Shooting a rebel, especially if I can find out who killed my family . . . no problem."

"Okay. We'll be going on a raid in the morning. I'll expect you to be ready and I'll be watching to see how you do."

"That's okay with me," replied Hans, "I'm ready now."

It was pitch dark when they got up, there was no moon the only light was from the stars. They didn't use any lanterns or lights but kept things dark just in case there were any spies nearby. After loading the trucks they drove, without lights, to an area near Lake Kariba. The rutted dirt road that ran alongside the length of the lake was rarely used because most people preferred taking the longer but quicker route on the blacktopped road.

The mercenaries had been watching this area for two weeks and knew it was this dirt road the rebels used frequently to make their escapes. So during the nights they had quietly worked and got everything set up for this moment, their moment, for an ambush. They came to a large tree right alongside the road.

"Well, Hans, this is going to be home for a while. Up you go," Keith ordered.

Looking up, Hans spied a small platform, crudely built, but not noticeable at all from the ground.

"Just shinny right on up and wait. There'll be some rebels come along, and when they do shoot. Be careful you don't shoot too soon. You want them to be your target not the other way around," Keith said sarcastically. "You have to be patient. Pick your target and then wait. They usually travel in groups of three or four, but occasionally they break up into twos. Wait until there are only two. Two kills are easy to do without being detected but if there are three or four your chances of getting spotted are higher."

Hans nodded and started up the tree. Once he was settled, he lowered a rope and Keith tied on a backpack loaded with dried meat, water, and supplies. This was to be his ration for the next few days.

"We will take up positions further down the road, close enough that we'll be able to hear your gunfire. If we hear repeated fire, we'll come running."

Not knowing when the rebel forces would come or if they would come at all, Hans was ready. He had his rifle and plenty of ammunition. He waited all day and saw no-one. A couple of times a family of kudu crossed the road.

"If I was in another place at another time, this would be a great place to go hunting," Hans thought to himself.

As he sat in that tree waiting, memories of his childhood flooded to the surface of his mind.

Edmund Grundey had been the kind of father every son would cherish. Time spent with his father was the best part of any day, and Hans's father always made time for his son. They spent long hours together, working side by side on the five acres they called home and then doing the things they loved to do after the work was finished. Hans's favorite pastime was to camp, hunt, and fish.

Edmund was a driver for the railroad, a job that demanded discipline and made no room for mistakes. Whether in work or in play, Edmund passed those same qualities to his son, never with a harsh hand, but always with a good balance of firmness and tenderness.

Hans was just fourteen when his father became sick. The doctors said the cancer had started in his lungs and by the time they found it, nothing could be done. Four months later, he was gone. After her husband's death, Karin Grundey retreated into herself. Laughter was gone from their home. With three children to care for on her own, life was a constant heavy load. As the eldest of the three children and the only boy, Hans bore a heavy responsibility at a young age. He did it well, without complaining, but always with a sense of loneliness and emptiness that nothing could fill.

When Hans became a man, discipline and responsibility made him a valuable asset wherever he worked and in whatever he put his hand to. But the void from his father's death remained. When he met Ingrid and they fell so completely in love, the loneliness and emptiness at last were gone. Life was good again. Now that she was gone, loneliness would have been a pleasant feeling compared to the anger that consumed him.

When night fell, Hans got as comfortable as he could on the small platform and tied himself in. Early the next morning he was awakened by the sound of a vehicle coming close. Looking down the road, he saw it was a truck full of men, all armed. He knew this was part of the rebel force. As he watched, the truck would stop every so often and at each stop three men would climb down. Finally reaching his tree, the truck stopped and just like all the other times three men got out. They each had a rifle and one was carrying a large round plate. The manner in which he carried it told Hans that it is was heavy.

The truck continued down the road leaving the three rebels just beyond Hans's position. He could hear them talk, but didn't understand the language. He wanted to fire, but with them being three and with others close by he didn't dare shoot. All he could do was to watch and wait. He knew he was safe where he was if he remained quiet and still.

One of the men started to dig a hole in the dirt road. It wasn't very deep and Hans wondered what they were doing. Then he saw the man with the large plate like thing fiddle with it and set it in the hole. Then he knew; it was a land mine. They talked the whole time they were working, grouped closely together.

Hans had an idea. If he shot the land mine the explosion would probably cover the shot and the others would think the three had made an error, blowing themselves up. As one man got down on his knees to cover the mine with dirt, Hans took aim. He squeezed off the shot, the explosion rattled the tree.

When the dust cleared he looked down and saw no one. The explosion must have thrown the bodies far off. Hans knew it would take a few seconds for it all to sink in and then the other rebels would swarm the area. He hurried down the tree and ran into the woods to hide.

From the ground he could see that the explosion even scarred his tree at the base and his good fortune was obvious. When he was quite a distance from the tree he turned to look down the road. He could see the vehicle just starting to move out, heading toward the explosion. He knew he was safe. Hans was tense but satisfied. His revenge on his enemy had begun. Keeping his head down, Hans moved from tree to tree and after fifteen minutes he saw Keith coming up on his left. As they drew close to one another Keith congratulated Hans on a job well done.

"I wish I had thought of that. If we had synchronized our shots we could have taken out nearly all of them, blown them all to kingdom come." Keith was talking excitedly. "Great job! When they all ran toward the explosion, it gave our men a way out. And we know exactly where they put every one of the mines. The men are making their way to this location. Tonight we'll go out and get rid of the mines."

As they were talking, the others appeared one by one, each taking their turn to either slap Hans on the back or shake his hand. They all told him he had done a good job and many commented that they wished it had been them. Hans was the hero of the day.

Hans found his new lifestyle appealing in many ways. He liked the camaraderie with the men he worked with. He also found he was good at being a soldier.

Night time was the hardest, though, when thoughts of Ingrid assailed him and sleep was long in coming. When it finally did, images of his wife haunted his dreams.

As time went on, Hans became more and more ruthless and adept at his job. His overbearing size was very intimidating to the locals and he used this to his advantage, primarily to extract information concerning the rebel hideouts. He soon became Keith's number one interrogator.

When rebel forces were encountered he had no qualms about killing them. Anger over the death of his wife and child was his motivating force. If Keith needed someone to go on a dangerous mission he knew Hans would volunteer. Each time, whether it was a suicide mission or not, Hans would go in and he always came back, multiplying his number of kills till his total far exceeded that of anyone else.

Despite his size, he could move very quietly in the bush. Amongst the Africans he became known as *Chipoko*, the Ghost.

7

New Life

INGRID PICKED UP LITTLE Nyasha from the shore and started walking. She knew that to the northeast the river broadened into Kariba Lake and there were no settlements going that way. She would be more likely to find a village in the opposite direction so she started walking southwest.

Her heart ached from her terrible loss. She clung to her baby thinking how tragic it was that he already had lost two fathers. Besides her head hurting, her neck, and chest were sore, as well as along the collarbone. It had probably gotten bruised from the seat belt when the car was thrown into the water. She felt cold all over from the dampness of her clothing and she was sure Nyasha was cold as well.

The accident kept replaying in her mind. She remembered seeing Hans look over at her as she made her escape from the car, but after that she focused all her attention on Nyasha. She had to get the baby out and up to air before he drowned. Then, just as she broke the surface, the log struck her head. She was amazed she didn't just sink and drown bringing the baby down with her. She had never been a religious woman, but she took time to thank God that she made it safely to shore. Now she just needed to survive. Her mother instincts had kicked in and she knew even without Hans, she had to go on. She had to be mother and father to Nyasha now.

Walking further, she was soon aware that there was gravel under her feet. She must have stumbled upon a road. As she looked around, the light from the full moon was enough so that she could see the road stretching out to her right and left. Now which way should she go? She had no idea where any village was or how far away it might be.

Meeting rebels was no longer a worry since she was on the opposite side of the river. She was relieved that she was on the Zambia side, away from the war heating up in Zimbabwe. She remembered the conversation she had with Hans just a few days ago. He had assured her the rebels were eighty kilometers away and would leave their area alone. He reasoned that they were not likely to be targeted because their team was on location to help the indigenous people. But in spite of Hans's reasoning, she had been getting more and more worried about the rebel forces.

"Some of the rebels don't care that we are helping the people." Ingrid said, "They see our skin color, shoot first and ask questions later."

"They aren't fighting against the white man in this war. It's a war between the predominantly Shona government and the rebels. I don't think they will cause us any problem at all."

"I guess Hans was right," thought Ingrid. "The mine was not necessarily meant for us, we just became collateral damage in this war." But the thought brought her no comfort. Tears came again as she dwelled on her loss. Hans was her strong tower during any crisis. How would she ever survive without him?

Shaking off the despondency Ingrid forced herself into action and decided that she would go left, hoping there was a town or village nearby. They hadn't eaten since their picnic and she was very hungry so she could only imagine how hungry Nyasha must be. She wished she had her Zambia cloth so she could put Nyasha on her hip and wrap the cloth around to hold him up, carrying him the way the African ladies carried their babies. Carrying him in her arms was very tiring.

She had been walking maybe six kilometers when she spotted a light down the road and to the right. It was a fire at a rural home. She hoped the people could speak English. If they couldn't, there would be no way to communicate with them. As she got closer she could see a lady cooking *sadza* over the fire. "Oh, please, please let them speak English."

"Knock, knock, knock," Ingrid called out in the African way as she approached the gate.

"Come in," said the lady by the fire. Ingrid was relieved that she at least knew a little English.

"Hello, how are you?" Ingrid asked knowing that you must start all conversations very politely with the proper greeting.

"I am very fine thank you, and how are you?"

"I am well, thank you." Ingrid replied as she reached out her hand to the woman. The lady clapped her hands twice, shook Ingrid's hand and then clapped again. Ingrid tried as best as she could to duplicate the greeting. She had never seen anyone greet like this. She assumed it was the customary way to greet in Zambia.

Feeling rather dizzy from the trauma of the day and the lack of food, Ingrid began to be unsteady on her feet. "Please sit down," the lady said motioning to the log near the fire. "My name is Susan Msipa."

"I'm Ingrid Grundey and this is my son Nyasha."

"You look like you have been through a lot. Oh my! Look at your head. It's cut and looks like it could use some stitches. I'm a nurse and I can stitch it up for you if you want. What happened to you?"

"Yes, please stitch it up," Ingrid replied as she gingerly touched the open wound. Susan went inside her hut and came out with water and a cloth. She bathed the wound and began stitching it up.

"Sorry I don't have anything to give you to numb it. It will only take three or four stitches and we'll be done."

While the lady sewed her up, Ingrid told her story. By the time she finished she felt totally exhausted and once again struggled to control the overwhelming sorrow.

"I don't even know where I am," Ingrid finished.

"You are near the Kafue River settlement in Zambia. My, you must have walked a long way. Or else the river carried you farther than you thought," Susan responded as she gently laid her hand on Ingrid's shoulder. That touch alone brought so much comfort.

"We have heard about the fighting in Zimbabwe and have been glad it has stayed on the other side of the river." After a pause Susan continued. "The cut is right near your hairline so there shouldn't be any noticeable scar when it heals. Okay, I'm all done. Would you like something to eat?"

"Yes, thank you Susan. We're famished and very tired. I've been walking all evening not knowing where I was heading, I . . . just kept walking, heading no particular direction. I don't know how I found you . . . or what I am going to do now. I don't have any travel documents or . . . anything. I worked for the Netherlands NGO in Zimbabwe, but I can't return there. I don't want to go back. There are too many memories, too much sadness. I'm so afraid. What should I do?"

"The first thing is to get you and your baby fed and into bed for a good night's sleep. Then in the morning we will figure out what to do." Susan started putting food on a plate for Ingrid and little Nyasha.

They ate, using their hands, African fashion. When they had eaten their fill, Susan showed Ingrid to a grass-roofed hut. Inside Ingrid found a bed with clean sheets and a blanket. The only other piece of furniture in the room was a table against the far wall. Ingrid expressed her thanks as Susan turned to leave the small room. Pausing at the door, Susan turned and gently smiled as she said "good night" and left the room.

Ingrid took off her outer clothes and stripped Nyasha down to his diaper. The two of them lay down on the bed together and promptly fell asleep.

Once they were asleep, Susan quietly entered the hut and removed their clothes. She washed them by hand in her washing tub and hung them out to dry on the line. Then she went to her own bed to sleep.

The next morning Ingrid woke up with a splitting headache. When she first began to awaken, she was just half aware of her head but the heaviness and sorrow were so strong. In that half–awake half asleep place she couldn't understand all these feelings. Then the memory flooded back upon her and she was fully awake, but wishing she could just sleep on forgetting it all.

Looking at her watch she saw that it was half past eight in the morning. She got up and noticed that their clothes had been washed and dried. She quickly dressed and went outside.

Susan was under a thatch roof shelter over to the side of the property wearing a nurse's uniform. It appeared as though she had a small clinic right there at her home. Ingrid walked over, carrying Nyasha with her. As she drew closer she saw Susan was busy taking a woman's temperature. Next she began checking a man's blood pressure and then she moved on to a young boy who had an extended stomach and looked like he was malnourished. Just as she began to examine the boy she looked up and saw Ingrid watching.

"Hi, Ingrid, how did you sleep?"

"I slept. Nyasha slept very well. The bed was comfortable. Thank you again." Ingrid realized her answers were very short and strained. She spoke again, consciously aiming to get past the pain and trying to just sound normal. "It looks like you have a clinic here. Is there anything I can do to help? I'm a nurse with the MAWFA."

"I don't know MAWFA, but I never turn down any help I can get. Go ahead and finish checking this blood pressure and I'll go tell my house maid, Nadia, to prepare some breakfast for you two. Here, let me take Nyasha with me. Nadia will be happy to watch him while we work."

Susan took Nyasha from Ingrid's arms and walked over to the thatch–roofed hut that served as her kitchen. The hut was round with a fire pit in the center of the floor. Inside she found Nadia, busy sweeping the floor. Nadia was more than happy to care for the baby. Susan had shared Ingrid's story first thing when Nadia came to work that morning.

Satisfied that breakfast would be provided in short order, Susan proceeded to the patient waiting area, some benches under a shade tree, to see if there were any English speaking patients that Ingrid could attend to.

"Do any of you speak English?"

"Yes, my sister and I do." Was one reply.

Another spoke up, "I speak English good."

"Well there are at least three who speak English. At least it will keep Ingrid busy for a while." Susan knew that Ingrid needed something to do to keep her mind off her tragedy.

"I speak little English." It was a small older woman. "I do."

Susan was satisfied that the woman would be able to make herself understood.

"I need you four to form a line near the shelter. Nurse Ingrid is here and will see to you. She only speaks English so you'll have to make yourself understood using only that language. Nurse Ingrid will see you as soon as she can."

The elderly lady stood up first and walked over to the shelter. Susan followed them and found that Ingrid had finished with the blood pressure and had also finished the temperature taking on the female patient, taking care to record both results on the proper medical cards.

The old lady sat down on the stool in front of Ingrid and smiled at her. She explained in very broken English that she had been having problems with her stomach and with her feet. "Is your stomach sore?"

"No" was all she said in response, not offering any further indication as to what was wrong with her stomach.

Ingrid went through a list of possible problems and symptoms and the old lady answered "no" to each one. Ingrid was getting a little exasperated. In her own clinic she always had an interpreter close at hand to help in these kinds of situations. Ingrid looked over to Susan and saw that Susan was smiling and trying to keep from laughing right out loud.

"Is this some kind of joke?" Ingrid wondered. Finally she asked the lady very slowly and as clearly as possible, "What is the problem with your stomach?"

The lady looked around to make sure that no one else was listening and leaned over close to Ingrid. "I keep getting air in it and it comes out my bottom." The lady was as serious as she could be, and it was all Ingrid could do to not laugh.

"Okay, we can take care of that with some pills. Now, what's wrong with your feet?"

"When I walk to church the feet hurt. This never happen before when I walk to church, but now it happen." She said in broken English.

"Is your church near your home?"

"Oh yes, only ten kilometers to church from my home. We have the best church in the world. I like to go there. Do you go to church? There are missionaries that come to our church, Mr. and Mrs. Perry. Do you know the Perry's? God is strong when they preach. We get excited. They are very, how do you say . . . prophets. They hear God. It is good, very good!"

Ingrid was at a loss what to say. The lady had asked at least two questions but then she kept talking so that Ingrid had no chance to respond. What did she mean when she said that they were "prophets?" She remembered in Sunday School the teacher talking about prophets in the Old Testament. They were the ones who heard God speak and then spoke to the people about what God wanted.

Did she really believe that these people could hear the voice of God? These missionaries must really have people hoodwinked. They hear from God!? God doesn't speak to people. God is just a figment of someone's imagination.

She had heard about missionaries exploiting the people, making them change their beliefs and changing their culture. She didn't have a very high opinion of missionaries in the best of times, but to hear this lady she thought they must really be telling a lot of lies to the good people of this village.

All she could think to say was, "Well that's nice."

Wanting to direct things back to medical issues, Ingrid began to question the woman about her age. The woman didn't know her exact age but they concluded that she must be in her late 70's to early 80's. Ingrid tried to convince her that ten kilometers was a long way to walk for someone of her age. Ingrid examined her feet and saw that they were wide and very flat.

Turning to Susan she asked, "Do you have any insoles for this ladies shoes?"

Smiling, Susan replied, "The woman doesn't wear shoes. Insoles would do her no good even if we had some, which we don't."

Ingrid went over to where Susan kept the medicine and took out a packet of antacid tablets and twenty pain relievers.

Handing the woman a pink tablet and a glass of water she said, "You must take this pink tablet now. It's for your stomach problem. Tonight after supper you should take another one. Do you understand?"

"Yes, yes, one pink now, one pink after I eat."

"That's right, these other pills, the white ones you should take when you have pain in your feet. They won't cure it but at least it will help with the pain."

Thanking Ingrid, the lady went on to say, "When the missionaries get here I am going to have them lay hands on me and pray for my feet. Then God will heal them and I will be able to walk good."

Again, Ingrid was at a loss what to say. She quickly dismissed the woman saying goodbye and immediately called for the next patient.

After working a short while Ingrid took a break to eat breakfast with Nyasha. The food, a simple meal of porridge and bread with tea, seemed to have no taste. Even being with Nyasha did little to bring comfort to the pain and emptiness inside her. Ingrid knew she would need to think things through at some point and decide what she would do and where she would go, but at the moment she just couldn't do it. At least when she was working the pain was pushed aside for a time. So as soon as she was finished eating, Ingrid went back to work and worked the rest of that morning seeing one patient after another.

All morning long, over and over again, Ingrid heard the same familiar comment. They couldn't wait until the missionaries came. Evidently the Perry's were coming soon and it seemed nearly the whole community was excited about it. Ingrid and Susan finished up with the last of the patients at lunchtime and Susan informed her new friend that the clinic was open only during the morning hours.

"Many afternoons I do home visits with those who are too weak to come to the clinic," Susan commented. "But my afternoon schedule is empty today so you will have time to rest, and later, if you would like, we can talk some more." Susan's tone and manner told Ingrid that she truly cared.

Ingrid found Nyasha still playing happily under Nadia's watchful care. He didn't notice any difference in the day or where he was. As long as his mother was nearby he was happy. Ingrid didn't have that luxury and the moment her hands were not busy, her mind was. The memory and pain came rushing back upon her, as strong as ever. The morning had kept her busy, but now in the quiet of the afternoon she was even aware of physical pain and bruises all over her body that she had not been aware of before. Her muscles ached and she felt exhausted. Taking Nyasha to her small hut for an afternoon nap, Ingrid lay down beside him, drawing him close and the two soon fell asleep.

When Ingrid awoke, the keen awareness flooded her mind that she was in a strange country and her husband was dead. She had to decide what she was going to do, which first meant she needed to find out exactly where she was. She remembered Susan saying something about the Kafue River settlement, but she had no idea where that was. As she moved from her bed she glanced over at the table and saw a small pile of baby clothes and diapers folded neatly. There were also a couple of tops and a skirt, apparently meant for her. Ingrid assumed they must have been placed there by Susan and wondered who had provided them. Susan had no babies and the two women were not the same size, so the clothing was not from Susan's own cupboard. Obviously, someone other than just Susan was responsible for this caring gift and the kindness touched Ingrid's heart.

Wanting to see Susan, Ingrid carried Nyasha from their hut and walked over to her small house. She knocked on the door and Susan opened it. She was drying her hair with a towel.

"Hi Ingrid, there's some water heating up so you and the baby can bathe."

"Thanks Susan. Thank you too for the clothes. Where did they come from?"

"Oh, this morning during clinic hours I put the word out to everyone I saw that you and the baby needed clothing. A couple of the women came by while you were sleeping with a few things. They're clean and they'll not need them back, so . . . use them."

"Thank you so much, and thank those women for me. I'm so touched," Ingrid replied with a lump in her throat. Then she continued, "I was just wondering, where exactly are we?"

"Well, like I said last night you're in the Kafue River settlement, we're about four hours by car from Lusaka."

"I'm just wondering what in the world is going to happen to me. I probably need to go to the Holland consul and see what I need to do." Overcome with grief and the huge burden confronting her, Ingrid collapsed in a heap and started crying. Susan knelt down beside her and put her arm around her shoulders.

"There, there Ingrid. It will be all right. Let me help. I know you are hurting with your loss. Come inside and have a cup of tea. There's something I need to talk to you about that I believe will help."

Ingrid just kept sobbing, so Susan helped her up and into the house. When they got inside, Susan directed Ingrid to a chair and left her to get the tea. The water was already hot, so it only took a minute to prepare things. Returning to the room, she set the tea tray down on the table and poured the tea. Reaching over, she took Nyasha from Ingrid's lap and set him on the floor. Then she gave Ingrid a cup of tea and sat down in the chair next to her. Having settled down a little, Ingrid took a sip of tea. Susan remained quiet and waited until Ingrid was ready to talk.

After a few minutes Ingrid spoke. "I miss him so. Why did this have to happen?" The tears started afresh and she could hear Susan talking very quietly. Not understanding what she was saying, Ingrid became quiet and asked, "What? What are you saying? I can't hear you."

Susan reached over and put her hand on Ingrid's shoulder. "I was just praying for you."

"Praying? To whom?"

"Well, that's what I wanted to talk to you about. As you were probably aware, our church is experiencing the move of God lately. The Perry's, our missionaries, have been coming here for several years now and in the last year our church has come alive?"

Ingrid interrupted here. "What do you mean your church has come alive? I went to church a few times as a child and a young girl, but it was cold and uncaring. In our country we have grown up and don't need a crutch like the church. When you say that your church has come alive it sounds like your building must have become a being and has a heart that is pumping blood to its brain, like Frankenstein. I'm sure that's not what you mean."

Susan was thoughtful for a moment. She had never met anyone as un–churched as this lady seemed to be. Nearly everyone in Zambia went to church or at least had gone to church when they were younger. If Ingrid had never been to church she would not understand a lot of the phrases and church words that were normally used. She realized she needed to choose her words carefully so she could express herself to Ingrid in a way that she would understand.

"Okay, what I mean is that changes are happening in the people that go to our church and we are growing in our spiritual lives and learning a lot about God. I heard what Mrs. Sayila said to you about being healed and I also saw the look on your face when she said it. You looked at her like she was from another planet."

"Well you have to admit; claiming that God was going to heal her so that she could walk ten kilometers to go to church sounds just plain crazy, especially for a woman her age. I don't have a very high opinion of missionaries anyway. In my opinion, all they do is exploit people in third world countries and I wish they would leave so that the NGO's could do their work without having to listen to what this missionary or that missionary said. They think they know so much. They tell people how to think and then they leave. By the time they leave, people have been so indoctrinated that they can only see one way to do a certain thing. Then when another group comes, like an NGO, and they want to do things differently it just causes problems. For instance, we don't take Sundays off when we are putting in a borehole but every time we are in the middle of a project and it falls on a Sunday we have to stop work in the morning so people can go to church. Sometimes these services last for hours and we never get back to work that day. We lose a whole day of work all because of people believing a fairy tale." Ingrid finished with a sigh and continued drinking her tea.

Susan knew that she was going to have to be careful how she shared her faith with Ingrid. She prayed a quick prayer asking the Lord to give her wisdom. She had such an assurance in her heart that it was no coincidence that Ingrid happened to find her house in the dark the night before. It was the hand of God. Peace settled all over her knowing that God would be faithful to complete what He had started. With renewed confidence she continued.

"Not all churches or missionaries are the same. The Perry's are hard working people who really love God and want to help the people of our nation. They have helped by feeding people during drought and they've started clinics and built schools in several areas where they work in Zambia. The reason they haven't started one here yet is because they have seen what I am doing and want to encourage me to do the work that God has given me. It's their policy never to start projects just to start projects because then, when they leave, who will continue the project? But, it is their desire to assist people so that they can run with their own dreams. When they find someone with a God given vision and they see that person has what it takes to finish what they start, then they do whatever they can to help. They are the ones who supply me with medicines. I am able to do what I love to do because of their help and encouragement."

Susan paused to gather her thoughts, "Let me tell you what happened here and then you can decide."

Ingrid was intrigued with what she was hearing, but "Okay, if you want to," was all she replied.

"About three years ago our pastor, Pastor Sayila, went to America for some training and while he was there he met Mr. Perry. At that time the Perry's were based in Zimbabwe. They became friends and started corresponding. When Pastor Sayila returned to Zambia he made a trip to Zimbabwe at Mr. Perry's invitation. He stayed a week with the Perry's, attending a seminar they taught on knowing God. While he was there, Pastor Sayila arranged a time for the Perry's to come and do the leadership training here at our church.

"Oh, by the way, our pastor is the son of the lady that you treated today. Anyhow, the Perry's came for two weeks. Mr. Perry taught on church leadership during the mornings and early afternoons. In the evening we would have a church service. Mr. Perry would speak and at first, although what he said was good, not much happened. But then during the second week there was a line of people waiting to be prayed for."

Susan thought about what she was saying and felt she needed to clarify it a little. "He had told us that God loved us and wanted to heal our physical sicknesses and so he had people come up front at the end of the meeting so that he could lay hands on them, I mean, he placed his hands on their heads and prayed for them."

"One night a lady went to the front to be prayed for. Everyone knew this lady and how badly she was crippled with arthritis. She was bent over so that her head was at the same level as her waist. Her hands and feet were very crippled and deformed. I watched and I saw Mr. Perry look over at her, skip her and move on to the next person. I think he was hoping that she would go away," Susan said with a chuckle.

"I don't think he felt that he had enough faith to pray for her. Finally the only person left to pray for was that lady, so he went over to her, placed his hand on her head and started praying. I remember that he said, "by the blood of Jesus," and all of a sudden the lady straightened up. She hadn't been able to stand upright in twenty years and suddenly she was standing straight, right in front of us, for everyone to see."

"We couldn't believe our eyes. Here was one of our own, a lady that we all knew, who had been bent and crippled for years, standing before us upright. Then someone noticed her hands. They were no longer deformed and her feet were straight. She was completely healed from the top of her head to the soles of her feet. She started running around dancing and jumping, something that she hadn't been able to do since she was a young woman. She would grab hold of people as she ran by them and have them dance and jump with her. It was truly amazing."

Susan paused briefly, and then continued. "Do you remember the lady that was herding the cattle along the road this morning? You greeted her and she greeted you back. She spoke to you in her language, Venda, so you didn't know what she said, but she told you that Jesus loves you."

Ingrid nodded at the memory.

"That's the same woman. Ever since that night our church has never been the same. This is why all of the people are looking forward to Mr. Perry coming. Those who are sick want him to pray for them. Mr. Perry teaches that if we would just abide, or stay with Jesus, then we would see these miracles happening all the time and we wouldn't have to wait for "the missionary" to come." The last comment was emphasized with fingered quotes.

Ingrid didn't know what to say. She remembered speaking to a lady who was herding cattle. At the time she was impressed that a woman her age was herding the cattle. She also was struck by the woman's smile and her obvious cheerful attitude. There was nothing wrong with her physically. In fact Ingrid had thought that the way that she walked and held herself made her seem to be regal, she stood so straight and tall. How could this woman have had such a crippling disease? She hadn't known Susan very long, but she liked her and had assumed she could trust what she said. Susan's comments filled Ingrid with lots of questions.

"I just don't understand. What is it that made this woman better? There aren't even medicines that can cure arthritis."

"It's the healing power of Jesus Christ. You see, the Bible tells us that, "Jesus, took our infirmities and diseases" and in another place it says that, "by his stripes we are healed." Jesus was beaten with a whip so badly that people couldn't even recognize him. It's those stripes that have carried our sicknesses and have healed us. Although Jesus had never done any wrong, he was arrested and put on trial. They beat him, made fun of him, spat on him, pulled out his beard and then they crucified him. To be crucified is a horrible, painful way to die."

Unsure whether Ingrid would even know what "crucified" meant, she went on to explain. "They hung him on a cross by nailing his hands and feet to it and left him there to suffocate and die. Jesus never fought back or protested. He allowed them to kill him and abuse him so that all people, all humanity, could live."

"What do you mean? I am alive. He didn't do anything for me," Ingrid commented in a questioning tone.

"Yes Ingrid, he did. Not so that you can live here on this earth, but so that after you die you can live forever with Jesus."

Ingrid sat there and thought about the words that Susan had said. She had forgotten all about her tea which was turning cold in the cup. They had churches in Holland, but she hadn't been to one since she was a little girl. She remembered it being cold and very unfriendly. Her mother had wanted her to go to Sunday school, but she was a very active little girl and after a couple of months the teacher asked her mother to keep her at home. So Susan decided to never go to church again. If that's what they thought of her then she wanted nothing to do with them. They didn't care about her so she wasn't interested in them. Now she was hearing about a different kind of church, one that seemed to care about people. Susan was one of the most caring people she had ever met. It suddenly struck her that the ladies who brought the clothing must also be from Susan's church. It was obvious people were excited about the missionary coming. She really didn't understand it.

What Susan was telling her about Jesus was new to Ingrid. She had never heard this story before. Jesus had died for her? Oh, she knew that he was hung on a cross; she had seen the pictures that all churches have. She always thought they were rather morbid and shouldn't be hung up in any public place. Something was tugging at her heart, a feeling she had never felt before, as Susan told her about Jesus. I'm sure it's only my emotions running away with me because of everything that has happened, she mused. She hadn't said anything and knew that Susan was quietly sitting there, just waiting. Realizing that she needed to say something, Ingrid pulled herself out of the daze she had slipped into.

Then, as if Susan knew what was going on in her mind she said, "Listen Ingrid, you don't have to say anything or make any decision right now. You are welcome to stay here with me for as long as you need to. I really enjoyed your help in the clinic and I like having you and Nyasha here. You've gone through a lot lately and it's not good to make any decisions while you're in this state. I know I don't have a lot of the luxuries you would find in the city, but you can get all the rest you need here. You need time to recuperate from your wounds. Nyasha needs a rest too. Please say you'll stay here with me."

Ingrid really wanted nothing more than to just stay where she was and recuperate. "Yes Susan, I'll stay with you. I don't have any money or any means to get anywhere else at the moment. It's probably best that I stay with you. I enjoyed the work this morning. It kept me occupied so I couldn't think too much. If you will put up with me I'll be glad to stay, for a while at least."

"Good! It's settled then. The Perry's are coming within the week and if you feel better then, they could probably give you a lift to Lusaka. I'm sure they will be happy to help you in any way they can. They know people all over and can make things happen. I'm so glad you are staying. Don't worry about money. The help you give at the clinic will more than take care of any cost. Most people pay the clinic in items such as chickens, goats or veggies. I'm never in need of food. We will have plenty to eat while you are here. Now, why don't you go into the next room. There's a bathtub in there. I have been heating water up and it's more than ready. You can soak awhile. That will help a lot. I'll watch Nyasha for you. Go on, there's a towel on the chair for you."

Ingrid walked into the room and found one of those old fashioned bathtubs that stood on legs right in the middle of the room. There was some cold water already in it and right next to it was a big pot with steaming hot water. Ingrid lifted the pot with a little bit of difficulty and poured the hot water in. She checked the temperature and it was just right. She got undressed and climbed in the tub. It felt so wonderful. She leaned against the back of the tub and closed her eyes. She thought about Hans and how much she missed him. The tears started flowing and she just let them come.

8

New Essence

INGRID AND SUSAN SPENT their days working in the clinic, making home visits and caring for Nyasha. On the fourth morning while the two ladies were busy in the clinic a car drove by. Ingrid had not seen a car driving by since she had been there. The bus or maybe a truck would drive by, but not a car. As soon as the car was past them, several of the patients got up and left the clinic without waiting to be seen.

"What's happening Susan, everyone is leaving?"

"The Perry's are here. That was them in the car. Everyone is going over to see them."

"In fact, I will probably close the clinic for a while, mostly because I don't want to miss any of the meetings but also because when the Perry's come, so many people get healed the clinic is not necessary. Ingrid, you must come along to see for yourself."

"Oh, don't worry I wouldn't miss this for anything. I'm quite the skeptic, so I have to see this with my own eyes."

That evening Susan and Ingrid walked the four kilometers to the church, taking turns carrying Nyasha in a sling made out of a long Zambia cloth.

Ingrid didn't know what to expect at the meeting. She had seen some of these so–called "faith healers" on TV and a lot of them wore flashy clothes and big rings on their fingers and they were always begging for money. She never watched the entire program. They always disgusted her so she would quickly change the channel.

When they arrived at the church, it was packed. There wasn't room for another person inside. There were people standing outside trying to see in through the small windows. Ingrid was a little disappointed. She wanted to see this man and hear what he had to say. Now it looked as though they wouldn't get to see him at all. Right then the car that passed earlier in the day pulled up. It wasn't a very fancy car. It looked to be about twelve or thirteen years old. It was in good shape, but she could see that the man didn't spend a lot of money on his vehicle. It stopped a short distance from them and two people got out of the car, a man and woman whom she guessed to be around fifty years of age. The man was bald and had a beard that was flecked with gray. The woman had short brown hair and a very kind look about her.

A third man came from the back seat of the car. Ingrid recognized him as the pastor of the church. She had met him once a couple of days before when he had come over purposely to meet the new nurse helping Susan.

The pastor had a very deep commanding voice, which came in very handy right at that moment. He shouted out so everyone could hear that they would hold the service under the big tree near the church building, instructing everyone to come out of the building and bring the benches with them.

As people made their way out of the building, Ingrid saw that many of them were being assisted. Some couldn't walk at all and had to be carried. Others were led out, obviously blind.

She thought to herself, "These people really are expecting to be healed by this man. I hope they won't be too disappointed."

Susan took hold of Ingrid's arm and led her to where the missionaries were standing.

"Mr. and Mrs. Perry. How are you?" She clapped her hands and shook theirs and then clapped her hands again in the customary greeting.

"Oh Susan, we are both very well. And how are you?" Mr. Perry seemed genuinely pleased to see them.

"I am doing well thank you. I would like to introduce you to Ingrid. She stumbled upon me a few days ago and has been helping me in the clinic."

"It's very good to meet you Ingrid. What does she mean that you 'stumbled' upon her?"

"It's a long story and I think you'll be needed at the service before I could tell it all."

Mrs. Perry put her arm around Ingrid and said, "Well, I want to welcome you to our church. We are so glad you could be here."

Ingrid liked this woman; there was just something about her that was real. She was "down to earth," and so was Mr. Perry. Mr. Perry was pulled away right then but Mrs. Perry stayed with her arm around Ingrid.

"Please Ingrid come and sit with me, you too Susan. I always like to have friends to sit near me." She paused for a brief moment and then continued. "Ingrid I think the Lord has something in store for you tonight."

"What do you mean Mrs. Perry? I must let you know that I haven't been to church since I was a little girl and so I don't know very much about it. In fact I don't like religion very much."

"That's alright Ingrid; I don't like religion either and please call me Lynn."

Now Ingrid didn't know what to think. Had she heard correctly? Did the missionary's wife just say that she didn't like religion? Weren't missionaries supposed to be religious?

Mrs. Perry took them toward the front of the group, over to the side a bit. Someone offered them chairs and they sat down. There were more people now than when Ingrid and Susan first came. People were coming by the hundreds.

Mrs. Perry still had her arm around Ingrid and she seemed to be talking to herself. Ingrid had learned through experience with Susan that Mrs. Perry was praying.

Just before the service started Mrs. Perry looked over at Ingrid with a strange expression and said, "Ingrid, we must talk, either later tonight or sometime tomorrow." There was such compassion on the woman's face all Ingrid could do was to nod her head yes.

The service started with a lot of singing. Ingrid didn't know any of the songs and couldn't understand the language they were singing in, but she could tell the people really liked to sing. The song service lasted over an hour while people danced and clapped their hands. It was all very surreal to Ingrid. She had heard the African's singing before in Zimbabwe, but it wasn't in a church service. She had always been impressed with the harmonizing in their songs, but the singing here was so much more enthusiastic. It was obvious they really loved their God.

At first the songs were fast and the dancing exuberant, but after some time the singing became slower and people raised their hands in the air as though they were reaching up to touch God. Ingrid had never experienced worship, but it was obvious to her this was what they were doing.

After they finished singing Pastor Perry got up and started talking. He started by telling everyone that before he came he was praying about the evening and asked God what He, God, wanted to say to the church. Ingrid thought this was strange. Did this man think that God talked to him? From a notebook he read what "God" had told him to say. Then he opened his Bible and started preaching. He wasn't a flashy preacher. He just . . . talked. He said God loved to talk to His people, if we would just listen. He read a verse in the Bible that said, "My sheep hear my voice."

"We are all His sheep if we have accepted Him as our Lord. And God speaks to His sheep. He speaks in many different ways. We just need to listen."

He then went on to say that God knew each one, and desired to spend time with them. Ingrid had never heard anyone speak like this before. It seemed this man really knew God. He didn't speak of Him as someone far away in heaven, but someone whom you could know.

He talked about knowing God and being intimate with Him. Ingrid thought to herself that she would really like to know this type of God, one who wanted to talk to her and spend time with her.

The Pastor spoke for just a short time and then he did a funny thing. He asked if there was a man named Lee in the audience. For a little while it was very quiet and no one said anything. He asked again if there was anyone named Lee. Still, no one spoke up. After a few minutes a woman pointed to the young man who was running the sound system, a simple system consisting of two speakers, a small sound–board and a microphone, run by a generator.

"We call him Lee," she said and everyone nodded his or her head in agreement.

"What is your name?" Mr. Perry asked the young man.

"My name is Leetonia, but most people call me Lee."

What followed was even stranger still. Pastor Perry pulled a golf ball out of his pocket and started talking about how he had found this golf ball the week before he came and it had the name Lee written on it.

"The Lord started speaking to me concerning this little golf ball," he said, holding the ball up for all to see. "There is no mention of a golf ball in the Bible, but a golf ball is something you use to play with. Lee, I think God is saying he wants you to "play" for him. He has made you a worshipper and you are to play your music for him."

He then pointed to a girl in the audience and started telling her about her mother and the difficult times they were having after the death of her father. He told her God knew all about it and was watching after them. As he spoke, tears came to the girl's eyes and all she could do was to nod her head in agreement.

Next Mr. Perry pointed to an elderly man and spoke to him about the loss of his wife. Again, the man was obviously touched by the words spoken. It went on like that for some time.

Ingrid didn't understand what was happening until Susan leaned over to her and whispered in her ear. "Pastor Perry doesn't even know those people or anything about them. God is the one revealing those things to him.

"I'll believe that only if he says something to me about the explosion," Ingrid thought to herself. "There's no way he can prove whether the things he's saying are true or not."

Mr. Perry proceeded to speak to several more people and then he looked right at Ingrid. It was such a penetrating look, like he could see right into her and there was such compassion in his eyes. She saw tears start to well up in his eyes. He said, "Ingrid, God knows your pain. He has felt your tears and wants to help you. He is saying to be strong, because He's not finished with what He is doing in your life. You will understand better in the future. He doesn't want you to worry when you go to the embassy. He has already put in place what you will need to work here in Zambia. He has now called you out of Zimbabwe and into Zambia for His good purpose." He was quiet for a few seconds and then he said something that was a complete shock.

"The explosion didn't take away as much as you think it did. It happened so that you could receive the signature of God on your life." The tears were running freely down his cheeks.

"He's crying, crying for me." The thought was startling. He really cared; she could see it in his face. She had been so intent on what the preacher was saying that she didn't see or hear Mrs. Perry praying as she held Ingrid in her arms. Mrs. Perry too, was crying. She had never in her life felt so loved.

Ingrid didn't know how long she sat that way, just being held by Mrs. Perry as the love of God washed over her, wave upon wave. She had lost all track of time.

Soon Mr. Perry became quiet again as though he was just waiting, listening. After a few moments of the most powerful silence Ingrid had ever experienced, the pastor spoke again.

"Anyone who needs to be healed by the power of God, please come to the front now."

The first person up and hobbling to the front as fast as she could was the old lady, Mrs. Sayila, whom Ingrid had treated that first day at the clinic. When she reached the front, all Mr. Perry did was to touch her with his hand and immediately she fell over like she was dead.

As Ingrid watched, she was puzzled, but not shocked. She was past shocked. She herself was experiencing something indescribable and beyond any reasoning, so nothing else that happened was going to be beyond belief.

One by one Mr. Perry prayed for each person, often laying his hand on him or her as he had with Mrs. Sayila.

After some time Mrs. Perry released Ingrid and joined her husband at the front. She, too, prayed for people in a similar way, only Mrs. Perry seemed to feel things more deeply and often would cry or sometimes even laugh as she prayed for people.

At different times Mr. Perry would start to sing a song. He had a striking voice and the people would sing along. Then as he sang he would lay his hands on people, just barely touching them and they would fall over.

After a little while Mrs. Sayila got up and started jumping up and down. Ingrid was glad to see she wasn't actually dead. She had assumed she wasn't but it was a relief to finally see the woman move.

Mrs. Sayila started running around at the front of the gathered group. She was shouting something in her language so Ingrid asked Susan what she was saying.

"She is saying 'I can run again! My feet don't hurt anymore!!' She is saying the same thing over and over."

Over on the left side of the assembled group were many people who had been carried to the meeting. Mr. and Mrs. Perry started walking through where they were sitting and lying. All they did was to touch them. As Ingrid watched she saw people who were crippled get up and walk. Since she was a nurse she could identify some that she knew for a fact were crippled. But after the Perry's touched them they were walking and jumping around.

Some of those who had been led up because they were blind were running around as if they could see. One man, she had seen when he came in, had one eye that was white with blindness and the other eye had an empty socket. That man walked by where she was sitting after he had been prayed for and she could see that his eyes were now clear. Both of them! The empty socket now had an eye.

She couldn't believe it. How could this be happening? Who were these people and where did they get such power? Becoming caught up in the excitement of what was happening, Ingrid leaned over to Susan.

"I've got to learn more about all of this. I can't believe what is happening here. This is truly amazing."

"It's just Jesus, Ingrid. He wants to heal people, and we just have to allow Him to do it."

Ingrid was so enthralled by everything that was happening around her that she didn't see Mr. and Mrs. Perry come up behind her. They gently laid their hands on her and although she was sitting in a chair, she fell forward face down on the ground.

She lay there not knowing what was going on around her. She felt such a peace and contentment pouring over her. It seemed to her that her mind had cleared and for the first time she could see who she was. She could see that she had a lot of things wrong in her life and it needed to be cleaned up. She also knew Jesus was the one who could clean it up. She kept asking, "How?" repeating it over and over so those nearby heard her questioning.

Ingrid didn't know how long she lay there, but when she got up things were still happening all around her. The Perry's were still praying for people and people were scattered, prostrate on the ground.

Ingrid felt such a peace, one she had never felt before. The pain from losing her husband was still there, but somehow it was manageable now. She really didn't know how to describe what she felt. She was just . . . filled up. Nyasha was sitting there on the grass beside her. She picked him up and held him close.

"I don't know what all this is about, but I know it's something that I need right now and something you also need my little one. How do we get this feeling to stay?" She knew while she was on the ground she had been in the presence of God and she wanted that in her life forever.

A few minutes later Mr. Perry stepped back up to the microphone. He quieted everyone down and started talking about the need for some to accept Jesus as Lord and Savior of their lives. He read several scriptures as he spoke.

"In John 3:16 it says, 'God so loved the world.' That means that he loves you. Out of all the billions of people in the world, Jesus loves you and brought you here tonight so you could meet him and experience his love. In Romans 3:23 it says, 'All have sinned'. In other words every one of us has done wrong things in our lives. In Romans 6:23 it says that 'the wages of sin is death.' If we have sinned, or done wrong in our lives, the penalty for that is death."

"Some of you think, 'Well, that's not fair. If all of us sin then we shouldn't all have to die.' God thought so too. The last part of John 3:16 says, '. . . He,' that is God, 'gave his only son, that whoever believes in Him will not die, but have everlasting life.' God didn't want any of us to have to die, but because of our sin we were dead already. So he sent his son Jesus, to this earth to take the penalty for our sins. The Bible tells us that Jesus never sinned, so he did not have to die. Yet he chose to die for us anyway. Because he died for us, He has given us a way out. Again, in Romans it tells us in chapter five verse eight that, 'God demonstrates His own love toward us in this; while we were still sinners Jesus died for us.'"

"Because He died we can live. All we have to do is believe in Him and confess Him as our Savior and Lord. That means we have received his forgiveness for our own sins like we would accept and receive a gift and we have made him boss of our lives."

"At the very first church meeting the Apostle Peter was preaching and it tells us the people wanted to know how to be saved. Peter told them in

Acts 2:38 '. . .Repent and be baptized, every one of you for the remission of sin and you will receive the gift of the Holy Spirit'. Now, if any of you would like to receive Jesus as your personal Lord and Savior, come up front so we can pray together and then our team will talk to you and share more."

The worship team started singing a song. "As I come into your presence, Oh Lord, I see your glory . . . "

Ingrid wanted to come into the presence of God again more than she had ever wanted anything else. She ran forward still carrying Nyasha. When Mr. Perry looked her direction, she saw him smile and nod toward her. A crowd was all around her, people wanting to be saved.

She looked up at the Perry's and saw them crying again, but this time it was with tears of joy.

Mr. Perry had them repeat a prayer after him, acknowledging Jesus as their Lord and Savior and asking Him into their hearts.

He then instructed them to move to an area off to the right and then other people came to talk to each one. They asked them if they really believed that Jesus was the Christ, the messiah, the anointed one from God and if they want Him to be the Lord or boss of their life. The team took their time with the new believers, not rushing, but wanting to be assured that each individual was sincere in their decision, not just wanting or expecting to receive a free gift from the visiting missionary. They had paper and pen and wrote down the details of each person. There were a lot of people who accepted the gift of salvation that night and one of them was Ingrid Grundey, a woman changed forever.

Ingrid was on cloud nine the rest of the evening and for several days after. Life was different and Ingrid wanted to tell everyone she met about Jesus. After they returned home from the service she and Susan talked late into the night. Susan was so happy for Ingrid and kept telling her so. Ingrid was so elated she couldn't keep quiet. She told Susan about her initial doubts and her thoughts concerning the explosion.

"It's almost as if he heard my thoughts. Did you hear what he said to me? He said, 'the explosion didn't take away as much as you think it did. It was the signature of God on your life.' I don't know what it means or what God is saying, but . . . he told me about the explosion. There's no way he could have known about it. You're the only one I had told and I've been with you every minute of the day. You never told anyone about it and I didn't, so God must have told him." In her excitement, Ingrid just couldn't keep it in.

"I only wish Hans were alive to hear this and see all that happened tonight." Ingrid stayed quiet for a brief moment. Breaking out of her reverie she asked, "Are we going to church again tomorrow night?"

"Yes. They are having services the rest of this week and the entire weekend. Today most of the people who were there were people who go to our church. Tomorrow night you will see many more people coming from all around. There'll be many more sick and there might be several who have been demon possessed."

"What do you mean demon possessed?"

"Well, let me start from the beginning. Satan used to be an angel of God but he rebelled and was thrown out of heaven. There were other angels that followed Satan and they were thrown out also. Sometimes these ex-angels, whom we call demons, will possess a person, partially controlling their behavior. A lot of the witchdoctors are possessed by demons. They think they have their ancestor's spirit and many times these witchdoctors are given the ability to heal the sick, but it's a counterfeit healing. People are only partially healed and have to continue going back to the witchdoctor. Very often these people end up being demon possessed as well."

"I have heard about places in Africa where strange things happen. Once I heard that someone had died and people in another village made food for the dead and for the mourners. After they were done cooking, the pot, with the food, lifted off the ground and flew to the village where the funeral was. Later the villagers where the person had died brought the pot back and thanked the village that sent the food."

"Yes, this type of thing happens a lot in Africa. It brings fear to the people, but the Bible teaches that 'perfect love cast out fear' and Jesus love was so perfect we really don't have anything to be fearful about."

"What's that again, 'perfect love casts out fear?' Why that's beautiful. Are there more things like that in the Bible?"

"Yes. Have you ever read the Bible before?"

"No, I've never even owned a Bible."

"Well here's a New Testament that the Gideon's gave away to the schools a few months ago. You're welcome to have it."

"Thanks Susan. Thank you so much." Ingrid took the Bible and held it close.

Susan and Ingrid arrived early to the service the next evening. They were surprised when Pastor Sayila met them and directed them to seats next to Lynn Perry again.

"Hello ladies," Lynn Perry greeted them warmly as they approached her. "I want you two close by this week, so come sit by me each night, would you please?" The two friends were eager to agree.

That night, just before the worship was to start you could hear the witchdoctor's drums starting to play. Mr. Perry went up to the microphone and bowed his head. He prayed a very simple prayer, "Lord, just confuse the enemy." Then he went and sat down.

The musicians started to sing and the singing seemed to Ingrid to be better than ever. Not even five minutes had passed and Ingrid was aware that the witchdoctor's drum playing had ceased.

When Pastor Perry got up to preach, his message that night was about how the Lord wants all of His children to be able to hear His voice. He used the scripture in John 10:1–5 where it talks about Jesus being the good shepherd and that his sheep listen to his voice. He explained that we are his sheep and as his sheep we need to know what his voice sounds like.

"We need to accustom our ears to his voice so we can hear him and follow his leading. In these last days the Lord is speaking more than ever to His sheep. Sometimes he is protecting us with a warning. A few years ago, when I had just started learning to listen to the voice of the Lord, I was traveling with my kids. I was driving at about 80 kilometers per hour when I heard the Lord say, 'Slow down.' I let up on the accelerator and the car slowed down. Just a little further down the road was an intersection where I had the right of way. As I got to the intersection an SUV was approaching from the right. The driver stopped at the stop sign only briefly and then pulled into the intersection right in front of me. I had to slam on my brakes and swerve into the other lane to miss the vehicle. If I had not listened to the voice of the Lord, I would have slammed right into the side of that car. There would have been serious damage to both vehicles, not to mention the injuries to my family or the other driver. We must be able to hear the voice of the Lord."

Ingrid had never heard anyone speak like this before. Could she really hear the voice of God herself? She had her little New Testament open to the scripture in John and she could see what it said. Maybe if she had known this before the accident, God could have warned them. Ingrid started praying, "Oh God, please speak to me. I want to hear you."

"Turn with me now to John 14:12. It says, 'I tell you the truth, anyone who has faith in me . . .

"Do you have faith in Jesus? If you have faith in Jesus, raise your hand. Raise it up high. All right, it looks like the majority of you have faith in Jesus.

"Now listen to what this says. '. . . Anyone who has faith in me will do what I have been doing.'" Pastor Perry stopped again and looked at the people.

"Did you hear what that said? If you have faith in Jesus you can do what Jesus did.

What did Jesus do?

He healed the sick. He did miracles. He raised the dead. He taught crowds of people. Those are the things that Jesus did."

The crowd cheered and shouted their excitement.

"Let's go on with the scripture. 'You will do even greater things than these, because I am going to the Father.'

Wow! Right here in the word of God it says we will do the things that Jesus did . . . and he did a lot of things. It goes on to tell us that we will do greater things than Jesus did.

This is so amazing! Doesn't that make you excited? Don't you want to see that happen in your own life? Don't you want to see healings and miracles when you pray?

First, we need to be in a place where we can hear the voice of God and then we just need to do what He tells us to do. That's the Kingdom of God and God means for every one of us to walk in that Kingdom power."

Pastor Perry paused for a moment, quietly praying and then he continued. "Tonight I want you to pray for one another.

Everyone who has a physical illness raise your hand. Keep it up. Now those of you who are near those people . . . lay your hands on them and pray. Remember, the word of God says you will do the things that Jesus did."

All around Ingrid people started praying for each other. Shouts rose up in different places as one was healed and then another.

Those that were healed came to the front to give testimony of what the Lord had done in their lives. Mr. and Mrs. Perry just sat and watched as people all around were getting healed.

Ingrid and Susan were near a man who had raised his hand to receive prayer so they laid their hands on him and prayed. He began to shake and sway, then he fell to the ground. They didn't know what to do then so they got down on the ground and kept praying for the man.

After a few minutes the man started shouting, "I can see, I can see." He had been blind, but the healing power of Jesus healed him. Ingrid was so excited. God had used her for this miracle. She and Susan took the man up to the front so he could share his testimony.

When Pastor Perry saw them coming he walked their direction to find out what had happened. They told their story and he was so overjoyed. He went to the microphone and told everyone that God had used Ingrid, who had just become a Christian last night, to pray for this man. The crowd cheered and praised the Lord.

Ingrid was given the microphone and said, "If God can use me, He can surely use you."

People all over were being touched by the power of God. Healings were taking place and people were giving their lives to the Lord.

Then it happened just as Susan said it would; a young girl started manifesting a demon. She looked like she was in her twenties, but when the demon started manifesting, she appeared so much older. She was thrown to the ground and began shrieking.

Pastor Perry went over to where the girl was writhing and rebuked the demon. "Let her go."

Right away she stopped writhing, with a cough and heave she lay still on the ground. The demon was gone.

During all this the worship had continued. Now it grew more intense as people were worshipping with all their hearts.

The following day, Ingrid and Susan spent most of their time discussing all these happenings. There was plenty of time for their discussion because the clinic was empty, the sick having been healed in the evening services.

"There's a scripture in the Old Testament that you need to see," Susan said as she turned in her Bible to Isaiah 53:5. "But he was pierced for our transgressions, he was crushed for our iniquities; the punishment that brought us peace was upon him, and by his wounds we are healed."

"Hey, that book isn't in my Bible." Ingrid had pulled out her New Testament from her pocket.

"No, all you have is the New Testament. I only had that small Bible to give you. We'll check around and see if we can find you a complete Bible with the Old Testament as well."

Ingrid was glad to hear that. She looked at Susan's Bible and realized that there was so much more she could read and learn if she had the entire Bible. Since the first night of the meetings, she was so enthralled with everything she had seen and heard, she would read her Bible late into the night. She was so eager to learn and grow. She had started from Matthew and was surprised that the next book started the story of Jesus all over again. She read quickly and had finished the entire New Testament in just a few days.

Ingrid was happy. She had found a family that she could work with and live with contentedly. Susan told her she could stay as long as she wanted. "I enjoy having someone close by to talk to about the Lord and to pray with."

Many amazing things continued to happen while the Perry's were there; lots of healings, signs and miracles.

The closing service on Sunday was a fitting climax. There were over two thousand people at the service. Pastor Perry delivered a message that encouraged the many new believers to seek God with their whole hearts. Many received personal words of encouragement as the Perry's shared from their hearts as the Spirit prompted. In closing they all took communion together.

Ingrid had read about the last supper and how Jesus had instructed His disciples to take the emblems to remember Him. She was so excited when they started talking about the Lord's Supper. She knew what they were talking about and when they read the scripture in Matthew 26 she remembered it. She took communion for the first time in her life, thrilled to be a part of such an eventful thing.

That afternoon, Rob and Lynn Perry paid a visit at Ingrid and Susan's home, anxious to hear Ingrid's story before their departure. Ingrid told her story, still very fresh, but somehow easier to tell in the light of all that the Lord had done in the past week. They were taken back when she talked about the explosion and the loss of her husband. They had been away from Zimbabwe for several months and didn't know things had deteriorated so badly.

"So, here we are, in Zambia with no passport or any way of getting one. I really don't know what I'm going to do," Ingrid finished.

"We're headed for Lusaka first thing tomorrow morning," Pastor Perry said with a sideways glance at his wife. Lynn stood there looking pleased as though she knew exactly what her husband was about to say. Pastor Perry continued, "Why don't you ride along with us. We've got business to take care of in Lusaka so we can take you to the embassy. We'll be there for a couple of days and then we will be coming back through this way. You can take care of your business and we'll drop you back off at Susan's on our way through."

Ingrid was very pleased with the idea. "I don't know how to thank you enough," she replied.

Susan had an idea of her own. "I'm sure the clinic is going to be slow for quite some time so my time is going to be free. Why don't I keep Nyasha for you while you're gone?"

Ingrid was so overwhelmed. Once again she felt thankful to be part of such a caring new "family."

9

New Existence

EARLY MONDAY MORNING THE threesome traveled the four hours to Lusaka. The four hours passed quickly as the three talked and sang the whole way. Ingrid had only met the Perry's a few days before, but now they seemed like old friends. In spite of all the amazing things that happened in their meetings and the attention that they got from crowds, they remained very down to earth and real. They were just ordinary people that loved Jesus.

Ingrid began to share all the things she had been learning as she studied the small New Testament that Susan had given her. She was especially excited about the book of Acts.

"Pastor and Mrs. Perry, I just want to live my life the same way the Christians did in the first church."

"Please Ingrid, just call us Rob and Lynn" Rob said.

"That's what we all need to do; live like the first church did. The early Christians bore the signature of God. Everywhere they went people knew they were Christians."

"What do you mean by that, how did people know they were Christians?"

"In Ephesians chapter one verse thirteen and fourteen it says, '. . . Having believed, you were marked with a seal, the promised Holy Spirit, who is a deposit guaranteeing our inheritance until the redemption of those who are God's possession . . .'"

"God's seal upon each of us is his Holy Spirit. People in the first church understood that the gifts they received were to be used in the church as well as their everyday lives. This is God's signature: living a life in the Holy Spirit with His gifts at work in our lives every day wherever we are."

"The early Christians had a reputation. Others who saw those gifts recognized the mark of Christ on his believers. Doing good, healing the sick and speaking forth God's word; those things were reality in the early believer's lives."

Lynn spoke up, "Ingrid, you also have received his Holy Spirit and he has given you a gift. Find out what it is and learn to walk in it. Listen to his voice."

"Wow! That's exciting. What gift do you think I have? How do I learn about other gifts?"

Rob spoke up again, "You can find the gifts listed in 1 Corinthians 12. You might have one gift, or you might have several. As you walk with God and grow in him, he will give you more gifts."

Rob paused for a moment and had that faraway look in his eyes. Ingrid had come to recognize that look on Rob's face as his "listening look." The Lord was speaking and Rob was listening.

Rob continued, "I believe that the Lord wants to do mighty things through you, Ingrid. I don't know what, but I hear him say that you will change a nation. I also think he is giving you one of the prophetic gifts. I keep hearing "words of knowledge." The Lord wants to speak to you. It may be audible, or it may be in visions or pictures in your mind. You may just hear that "still small voice," that gentle whisper in your heart. However he chooses to do it, I know he wants to talk to you."

"Oh my! That's an awful lot to take in. I've only been a Christian for a very short time. Why would he want to give me this gift?"

"Because he loves you and he loves to give his children good gifts. He also wants to use you to speak to others. When he does, just ask him what to do with it and he will show you."

Ingrid wasn't sure what to say. She remained quiet just contemplating all that Rob had said.

Arriving at the Netherlands Embassy, Lynn got out of the car to give Ingrid a hug good–bye with Rob following close behind. "Why don't you plan on staying with us while we're here in Lusaka? We have a friend that allows us to stay at his guesthouse whenever we are in town. His son was healed of Muscular Dystrophy in one of our meetings a few years ago. Ever since then he has insisted that we stay in his cottage whenever we are in town."

Ingrid was elated. On the trip there she had been praying for the Lord to provide a place for her to stay while in Lusaka. Here was the answer to her prayer.

Lynn handed Ingrid her cell phone, "I want you to use this while in Lusaka. When you're finished at the embassy just call Rob's phone and we'll come to get you. His number is in the phone under Rob."

"Thank you so much." Ingrid hugged them each one more time. "I'll phone you shortly."

As they started away Lynn looked over to Rob and said, "Do you remember at the first service the word from the Lord you had for Ingrid?"

Lynn looked expectantly at Rob and then continued. "I also heard from the Lord for her. You had said, in your word, that she hadn't lost as much as she had thought. The Lord told me that she was in for a big surprise. I have a feeling that maybe Hans is still alive somewhere. What do you think?"

"I don't know. I remember crying for her and, although my tears were for her loss, I also felt that there was something else that God was going to do in her life. I hadn't thought about Hans being alive. Maybe that's it. I think we should keep this to ourselves though. I wouldn't want to get her hopes up."

Approaching the embassy, Ingrid was stopped at the front by a security guard.

"May I see your ID please?"

"I . . . lost my ID," Ingrid stammered. "That's why I'm here, to get a new ID."

"I'm sorry, but without any ID you may not enter the embassy." The guard was very firm.

Ingrid didn't know what to do. She knew of no other way to obtain the paper work she needed but this guard wouldn't let her in.

"But I have to get in. How else am I going to get my ID and passport?"

"I'm sorry ma'am but I can't let you in without a picture ID. You'll have to leave."

Just as Ingrid turned to go a voice called out from inside the doorway.

"Ingrid Grundey, is that you?"

Ingrid turned toward the voice and recognized a fellow nurse, Corrie Filer. The same Corrie that had arrived with her in Zimbabwe when she first came. Ingrid hadn't seen her since she took this job in Zambia.

"Hi Corrie! Oh, it's good to see you. Can you help me? The guard won't let me in."

"Kenny, this is a friend of mine. I will vouch for her. She is a citizen of Holland. We came to Africa together. You can let her in."

The guard looked at Ingrid suspiciously but opened the door for her to enter. Ingrid entered the lobby and hugged her friend.

"Tell me, Ingrid, what is going on? We got word from the embassy in Zimbabwe that you and your family were missing. They found your vehicle at the bottom of the river. We heard it hit a land mine. The police report even said you were dead. Now here you are right in front of me."

Corrie's words cut Ingrid to the heart. Since the explosion, Ingrid had just one small shred of hope; that when she got to the embassy she would hear news that Hans was alive after all. Now even that shred was gone.

"Oh Corrie it was so horrible. We had gone on a picnic and on the way home we hit the land mine. It threw the car into the river. I grabbed Nyasha and got out, but as soon as I broke through the surface a log hit me and knocked me unconscious or at least semi–conscious. When I came to, I was on the Zambian side and I couldn't find Hans anywhere. He must have drowned in the river. He was probably looking for me and now he is gone."

"Oh, my goodness. How horrible. What can I do to help?" Corrie led the way to her office on the second floor.

"I have nothing; no ID, no passport and no work permit for Zambia. I need all my papers and then I need to talk to the NGO to see if I can set up work here in Zambia. I don't want to go back to Zimbabwe now. I had told Hans it was getting too dangerous."

"Okay, I can help you get your passport and ID. It's going to take about a week to get it all done. We'll get that started now and then you'll have to contact the NGO. They will have to process a work permit for you. That could take even longer. Let's work on what we can get done here first. Once we get the paperwork started you can go to the NGO and get things started with them. I'll get you a letter of introduction from the consul. They all think you are dead so if you just show up it might put a fright in them."

Corrie opened her desk drawer, pulled out the forms and they started filling them out. It only took about a half an hour and then Corrie excused herself to go down the hall to the consul in order to get the letter.

"There are vending machines in the next room if you want a Coke or a snack," Corrie explained as she rose to leave the room.

"That would be nice except I have no money."

Reaching in her pocket Corrie handed some change to Ingrid. "Here you go. It's on me."

Just that simple thought brought back memories of Hans. She and Hans had no refrigerator at their place in Zimbabwe, so a cold Coke was a treat reserved for special occasions when they traveled to town.

Dropping the coins into the vending machine, Ingrid pressed the familiar logo button. Quickly popping the top she took a long drink. It was cold and tasted so good. She thought about getting a snack from the other vending machine, but then decided she would rather have another Coke.

As she drank, her thoughts returned to Rob's comments in the car about hearing the voice of God. She was thinking to herself, and then voiced her thoughts out to the Lord.

"Okay Lord, if you want to speak to me, I am ready to listen. I don't know how to do this at all; you'll have to teach me. Please, Lord, speak to me. I want to hear you."

Almost immediately Ingrid saw a picture in her mind. She saw Corrie in a meadow walking with an older man and woman. There was a split rail fence that needed painting over to one side and a big apple tree next to it.

She wondered what that was all about. She remembered what Rob had told her, so she asked, "Lord, what do you want me to do with this?"

She was quiet for a minute and then she heard that still small voice. "Tell Corrie what you saw." That was all.

A little bit later Corrie returned with the letter.

"Now you need to go to the NGO office. It's just a block away. Go out the front door and turn left. You can't miss it."

Nervously, Ingrid took a step of faith to relay to Susan what she had seen. "Corrie, before I go I need to tell you something."

Taking a deep breath she plunged ahead, "A few days ago I became a Christian and I have learned that God can and wants to speak to us. He showed me something and I feel like I need to share it with you. Is that okay?"

"I guess so. I have no idea what you're talking about. I've never been to church in my life so I don't know what God would want to say to me."

"I don't understand what he showed me, but maybe you will."

Waving her hands in the air she said, "I saw you walking in a meadow with an elderly gentleman and woman. There was a split rail fence on one side with an apple tree next to it."

As Ingrid shared the picture the Lord had given her, Susan's eyes got wider and wider.

"You just described what my family farm looks like? How could you know? The meadow with the fence and tree is my favorite place on the whole property. I can only imagine that the older man and women are my parents. We used to take walks in that meadow. I just got word from my mother that my father is sick. The doctors don't expect him to live very long." Corrie's eyes began to fill. "I am supposed to go back to Holland in another week. I have a two week leave to go see them. Do you think your vision, or whatever, means that my father is going to be okay?"

Ingrid said a quick prayer to herself, "Lord, is that what it means?" Right away Ingrid felt the tangible peace of God flood over her. Looking into Corrie's eyes, she could see hope there mixed with fear.

"I suppose that's in God's hands alone, Corrie. But something tells me your father will be fine. There's one thing I know for sure. God cares for you and he wants to keep your heart in peace if you will let him."

Reaching out to her friend, Corrie clung to Ingrid and cried.

"Oh Ingrid, I do hope you are right. My father and I have had some problems in the past and I want him to live so I can make things right between us. Thank you so much for giving me this hope."

Ingrid put her arms around Corrie and held her. "Corrie, God loves you and just wants you to know it." She felt Corrie's shoulders shaking even more as the tears came. They stood together in each other's arms for several minutes, and then Corrie pulled away.

"Thank you again. I'll write to you when I arrive back home and let you know what is happening."

Ingrid knew it was time for her to go. She had done what she knew the Lord wanted her to do. "Okay, thanks for everything Corrie, I'll never forget it. I will continue to pray for you and your father. Have a safe journey home. God bless you."

She was amazed that through that one little picture God was able to do so much.

Leaving the building, Ingrid proceeded down the street. She found the NGO office right away and went in. Ingrid handed the letter of introduction to the girl at the front desk who quickly glanced through it and then asked Ingrid to have a seat. Within five minutes she was shown into the director's office. Ingrid had met Mr. Hertzog only once before, but she remembered him. He was a large man with thinning gray hair.

"Ingrid, it's good to see that you are alive. We heard that you had drowned. I'm so glad that the story wasn't true."

"Hello Mr. Hertzog, it's good to see you again. There was an accident and Hans was killed, but my baby and I are fine."

"Oh yes, you have a baby, where is he?"

"I left him with a friend in the Kafue settlement. That's where I have been the last several days. The lady I am staying with has started a clinic and it looks like a good place to establish a permanent one. Can you help me? I need to get a work permit that will allow me to continue my work here in Zambia alongside my friend. "

"The Kafue settlement, hey? We don't have any work out there just yet. We have been wanting to, but the chief in the area hasn't allowed us in. He is blocking our progress. If you can get the approval of the chief then, yes, I'll get you a permit to work here."

"Okay that sounds great! I'm sure I can persuade him. Another thing, is there a vehicle I can use to travel out there and back? I had to hitch a ride with some people to get to Lusaka. I could really use a vehicle."

"Let me think. There's an old Land Rover out in the lot. You can use that if you want." Mr. Hertzog reached in his top desk drawer and found the key. "Here you go; it should be full of fuel. Let me process the paperwork for it and you're good to go. How are you with money? "

"I lost everything in the accident sir, I don't have anything."

"Okay, let me see what I can do." Opening a drawer he removed a cash box and opened it. I don't have a lot, but here's a bit." He handed her a roll of Kwacha, the Zambian currency. "It's not really worth very much, but you can get some groceries and supplies. There's probably even enough to pay for a place to stay for the night."

"Great, I really appreciate all you are doing for me." Ingrid made her way around the desk and gave the man a big hug. "I'll check with you to-morrow before I go back to Kafue. Thanks again Mr. Hertzog."

Ingrid was elated as she walked out to the parking lot and found the Land Rover.

"Hertzog was right, it is an old vehicle. Probably older than I am," In-grid thought to herself as she climbed into the front seat. "As long as it runs."

Ingrid called the Perry's and briefly told them her good news, finishing with her description of the car she had acquired. She then timidly told Rob a bit about the word she had received for Corrie. Rob was overjoyed. After getting the address and directions to their place, she was ready to go.

"I should be there in just a few minutes," Ingrid said and then hung up the phone.

The next day, after checking back with Mr. Hertzog, Ingrid drove to Kafue, excited to get back to Susan, her new home and especially Nyasha.

When Nyasha saw her, he squealed with delight. This was the first time they had been away from each other for any length of time and they were both glad to be together again.

Susan's excitement matched theirs when she learned that the vehicle Ingrid was driving was a permanent addition to the clinic.

All Ingrid's new plans played over and over again in her brain and she was anxious to set things into motion. She was sure everything was going to work out well. Although it would be a whole week before the paperwork would be done, Ingrid decided to go ahead and approach the chief and dis-cuss plans with him.

She learned from Susan that the chief was a member of the church and Susan knew him well. The next morning, with Susan directing the way, they drove to his house. Ingrid was surprised upon meeting the chief. She imagined the chief would be an older man, but the man Susan introduced was a young man, probably in his mid–thirties.

"I guess a chief has to be young sometime in his life," thought Ingrid to herself.

"Hello Mr. Msipa. How are you?" Ingrid clapped her hands, shook the chief's hand then clapped again, thinking she was getting the hang of the new greeting. She was a bit surprised when the chief did it differently.

He clapped, shook hands, clapped, and then shook hands and clapped once more. Ingrid just followed his lead and did what the chief did. After the greeting, the chief sat down and motioned for her to sit as well. Looking around, Ingrid found the only available place to sit was on the ground as she often saw the African women doing.

Susan quickly pulled a Zambia cloth from her bag and handed it to Ingrid. Unfolding it, Ingrid placed it on the ground and then sat upon it in the same way she'd seen other women do hundreds of times before.

Once seated, she began to speak to the chief about the work she had done in Zimbabwe.

"Since I am now in Zambia, I would like to continue the work I was doing. The NGO will pay for everything. Susan has been running a clinic out of her home and I have been helping her. She works out of a thatched roof shelter but I am hoping the NGO will pay to have a proper building put up. They will also help with a school for the area and possibly dig boreholes."

At that, Ingrid's heart stuck in her throat. It was Hans who used to dig the boreholes, and now he was gone.

In spite of her new life in Jesus, mourning her loss was fresh, especially when she was alone in her bed at night. She would lie awake thinking of him, wishing he could have been here to see what God was doing. She knew he would have loved Jesus just as much as she did.

Quickly pushing aside her feelings, Ingrid continued. "We need your written permission to be allowed to come into your area."

"I am happy to give you my permission to come and help us in any way you can. We need a clinic, and a primary school here. The nearest primary school is ten kilometers away. It's much too far for the small children to walk."

The chief paused for a moment, apparently thinking, and then he continued. "If we had a primary school here we would need a borehole for the school which would help the entire area. So, yes you may come and work. I will write a letter and you can take it back with you to your NGO."

With that he went into his hut and returned with paper, pen, stamp and inkpad. He took his seat again and began writing the letter.

Writing in English was difficult and time consuming for the young chief, but such an official letter had to be written in formal English. When it was completed and the chief was satisfied with the results, he then took his stamp and inkpad. He first applied ink three or four times to make sure there was enough on the stamp, and then he stamped the paper making it official. After folding the paper he handed it to Ingrid. She took it and put it in her Bible to carry home.

Once business was completed, the chief offered Ingrid and Susan tea. Ingrid knew it would be very bad manners for him not to offer something to such a special guest and it would be equally disrespectful for her to refuse. They sat together under the shade of a tree drinking their tea and afterwards Ingrid, Susan, and Nyasha returned home.

The next day, Ingrid and Susan heard a car in the distance, a sound rarely heard in the area. The sound of the bus was an everyday occurrence but an approaching car always caught attention and brought excitement to everyone, Ingrid included. When the car drew near enough, the ladies recognized it as the Perry's and were very pleased when the car pulled up to their house. Everyone greeted one another warmly and then went into the main house to visit.

"We're headed back to Zimbabwe within the next couple of days," Rob said after a while. Although Zambia was where they resided since the outbreak of fighting, they still considered Zimbabwe home.

Continuing, Rob asked, "Is there anything we can bring you from your house in Zimbabwe, Ingrid? We are planning to go to *Silobela* and then to our own home in Gweru so we will be traveling near where your home was on the way through."

Ingrid was touched by the offer and she gave them a list of items that she wanted from her house.

"I have no idea who is staying in the house or even where the key is. You can talk to James Mabhutu. He was working with the NGO under Hans and will be able to help you."

"Please let everyone know that Nyasha and I are doing well. Tell them that we miss them, but are going to stay in Zambia for a time."

Leaving Ingrid and Susan's place, the Perry's traveled the rest of that day.

"The whole time we were with Ingrid I kept wondering what the Lord has planned for her and what he meant when I heard him say she hadn't lost as much as she thought," Rob shared with Lynn.

"I'm thinking the very same thing," Lynn replied and then continued, voicing her prayer to the Lord. "Lord, have your way. Let your Kingdom come and your will be done in Ingrid's life."

They stayed the night in a little hotel near the Kafue River. "Rob, I just keep getting an inkling that God is going to be doing such a work in Zimbabwe when we get back. I'm really excited! I know the war is getting worse, but I also know God wants us there right now."

"I know. I get that same feeling. There is something very special God wants us to do, I'm just not sure what it is. We'll just continue seeking His presence night and day and . . . he will do it."

The next day they traveled on to Zimbabwe. They got right through the border with no hassles, and then drove on to Karoi. Just before town they turned off the main road heading to Ingrid's home.

They had been in this area years ago. There was a mission hospital close by where friends of theirs stayed and worked. In years past they would go up once or twice a year to visit, sharing many holidays and good times with their friends. There was a special bond between the two missionary families, one that comes from sharing like backgrounds and similar circumstances. So although the area was familiar, the trip was very different this time.

They could see where land mines had exploded and they wondered if one of those places was where Ingrid's car had been thrown into the river. Both of them wondered if they should be driving on this road or not but each remained quiet, not wanting to voice their own fear. Rather, the two voiced it to the Lord and soon his amazing peace and presence filled the car and the couple was confident in proceeding.

They soon arrived at the mission hospital and talked to some of the staff at the reception area. The Perry's were glad to hear that the authorities had just removed all the land mines and for the time being, the roads were safe.

"The rebels are no longer in the area so things are pretty safe," said one of the nurses. "*Chipoko* is far away as well."

"*Chipoko*? Who is *Chipoko*? Doesn't that mean ghost?"

"Yes, it does. There is a white man, a mercenary, who is fighting against the rebels. They say that he moves like a ghost. He moves quickly and strikes as if out of nowhere. They say he's a very big man, but he moves silently through the bush and kills with no feeling."

Lynn and Rob weren't sure how to react to the description of "*Chipoko*." They knew from experience that often people exaggerated stories and fear was a motivating factor.

Changing the subject Rob asked, "Do you know where the Netherlands NGO, MAWFA, is located? We need to go there for some things but we have never been there before."

"Yes, it's just over the next hill. I can take you there if you like," an older man replied.

The Perry's knew that the "next hill" could be four hours away so Rob said, "We aren't coming back this way. Would you be able to get home from there?"

"Yes, I need to go to that area to look at some cattle my young brother is selling, I want to buy them. I will be staying with him for the rest of the week and come back on Sunday morning for church."

They learned that the man's name was Stillwell and since he didn't need to take anything with him, the Perry's were quickly back on the road and headed "just over the next hill." The trip wasn't too bad, only an hour away.

After arriving, they thanked Stillwell and went into the Netherlands office. Rob asked to see Mr. Mabhutu and was told that he was no longer with the NGO.

"He left to join the rebels" the man said with a disgusted look. "What can I help you with?"

"We have just come from Zambia and one of your people asked us to get some of her things." Rob told him all about Ingrid and what had happened. The man was shocked and excited at the same time. He was so glad to hear that mama Ingrid was still alive.

"She plans on staying in Zambia until things cool down in Zimbabwe," Rob informed him. "She wanted some of her stuff from her house."

Rob pulled out the list and gave it to the man. "She said she didn't know who would have the key or if anyone was living in the house. That's why we asked for Mabhutu. She said he would know."

"Yes, Mabhutu would have known, but there is a problem. The night of the accident Baba Hans came back to the station. He went into his house for a short while and then we heard a scream. No one saw him after that. We assumed he ran away. The house burned to the ground that night. All we could figure is that he knocked over a candle or lamp and it caught the house on fire. There was nothing left after the blaze."

Rob and Lynn looked at each other, Hans was alive! Excitement filled them and they praised the Lord together, out loud, not worrying what the man thought.

"I knew the Lord had something more for Ingrid. She will be so excited to find out he's alive." Lynn commented. "We'll have to write to her and let her know."

The man behind the desk wasn't sure what to say. Evidently these people hadn't been keeping up with the news in Zimbabwe. "Uh, well, things are a little different now with Mr. Hans. We hear rumors about him. People say that he is the one called *Chipoko*. He has joined the mercenaries. Some think that after he left here he died and it's his ghost trying to get revenge on the rebels who killed his wife. I don't know how you will find him. He has been seen here and there, but never twice in the same place."

"Well, thanks for the information. We will pass the news along," Rob replied and they turned to go. "Since there's nothing for us to pick up for Ingrid, then I guess we will be on our way."

After they got in the car Rob said, "We'll have to pray very hard about how to find this man. It sounds like he's the kind that would shoot first and ask questions later." The Perry's were happy for Ingrid, but sad at the same time. This *Chipoko* didn't sound like the same man that Ingrid had described to them.

They traveled the rest of the way to their house in Gweru praying and worshiping the whole way. They needed a few days rest before they went out to *Silobela* and it felt very good to be in their old place again.

The next morning Lynn wrote a letter to Ingrid telling her the good news: that her husband was alive. She took the letter to the post office in town and mailed it.

Later that day the truck came to take the mail but on the way to Harare it was stopped at a police roadblock. Only it wasn't a real police roadblock. Rebels dressed as police manned it. The real police officers lay dead a few meters away hidden in a ditch. The rebel forces were hungry and driven to extreme measures. With each vehicle that passed the roadblock, the rebels harassed the motorists for food or money.

Just before the rebel manned roadblock, the mail driver had stopped at a shop beside the road and bought a hamburger and coke. The "police" stopped him and when they saw he had food they asked for it. He refused, so they pulled him out of his car, kicked and beat him, and then took the little bit of food that he had. They left him lying wounded by the road and then set his truck on fire. Leaving the truck burning in the road the rebels disappeared into the bush. By the time the authorities came the truck was completely burnt.

Ingrid never received the letter.

Time moved on bringing with it many changes and the reality of Ingrid's hopes and plans for the Kafue region. Susan and Ingrid remained very busy, working hard to see things come together.

The NGO built a much nicer building for the clinic in a nearby location. Susan was put on their payroll, which was a huge financial blessing. The next project was to build the school and borehole the chief wanted.

Ingrid was elated that everything was going so well. She was content with her life and grew more in love with the Lord every day. Each morning

Ingrid, Susan, and the other workers at the clinic would get together and pray for the day. Their prayer times were very special. They didn't just have a prayer circle where one person would pray for the day and then be finished. They spent time in the presence of God, asking him to touch each person that came to the clinic. They waited on God, practicing his presence and soaking before him.

While they were seeing patients they would ask if it was okay to pray for them and most everyone said "yes." Sometimes God would heal the person on the spot. At other times the patient would return home with the proper medication and a promise that those at the clinic would continue to pray.

One day a woman came to the clinic complaining of severe headaches. Ingrid took her blood pressure and found it to be very high. During her years in Zimbabwe and now in Zambia, Ingrid had found that high blood pressure was very prevalent, so she always kept the clinic well stocked with blood pressure tablets. After asking the woman's permission, Ingrid called Susan to come so they could pray together for her healing. As they prayed the woman began to jump in her seat. They didn't understand what was happening but then the lady quieted down. They finished praying and Ingrid re–checked her blood pressure, finding it was normal.

"It was like fire burning through my body," the lady exclaimed excitedly. "It made my whole body hot, even the tips of my fingers. But, praise God, I am healed."

Susan and Ingrid were overjoyed to see God working in their village even when the Perry's were not there.

To be used of God in such a way and to see him work through their prayers was an exciting feeling. Each time someone was touched by God and went away from their clinic praising his name they were even more encouraged to continue to pray for the people who came to them for treatment. To love Jesus more and to be used for God's Kingdom purposes was their greatest desire.

Hans had been gaining in notoriety as a mercenary. He was becoming known as one who had no fear of death and no feeling for the African.

His comrades thought it strange that for many years Hans had worked alongside African men and had gotten along with them quite well. Now it seemed that all he wanted to do was kill them.

His skills as a sniper were sharp and he would wait in a tree or on a hill for any length of time just to make one kill. He had read in western novels that the cowboys of old used to put a notch in their gun butts to keep track of how many people they had killed and he had adopted this counting method as his own. One side of Hans's rifle had been notched completely and the other side was almost full. Soon he would need a new gun or a new way to count his kills.

He was ruthless in all of the campaigns. If he learned that a village had been used to hide the rebels, Hans wanted to kill everyone who had helped them and Keith would be hard pressed to keep him from doing so.

The only thing he enjoyed more than killing his enemy was when they would capture one of the rebels and he was allowed to "question" them. His questioning consisted of beating them almost senseless and then asking his question. He always got quick results.

As soon as the enemy saw Hans they cringed. They knew he didn't care if he killed them while "questioning," so very often the captive would start telling all they knew before Hans had a chance to begin. They would readily reveal where the rebels were located, campaign strategies and other valuable information.

The most important thing to Hans was to find out who was responsible for putting the land mine on the road that had killed his wife and child. He had the feeling he was getting close.

One day Hans was up in a tree waiting when an enemy truck stopped right under him. There were three of them and they had just stopped to relieve themselves. In his months of fighting, his mastery of the Shona language had greatly improved. He knew a little before, but with interrogating the rebels he had learned a great deal more. As he listened to the three below him he realized they were talking about him. It kind of shocked him but also pleased him.

"I heard that *Chipoko* used to work alongside Africans."

"Yes, I have heard that too. They say he worked for an NGO and used to build clinics and drill boreholes for our people. I was told that he had a wife and child and they were killed by some of our people and now he is getting his revenge. The story goes that all three of them were abducted and he was beaten, his wife raped and then he had to watch while they killed his baby and wife."

"No, I heard that wasn't true. I heard that he and his family were driving down the road and ran over a land mine. It threw the car into the Zambezi, he was able to get out, but the wife and child drowned."

"Where did that happen?"

"Over by the Maguchi settlement."

"Oh yes, I remember. We had a new guy who didn't understand where we wanted the mines to be placed and put them on the wrong road. One of our trucks got blown up on that stretch of road also. There weren't supposed to be any mines there at all. He just put them in the wrong place."

Hans could take no more. The rebels had gathered together close enough that he could shoot all of them with no problem. He shot two of them and then purposely wounded the third. He was the one who had got the story right and Hans wanted to question him.

Hans grabbed the man by the collar and shook him. "Who was it that set those mines? Answer me!"

"What, what are you talking about. What mines?"

Hans landed a blow with the butt of his gun to the gunshot wounded causing the man to scream with pain.

"I heard you talking about the person who set the mine that killed my wife and child. Who was that man? What was his name?"

"Uh, uh, I think his name is Sam. I don't know his surname. Please, oh, please don't hurt me anymore. I can find out where he is."

"No. There's no need for that." Hans then pulled out his handgun and shot the man again, killing him instantly.

Sam. Now he had a name attached to the killer. Hans dragged the bodies off the road and covered them over with a little dirt.

"The scavenger animals will clean up this mess," he said to himself with a measure of satisfaction. Then he got in the truck and drove back to his team.

"Now I'll take care of Sam."

10

Retaliation

Looking at the calendar Chipo realized it had been over a year since her father had taken her baby boy from her. She had been living in Harare the whole time, never seeing or hearing from her father or any of her family members.

She denied forgiveness for what her father had done and the bitterness and hatred ate away at her. She didn't know what was happening at her home with her brothers and sisters and really didn't care. She was angry at the world.

Ethan's silence convinced her that he never loved her at all. All that he wanted was the sex, to use her just like all her male clients.

"Well he got what he wanted from me." She thought, "I really don't care what happens to him or to me anymore. What is there to live for anyway?"

Despondency and depression were her closest companions. Prostitution made her feel dirty and ashamed. She only did it for the money, having no other means to keep food in her stomach and a roof over her head. She really didn't want to be like this. She often thought of what she really wanted to do, but modeling had been a dream and her present life was a shameful reality.

The few pleasant memories of her childhood, her mother, and going to church, were now her only comfort. Those memories were always pushed out the back door of her mind when truth and reality crowded in the front door. "The church probably wouldn't even let me in now," was always the thought that slammed the door shut.

Even though she hated prostitution, she was good at what she did. She was able to make enough money to live comfortably, even a bit luxuriously. She had maintained a nice figure and a pretty face even after the baby. She was desirable enough that she was able to put together a distinctive clientele, able to choose those who were more desirable to be with, not just any man off the street. Most of her clientele were businessmen or visiting CEO's. This was better for Chipo, a safeguard against diseases. Sometimes she was only required to act as an escort, accompanying her client to a special event or gala. Her wardrobe was to be envied by nearly any woman, most of it having been purchased for her by different clients. She could dress formally in many different colors or, if the occasion called for it, her casual dress wardrobe was just as impressive. Her knowledge of men had grown in the last year, as well as her feminine prowess. She could use it to get almost anything she wanted.

Even still, she wasn't happy. She missed her baby. She didn't know what had happened to him and wondered where he was and who he was with.

Chipo also missed her grandparents, her mother's parents, Pastor Alex and Mary Dube. They had been so kind to her after her father took her child. They had always been kind. She had written several letters to them, but never mailed them. She knew that they would never approve of the lifestyle she now lived.

"Hey, don't forget to get in contact with my friend Steve. You still have his phone number that I gave you, don't you?" Ethan asked his younger brother Sean.

"Yes, I have it. You've asked me three times already." Sean was a little frustrated at his big brother. When Ethan had gone to Zimbabwe two years ago he only had their mother and father to worry him. Now Sean had both of them, plus his brother that kept pestering him to look up all his old friends. That wasn't what Sean wanted to do. He wanted to make his own friends, put his own mark on Zimbabwe, live his own adventure. Yes, he wanted to see the animals and travel the country, but he wanted to do it his way. Trying his luck at the new casino in Vic Falls was at the top of his "to do" list. He wanted to spend money on wine, women, and whatever else that came along. He had seen the picture of Ethan's "supposed" girlfriend and thought if all the girls were even half as hot as she was he was bound to have a good time.

Ethan had such great memories of his Zimbabwe trip. Yes, there was some sadness, but things had all worked out for the best. He was married to Lisa and his life was good. He had all but forgotten about Chipo, happy as he was with his present life and plans for the future. His Zimbabwe adventure was such a long time ago. Chipo had died and a part of him had died with her. Now, he had a new life. He was happy and content.

His parents were a bit more cautious with Sean's plans because of the violence they'd heard of in the country. They phoned the new British Ambassador, a close friend of the family, to inquire as to whether it was safe or not. They were informed that most of the violence was confined to isolated areas of the country and travel advisories were limited mostly to those areas. He assured the Benhams that a car and a driver would be provided for their son and he would be well looked after. He also assured them that the Zimbabwean government would be informed of their son's visit on a diplomatic visa. So Sean's arrival was very expected and a grand welcoming was planned.

When Sean finally arrived at the Harare international airport the traditional dancers and singers were on duty to greet him. The customs and immigration people were told of his visit and to make his reception as hospitable as could be. A delegate from the government was assigned for the welcoming of this distinguished visitor into the country. The airport was a bustle of activity for Sean's red carpet arrival. He gave polite attention to the traditional dancers and singers and then was quickly ushered through customs and immigration.

The promised driver and car, a short limousine, was waiting at the front entrance. Sean would have preferred a Hummer Limo, but this would do. As they drove from the airport, Sean noticed that there were small Zimbabwe and British flags on the light poles along the road as they left the airport. His picture was hung on every second pole while the president of Zimbabwe's picture was on the other ones.

"Ha, look at that, they've got my picture up on those polls." Sean directed his comment to the driver.

"Yes sir, you are an important man visiting so the government wants to make sure you know they respect you. Many others have had their pictures up there, President Nelson Mandela of South Africa, President Bill Clinton of America, and even Prime Minister Tony Blair of Britain."

"They had a dance troupe and some singers meet me at the airport. Plus some government people were there. I don't remember who they were." Sean flippantly spoke trying to act unimpressed, but secretly he was quite impressed, mostly with himself.

"I have been instructed to take you to your hotel to let you rest and get dressed for tonight. They are having a grand reception for you this evening."

So that's why mom insisted I bring a tux.

"I hope that meets with your approval?"

"Carry on, my good man," Sean replied as he stretched out in the back seat feeling pleased with himself.

Reservations had been made for Sean at the Monomatapa, the same hotel his brother had stayed at. The view from his room overlooked Harare, a very beautiful city, modern and clean. The rains hadn't been as good through the rainy season and things weren't quite as green as Ethan had described, but that didn't bother Sean. He wasn't there for the scenery.

Later that night, after the embassy reception, he fell asleep remembering the beat of the drums from the dancers echoing in his ears. He was ready to have the time of his life.

Waking late in the morning the following day, Sean was ready for a swim. The weather was beautiful and the sun felt great, just like his brother said it would be. He kind of wished he had chosen a country, other than Zimbabwe for his graduation trip. Following along behind his brother he felt that all the exploring had been done. This really wasn't true. There were a lot of things Ethan hadn't seen or done, but Sean allowed his feelings rather than common sense to dictate his thinking, a common mistake where his older brother was concerned.

After swimming a few laps and working the kinks out from his long trip, he found a shaded lounge chair and sat waiting for the waiter to come take his drink order. Now that was one of Ethan's many bits of information that he was interested in. Drinking! He wanted to drink until he was drunk and then drink some more. He wanted to go to parties, not a cook out at a farm, but real parties where guys and girls get together and have a good time. The waiter finally came and he ordered his beer. He had three more before lunch. Stumbling up to his room, Sean ordered room service, ate and promptly fell asleep.

Emerging from the dress shop with her newest designer purchase, Chipo headed down the street toward her flat. Passing the newspaper vendor on the corner, a familiar face caught her attention. The picture gazing at her from the corner of the front page looked just like Ethan Benham.

Snatching the paper up, she read the caption beneath the picture. "Visiting Dignitary Makes Splash at Airport." The brief caption directed readers to the "Social Events" columns.

Thumbing the pages, Chipo quickly glanced through the article. It wasn't Ethan. It was his younger brother, Sean. She remembered Ethan talking about his little brother. Starring at Ethan's likeness, memories flooded back; days and nights spent with him what seemed a lifetime ago. The article said that Sean was staying at the Monomatapa Hotel, the same place that Ethan had stayed. She wondered if he was staying in the same room. Should she try to see him? What would be the reason for that? She remembered

Ethan telling her how much he cared for his brother and how he always tried to protect him and keep him out of trouble. A new thought followed that one, a scheme quickly taking shape in her mind. If she could use Ethan's younger brother the way Ethan had used her, it would go a long way toward revenge.

"He's not here to protect little brother now is he," Chipo mused, "and what little brother does is his own problem." She decided she would go and visit Sean Benham.

Arriving at the Monomatapa that very afternoon, Chipo had a hunch Sean might be at the pool so she headed there first. She was ready for anything. Chipo was not the same girl she had been when Ethan met her. Not only had her appearance changed but also her demeanor. Gone was the quiet, reserved girl who had just moved from the bush. In its place was a woman who knew how to attract a man's attention and how to use it to her best advantage. She had put her bathing suit in her purse just in case she needed it. Spying Sean in the pool, she went to the changing room and put it on.

As she looked in the mirror at her image she remembered the bathing suit she had worn when she came swimming with Ethan and how shy she felt in that old, very modest suit. Now the shyness was gone and the suit she now wore was far from modest.

Coming out of the changing room she walked toward the pool. Many heads turned to look at her as she walked past, Sean's included. She wore sunglasses and her hair, or rather her hair extensions, framed her face making her look even more alluring. Laying her glasses on a table as she walked by, she went to the deep end of the pool and dove in.

When she came out of the pool with the water dripping off her body, she saw Sean watching her with desire. She went over to one of the chaise lounges and sat down. When Sean immediately followed, she knew she had him.

"Hello, my name's Sean."

"Hi Sean, my name is Gloria. It's very nice to meet you." Chipo didn't want to give her real name in case he'd heard it before.

"This may be a little forward of me, but you are the most beautiful girl I have ever met."

Chipo lowered her eyes in an assumed gesture of modesty, but inwardly she was gloating.

They sat and talked for a long while and Sean spoke of England and his family. "My parents are Lord and Lady Benham." Chipo feigned interest just to keep him talking, wanting to hear news of Ethan. "I have one older brother named Ethan. He got married last summer to his high school sweetheart."

The words were like a slap to Chipo's face. She had not ever thought of Ethan being married. How could he have been so cruel to her, promising her so much when it was all a lie? She was angry all over again and wanted to hurt Ethan. But how? How could she play this cocky younger brother so that Ethan would know it? A photo! A photo of her with Sean. She was sure Ethan would recognize her. He would see that she was doing just fine without him and that he wasn't the only boy in the world.

The two chatted the hours away until Sean realized it was getting late in the day.

"Would you care to join me for supper," Sean asked.

"That sounds great. Just let me get changed first."

"You're welcome to come up to my room and change if you would like."

"Okay, that's fine. Then maybe we could just order room service," Chipo said rather coyly.

Sean thought, Wow! This is better than what I had hoped for. I thought I would have to wine and dine her first.

"That's fine by me," Sean replied with a sly smile.

They gathered their things by the pool and walked into the hotel. Once in the elevator, Chipo leaned forward, kissing Sean, full on the lips. He was taken back at the girls' forwardness, but enjoyed the kiss nonetheless. He put his arms around her and kissed her right back, breaking apart only as the elevator doors opened.

Once they were in Sean's room, Chipo asked, "Is it okay if I use your shower? I want to rinse the pool water off." The thought of this beautiful girl in the shower was an appealing one to Sean.

"Yeah, go ahead. I'll order the food."

"Order me a steak with salad," Chipo replied as she made her way toward the bathroom.

"Sounds great. I'll order a bottle of wine to go with it. There's a robe in there for you to use when you're done." Thinking for just a moment he added, "Just call if you need any help." There was a delightful chuckle as he heard the water turn on.

Sean couldn't believe his luck. It was going to be a great night. He dressed quickly and then sat waiting for the food and the girl. The food arrived first and he called "Gloria" to come for supper. She came out wearing the robe. It was one of those bulky terry cloth ones, but she made it look good. They sat down at the table and started eating.

Chipo told him about her "family," a make believe family, spinning her tale while they ate. She had become very good at lying, a tool of the trade that always helped in getting her own way. Just as they were ending the meal she reached her hand across the table and took Sean's. "But my family lives so far away these days and I'm so lonely."

Sean took that as his signal and directed them to move to the couch. Chipo advanced towards him in the way that Sean was hoping for. She draped herself across his lap to reach for the lamp switch. Sean swallowed hard, once, then, as she started to sit back up she turned her face toward his. That beautiful face, only an inch away from his, he wanted so much to kiss her. They looked at each other for just a moment, then, Chipo smiled, closed her eyes and their lips met.

In the morning Chipo was the first one to wake. She had purposed to wake first, her motive and plan firm in her mind. She quietly got out of bed and dug her camera out of her purse. After setting the timer she placed it on the table and focused it on the bed. Then she climbed back into bed and snuggled up to Sean, still sleeping and clueless. Chipo draped Sean's arm around her and smiled at the camera. Quietly getting out of bed again without waking Sean, she got dressed and left the room.

When Sean woke up a couple hours later, he was unhappy to find the girl gone. He knew they had connected, so he expected they would meet again. That afternoon he went to the pool hoping to find her, but she never showed up.

His itinerary took him all over Zimbabwe in the short weeks that followed and everywhere he went, he kept looking for her, hoping she would come strolling in. He met other girls and had a good time with several, but none of them compared to Gloria. She stuck in his mind like a song that just won't get out of your head. At the end of his month long trip he returned to the Monomatapa, hoping against hope that she would be there. But he never saw her again.

The day before his departure, as he walked by the front desk, the concierge stopped him and handed him an envelope. He looked at it, wondering who it could be from. Opening it, he found a picture of himself in bed with Gloria. On the back was a note.

"Please show this picture to your brother. No one else but him," and it was signed "Chipo." He didn't know who Chipo was, but the picture was an amazing one. Yes, he would show it to Ethan, and revel over his conquest.

Sean arrived home feeling tired and rather unwell. His mother assumed it was probably from the poor drinking water in Africa and sent him straight to bed. While he was unpacking, Ethan entered the room ready to talk.

"Well, did you have a good time?"

"Yeah, it was great. I saw all the sights. I went to this one place just outside the city of Gweru called the Antelope Park. It was awesome! I got to ride an elephant and I walked with some lions. I don't think you had that one on your itinerary," Sean said gloating to have one up on his brother. "I have pictures. They're on my camera in the suitcase if you want to look at them."

Ethan went over to the suitcase to find the camera. Right on top there was an envelope, obviously containing pictures. Assuming it was a professional picture of Sean walking with the lions, he collected it with the camera and took a seat. He started with the pictures on the camera, scanning through them one by one, remembering familiar sights and interested in the not so familiar ones. When he had finished with all the pictures on the camera, he opened the envelope and drew out the picture from inside. It was a picture of Sean, in bed with . . . Was that Chipo? He stared at the photo trying to make sense of what he was seeing.

Ethan had been talking non–stop since coming into Sean's room. For every picture he had some comment and lots to say about Zimbabwe, reminiscing about his trip. Then suddenly he was quiet. Too quiet. Sean looked over to see why and saw that Ethan had gone as white as a sheet.

"How did you do this? What is this? I don't understand. She's dead." Ethan was speaking but Sean could make no sense of what he was saying. He walked over beside his brother to see what photograph he was looking at.

"Oh, that's a girl I met at the hotel. Man was she hot. We got together one night and then I never saw her again. Then, just before I left, that envelope was delivered to the hotel. She must have sent that picture to me. Her name is Gloria. Pretty hot isn't she?"

"Her name isn't Gloria, it's Chipo and that's the girl that I was in love with. I wanted to marry her! I was going to send for her to come here so we could get married but I got a letter from her cousin. She told me that Chipo had died in childbirth. It was my baby. I don't understand what this is about."

"Look on the back, there's a note. I didn't understand it, especially since it wasn't signed Gloria."

Ethan turned the picture over and he saw the familiar handwriting. It was signed "Chipo."

"So she isn't dead. Why did they lie to me and tell me that she was dead?" He turned to his brother, "Why are you in bed with her? What is the matter with you? This is the girl I loved and you are treating her like a tramp."

"Now wait a minute, don't blame me. I thought she was moving really fast. I figured it was my charm and good looks, but maybe she was just getting back at you for something," Sean paused briefly then continued. "Now that I think about it, she did keep asking about you; where you lived and what you were doing. When I told her you were married, she got such a strange look on her face. I thought maybe I had said something wrong, but I couldn't figure out what. Then we had supper and one thing led to another."

Ethan calmed down a bit realizing his brother wasn't at fault. How was he to know? Chipo looked completely different from his photos of her. Only someone who knew her well would recognize her.

"Okay, I guess I can't really blame you. She looks a little different in this picture, but I can tell it's her. You didn't know her. I didn't say much about her to anyone. Mom and Dad sort of made me keep it quiet." The memory of his parent's reaction pressed briefly on his heart, but no longer with any bitterness. Rather, in its place, the anger was now directed toward Chipo.

"I just can't get over that she never wrote to me. I guess the driver was right all along. All she wanted was a way to get to England. She was just a gold digger." Ethan took a deep breath, ready to direct his thoughts elsewhere.

"I'm over her now and I'm happy with Lisa. I hope that she finds happiness someday, as I have." Ethan looked over and realized that his little brother had fallen asleep. Taking the picture with him, he made his way to the den. Coals from the evening fire still burned in the fireplace. Tossing the picture onto the coals, it blazed up quickly. He watched as the corners curled up, the picture turned black and floated up the chimney. That chapter in his life was finished, completely closed.

Returning to her apartment, Chipo felt dirty all over. Fresh guilt and shame came each time she thought of what she had done to Sean. Images of her life played through her mind. After a time, a new thought followed close behind the old ones.

Who is this person I've become. It can't really be me living like this and doing these terrible things. I'm better than this.

That night Chipo made a decision. She decided she would return to the rural area, not to her home area, but to her grandparents. She thought, "Maybe they will let me come back home if I offer to work in the fields and the kitchen. All I would require is food and a roof over my head."

Her apartment had come fully furnished, so leaving it would be a simple matter of packing her personal belongings and dropping the key off at the landlord's. She couldn't wait until the next morning when she would return home. That night Chipo slept more soundly than she had in a very long time.

11

Homecoming

PASTOR ALEX DUBE AND his wife, Mary, were very ordinary people. They lived in the Makoronga village in the *Silobela* area. Their home was laid out much the same as most rural homes with a main house and several small rondoval huts inside a fenced in enclosure. Each rondoval was distinctively decorated on the outside with zigzagged lines circling the hut in vivid colors, a taste of Mary's flair for colors.

It was obvious the Dube's never thought of themselves as better than others. Alex never used his position as pastor to get ahead or receive special treatment from anyone, a rare quality in Zimbabwe even amongst church leaders.

"What are you thinking about dear?" Mary had seen Alex sitting in the shade of the mango tree with that far off look in his eyes.

"I was just thinking and praying about Chipo, wondering how she is doing."

Mary knew that her husband loved Chipo dearly and worried over her. Looking into his eyes she could see that he had been crying that morning. "Alex, it's been over a year since we have heard from her. No one has seen her, not even Peggy."

Alex put his arm around his wife, "It's just so hard, she's the daughter of our dear Martha . . ." That was all he could say, his emotions got the better of him.

"I know, I know." Mary patted her husband's shoulder. "Let's pray for her. The Lord knows where she is and can protect her."

Alex nodded his head and closed his eyes. Mary knew it was too hard for him so she prayed out first. "Dear Lord, be with our little Chipo, help her to find her way back to us and back to you . . ."

Just as they finished praying they heard the car. Alex wiped his nose with his sleeve and stood up. "It's the Perry's, I can tell by the sound of his car."

They had been excitedly anticipating their arrival for several days and now they were coming. Sometimes being a pastor was a lonely job and Alex needed someone to talk to, someone to be his pastor.

Mr. Perry was more than just a pastor to Alex Dube. Alex looked to him as his spiritual father even though he was much older than Rob. Rob Perry was a compassionate and understanding man with a good measure of Godly wisdom. He also knew how to listen to the Lord and hear God's heart in each situation. Alex was very happy they were coming.

Getting out of the car, Rob and Lynn shook hands with everyone and then Alex invited them into his house for tea.

"Tea sounds good!" Rob exclaimed. "I think the drive gets longer and bumpier every time I drive it."

Rob smiled to himself remembering the time he first met Mr. Dube. He must have been the age that Rob was now, but he really hasn't changed at all.

"What has been happening in your life, Alex?" Rob asked when they were comfortably seated in the house.

"I'm glad you asked. We've been worried lately and really need you to be praying for us," Alex said, not wasting any time. "A little over a year ago, our late daughter's daughter, Chipo, had a child out of wedlock and her father gave the baby away to a foreign couple. Everyone in her home area thinks that she died in childbirth because that's what her father told people. But after the baby was gone she came here and spent the night, so we know this story was not true. The following morning, she left and we don't know where she went or if she is okay."

Alex eyes glistened with tears as he spoke, "Like I said, that was over a year ago and we still haven't heard from her. We didn't concern ourselves too much at first, but now so much time has passed. We are really worried about her. I'm sorry to dump this on you all at once, but we need your prayers. We need you to hear the Lord. It's hard to hear for ourselves when we're so close to the situation. Maybe the Lord will show you something that could help us find her."

Mrs. Dube sat there with tears in her eyes as her husband shared all that had happened. Lynn reached over and put her arm around Mary.

"I'm sure it will be alright."

At that Mary broke down and cried. Lynn held her and looked over at her husband. "We need to pray right now."

"Okay, let's pray. Dear Lord . . . " Rob began and they continued to pray for about an hour. They prayed for Chipo to be safe. They also prayed that she would contact the Dube's soon. After praying out loud for a time they became quiet before the Lord, waiting, listening. They sat for a long time in silence, saying nothing. Then Lynn spoke up.

"I saw a picture of a person getting on a bus. I couldn't even tell if it was a man or woman. I'm not sure what it means, though."

Rob looked up at his wife with a smile, "I heard from the Lord as well, but was a little afraid to say what He told me. But after you shared your picture I know that it must be God."

Rob paused a moment, still feeling a bit apprehensive. "I believe I heard God say that Chipo is coming home tomorrow. I guess we'll wait and see, but no matter what happens we will keep on praying and believing God for a miracle."

Mr. Dube had been very quiet during this whole exchange. "I believe you are right. I have felt in my spirit that she was okay and now that you say she will come back tomorrow, I think that you are hearing right. I will wait, though, and if she comes back we will celebrate. If she doesn't, then the Lord is still in control and I know He will continue to take care of her."

As quietness fell in the room, the foursome naturally found themselves with bowed heads, once more beseeching the throne of God and thanking the Lord for His protection over Chipo, leaving her in God's hands.

The next morning at 6:00 am the bus came. Mr. Dube was waiting by the gate to see if his granddaughter was on the bus, but she wasn't. She would have had to leave Harare at one in the morning to have been on that bus so he really wasn't expecting her, only watchful just in case.

The four of them had a full day. People from all over had gathered for the meetings. The morning was spent broken up into two groups; the men's group that Rob taught, and the women in the other group, with Lynn teaching. Alex and Mary acted as their interpreters. After the teaching, they provided time for questions and answers. It kept them busy so they weren't thinking about Chipo all day.

In the afternoon they had lunch and rested for a couple hours. At 3:30 pm everyone assembled together in the school classroom. The agenda for the late afternoon session was loosely put together since the leadership planned for this time to be led by the Holy Spirit. They began with singing and soon times of prayer were intermingled between songs in a true spirit of worship. The presence of the Lord was tangibly awesome. Soon healing fell in their midst. Many began to weep as they realized the blood of the Lamb, Jesus Christ, had healed them. No one had touched them, only God's presence. As more and more were healed, people began to call out what God had done and then the room would explode with shouts of praise. It was a very good meeting. No one was concerned about the time. The meeting just kept going. People didn't want to stop.

After a while Rob noticed that Alex left the room. He didn't know why, but Rob assumed he had a good reason and left it at that. Then he heard it; the sound of the bus coming.

"Now I understand," Rob said to himself with a smile. "He must have heard the bus when it was much further away."

Rob got up and left the classroom following his friend toward the road. He heard a noise behind him and turned to look. His wife was following him with Mary by her side. They got to where they could see the road right as the bus came, but they were on the wrong side and couldn't see who was getting off. They were sure someone was getting off because luggage was being removed from the top of the bus.

When the four of them left the classroom the assembled group assumed the meeting was over, and curious as to where the four were headed, they followed behind. They crowded together by the road, waiting to see what was going to happen. Finally the bus started up again and pulled away.

After the smoke from the diesel engine had blown away they could see Alex holding a young lady in his arms like he would never let her go. It was his Chipo, his granddaughter that he thought he had lost forever. Both of them were crying and laughing at the same time.

The people didn't understand what was happening or even who this young girl was. Mary turned to the crowd and through tears said, "It's our granddaughter, Chipo, our Martha's girl. She's home!"

The congregation broke into a loud cheer startling some donkeys pulling a scotch–cart. The driver just managed to keep them under control. "Whoa," he called to the team, anxious to find out what all the commotion was about.

The crowd of people ran to Alex and Chipo, greeting Chipo and slapping Alex on the back. They had all been praying for her safe return. Some were awed at the power of God, having already heard the word that Rob had spoken about Chipo returning that day. All Alex could do was to hold on to his girl and cry.

The evening meeting was canceled in order to make time for a celebration and to provide a chance for the Dube's to be alone with their granddaughter. Rob and Lynn tried to make themselves scarce so the Dube family could be alone, but Alex and Mary wouldn't hear of it.

"You're family. We want you to be a part of our reunion."

The conversation in the Dube home that evening was sometimes excited, sometimes subdued, but mostly in Ndebele, the local language, so Rob and Lynn understood only a little. During those times the couple remained silent and in an attitude of prayer knowing God was doing an amazing thing. Alex would pause now and then to translate the important things. Sometimes Chipo spoke in English, so Rob and Lynn understood that Chipo was repentant and asking forgiveness for how she had behaved.

"I've been living a horrible life and I know I need forgiveness, not just from my grandparents but especially from God," Chipo said through the tears now flowing.

In honor of Chipo's return the ladies had killed a goat and prepared a real feast. During supper they didn't talk as much, but Rob noticed that Mary and Chipo stayed in the room and ate with the men, very out of character for the culture. Chipo sat next to her grandfather on the couch and the compassion on Alex's face was plain to see. He was so glad she was home and safe. She looked way too skinny, but he knew that kids in the city tried to stay thin for some reason. His wife was short and plump and that's the way he liked her. Chipo needed some meat on her body and he was determined to feed her well.

Chipo had wiped her tears away when the food arrived but as they were eating they started all over again. "What is the matter, Chipo?" Alex asked.

"It's nothing. I'm just so happy to be back and glad that you are willing to let me stay. I keep thinking about the crowd at the bus stop. It looked like you were welcoming a celebrity instead of your wayward granddaughter. I was afraid you would send me away. I don't think my father would ever let me come back."

"Let's not talk of your father tonight. We will have to talk about him sometime, but not right now."

After the meal was finished the five of them joined the rest outside. Everyone got down on their knees thanking God for Chipo's safe return. Chipo prayed and asked God to forgive her for her many sins. Her grandfather spoke gently to her, inviting her to give her life to Jesus. As she did, tears welled up in her eyes, first because of the heaviness in her heart, but then after some time they turned into tears of joy.

Rob, Alex, and the other church leaders gathered around her to bless her and pray for the fresh anointing of the Holy Spirit. Alex shared scriptures with Chipo about water baptism and Chipo knew that was the next step for her. Plans were made for that event on the following Sunday. After prayer they all went to bed. Tomorrow was a new day, not only for Chipo who had just become new again, but also for the Dube's. Their lost grandchild had returned.

❖❖❖

The following Sunday the church was packed with people from all over. People came from areas that were over fifteen kilometers away. Some had heard about the healings, but most had heard about Chipo's return and they wanted to see for themselves.

When news of Chipo's return reached the ears of her two younger brothers, Simba and Dumisani, they didn't know what to believe. Their father had told them that Chipo had died in childbirth and they had buried her. There was a grave with a gravestone bearing Chipo's name telling the world that Chipo was dead. Now they heard that their sister was alive at their grandfather's home. Simba, the eldest of the two, didn't believe it. He was sure that Chipo had died. He had heard the stories of her ghost wandering around looking for her dead child, but he had helped dig the grave and bury her. He had lifted the heavy coffin where mother and baby laid together.

Dumisani never wanted to believe that Chipo had died in the first place and now that news had come to the contrary, he was easily convinced. Chipo was like a mother to him and he missed her very much. Upon hearing the news, he immediately started out the gate to go see her but Simba stopped him and they argued.

"You are crazy to believe such things. She is dead. We buried her."

"No, I know she's alive. She has to be. I'm going to grandfather's to see her." Dumisani said with resolve.

"Don't be a fool Dumi, it's too far to go today, it will be dark way before you get there. If you wait I'll take you to grandfather's tomorrow for church. Then you'll see, you'll see she is dead."

The next morning Dumisani and Simba got up early and headed to the church. It was only seven in the morning when they left and they knew they would only get there just as church started at ten.

When they arrived the service had already begun. Entering the church, their eyes had to adjust to the darkness in the thatched roofed building. Then they saw her. There sat Chipo . . . or her ghost. Fear held them in the doorway, as Simba whispered into his brother's ear.

"This must be Chipo's ghost come to possess either you or me." Sitting down they continued to stare at this apparition.

During the service Mr. Dube talked about Chipo and how they had missed her and now were overjoyed at her return. He talked about the word that Rob had given and how it proved true, causing shouts and cheering from the assembled group. Next he asked Chipo to come forward. Feeling shy, Chipo timidly rose and stood beside her grandfather. Putting his arm around her shoulders, Alex asked "Chipo do you want to confess Jesus as Lord and Savior?"

"Yes I do."

"Could you please share what it is that you believe in your heart about Jesus." He said with a catch in his voice.

Looking up at her grandfather with a questioning look she whispered, "Do you want me to tell everything I have been doing?"

"You say whatever you feel you need to share Chipo, however much you feel you need to share."

Glancing up Chipo saw many faces that she knew, people she had met in this very church building. "What will they think of me?" Chipo thought to herself. Then she saw them, her two brothers were sitting toward the back. She gave a start and ran back to them.

Falling on her knees she hugged both of them. "Simba, Dumi, I've missed you so much. Please forgive me for running away from you. I'm so sorry for leaving you and not even contacting you. I was angry and confused. I've done many very bad things, evil things that I'm not at all proud of. Please, please forgive me."

Through tears of joy Dumisani responded, "Oh, Chipo, you're alive! We thought you were dead."

Simba took her by the shoulders and held her at arm's length. Looking into her eyes he spoke as an older brother would. "Chipo, I really thought you were dead. We buried you. I helped dig your grave and carried the casket with you and your baby in it. When you died I felt abandoned and alone, knowing that now it was me who would have to help Dumisani grow up." With tears streaming down his face he continued, "Chipo, there is nothing that you could have done to make me love you more than I already do. You're my sister, my own flesh and blood. I'm just glad you're back."

As he fell into her arms there wasn't a dry eye in the place.

Rob pulled out a handkerchief and wiped his nose, "That's the best example of confession and forgiveness I have ever seen. We have just witnessed a true Bible story, the story of the prodigal son, except it's a sister coming back to her brothers. Simba's reply was such a God spoken word. He said, 'there was nothing more that she could do to make him love her more than he already did.' Brothers and sisters this is exactly how God feels about you. There is nothing more that you could do to make him love you more than he already does." Looking directly at Chipo he asked her, "Chipo, will you allow Jesus to become the Lord of your life?"

Chipo was still on her knees holding her two brothers. "Yes, yes I want him to be the Lord of my life."

By then Alex had regained some composure. "Let's pray then." As everyone bowed their heads Alex looked in his granddaughters eyes. "Father, thank you for bringing my girl back to me, thank you for bringing her back to you too, you have made us a family again." His voice was trembling with emotion. "I've got so much I am thankful for right now. Praise you."

When Alex had finished praying, it was very quiet in the building. No one moved, no one spoke. Then Chipo started to sing. "As we gather at the foot of your throne, we sing with the host of heaven. As we gather at the foot of your throne, we worship and praise the most high. Hallelujah, you are worthy to be praised. Hallelujah, you're the one that was slain. Hallelujah, hallelujah to the Lamb." As she sang the rest of the congregation joined in and the room was filled with praises to the King.

All during the service Simba had wrestled with questions, doubts, and fear. Could this actually be his sister? Could she really be alive? But when she ran back to them, held them in her arms and spoke to them he knew it was her. Now that he heard her sing there was no doubt. That was Chipo's voice. It was the voice that used to sing him to sleep. As people joined in with the singing, he stood up and walked up to the front where his grandfather was. Chipo and Dumisani followed along with him. Taking his grandfather's hand he spoke quietly to him. "Grandfather, I have not done well since Chipo has been gone. I blamed God for her dying and my mother dying. I told him if that was the way he loved people then I wanted nothing to do with him. I was wrong. Please pray that he will forgive me and love me again."

"Simba, all you have to do is ask forgiveness and he will forgive you. Like you said, there's nothing more that you could do to make him love you any more than he does now." He smiled at his grandson knowing the immense truth that he had spoken to the church that day. "Could you pray and do that now? Just ask him for forgiveness."

Simba bowed his head, "God, I'm sorry for the things I said to you and the thoughts I had about you. I want you to be my Lord too. Can you accept me?"

When he asked that question Alex grabbed him and held him tight. With tears streaming down his face there was nothing he could say.

Simon got word that Chipo was back and staying with her grandparents. At first he didn't know what to do. In the end he decided to do nothing.

"I have said she was dead for the last year and she is still dead to me. I won't even acknowledge her if I see her. That old man is crazy anyway. He'll probably tell everyone that he raised her from the dead. I'll just say it's not really her. To the day that I die I will never admit that this girl is Chipo."

Chipo was so happy to be back with her grandparents. Life was good again. Giving her life to Jesus was the best part. All the months of shame were gone and she felt clean, cleaner than she'd ever felt before. Since she had become a Christian, Chipo had been reading her Bible and going to church as often as possible. When she wasn't doing either of those things, she was helping her grandparents around their home.

Her grandmother was so good to Chipo and she loved spending time with her whether it was cooking, working in the field or just going for a walk together. They spent many hours talking, sometimes about simple things but most often about things that counted the most in life. They spoke of Chipo's baby and hoped and prayed that he was doing well with his adoptive parents.

The experiences of the past year and her new life in the Lord worked together in Chipo's heart, causing her to realize that her baby was better off where he was than if she had been able to keep him. She knew raising a mixed race child as a single mother in the rural area would be very hard.

Mixed race children were often ridiculed by other children and always lived a difficult life. Watching the loving relationship between her grandparents made Chipo long for the same kind of marriage and the prospects of that were very slim for a single mother. She wanted a husband who would treat her with kindness and gentleness the way her grandfather treated her grandmother. Chipo sensed the special ingredient in her grandparent's marriage was their relationship with Jesus and she prayed for the same kind of relationship with a man.

Chipo hadn't been feeling well lately and just couldn't seem to shake whatever it was. At first she thought it was a cold or maybe the flu. When her grandparents left for Nkayi along with the Perry's she opted to stay at home, not feeling well enough to travel. One evening she had finished her supper and was cleaning the dishes when it suddenly dawned on her. She was pregnant!

She had always been very careful, practicing "safe sex" without fail. Every time, that is, except that last time with Ethan's brother. She was angry, and a little crazy, so she hadn't thought to use any birth control. The realization hit her hard and she knew even before taking a pregnancy test that she was definitely pregnant.

The bitter tears flowed much of the evening and into the night. She was thankful that she was alone. The shame from her past flooded back upon her with all its ugliness and it caused her to want to hide. She needed her grandmother, especially right now, but she didn't know how she was going to face her. She tried praying but found it difficult. She longed for that peace and acceptance once again but it seemed unattainable. She prayed that the baby would miscarry, but that didn't happen. She had to figure out what she was going to do. She didn't want to bring this shame on her grandparents.

"What will they say?" she wondered. "Will they kick me out? Will they send me away? What am I going to do?" She had just become a Christian and now what kind of testimony would she have. "What will everyone think?" She and her grandfather had been talking about Chipo teaching the children at church, but now . . . she could just see herself standing in front of the children trying to teach them about Jesus . . . but they would know how bad she was. There was no way she could teach the children now. So many thoughts ran through her head making prayer impossible and the Lord seem so far away. She remained in her hut most of the long lonely weekend.

When her grandparents and the Perry's returned, Chipo forced herself to emerge and greet them as though nothing was the matter. It was one of the most difficult things she had ever done. She tried to put on a happy face, but inside she was far from happy. They talked excitedly about the week-end in Nkayi, all the miracles and wonders they had seen. But all Chipo could think about was how she had failed God. He couldn't possibly love her anymore.

Although sensing that something was very wrong with Chipo, Mary remained quiet waiting for the opportune time. Rob, Lynn, and Alex were leaving the next morning to go to a new area in Botswana, checking out the possibilities of starting a church. Once they were gone and she was alone with Chipo, Mary knew she would be able to have a good talk with her granddaughter. The others would be gone for a whole week.

Everyone went to bed early that night, the threesome planning on leaving around four in the morning. Chipo was relieved. It was hard for her to pretend everything was fine, but she thought she had fooled them all. She hoped the coming days alone with her grandmother would present an opportunity for them to talk. Maybe her grandmother would understand. Then Chipo remembered her mother talking about when she became preg-nant with Chipo. Martha too, had been in the same situation, having no husband. When Alex was told his daughter was pregnant, he was angry and stormed out of the house. Mary wouldn't look at her daughter for a week. The memory of her mother's words stripped Chipo of all hope of under-standing from her grandparents but she knew her exposure was inevitable.

The next morning, after the others had left, her grandmother turned to Chipo.

"Why don't you bring your things from your hut and stay with me in the main house. My room is too big without your grandfather here. We can have more time together, talking into the night like we did when you were small."

Chipo was glad for the attention but was sure her grandmother would change her mind when she knew Chipo's secret.

"Okay *Gogo*," answered Chipo calling her grandmother by the familiar African name. Chipo left to get some of her things from her hut, moving them to the big house. It was still very early so the two decided to go back to bed and sleep just a little longer. Chipo was glad. She hadn't slept very well that night and was quite tired. They shared the big bed her grandparents slept in, a comfortable bed, soft, and holding so many pleasant memories. She remembered as a girl when she visited her grandparents that they would allow her to come into their bed and snuggle with them early in the morning. She would pull the covers up over her head, feeling protected and safe. It was one of the few fond memories she had of her childhood. Crawling into bed next to her grandmother, Chipo pulled the blankets up and within a few moments she was asleep.

When she awoke, her grandmother was gone. The sun was coming in the window warming the room up nicely. It had been cold in the night and the warmth of the day felt good. She heard her grandmother over at her kitchen rondoval, working. Mmm, breakfast. She could smell the aroma from the kitchen and for one brief moment, her thoughts were pleasant as she lay there in her grandparent's bed. Then she remembered her secret. What was she going to do? How would she tell her grandmother? Just then Mary came into the room and saw that Chipo was up.

"Good morning, Chipo, how did you sleep?"

"I slept very well, grandmother. Your bed is so comfortable and I have so many wonderful memories in this bed. Do you remember the time we woke up before grandfather and snuck out to have a cup of tea? Grandfather was a sleepy head that morning so we threw a cup of water on him to wake him."

They both started laughing at the memory of that day. "Yes, I remember. I remember we used just a little too much water and that night he had to sleep in a damp bed because it hadn't dried completely. He wasn't very happy then."

"But I don't remember him ever getting angry, not that time or even when my brother broke his favorite cane. You remember that don't you? Simba had been playing with it, walking around pretending he was grandfather and somehow it broke."

"I'll tell you a secret, Chipo." Mary leaned in closer to her, "Your grandfather used to get very angry. He was never a violent man, but at times things would make him so very angry he would just blow up. Usually this happened when he was tired or overworked. He would get on edge and even the littlest things would cause him to be angry. It all came to a head when your mother got pregnant with you. It was the last straw. Your grandfather was mad enough to kill someone and of course he wanted to kill your father. He walked out of the house and was gone for two days. I didn't know where he went. It turned out he went to Gweru to the missionary's house. Mr. Perry wasn't home that day, but Mrs. Perry was. He told her all about it and she talked to him about what our children mean to us. She told him that no matter what they do we still needed to love them or run the risk of losing them for good. Your grandfather opened up to Mrs. Perry that day and talked about his anger. The episode with your mother made him realize the seriousness of his problem. They talked a while longer and then they prayed together. Something happened to him that day that changed him forever."

"What was that *Gogo*. What changed grandfather?"

"It was the Holy Spirit. We had been in the church for many, many years, but we had never received the fullness of the Holy Spirit. The previous missionaries had never talked much about the Holy Spirit and so we didn't know anything about Him. Mrs. Perry told your grandfather the Holy Spirit wanted to help him, to counsel him, and comfort him in times of trouble like what he was going through at that very moment. She said it was the Holy Spirit who could help him to forgive your mother and your father and who would empower him to overcome anger. She also talked about gifts that the Holy Spirit gives. Mrs. Perry prayed for your grandfather and asked the Holy Spirit to come on him with power and to give him the gifts he needed.

He was only there for a couple of hours and then he took the bus back home. He should have been home that evening, but the bus broke down and he had to sleep in the bus that night until another bus came along. Ordinarily the situation would have caused your grandfather much anxiety. But like I said, he was a changed man.

He began praying, nothing new for your grandfather, but this time he began to hear the voice of the Lord speaking to his spirit. Nothing bold or audible, just that still small voice. He spoke into the situation, and then, right there, sitting on that broken down bus the Lord began to speak to him about your mother. He realized that although your mother was at fault it wasn't completely her fault. He had been so busy with the church work he didn't know what she was doing and wasn't watching out for her as he should have been.

When he returned home I noticed right away he was different. He was quieter, and gentler than he had ever been before. By then it was too late to save your mother. When your grandfather flew off the handle at her, she packed her bags and ran off to your father's place. Your grandfather tried to make it right, but he and your mother were never close again. It hurt him very deeply and then when she died it hurt even more. When your mother died, a part of him died also. It is only by the grace of God and the Holy Spirit that your grandfather is now as strong as he is. He has had to depend on God to be his strength. I think if he didn't have Jesus, he would have given up on life a long time ago."

"I never knew that about grandfather. He has always been the gentlest man I have ever met."

Chipo's grandmother was pleased with their conversation but she knew this was trivial compared to what they needed to talk about.

"Chipo, I know there is something wrong. Please don't try to hide it from me. The Holy Spirit told me yesterday you were in great anguish over something and I needed to talk to you. I think I even know what the problem is. Please . . . tell me."

At this Chipo's eyes filled with tears. "Oh grandmother, what am I going to do? I have been here all alone the past four days and I just want to come clean. I think I'm pregnant. I haven't taken any test to find out for sure, but I'm certain I am. You understand don't you grandma, you sometimes just know these things."

"Yes, I understand. Chipo I am so sorry. Please allow me to help you."

Chipo didn't know what to say. She expected anger or at least a look that meant she was in trouble. None of that happened. "Oh grandmother, please forgive me."

"Child, it isn't me you need to ask forgiveness from. Have you asked God to forgive you yet?"

Chipo nodded her head.

"What about the child's father? Do you need to send him a letter or contact him somehow?

"No. It was just a one–time thing and he isn't even from Zimbabwe. He's gone now," Chipo replied feeling the deepest shame. "The worst part is the man I was with, the father of this baby, is brother to the father of my first baby. I was foolish and angry. I was trying to get back at Ethan, the first brother. He hurt me so much and I just wanted to get back at him by using the younger brother. I really messed up, didn't I?" Her grandmother nodded her head in agreement with her.

"Sometimes in fits of anger we do things we are very sorry for later, but even so we have to face the consequences. You were angry and did something very wrong. Now you are pregnant and will have to face that fact."

"*Gogo*, I know that now. I am so sorry for what I have done. Just a month ago I was on top of the world with my new found faith and trust in Jesus. Now I feel like He must hate me."

"No my child, He doesn't hate you. He still loves you and in fact He still wants to be with you. I'll bet that since you realized you are pregnant you haven't been praying or reading your Bible like you were doing before."

"Ya . . . yes, that's true." Chipo stammered out, "I've felt too guilty to be able to pray. I have felt like He has abandoned me."

"No, He hasn't abandoned you. Look what it says in James 4:8. 'Draw near to God and he will draw near to you.' This works the same as it does with you and me. If I walk closer to you, you are closer to me, but if I walk away from you, you are farther from me. It's the same with God. If we are closer to Him, He is closer to us. We are the ones who walk away from Him. He doesn't move. He is always there waiting for us. Sometimes people get so far away they can barely see God, but He has not moved. All we have to do is walk back to him."

Chipo thought about that for a while. "Then if we walk back to Him, will he forgive us?"

"Yes, He always forgives. In fact, if you walk back to Him you will automatically have a desire to ask forgiveness. Being close to the Lord just has a way of working out like that. You can't stay in sin if you are close to Him. A lot of people don't see it this way. If they sin they stay away from God and the sin builds up and they go from one sin to another. If they would only go toward God they would see that He forgives, drawing us close once more. Our Lord is not some mean, angry God sitting up in heaven waiting for us to do something wrong so he can throw lightning bolts at us. He's a loving God that wants us to know Him and spend time with Him."

"Are you serious? He wants to spend time with me? I feel as though He has turned His back on me, never wanting to look at me again."

Chipo had moved near her grandmother and was sitting on the floor with her arms in her grandmother's lap looking up at her. Mary smiled and looked at her granddaughter with such love in her eyes. "Chipo, when God created the earth he looked at it and said it was good. Then he created man and woman and when he looked at them he said it was very good."

Reaching for her Bible she continued, "We can read in Genesis chapter three where God used to come to the earth and walk with Adam and Eve. He probably walked with them many times in the garden, just as you and I sometimes do when grandpa is away."

Smiling through the tears in her eyes, Chipo remembered those times. "Yes *Gogo*, I love those walks in the garden."

"I know you do, and I love them too." Mary looked deeply into Chipo's eyes. "And our Father loved those walks with Adam and Eve, but then sin came into the picture. They ate of the tree God had warned them not to eat of."

Mary placed her finger on a verse, "Look what it says in verse eight, God was walking in the garden in the cool of the day. But Adam and Eve had just sinned, the very first sin ever to be committed, and they wanted to hide from God. He didn't allow them to do that. He called out to them, 'Adam, where are you?' Now, God didn't need Adam to tell him where he was; he knew where he was. He knew they were hiding from Him because they had disobeyed His word. God punished them for the sin, but he still wanted to walk with them. Sin would not allow that and that's the reason Adam and Eve were removed from the Garden."

Mary reached out and patted Chipo on the head. "Sin has been around for a long time and Adam and Eve did exactly what we do when we sin against God. They hid. Just like you did this weekend Chipo, you were hiding from God."

"We have to realize that we can't really hide from God. He knows where we are. He may call our name to see if we will answer, but He already knows where we are hiding and the reason we are hiding. Even though we look at ourselves and think that what we did was so bad that he could never forgive us, he still wants to walk with us. He desires to spend time with us. He wants us to want to spend time with him.

"Chipo, sin made it impossible for that to happen with Adam and Eve, but through the redemptive power of Jesus, we are able to walk with God again."

Mary placed her hand under Chipo's chin and lifted it up so she was looking right at her. "All we have to do is repent and confess our sins and the blood of Jesus does the rest. So don't run away from him, run to him. He is waiting for you to come back to him."

Chipo was crying as she heard these words from her grandmother. She had never realized how much God wanted to be with her or that He loved her that much.

"Chipo, why don't we take this time just to pray and you can ask him for forgiveness and I will agree with you, okay?" Through her tears Chipo said, "Yes" and they began praying.

"Dear God, please forgive me for my sin. I know I was wrong and I should have never done many of the things I have done in my life. Please, Lord, forgive me." Chipo didn't know how else to express her sorrow and repentance.

Her grandmother was quiet for a little while and then said, "Lord, you know our hearts; you know our thoughts and all the sins that we do and hide from everyone else. Yet you still love us. I know you still love Chipo and want her to know that you do. Lord I ask that you just show her your forgiveness and love."

Mary was quiet for a few moments and then she spoke. "Chipo, were you already pregnant the day you returned to us, the day you gave your life to Jesus?" Mary already knew the answer to her own question. Her purpose in asking was for Chipo, not herself.

Chipo nodded her head yes and then reality dawned slowly upon her. The Lord knew all along that she was pregnant even when she hadn't known. The day she gave her heart to Jesus, she was pregnant and the Lord accepted her just the way she was. The Lord's redemption was hers no matter what.

Mary was speaking her heart silently to the Lord as well. "I want to bless her now, Lord. She is a lovely woman and I am so proud of her. Lord, she has gone through some very hard times. She has known heartache and loss. She has known suffering and abandonment. Bless her now Lord."

Mary looked at Chipo and lifted her granddaughter's head with her hand. "Chipo I just want you to know that I am very proud of you. You are not forgotten. I have never forgotten you. God has never abandoned you. He has always watched over you. Even when you were far away from Him, He watched over you. I know your father hasn't been very good to you. Part of his problem is that he sees in you too much of your mother. Your father really did love your mother and I know deep in his heart he loves you. Your grandfather and I love you. God bless you Chipo."

All Chipo could do was to cry. She was so happy to know that her grandmother and grandfather loved her so much. They really did care about her no matter what she had done. As her grandmother was praying Chipo saw a picture of herself walking in the field with Jesus. They were holding hands and just walking. It was so real and spoke straight to Chipo's heart. He really does care for me. He wants me to be close to him, Chipo thought to herself. When she was able to speak, her only words were, "Thank you Jesus, thank you Jesus." Once again, the tears that had begun as tears of shame and remorse, by the Lord's grace, were turned to tears of peace and acceptance.

Chipo's grandfather returned with the Perry's the following week. Chipo sat down with all of them together and told her story. They were all so kind and tenderhearted, no looks of disgust or even disapproval. Alex was especially tender to her as she shared her heart. He was in his chair with Chipo sitting on the arm of the chair. As she talked he put his arm around her and just held her, rubbing his hand up and down her arm or patting her on the back. Tears welled up in his eyes as she spoke. He had been here before, but the first time he became angry and lost his daughter. He had determined in his heart he would never do that again.

After a few minutes, Lynn spoke up, "We need to make sure this baby is covered by the blood of Jesus. Chipo, since your baby was conceived in a wrong situation, Satan assumes he has a right to bring cursing. We don't want that, so we need to break this curse. God has given you the authority as the child's mother. Now that you have asked forgiveness you need to renounce sexual sin and iniquity. Do you understand the difference between sin and iniquity?"

Chipo shook her head "no."

"Sin is like the fruit on a tree, but iniquity is like the roots of the tree," Lynn continued. "We are born with iniquity, passed down to us from the sins of our parents or grandparents. Have you ever noticed that if a father is an alcoholic a lot of times his son will become one too. Or if a mother or father is abusive to his family the children become abusive to their spouses and children when they grow up. This is iniquity."

Lynn looked right in Chipo's eyes, "As children of God, we don't have to allow this to stay with us. What we can do is renounce this and repent of it. Even if it's not our fault, a person can repent even if they are not wrong. Repentance means to turn away from something. So when we repent of an iniquity we are turning our back on it.

We don't want to stop there though we need to renounce it also. Renouncing closes the door to iniquity. To renounce means to say, 'get off of me.' When we shut the door, then we break the foothold Satan assumes. Does that make sense?"

Chipo nodded her head and everyone else agreed as well. Chipo had never heard of "renouncing" before and wasn't sure what she was supposed to do.

"Uh, Mrs. Perry, this may sound stupid, but I don't know how to renounce my sin. I wouldn't know what to say to God.

"I'll help you Chipo," Lynn replied. I'll pray and all you have to do is repeat it. If I pray something that you don't agree with or you don't understand just let me know and we'll pray another way, okay?"

"Okay."

Rob remained very quiet during this exchange, silently praying. He knew his wife was gifted when it came to prayer for deliverance and inner healing. She knew how to pray what the Holy Spirit led, and she was right on every time. Rob and Lynn both got down in front of Chipo. Lynn took hold of Chipo's hands and Rob laid his hand on her shoulder. Lynn prayed and Chipo repeated what she said, repenting, renouncing, and closing the door to that act of sexual sin and to generational iniquities in her life. After they had finished praying Rob began sharing his heart.

"You know, Chipo, in Biblical times the father would give his blessing to his children. This was done on several occasions. The first was at the conception of a child. Now I don't know what you did when you realized you might be pregnant, but I'll bet you didn't think to bless this life."

"No I definitely didn't bless what had happened, I was angry, scared, and confused all at the same time. I even hoped that the child would abort."

"Okay, then we need to take time to bless this child. Of course the father of the child isn't here, but ultimately the father's blessing comes from Father God. You could give the blessing, but I think it would be better if your grandfather would bless this child. Does that sound okay to you?"

Chipo wanted nothing more than for this baby to be blessed. She was unsure if her grandfather would be willing. "Grandfather, please, will you bless this baby?"

"I would be proud to bless this child of yours," Alex said. "I think we also need to bless your first child. Do you think that's a good idea Rob?"

"Yes, that's a very good idea. In fact if there are any troubles or issues in his life, a blessing from you could change that."

Alex looked again at Chipo, "Did you name that first child?"

"Yes and no. I didn't get the chance to properly name him, but I was going to name him after his father. His name was to be Ethan."

"Names are important and the meaning of our names can reveal a lot of what God will do in our lives. Your name, Chipo, means 'a gift'. My name, Alexander, means 'brave protector'. Your grandmother's name, Mary, literally means 'myrrh', but spiritually, it means 'living fragrance'. Rob, do you know what your names mean?"

"Rob is short for Robert which means 'shining with fame or excellent worth'. Lynn literally means 'from the pool or waterfall' but spiritually it means 'refreshing one.'"

"Can you see how each of us has lived out the meaning of our names, the ones that our parents gave to us when we were first born? As I was growing up I had no idea what my name meant, but the Lord saw fit to mold me into what my name means. I am the protector of all twenty-three churches that He has put under my care. Look at Rob, he never wanted fame, but the Lord has given him such a great gift in his ministry. People all over the world want him to come and minister. How many people have been touched by your grandmother's fragrance? After Lynn prayed for you, did you feel refreshed and free? Now all we need to do is find out what Ethan means so we can pray that for him."

Lynn got up right then and said, "I think our name book is in the car, I'll go see." She went out and a couple minutes later came back in with the book already open to the name Ethan.

"The literal meaning is 'firm or strength' and the spiritual meaning is 'steadfast in truth or a steadfast heart'. Oh, listen to the scripture that goes with this name. It's in 1 Corinthians 15:58 and it says, 'Consequently, my beloved brothers, be steadfast; immovable, at all times abounding in the Lord's service, aware that your labor in the Lord is not futile.'"

Chipo thought about these words and although she didn't know the little baby that was taken from her by her father, she remembered the father of the baby. He was steadfast, a very strong man and would go far in the world. She hoped he would find the Lord someday and come to know the joy she had found. "Could we also pray for the fathers? I don't necessarily want them to come back to me, but I do want them to know the Lord."

"Yes Chipo, we can pray for the salvation of the fathers also. They need to know Jesus and accept Him as their personal Savior." Lynn waved her arms around, "God's arm is not too short that he can't save them even if they are all the way across the ocean."

"Okay, I'm ready, let's bless these babies," Lynn said, anxious to see God touch their lives, the baby growing in Chipo and little Ethan whom none of them knew and the fathers.

Alex instructed Chipo to sit on a chair across from him and he took both her hands in his. He looked straight into her eyes and started to bless her children. Beginning with the baby inside her he said, "Father, we want to bless this baby growing in Chipo, right now. Your word says that 'you formed us in our mother's womb'. You are forming this little one right now. I pray you will bless the conception of this baby. Even though it was done in a wrong way, a child has been created out of it. We don't know the gender of this child, but Lord, I ask that you will make this baby what you want him or her to be. Help this child to grow up knowing you and having such a desire in his or her heart to serve you all the days of his life. Thank you for this little baby and bless him."

Reaching over to Mary, Alex took her hand in his, " Now Lord I want to also bless little Ethan. We don't know where he is, but he is Chipo's child. Father just bless his conception and birth. I know when he was born there was turmoil. Please change that and let there be peace in his heart. Let him know he is loved and accepted. We thank you that you made him a boy, who will grow up to be a man who is steadfast and true. We thank you that he will always be abounding in the service of the Lord."

Turning back to Chipo, Alex continued, "And Lord, I also want you to bless Chipo." At this Chipo gave a start. She didn't expect her grandfather to bless her. "She is a gift from you. You gave her to us when we were hurting. Father, you made her the woman she is today. Now I ask you Father, to empower her to prosper. We bless her conception, which we didn't do when we found out about her. We bless her birth. We bless her growing up years and when she became a woman. And Lord, we bless her new life in Jesus. Father we ask that you bring into her life a strong Christian man who will love her as we do and who will marry her and take care of her the rest of her life. Father we ask you to touch the two men who are the fathers of these two babies. Bring them to you, Lord; let nothing stop your salvation from reaching them. Your arm is not too short to bring salvation to these two men."

Chipo knew in her heart that what her grandfather was doing was very right. As he blessed her, emotions welled up inside her. When he asked God to bless her womanhood, she could hold it in no longer. She burst into tears and didn't hold back. God was touching her. When Alex began blessing a man in her life it made her start again and even blush a little. Does God even care about my future husband? This was all new to her, but she sensed it was right and good, bringing change in the spiritual realm.

Chipo had one last question. "Grandfather, is there any way you can find out who my father gave Ethan to? I don't want him back, but after this baby is born I thought maybe they would like to adopt him . . . or her as well. I'm not angry anymore and I'm thinking maybe my father actually did what was best for my baby. I want to do what's best for this child as well."

"I'll see what I can do."

12

Prayer

ACROSS THE BORDER 370 miles away Ingrid had been at her wits end. Little Nyasha was growing up. He was a toddler now and would get into mischief all the time. Sometimes Ingrid thought he was just too much for her. "It was so much easier when Hans was alive," was her frequent excuse. With him gone, little Nyasha was always surrounded by women and she sometimes felt he really needed a man's firm hand. One day Ingrid was very busy and Nyasha kept asking to go for a walk. Ingrid had told him "no" several times when he asked to be taken, but he still insisted. Finally, he was playing contentedly in the yard when Ingrid went into the medicine room to get some antiseptic. When she came out he was nowhere to be seen. "Susan, Susan." She called excitedly, "Have you seen Nyasha?"

"No, I've been over at the clinic and haven't noticed him."

"He has been asking me to take him for a walk all morning and I just haven't had time and now he's gone."

Although the road was a dirt road there were so many footprints there was no way she could track him. She went one direction and didn't find him so she turned around and went the other way with no better luck. There were many footpaths in every direction and Ingrid couldn't even begin to know which one to take. Finally she stopped and sat down. She felt like crying, but knew that wouldn't help. She decided to pray.

"Lord, please keep Nyasha safe and bring him back home. Watch over him and guide me to find him."

The thought immediately came to her mind that he may have returned home by now. Quickly picking herself up off the ground, she headed for home. When she got close enough she could see him in the yard playing in the sand exactly where she had left him earlier. She ran to him and didn't know whether to scold him or hug him. So she did both.

Sometimes she just didn't know what she was going to do with the child. He had a mind of his own and he did whatever he wanted to do. It didn't matter how much she scolded or disciplined him with "time out," he would still do what he wanted. His overly strong will was bad enough but on top of that he was beginning to display a tendency toward violence, especially when he didn't get his own way or when Ingrid corrected him. He would break things when Ingrid wasn't watching and a few times he even became aggressive toward his mother.

During nursing school, Ingrid had studied a bit about Reactive Attachment Disorder, common among adopted children, especially interracial adoptions. Thinking that might be the problem, she had prayed together with Susan several times but with no apparent results.

Then one day, he changed, suddenly, as if overnight. Ingrid didn't know what had happened. She woke up one day to find a gentle natured, obedient child. The violence was gone as well as the strong will. He no longer ran off by himself or became aggressive. It was like night and day. Now he was a very polite, outgoing little boy. She didn't know for sure what had gotten in to him, or possibly out of him, but she knew in her heart that God had worked a miracle.

Ingrid enjoyed her work with the NGO in Zambia. The work was easier somehow. She didn't know if it was because in Zambia people just didn't work as hard as they did in Zimbabwe, or if it was because when people came to them for care, they would first offer to pray for them, many times resulting in healing and no further need for treatment.

When Pastor Rob had been in Zambia, he taught the church about abiding in Jesus and walking in the Holy Spirit. "We would see miracles and healings all the time if only the church really believed what the Bible says. Jesus taught that if we only have faith in him, we would do what he did and even greater things. Why is it so hard to walk in His ways? Why is it so hard to understand that we are as much spiritual beings as we are physical beings? We are part of a spiritual world. We can't see it but it is there. Jesus said, "wherever two or more of us are gathered in His name, He is there in our midst." We don't see him but we believe that he is with us. That's the spiritual world. It really exists and we need to be aware of it and enter into it daily, even moment by moment.

"God is a Spiritual being and he has given us his Spirit to interact with our spirits. We need to learn to interact with God's Spirit more, just as Jesus did. Jesus was human just as we are a physical being as well as a spiritual being. Jesus told us that he only did what he saw his Father doing. He 'saw' what the Father was doing in the spiritual realm with spiritual eyes. We can do the same thing.

In fact, in John 17, Jesus prayed that we would be one with him just as he and the Father are one. Get closer to Jesus. Become one with him so you can 'see' what he is doing just as he 'saw' what his Father was doing. As we become one with him, he places his signature on us, the power of his Holy Spirit."

It had been months since the Perry's last visit. They had been in Zimbabwe for a long time working with churches there. They were supposed to be coming back to Zambia before too long and Ingrid couldn't wait. Since she had become a Christian eight months ago she had learned so much and most of it was through the ministry of the Perry's. She had grown to love and respect them.

One day Ingrid and Susan had been busy with patients all day. It was unusual to have as many patients as they had that day. Usually their afternoons were free. Most days they didn't even open the clinic after lunch, but this particular day there were just too many people to be able to close in the afternoon. That was until Mrs. Moyo came to the clinic.

Mrs. Moyo was a very simple lady. She had no formal education past seventh grade and had lived her whole life in the rural area. She couldn't drive a car, nor could she speak English. That afternoon Mrs. Moyo was walking by the clinic and noticed all of the people waiting to be treated. She decided that she should help if she could. She walked over to the waiting area and saw a man who had been brought to the clinic in a wheelbarrow because he was too weak to even walk. Mrs. Moyo talked to him for a few minutes as Susan and Ingrid looked on. Soon she closed her eyes and started praying. She took her time praying, wanting first to simply find the presence of the Lord. She worshiped Him, sometimes in prayer and at times singing right there in the clinic waiting area. Soon she felt the tangible presence of God. She began to ask the Lord what he wanted to do, interceding for those around her, confident that he would speak through his Holy Spirit. Then she began to pray for those waiting, first this one and then another, skipping this one and moving on to that one, obviously moved by the power of the Holy Spirit. For some, she didn't even actually pray. She only spoke to them telling them to "Be healed in the name of Jesus" and they were.

Ingrid stood watching Mrs. Moyo the whole while as Susan interpreted the highlights of conversations and prayers. They observed that Mrs. Moyo didn't pray for every person in the waiting room, only certain ones. They also noticed that all of those people left after Mrs. Moyo prayed for them. Ingrid and Susan were very happy to be able to close the clinic at around four in the afternoon and as soon as they did they went to see Mrs. Moyo.

Once they were seated comfortably in the shade of a big *Msasa* tree, Ingrid asked, "How were you able to bring healing to all those people like you did?"

Susan acted as interpreter as Mrs. Moyo gave a simple explanation.

"In Mark chapter sixteen it tells me I can heal the sick. So that's what I did," Mrs. Moyo replied with Susan translating. "Actually, it is not me who does anything at all," she continued. "I only listen to what the Holy Spirit tells me to do and then I do it."

Ingrid was so amazed at how God used Mrs. Moyo that day. She learned that God is no respecter of persons. He could and did use anyone who was willing to do whatever he asked.

Still, Ingrid missed Hans. The pain was no longer at the forefront of her mind, but some days still seemed so heavy. He had been such an important part of her life before the accident. It was hard for her to think of raising little Nyasha by herself. She knew that he needed a dad. She wasn't going to be able to be both mom and dad to him. She had read in the Bible that God would be the father to the fatherless, and a husband to the widow, but still how did that apply in a tangible way? At times she still cried herself to sleep. Although prayer and listening to the voice of God had become her source and help in every situation, this was the one area where she found it hard to trust and hear. So she did what a lot of people do; she filled her life with work. Her life consisted of her growing relationship with the Lord, Nyasha, and work, lots of work. She put her whole self into what she was doing.

It was exciting work, because sometimes people were healed after she prayed. One day a man came carrying his child, a boy, with a broken leg. It was a very bad break; the bone was nearly sticking out of the skin and it was going to take a lot to put the bone back in place. In other circumstances, Ingrid would have immediately transported someone with such a severe injury to a hospital in the city. But she had found the hospitals in the city were no better equipped than her clinic and often they were less capably staffed. She had learned that lesson the hard way.

Once, several years ago, when she was first in Zimbabwe, a woman came to the clinic. She was in the early stages of pregnancy and the baby was miscarrying. Ingrid knew the woman would need a DNC, so she sent her on to the hospital in a nearby city. When the woman arrived at the emergency room, the nursing staff questioned her concerning her method of payment. They learned that she had no insurance, common for most people, especially those who lived in the rural areas. Since proper surgery in a sanitized theater was not affordable, the doctor opted to perform the DNC right there in the emergency room with nothing but a curtain separating them from the dozens of sick, infected patients in the waiting area. Immediately after surgery, the woman was discharged from the hospital. She returned home and within a week she died from a uterine infection.

Since Susan was away for the afternoon, Ingrid knew she had to set the bone by herself. She had injured her wrist the evening before and didn't know if she would be able to pull the bone back in place or not. Ingrid knew from experience that parents many times have trouble seeing their children in pain so she asked the father of the boy to go out to the waiting area. Once alone with the boy, she decided the first thing to do was pray.

Bowing their heads together Ingrid prayed quietly but powerfully. The only other sound was the boy's soft whimpering. After praying for some minutes, pressing in to the heart of God, her heart was filled with peace and only then did she make preparations to set the bone trusting that God would intervene somehow.

Once everything was in place she got into position and began the task of setting the bone. Just as she began to pull slightly on the leg, it was if the hand of God took over and set the bones without any effort on her part. The bones began to move as if on their own. She looked at the boy's face and could see in his eyes that he was amazed and a little bit frightened. Soon he put his hands over his eyes. As Ingrid watched even the skin returned to normal and when she re-examined the leg she found the bone was no longer broken. She was amazed at what God had done. When Ingrid and the boy walked side by side into the waiting area, the father began to praise the Lord along with Ingrid.

"Praise God! He has heard my prayer! He has healed my son!" The waiting room was soon filled with the awesome presence of God as the three worshiped the Lord together.

But still Ingrid often felt tired, very tired, overwhelmed with work. She often added to her workload, unconsciously using it to escape her pain.

Susan had noticed that Ingrid was using work as a crutch and decided to confront her.

"Ingrid, you are doing too much."

"No I'm not. I really enjoy doing this work. It fulfills my life."

"I'm glad you like the work, but I can see that you are not getting enough rest. You have bags under your eyes and are sometimes short with the patients."

"Susan, you worry about yourself and let me worry about myself." Ingrid flared up angrily, "You don't know what it's like to lose your husband, you've never even had a husband."

As soon as she spoke the words she wished she hadn't. "I'm sorry Susan, I didn't mean it."

"I know you didn't mean it but that's exactly what I was talking about. I think you need a break. Why don't you go to Lusaka and visit your friend Corrie. I know you get along well with her. Take a week and just spend it with her. The two of you could go shopping and out to restaurants, just go and have a good time. I'll watch Nyasha so you won't even have to worry about him."

Ingrid made a sound like a tire deflating and closed her eyes. "I have been very tired. Nyasha is obeying now but it's just . . . "

"I know, I know. I really do understand. I did have a husband once but he was killed during Zimbabwe's war of independence."

Ingrid looked up in surprise. "What, you had a husband? You never told me that."

"I didn't think it was important at the time. Your loss wasn't about me, it was about you. The Lord has helped me and through prayer I am able to carry on. Time will never take away the memory, but it does deaden the pain."

"Oh Susan, I'm so sorry, I've made this all about me. Are you okay?"

"It was a long time ago. The Lord helped me to get past the initial pain and I know he will help you too. Enough talk about this. I want you to go phone Corrie and make a plan with her. Go, go on now." She said shooing her away.

Ingrid started walking over toward a tree where they could get a cell phone signal and found that it wasn't working. She started walking down the road watching her phone hoping at least one of the towers was working.

After walking down the road and around a corner she got a signal, but it was a different cell phone company than she had. Running back home she rushed into her house and picked up a Sim card that was on her dresser. As she walked back out of the compound she took her battery and old Sim card out of her phone and replaced it with the one she just picked up. She got the battery back in just as she arrived at the place she had received the signal.

"Hello."

"Hello Corrie, it's Ingrid."

"Hi Ingrid, the connection isn't very good."

"I know, I'm walking a little bit to see if I can get a better connection. There, is that better?"

"Yes, that's better. How are you?"

"That's why I'm calling. I need a break and was wondering if I could come and stay with you for a week. Just relax and do some shopping and things like that?"

"That would be great. I've got some vacation time saved up I would have to work a little, but I could probably take off some days."

"Don't take any off yet, wait until I get there so we can make some plans."

"Okay. When are you coming?"

"Is today too early?"

"No that's fine. If you get here before five come to the embassy. Today is our late day so I'll be here."

"It's early yet so I should be able to get there before five. I'll see you then."

"Great, bye."

"Bye."

Ingrid rushed back home and started packing. After loading up her vehicle she went over to where Nyasha was playing and held him in her arms.

"Honey, I'm going to leave for a few days then I'll be back. Aunty Susan will be taking care of you while I'm gone okay?"

"'K, Mommy. See you." He hugged her as quick as he could so he could get back to playing in the dirt with a friend.

She then went over to the clinic where Susan was taking a child's temperature. "I'm all packed up. I'm not sure what we will do, we're going to make plans after I get there."

"That's okay, you take as much time as you need. Have a great time. Don't worry about us we'll be fine." Susan looked up at Ingrid and smiled.

Ingrid could feel the warmth that emanated from the love that Susan had for her. "Thank you again. You are the best friend I have."

After a hug Susan went back to work and Ingrid got in her car and left.

They planned for Ingrid to spend a couple of days in Lusaka with Corrie and then the two would return together to Ingrid's home at the Kafue settlement. Corrie had not been out of the city since arriving in Zambia and she was excited to see the settlement area and the NGO site in Kafue.

When the two ladies worked together in Zimbabwe, they were posted on a compound in the city that was built by the NGO. The houses were all miniature models of houses back home. Even the roads in the compound were laid out just like in a suburb of Amsterdam. Ingrid had explained that the Kafue compound was nothing like that, but still Corrie was anxious to see it. In all her years in Africa, Corrie had never been posted in a rural area. Having been trained in office work as well as nursing, she was better suited for work in the city. So this would be her first real outing to a rural area compound and although she didn't know what to expect, she was excited nonetheless.

Leaving Nyasha in Susan's capable care, Ingrid left for the first day of her holiday. The day was beautiful with perfect weather. Alone in the car with nothing but the sunshine for company, Ingrid turned on her favorite worship CD. After stopping for fuel in the settlement, she was soon flying high with the praises of God in her heart, the breeze from her open window in her hair, and a cold Coke in her hand. Life couldn't get any better than that . . . "Except if I could only share it all with Hans," came Ingrid's uninvited thought.

In Lusaka the two friends spent the next couple of days shopping, eating out, and taking in a movie at the movie theater.

"Tomorrow we'll head out early to return to Kafue, so we better get to bed early."

"I'm so excited Ingrid, I've never done anything like this before. Oh there was the time I went to Victoria Falls in Zimbabwe, but we flew and a limo picked us up. We stayed at a five star hotel and although we saw animals it felt like we were in a zoo."

"You're in for a treat then. The animals in the Kafue Reserve live like they have lived for hundreds of years. We're going to have a great time."

Although they went to bed early anticipation made sleep long in coming for Corrie. She couldn't wait for the next day's adventure.

In spite of the short night, Corrie was up early getting last minute things done. Ingrid got up at a normal hour and they loaded the car and headed out.

Ingrid was anxious as well, but for totally different reasons. Over the months of their growing friendship, Ingrid had prayed often for the chance to speak to Corrie about her relationship with God. There had been opportunity a couple of times for a brief comment concerning her faith, but not any real heart to heart sharing. She sensed that Corrie was not totally closed to the topic, so as they started out, Ingrid prayed for the right moment. After talking for many kilometers about one thing and then another, there finally came a lull in the conversation. Ingrid took the moment and plunged in.

"Corrie, I need to talk to you about something very important to me, is that okay?"

"Sure we have a long trip so we can talk all we want. What's on your mind?"

"Well, I'm not sure how to start; I've never done anything like this. You know that I have become a Christian. God is so important in my life now. I want you to know the joy I have in Jesus."

"Whoa, girl, I know your new found faith is exciting for you, but I really am not interested in religion right now."

"I'm not talking about religion. Lynn Perry told me that what we have is not religion, but a relationship with the Lord. This isn't making any sense is it? I'm really messing this up."

"I don't know if you're messing things up or not, but let's change the subject. I really don't want to talk about this right now."

"Okay, what do you want to talk about?" Ingrid was kicking herself for messing up her opportunity to talk to Corrie about Jesus. Silently she sent up another prayer, "Lord, I'm sorry, I really didn't do that very well. Please give me another chance."

"I want to talk about seeing some animals. How long before we get to the Kafue Reserve?"

"It's not far," Ingrid replied, "In fact there's a nice place in the reserve where we can get out of the car and have our lunch. How does that sound to you?"

"I don't know. Is it safe? I want to view the lions, not get eaten by them."

"No, it's perfectly safe. The area is fenced in on three sides with the Kafue River on the fourth side. There are some thatched roof shelters with tables that face the river where we can have our picnic. Hopefully, we'll see some game on the other side of the river. This place is a favorite watering spot this time of year. We might see hippos or elephants in the water. That would be fun. The elephants are so fun to watch in the water."

"That sounds great! Let's do it."

A few kilometers up the road Ingrid took the turn off to the reserve entrance and soon they were at the gate. The entrance fee was one thousand Kwacha, less than one U.S. dollar per person.

"So, Learnmore, where's a good place to find game today?" Ingrid inquired of the guard after reading his name badge. She never ceased to be amazed at the creative names the African people gave their children.

"Well, I think if you stay on the main road you won't find many animals. It is better to take one of the dirt roads. Take the second road on the left. That road takes you near the water holes and usually there are animals there. No promises, but hopefully you will see some game. The road winds around a bit but eventually loops back to the main road. It's a little bumpy in places but with the Land Rover you won't have any trouble getting through."

Ingrid thanked the man and they started out on their "African Safari," the grand title that their road trip had now been dubbed. Corrie dug her camera out of her bag ready to get some good pictures.

It was several kilometers before they came to the second road on the left. Making the turn off the blacktopped road onto the dirt road, they determined that Learnmore's description of the dirt road had been seriously misleading. The road wasn't a little bumpy; it was a washboard!

"It's a good thing we have four wheel drive!" Ingrid yelled over the rattling of the Land Rover.

They rounded a corner and there, right in the road was a huge giraffe. It was such a beautiful sight. Ingrid stopped the vehicle and Corrie quietly leaned out the window in order to get a good shot of the magnificent creature. As they were watching the giraffe, out from the bush came three more giraffe, two more adults and one young giraffe. Corrie was beside herself with joy and took more than enough pictures.

After some time, they drove on down the road and came to one of the water holes. Spotting a viewing hide up on a platform, Ingrid maneuvered the vehicle as close as she could possibly get. Cautiously the ladies got out of the car and climbed up the steps. The view was magnificent with plenty of game at the water hole. They identified most of the different species and Corrie wrote each one in a small notebook. There were impala, kudu, sable, and a few of the smaller antelope which they didn't know all the names of. While they were watching and taking pictures, a crocodile suddenly appeared aiming to have one of the smaller impala for lunch. He wasn't successful though, much to Corrie's relief.

"Okay, I'm ready to move on. I don't particularly want to see that much of the wild."

They continued on down the road and saw a number of other animals; wildebeest, monkeys, baboons and zebra. Corrie was having the time of her life.

"Now this is what Africa is supposed to be like," Corrie exclaimed, "animals roaming around like they have for centuries."

Just when Corrie thought the adventure could get no more exciting, the most magnificent sight she had ever seen came into view. Right in front of them was a lion, a great, big male lion. His mane was dark brown, almost black. He was just walking down the middle of the road as if he were out for a morning stroll. Corrie began taking pictures as fast as she could, this time through the front window instead of the side, having rolled the window up the minute they spotted the lion. Winding her window up as well, Ingrid drove slowly, creeping closer and closer to the lion. By this time he had moved to the side of the road and seemed to take no notice of them at all. Drawing nearly parallel with the lion, they realized how immense he was. The Land Rover was a fairly large vehicle so the seats were pretty far off the ground. Nevertheless, the lion stood level with their door able to look them straight in the eye. They continued down the road together side by side, until the lion suddenly decided he didn't like them so near. He stopped, looked over at the vehicle and gave a loud roar. Then he took off into the bush.

"That was so amazing! Have you ever been this close to a lion before?" Corrie asked breathlessly.

"No! And he was huge. Did you see how big he was?"

"You know, I love cats, but that one really made me respect who he was. I never knew that a lion could be so big, and he was so regal. He just walked right beside us like he owned the road. I'm glad I got pictures of it all. I don't think anyone would believe me if I just told them about this. Ingrid, thank you so much for taking the time and going through the reserve for me."

"Just wait, we're almost to the area for our picnic. Hopefully we'll see elephants."

"Ingrid, you are so good to me. I will cherish this day forever."

In five minutes they arrived at the enclosed area. The ground sloped upwards from the river to the shelters, allowing a good view of the other side of the river with a short wall just a few meters from the water's edge on their side. The remaining three sides of the enclosure were surrounded by a high fence except for the entrance from the road, which was closed by only a boom. A man approached them from a booth beside the entrance and lifted the boom.

"I wonder what that chap would do if one of those big lions came up the road to the entrance." Corrie said as they drove on into the enclosure.

"He'd probably close the door to the shelter and hide. That boom wouldn't keep very many animals out though would it?"

Both girls looked at each other wondering, but neither said what they were thinking.

Looking around first to make sure there were no animals near them they got out of the car happy to stretch their aching limbs. Even though they had their windows open, except when the lion was near them, traveling so slowly over ruts and bumps didn't allow much air to come in. The breeze off the river felt nice. Opening the back hatch they retrieved the food basket and cooler carrying them toward the thatched roof umbrellas, shading picnic tables beneath them. They were the only ones there so they got their choice of which table they wanted. They chose the one closest to the water. Ingrid put a tablecloth on the table and started getting the food out while Corrie walked around to see what there was to see.

"Ingrid, look, there are elephants!" Corrie called excitedly.

"Yes Corrie, but don't be too noisy or they will leave. They have those big ears and they can hear very well."

In a loud whisper Corrie said, "Oh, okay, I'll be quiet."

Returning to the table, she sat down. The food was ready to be served but Ingrid hesitated a moment.

"Would you mind if I prayed over the meal first?"

"No, not at all," Corrie replied with raised eyebrows.

Ingrid prayed a short prayer thanking the Lord for the food and the beautiful day as well as all the animals they had seen and then they dished up the simple lunch.

As they ate, they watched the elephants. There must have been fifty elephants in the herd. There were some little ones that were the most fun to watch. They would run into the river, splash around and then run back out. The older elephants were more sedate and seemingly "dignified." They would amble slowly into the water, lie down for a while, spray water on themselves and then get up and walk out. They made for very good entertainment while eating lunch.

"I would really like to see rhino in the wild. Do you think we will see any?"

"They're harder to find but I'll go ask the man at the booth if there are any around."

Ingrid approached the man and asked about rhino.

"Oh, sorry madam, but the rhino are very hard to find. They usually hide deep in the interior because of poachers. They are seen only rarely." Ingrid thanked the man anyway and returned to Corrie.

"Sorry Corrie, the man said they usually hide in the interior part of the park." Ingrid relayed the whole conversation.

"I really wanted to see at least one rhino in the wild before I left Africa," Corrie replied with a pout.

Ingrid had an idea. "I'll tell you what, let me pray and ask God to make this happen for us. He knows where they are and I'm sure if we ask He will move them into our path."

"If you pray and we get to see rhino, then I'll listen to you a little closer about this God thing you're into."

Ingrid bowed her head right then and prayed, "Lord, Corrie would love to see a rhino. Could you make it possible for her to see one in the wild? In fact could you let us see a family of rhino, a male, female, and a little one? Thank you, Lord, for listening to my prayer."

"Is that it? Shouldn't you have a lot more to say? I mean, it's been a long time since I went to church, but I remember the priest going on and on in his prayer. It was a sermon in itself."

"No, I don't have to make a big flowery speech. God just wants me to talk to Him and I have been amazed at how many times He has answered my prayers. Let's head out and maybe God will allow you to see some rhino."

They drove out of the enclosed area and started down the dirt road. It soon ended turning back onto the main road, the same road that Learnmore had told them held little hope of viewing any game. Ingrid thought maybe she should take one of the dirt roads and go around the back way again in hopes of seeing rhino. But it was getting late in the day and she didn't like driving at night, so she chose to stay on the blacktopped road. They had a nice drive and were not far from the exit when over to their right they spotted three rhino; a male, a female, and a young one.

"Look, look! There they are just like you prayed." Corrie was so excited, she had her camera up taking pictures as fast as she could. "I can't believe it. There are three just like you prayed. How did you do that?"

Ingrid replied, "It wasn't me, it was God. He enjoys making us happy."

They pulled over to the side of the road and watched the rhino. They were busy wallowing in a mud hole when the vehicle approached. Ingrid knew to leave a good distance between them, but even so the male positioned himself between the car and the mud hole acting as the strong protector of his family. Corrie got a lot of pictures of the rhino and was very quiet the whole time they watched them. After a short time the male let down his guard a bit and moved to the side so the female and the young one were plainly visible, allowing Corrie to get photos of all three together.

"This is just amazing, Ingrid," Corrie whispered. "All you did was say a very simple prayer and, *viola*! Here are the rhino. Maybe there is something to this God of yours. Maybe we need to talk again."

The remainder of the trip was spent talking about Jesus. Ingrid shared scriptures that she knew by heart, relating much that she had learned. Soon she began to describe the crucifixion of Jesus and why He endured such agony, laying down his life, all for our sake.

"I didn't know, I didn't know," Corrie said shaking her head.

Ingrid was quiet for a few moments and soon Corrie continued, struggling to get past the lump in her throat. "I went to church most of my childhood, even at Easter time, but I never heard this story. I never heard of what Jesus did for me."

Ingrid finished by telling her the plan of salvation and then she asked, "Corrie, are you ready to give your life to Jesus?"

With tears in her eyes Corrie said, "Yes, oh yes!"

Ingrid pulled the car over to the side of the road and together they prayed. Corrie tearfully confessed that she was a sinner, asking forgiveness and declaring Jesus as her Lord and Savior. Ingrid prayed for her and asked for the filling of the Holy Spirit to come upon her dear friend. When they had finished the two friends embraced one another, both of them crying and laughing at the same time.

Dusk was upon them as they were nearing the Kafue settlement and the settling darkness made it harder to see the road ahead. Suddenly, as they rounded a curve in the road, a huge bull elephant stood right in the middle of their lane. Ingrid swerved quickly to avoid hitting it, slamming on the brakes at the same time. The car skidded onto the gravel shoulder and finally came to a stop a few feet off the road. Once her heart slowed a bit, Ingrid looked out the window, shining her flashlight all around to assess where they were and what to do. Panic seized her heart when she found that they were perched right on the edge of a ledge with a ten–meter drop to the bottom. Corrie took the flashlight to determine how things were on her side of the car, the side closest to the drop off. When she turned her face to Ingrid again it was ashen.

"What? What is it?" Ingrid asked through the knot in her throat.

"Our rear tire is right on the edge, half on solid ground, half over the edge. I don't know how we are going to get back onto the road without plunging to the bottom."

Grasping hands, the two ladies again approached the throne of heaven. After several minutes of prayer, Ingrid decided to try to ease back onto the road, trusting that the four-wheel drive would see them to safety. At first it appeared to be working, but then the back tire seemed to slip and for an instant it seemed that they would go over the edge. Ingrid called out "Jesus" at the top of her voice and in a split second they found themselves righted again and soon back on the road.

Shaking from head to foot, Ingrid pulled the car over a few meters down the road where the terrain had leveled out and there was plenty of space to park the car off the road. The two found themselves praying again, this time with much thanksgiving, shouts of praise, and even laughter. As they prayed, an amazing peace and presence of the Lord came upon Ingrid and she became quiet, taking it all in. In that stillness, she heard the voice of the Lord speaking to her heart and knew his tangible presence. In an instant she recognized a lie of the enemy that had held her heart captive for many months now. All these months of missing her husband, the pain and the loneliness, she was convinced that God couldn't really, tangibly be a "husband" to her and a "father" to her fatherless child. But there, perched on that drop off, with no-one else to call upon, she had called out to God and he was there, tangibly, caring for her in a way that Hans would never have been able to do. Ingrid remembered that split second when it seemed as though the car would plunge over the edge, when she called out to Jesus it was as if a mighty hand nudged the tire back onto solid ground. Tears flowed, tears of healing and release.

That night in her bed, Ingrid again remembered the near tragedy and the Lord's amazing intervention. With tears of repentance for not learning to trust the Lord sooner, Ingrid laid it all down. The months of pain and loneliness, all the worry, especially concerning her fatherless child. Again the tangible presence of God flooded her heart and Ingrid knew she would never be lonely again.

Corrie's new found faith changed her. Before, she was a very shy woman, but now she wanted to talk to everyone who would listen to her about Jesus. The first two weeks of her visit in Kafue passed quickly for Corrie as she kept herself busy helping in the clinic and with whatever else she could find to do.

Her favorite thing was spending time with little Nyasha. She was amazed at what a well–behaved little boy he was and her heart always melt-ed when she heard his little voice calling, "Aunty Corrdeeeea." When Ingrid told her stories of how he used to behave she couldn't believe it was the same little boy and agreed with Ingrid that God must have worked a miracle.

She loved Ingrid's "house." It consisted of three round mud houses with thatched roofing in a fenced in area, similar to all the neighboring houses. One of the rondovals was the bedroom, one was the kitchen, and the third was the "sitting room."

The kitchen impressed Corrie the most. The walls were lined with shelves and cubbyholes formed from the same mud mixture that the walls were made of. Those shelves and cubby holes held Ingrid's dishes and sup-plies all arranged attractively as though on display in a department store. The floor sloped to the center of the room and right in the very middle was a large, round, dish–like pit for the cooking fire. The grass "ceiling" in the kitchen was blackened from smoke. This was the winter kitchen. In the summer Ingrid cooked outside under an open thatched shelter. Corrie was most curious about the floor in each of the rondovals. It looked like concrete, but wasn't smooth like a concrete floor would be.

One night while they were lying in bed she asked, "Ingrid what are the floors made of?"

"It's a mixture of anthill dirt and cow dung. Once it dries it becomes very hard, almost as hard as cement."

"Eww! You're kidding aren't you? Dirt and cow poop?"

"No, that's really what the floors and walls are made of. I have found though that in the summer a certain bug is in season and they like to make their homes in the flooring. They dig holes in it and live there. If you put something on top of their holes they will continue to dig around until they get out. Before I bought my bed I slept on an air mattress on the floor. I didn't know it, but I had put the mattress on one of the holes. Before I went to sleep I kept hearing a scratching noise. I turned on my flashlight and looked, but I couldn't find anything. I finally fell asleep until about one in the morning. The bug had scratched a hole in my mattress and I was lying on the hard floor. It was a very long night. I have since learned not to put things over their holes."

"Ha, ha, oh Ingrid that is priceless."

"Yes, but these bugs cause me more work. I have to repair the floors once a year. I go out and collect the material, mix it with water and plug the holes. Usually during the day the bugs have gone out. If any are still there they dig until they get out and then I have to do the job again." Shrugging her shoulders she continued, "It's not too bad. There's no smell of the cow dung once it dries and it makes a very nice floor."

"Well, that's really more information than I wanted. I didn't know I was sleeping on manure. But you're right; it doesn't smell at all." Corrie looked thoughtful for a second and said, "Not to change the subject, but I remember you telling me about people who have been healed when you prayed for them at the clinic. I've been here two weeks and haven't seen one healing. What's up with that?"

"I really don't know, I've been wondering about that myself. I've prayed for lots of people this week, but no one has been healed." Ingrid stretched and gave a big yawn, "Mr. Perry says that we are told to pray for people and it's up to God to heal them. All I know to do is to keep praying. Maybe tomorrow something will happen. Good night Corrie, have a nice night's sleep."

"You too Ingrid, sleep well."

The next morning it was business as usual in the clinic; a headache here, and a stomach ache there. There were just a few people, and no real serious cases. Susan and Ingrid were talking about closing early and taking a nice long walk when a young boy came running in. He was very excited and speaking very fast in Venda.

"Slow down a little. Do you speak English?" Susan asked.

The boy took a big breath and said between gasps, "My father is hurt. It's very bad. Can you come and see him? Please, come quickly."

The ladies looked at each other and nodded in agreement. Ingrid left instructions with the clinic assistant to care for Nyasha and then grabbed her medical bags. They decided to take the car because they didn't know how far this boy had come. Ingrid told the boy to sit in the front in order to give directions and Susan piled into the back seat beside Corrie.

The boy's home turned out to be in a nearby village. When they arrived, they found a crowd of people standing under a big shade tree. The boy pushed his way in leading the ladies. When they got to the boy's father they saw what everyone was looking at. The man had evidently been chopping wood, somehow missed the log and struck his foot with the axe. The sharp axe was imbedded into the top of his foot and ankle. There was blood everywhere and you could see the man was in serious pain. Ingrid could tell from his eyes and the fluttering of his pulse that they needed to act fast. A moment of panic seized her heart.

This was one of those times when a speedy ambulance on city streets could mean the difference between saving a limb or even a life and the alternative. But they were far from the city and the nearest thing to an ambulance was her rattley old Land Rover. As Ingrid looked around at the circle of people standing there, she saw fear in each face.

No one had tried to help in any way. Ingrid had seen this reaction before. So often when tragedy struck, fear of the spirits would totally immobilize people. It was believed that if one became involved or tried to help then they could very possibly be the next victim. This way of thinking was very prevalent, especially in the rural areas where animism was so common. Ingrid and Susan got down beside the man to examine the wound and see what they could do. When Ingrid looked up into Susan's eyes she saw faith there and as quickly as it had come, the panic disappeared and faith rose in her own heart.

"Let's pray. Corrie come on over here and pray with us." Susan and Corrie both laid their hands on the man's leg and started praying. As they prayed Ingrid got a towel and started cleaning the wound. There was so much blood! Ingrid knew that when the axe was removed the bleeding would probably increase. It would be better if they were in a clinical setting, but they were far from that and time was of the essence.

Placing towels under the leg, Ingrid made ready to remove the axe. Closing her eyes for one more quick prayer, she then placed her hands on each side of the axe blade and began to pull. Suddenly, Ingrid was enveloped with the power and the presence of the Lord and it was as though another pair of hands were there on top of her own, easing the axe from the man's leg as easily as a knife from butter.

"Oh, dear Lord!" Ingrid gasped!

Susan and Corrie knelt praying with their eyes open and soon gasped with astonishment as well. Right before their eyes, the wound closed up and the skin came together. The only indication that there had ever been a problem was the blood on the ground and on the towel.

For just one moment there was total silence as people watched in amazement. Then the atmosphere turned to a bedlam of activity. Some women began to scream while others fell to their knees and began to pray. Many just stood there motionless. The man, whose leg was now whole, only sat there in amazement. His eyes were clear and strength was visibly returning to his body.

Ingrid was standing by now just observing all that was taking place around her. Once again she felt the power of the Lord all around and sensed that he was not finished. She began to intercede, one moment in English and the next in a heavenly language not her own. Then an old woman started screaming, but this time it was a scream of joy. The cane she had come walking with supporting her bent body was now raised above her head as she slowly stood erect. Soon she was jumping for joy, straight, and tall.

Nearby another lady began to weep as she removed her child from the sling on her back. Susan learned later that the mother had been on the way to the clinic with her sick child when she came upon the accident under the tree. The little one had been burning with fever and the only sound coming from his mouth was a raspy, wheezing sound. Now the bright eyed baby was laughing and chattering in his mother's arms.

Next a man began shouting. Looking his direction, Ingrid noticed that he had his hand to his face over his eye. The man kept shouting the same thing over and over again in his own language. Ingrid saw amazement on the faces of those around her and was very curious to know what he was saying.

"What's going on?" Corrie asked Susan before Ingrid had a chance to voice it herself.

"He is saying, 'My eye, my eye.'"

Not understanding the situation any better herself, Susan began to quiz those around her. Ingrid and Corrie watched the excited chatter going on all around them. Their curiosity got the best of them when Susan became as animated and excited as all the others.

"What is going on!?!" the two ladies repeated together as if on cue.

"The man had no eye! He said he felt something happening, like movement in the empty socket, so he put his hand to his face and felt an eye. When he removed his hand he could see clearly! He has a perfect eye where the empty socket used to be!"

The crowd soon became quiet, huddled together under the shade tree, but no one made a move to leave. Amazement and curiosity held them where they stood. They knew the nurses had prayed for the man with the axe wound and that's what started it all. Soon the group began questioning the three ladies.

"How did you do this?"

"Are you witchdoctors?"

"Do you have special powers?"

The questions began slowly at first but soon the ladies were being peppered with them as the crowd pressed in closer and closer. Susan was the first one to speak.

"Greetings to all of you. No, we are not witchdoctors, nor do we have special powers. What you saw is from God the Father and our Lord Jesus Christ. All we did was pray that God would heal this man and it seemed that He wanted to do something more than just heal one person. May we share with you what the Bible says?"

The villagers all agreed that they should talk to them about what had happened. The old man with the new eye spoke up.

"We need to send for the chief and the head men. They must hear also," he said first in Venda and then in English.

A young boy was sent to bring the village leaders. While they waited, the lady of the house made tea and the ladies sat together with several of the village people sipping their tea and making polite conversation. They understood that to speak of anything of importance before the leaders were assembled would be uncustomary, even rude.

Just over an hour, after they sent the boy he was back with the chief and several other men all walking together with their canes in hand. Although the men were all older, the canes were not for assistance in walking, but rather they were ceremonial canes signifying the importance and prestige of each of those carrying them. Everyone greeted the chief and his men properly and after the leaders took their seats then the whole assembly sat down as well.

"Now what is this young boy babbling about?" the chief began the questioning. "He says that Chikwanda's foot had been cut and then right in front of his eyes the wound closed up. And what is he saying about Sibanda's eye?" The conversation went back and forth between Venda and English for the benefit of the two English–speaking ladies.

Sibanda got up and walked over to the chief. Bending, he looked the chief right in the eye. "My eye has grown back! Look!" The chief and his men were startled at the sight of it. The chief had seen a glass eye before and wondered if that was what he was now seeing.

"Sibanda, put your hand over your good eye."

Sibanda complied. Holding up three fingers in front of his face the chief asked, "How many fingers am I holding up?"

"Three," Sibanda replied with a huge smile.

The other men started holding up objects for him to see and he identified every one of them. The chief and his men were baffled. They had known Sibanda from his youth when he had lost his eye in an accident. They gathered that the three strangers in their midst had something to do with the situation, so it was to them that they turned for answers.

"Please tell us what has happened here." The chief addressed his comment to Susan. Susan again told what had happened and asked if they could share a little more about Jesus.

The chief had never seen such power before. He had seen the witch-doctors do a lot of things, but never had he seen them restore an eye. He had been to church as a child and occasionally as an adult, but he had never seen any power in his church. He was eager to hear what Susan had to say.

"Please tell us about this Jesus of yours."

Beginning with the life, death, and resurrection of Jesus, Susan presented the gospel message. As she spoke, Ingrid was aware again of the supernatural, tangible presence of God. Looking over at Corrie, she could see on her face that Corrie, too, felt His touch. Tears were streaming down her cheeks as she lifted her face toward the heavens.

Everyone listened very quietly and when Susan finished she asked, "Do any of you want to serve Jesus and become a Christian?" All eyes looked to the chief. Standing to his feet he replied, "We have heard what this lady had to say. We have seen ourselves the power of their God and His Son, Jesus Christ. We all need to accept Him and become Christians."

Like one huge wave, the entire group were on their feet cheering, pleased that the chief had agreed. That day one hundred thirty-seven people came to know the Lord and were baptized in the old water tank by the school. Susan and Ingrid did all the baptizing. Corrie had not been baptized yet, so she too joined the others.

"We would like to have more teaching about this God and His Son," the chief commented at the close of the baptisms. The ladies agreed to return.

"We will also bring our pastor. He knows so much more than we do and will be able to help you with your questions." The chief was pleased with the idea and smiled his agreement. Plans were made to meet on Thursday afternoon.

Rising to his feet, the chief got up, walked over to Susan and Ingrid and hugged them. His men followed suit. The ladies were very surprised at the gesture so uncommon in the Venda culture. Ingrid prayed once more and then they all went to their homes.

"Wow! That was awesome," Corrie said once they were in the car heading home. "Does this happen every time you go some place to help people?"

"No, this is the first time I have ever seen this happen since I have lived here. Susan, have you ever seen anything like this before?"

"No, I've never seen anything like this happen before. I was so scared speaking to all those people. I'm not a preacher. In fact I've never shared any of that before. I guess they understood what I said. It looks like we helped start a new church. I hope Pastor Sayila doesn't mind."

They all laughed together remembering the pastor's last visit.

"I need help," he had confessed openly to the ladies. "The churches are growing so fast. I just can't keep up with it all." They all agreed it was a good problem to have, but a problem nonetheless. A prayer time had followed as they asked the Lord to raise up workers and Pastor Sayila had left, challenged and prepared to do some training with those the Lord had laid on his heart. The women knew he would be challenged again when they told him of the day's events.

Corrie was the most excited and talkative on the return trip. She had hoped to see miracles and boy, did she see some miracles. This had been a day she would never forget. Although the miracles were amazing, Corrie shared that she was most touched by what had happened to her.

"It was as though the very hand of God touched me, changing me. I feel so free. This holiday has turned out to be more than I ever dreamed of."

The rest of the trip home, the three women sang their praises to God, first in English, then in Venda and then as only the Spirit can give utterance.

13

Resolution

CHIPO WAS BEGINNING TO understand the Biblical saying "heavy with child." Her stomach was so large she couldn't even see her toes. Every move was a labor and her walk was more like a waddle. She didn't remember being this big with her first pregnancy. She was due any day now and the issue that pressed most on her mind and stirred her heart was finding the couple that had adopted her "little Ethan." The closer the time came for her baby to be born, the more she was sure the best thing for this baby was to be in the same home as his older brother.

Chipo kept these feelings to herself most of the time because the idea of adoption was so foreign to her culture. She knew everyone would do all they could to persuade her otherwise. Although she had expressed her wishes to her grandparents and they had initially agreed, as the time drew nearer their resolve grew thin.

The only other person she had tried speaking with was her father. She hoped to persuade him to tell her who he had given "little Ethan" to, but when she found him alone in his house he acted like she wasn't even there. He walked right by her without saying a word or even acknowledging her presence. Chipo was hurt and realized anew how deep her father's bitterness toward her ran.

Her two brothers had also left home and were now living at their grandparent's in order to be close to Chipo. Simon Sibanda was angry when his sons left. Although they didn't have much contact with him at least their father would talk to the boys when he saw them. He wouldn't even look at his daughter. Chipo decided she would have to try another avenue in order to find the adoptive family.

That evening she approached her grandfather, "Grandfather, are you busy?"

"Sit down child," laying aside his Bible he'd been reading, he moved some papers off the couch for her to sit. "I'm never too busy to talk to my granddaughter. What can I do for you?"

Looking down at the cement floor she wasn't sure how to begin, but then just spoke. "You know that my father gave my first baby to a family that was working in the area drilling boreholes?" It was a question, but she knew that he knew all about it. Looking up she saw him nodding in agreement. "Um . . . well ummm." Again she was at a loss for words so she just blurted out, "I want to find them so I can give them this baby too."

"But Chipo," Alex began his argument, "this time your grandmother and I are here. We will help with the baby."

"Grandfather, I can't keep this child. Even with your help, I know that life will be very hard for a child with no father." She had seen other single African mothers and their children shunned by the community as being wrong or dirty, always made to feel "unwelcome" wherever they went. The children often suffered the most, becoming the brunt of every cruel joke at school, outcasts, targeted by not only their peers but also the teachers.

"Besides," Chipo continued, "no African man would want a woman with a child, so my hope of ever marrying would be next to nothing if I choose to raise this baby." As Chipo gently explained all this to her grandfather, she saw the light of understanding dawning in his eyes.

Alex spoke up after a thoughtful silence. "I know who has your first child," he said with his head hanging down as though the memory was as real and heavy as the day it happened. "That day when you came to us angry and out of sorts, I went to your father and talked to him. He told me where he had taken the baby. My plan was to go to them and get the child back. But . . . the next day you were gone. I didn't know what to do, so I just left it. I had heard people speak about the couple that took your baby and I knew he was in a good home. So, like I said, . . . I . . . just left it."

Alex raised his head and met Chipo's eyes as he continued. "I was more worried about you at the time. You had left and we didn't know where you had gone or when you would come back."

Sighing deeply, Alex carried on, "Some months later I told your grandmother who had the baby and she went to see how he was, how they were treating him. When she arrived at their home she saw the three of them sitting on a blanket in their yard, playing. The husband was holding the baby up in the air and the baby was chattering and laughing. It was in your grandmother's heart that day to somehow get her grandson back. But as she watched them, the Lord gave her peace and confidence that the baby was right where he should be. So we have left everything as it has been."

"So, grandfather, who has the baby? I need to know. I must talk to them and see if they will take this baby too."

"I'm not so sure that's a good idea. It would probably be better if you didn't see your other child. If you saw him you might not want to leave him."

Chipo thought about this and agreeing said, "Yes, you're probably right. So how can we get the baby to them?"

"Tomorrow the Perry's are coming. They are staying for a little while and then they are leaving to go to Zambia. You are due to have the baby while they are here. Once you've had the baby we need to get it to someone who can take care of him temporarily until the Perry's leave. I know how strong mother instincts can be and if you have the baby near you, you will want to keep him. On their way to Zambia the Perry's will pass by the area where the couple lives," Alex said being careful not to reveal the name Grundey. "We will ask them to drop the baby off." Alex was quiet again, as if thinking things through. "The only problem would be if they didn't want another baby. We'll talk to the Perry's when they arrive and see what they think."

Chipo's grandmother wasn't as easy to convince as her grandfather had been, but after a bit of talking and explaining, Mary finally understood what her granddaughter needed to do and why she needed to do it. Even still, letting go was a difficult thing. Mary loved children, especially her own grandchildren. Now, here she was, expecting her second great grandchild and she wasn't going to get the joy of holding either of them or watching them grow.

The next day the Perry's arrived in the afternoon. As always when they first arrived in *Silobela*, the first several minutes were spent just greeting all those who were there to welcome them. They were surprised at how big Chipo was and the usual jokes were made about her swallowing a pumpkin or watermelon. After all the greetings were made and hands were shaken, they sat down in the shade of a tree to visit and enjoy a cup of tea. They chatted about their travels and the continued violence in the country.

Finishing their tea, Alex quietly told Rob he needed to talk to the two of them privately. Since the afternoon was a pleasant one, not too hot and not too cold, they decided to take a walk. Lynn quickly ran to change into a pair of walking shoes. The sandy terrain made walking a chore if you wore the wrong shoes. Lynn had found that out the hard way long ago and always came prepared with a pair of simple canvas shoes, none too dressy but very practical.

"As you can see, Chipo is close to having her baby," Alex began once they were on the road.

"Well, you sure couldn't miss that. She looks like she about ready to explode," Lynn commented with a chuckle.

"She wants to give the child up for adoption," Alex said not wasting any time.

Rob was surprised. He knew the culture and the taboo about adoption so he never imagined Alex taking his granddaughter's idea seriously. "Well that's not a bad idea," Rob replied thoughtfully. "She's still very young and it would be very hard for her to find a husband if she already has children."

"Yes, that's what we have discussed. You remember she had another child and her father gave it away."

"I remember. I thought it was very cruel of her father to do that. Didn't he also tell everyone that she and the baby had both died in childbirth? What is he saying now?"

"He says this isn't Chipo. He claims that another girl is pretending to be Chipo." Seeing the amazed expression on both Rob and Lynn's faces he continued. "I know it seems like such an incredible story, but that's what he is claiming. Nobody believes it though. Everyone knows Chipo . . . is really Chipo. There was always something about her people were drawn to. That hasn't changed. She still draws people to herself, especially the children. They all love her." Alex hesitated a little before continuing on. "She wants to give the child to the same couple who have her first child. Then at least the two children could grow up as brothers."

"Oh, so we think this baby is a boy, is it?" Rob was all smiles.

"The doctor at the clinic is fairly certain it's a boy," Alex replied, all smiles himself. Quickly the smile faded and he continued with his plea. "We don't know if this couple will want another child or not, but I feel we need to try for Chipo's sake."

"You should try as much as you can to find a good family for this baby, for Chipo's sake as well," Lynn responded. "It probably would be good if the children could grow up together as siblings. Do you know who has the older child? Do you know how to get in touch with them?"

"Yes, I do. They stay in a village up by the Zambezi River."

"Well then maybe you need to talk to them and see if they want the second child."

"That's a good idea, but they are quite a ways from here. Chipo is due any day and once she has the baby we need to get it away from her as soon as we can, which will hurt more than anything. But if we don't remove the baby as soon as possible, she will grow attached to him and then she will never give him up. I know she really loves this child and she wants what's best for him." Alex stopped walking and turned to face the couple beside him. "I am wondering if you could help."

Rob was a little hesitant at this. "What is it that you need our help with?"

"When Chipo has the baby, we have decided my sister, Alice, will care for him until you leave. When you leave we want you to take the baby and Alice with you. The village where the couple stay is on the way . . . well, sort of on the way to your next stop in Zambia. You will be able to meet them and speak to them about taking the baby. If they won't, Alice will take the bus back here with the baby and we will figure out something else to do. What do you think?"

Rob and Lynn looked at each other. Lynn spoke first, "Is this okay with Chipo? We don't want her to get all worked up and take off like last time. If she did that you may never see her again."

"Yes, yes, this is Chipo's idea. Well at least finding her other baby's adopted parents is her idea."

"We are first going to another village for two days before heading on to Zambia. Will that be okay?"

"I'm sure it won't be a problem at all. Alice will be there to take care of the baby so all you would have to do is drive them."

Rob and Lynn looked at each other again. Lynn could see in her husband's eyes that tender hearted look so she knew she was right in responding. "Okay, we can take the baby with us, just as long as it's okay with Chipo."

"You can talk to her later and she will tell you its okay."

"Who are the couple we need to get the baby to and where are they?"

"It's a couple that works with the Netherlands NGO over on the Zambezi River. He's a real big guy and she's a small lady. Their last name is Grundey."

Rob and Lynn stopped in their tracks and both uttered a sound of exclamation.

"Oh, it can't be."

"But then look at their child. He is dark."

"But I thought that he was dark because her husband was dark." Both Rob and Lynn spoke these things to each other, but neither one was really listening to what the other was saying as the comments rolled off their tongues in shock and awe. Alex didn't understand at all what was happening.

"Alex, we know this lady," Rob finally explained. "We have met her and her child. They no longer live in Zimbabwe, but are in Zambia. We've been trying to piece together what happened to them. All we can figure is that there was some kind of explosion on the road and it threw their car in the river. They, the husband and wife, each thought the other had drowned. Ingrid, that's the wife, ended up on the other side of the river in Zambia. Because of her loss, well, her assumed loss, she didn't want to come back to Zimbabwe at the time. So she got a job in Zambia with the NGO and is working there. We were able to help lead her to the Lord."

"Well, that's great! She's a Christian! That will make Chipo even happier. But you said the husband and wife thought each other dead. What's happening to them now?"

"We don't know," Lynn continued with the story. "She asked us to get some of her things from their old house, so we stopped by on our way back into Zimbabwe. We were told the house had burned down and the husband had run out screaming. He is now fighting with the mercenaries against the rebels. He is the one they call *Chipoko*."

At hearing the familiar name, it was Alex's turn to be shocked.

"Yeah, we were shocked at that one too," Rob continued. "When we were sure about the information, we wrote her a letter but have never heard back from her. We don't know if they have found each other, or what is happening with them."

"This causes a problem. We can't keep the baby here or Chipo will not let it go when we have found the family. You can't take the baby into Zambia with you. He won't have a passport or visa. What can we do?"

Lynn spoke up again. "Let me make a suggestion. We'll go ahead and take the baby and your sister. We will go to the village where the NGO station is first since it's not too far from the border. Your sister will have to stay there with the baby while we go on to Zambia. We know a family she can stay with. When we get to Zambia, if Ingrid is still there, hopefully with her husband by now, we can talk to them about the baby and see if they will take him. If they want the baby, we'll send them on to get it. If they don't, then we'll get word to your sister and she can come back here with the baby. How does that sound?"

"That sounds alright to me." Alex assured her, "I'm sure Alice won't mind staying in the village for a little while. The only thing that can go wrong would be if they don't want the baby. But we'll never know if we don't try. My heart is at peace with the plan. How do you feel?"

"Excited!" was Rob's response to Alex's question.

Rob and Lynn gave each other that knowing look again. In their hearts they were sure it was no coincidence that their friend Ingrid was the very one they were looking for. Neither of them was sure what lay ahead, but they were confident God had bigger things in store for everyone involved than what was apparent. Excitement filled their hearts, anticipating the things to come.

So plans were made. Three days later as if on cue, Chipo had her baby. It was a girl, much to everyone's surprise. Chipo would have named her Precious, but her grandmother wouldn't allow her to do that. She knew Chipo had to live her life without knowing this baby and giving the baby a name would only make things more difficult. Alex's sister came and took the baby to her house.

The pain of separation was almost more than Chipo could bear. But her resolve held knowing she was doing what was best for her baby. She cried into the night, mourning her loss, knowing she would never see her baby girl again. Chipo slept in her grandparent's bed that night with Mary. Mary consoled her all through the long hours, praying and singing songs of praise and by morning Chipo was better, experiencing the comfort that only the Holy Spirit can bring.

Two days later the Perry's left, stopping only to pick up Alice and the baby. She was a beautiful baby and they believed if Ingrid saw her she would want this baby as her own.

14

Truth

HANS HAD BEEN ON the move for a year and a half now. He and his comrades had done a lot of killing. The rebel forces had slain many people as well, even non-military casualties and the feeling in the country was changing. People were tired of the violence. Jason Deke was no longer seen as the hero they had once looked up to.

Out of the original eleven men in Hans's group, only five remained. That was one of the hardest parts of this fight; losing one of your own. With every loss, hatred was stirred in the hearts of those remaining, driving them all the more to destroy the enemy.

Hans had never been a violent person. He was just thrown into this war. At least that is what he kept telling himself. He still hadn't found the man named Sam, the one who had killed his wife and child. He was searching, but for some reason Sam had alluded him, always just one step ahead. Hans traveled up and down the border area of Zimbabwe and Zambia trying to find him, but with no success. One day he had heard that Sam was near Victoria Falls, so following the lead, he went there making the long, rough trip in as short a time as possible, pushing and driving himself and his partner. But there were no rebel forces anywhere to be found.

He did however see a lady with a small child and it reminded him of Ingrid and Nyasha. He wondered what his little baby would be like if he were alive. He knew he would be walking and talking by now. How he missed his family. The pain was as deep as ever and it made his resolve even stronger to find this man who was responsible. He followed every lead he heard about, always hoping to locate him, but never succeeding. Every hopeful high was followed by the low that despair always brings, followed in turn by the bottle, an endless cycle.

Hans's obsession often caused problems among the men he fought with, especially with Keith. Keith had been commander of this group for ten years. They would lose a man here and there, but never so many in such a short time. Although indirectly, Keith knew some of the blame for their loss was due to Han's obsession. There were times when Keith was expecting Hans to be at a certain place at a certain time and he wouldn't be there because he was out looking for this Sam fellow. When that happened, Keith was forced to make adjustments; adjustments that were second best for the good of the group. He had lost two of his men, good men, on account of those adjustments.

Hans was supposed to be the backup for a mission. He was in charge of the mortar rounds and good at his job. When the men were in trouble and they called in for mortar fire, accuracy and speed were of utmost importance. Hans could deliver accuracy and speed . . . when he was there. But more and more frequently, Keith was forced to depend on others who were slower and much less accurate. All because Hans had left to go look for Sam in a remote area where no rebels had ever been. Keith reprimanded Hans more than once. He wasn't in the habit of losing men, and Hans's excuses were wearing thin.

When Hans first joined them, Keith felt for Hans's loss, but as time went on his patience diminished. Finally, he gave him an ultimatum; to do his job with them or go and fight his own war. Hans was very repentant and said he would be more careful and take care of business before going off to look for Sam. Keith understood what Hans was going through. He knew Hans was angry and just wanted to get revenge for his family, but if it was going to endanger a mission or the lives of his men, he was not going to allow it to happen ever again.

They had been camping near Kariba, engaging the enemy along the border. It looked as though Jason Deke was losing popularity with the people. He had started out as a "Robin Hood," but as time went on the people started realizing that all he was doing was disrupting life as it should have been. In the beginning Deke had told them they deserved more and he was going to give it to them. All he had done so far was make things harder for everyone.

The rebel forces traveled in convoy and when they came to a village, the men would take what they wanted, whether it was food, money or women. On the farms they disrupted harvest time and sowing season. That, combined with increased taxes to fund defense was taking its heavy toll on the nation bringing suffering to the indigenous people.

The government depended much upon mercenary groups in subduing the rebel forces. They were able to get information the government troops couldn't get. People would talk to the mercenaries, especially Keith. Keith had a way with people that made them trust him.

Moving on to the next village, Keith and his men found the rebels had been there, but had moved on.

"Keith, just let me take the headman out in the bush. I'll make him talk," Hans said through gritted teeth.

"No, Hans. I'll deal with it." Keith said, his eyes resolutely piercing him from beneath his firm brows.

Joining Mr. Shumba, the headman, under a tree, Keith soon had him totally at ease. Evening came and they were still talking. Mrs. Shumba brought them supper; a plate of *sadza* and relish, just one for them both to share. Keith had long ago adopted the local custom of eating from the same dish and casually took a handful of sadza, dipped it in the relish and ate. After the two finished the huge plate of sadza, Mr. Shumba told Keith what he wanted to know.

"I was waiting to see if you would eat with me or if you would be too proud. Neither you nor your men have stolen anything from us since you entered our village. None of you have touched our women or killed our cattle. Since you have shown me that you are really a friend to our people I will tell you what I know. I have heard that Jason Deke is on his way to the Sanyati area to meet with some foreigners, hoping to raise funds. Sanyati is a big area and I don't know which village in Sanyati he will be in, but my source is very good. He will be there."

"*Ndatenda, baba*; thank you, father," Keith answered with the familiar term of respect. "This information is very important for us. If we could get Deke we could end this conflict and the troubles would be over. *Baba*, I'm also wondering if there was a man named Sam in this group. One of my men has a very personal debt to settle with this man."

"Yes," Mr. Shumba spat on the ground, "there is a man named Sam. He came into my home and stole my ancestral necklace. If you find him could you please get it back for me?"

"I would be happy to retrieve your necklace for you. If we find these men where you say they are many people will be overjoyed and it might even mean a promotion for you from headman to chief."

Keith was pleased. Walking over to the men he gave the orders. "Men, get your gear, we're heading to Sanyati. I have just received some of the best intel that we have ever had. It could be the deciding factor in this war. If it proves true we might just be able to end this war with one blow." Turning toward Hans he said, "And Hans, you might get your revenge, Mr. Shumba said Sam is there too." Turning back to the rest of the men he exclaimed, "Let's get going, I want to move within the hour."

The men groaned, they were tired and had expected a bit of a rest, but they knew Keith would not be so adamant if he was not sure of his information. They were a loyal bunch and whatever they needed to do they would do it.

Keith pulled Hans aside and warned him. "Hans, we might be able to finish this war and you might get your man, but first off is to do your job. You can find Sam after we get Deke. That's an order, do you understand me?"

"Yes sir, I understand, but when I get him he's going to suffer."

"I don't doubt it Hans, just make sure you obey orders."

The trip to the Sanyati village was a long and dusty ride for the Perry's, Chipo's aunt and the baby. It was just a few months into summer and the rains were getting ready to start. It hadn't rained since the beginning of the year and the heat was becoming unbearable before the expected rains.

The first rains were always welcomed with joy. Relief from the heat was enough to make people happy, but even more significant, that first rain signaled the time to get the crops in, the beginning of a new farming season. The rains hadn't started yet and people weren't happy, they were just hot. Arriving at the village in the late afternoon, Rob spoke to the area pastor, Pastor Jacob Chinyoka.

"Hi Jacob, How are you? It's good to see you again."

Rob and Jacob exchanged greetings along with several others who were present. Rob then pulled Jacob aside to talk to him about the baby and her aunty.

"Jacob we have a very interesting situation. We have a lady and a baby who will need a place to stay while Lynn and I travel to Zambia." Rob went on and told him the whole story.

"We hope to get things worked out and be able to return within two weeks," Rob said in conclusion.

"No worry. The baby and aunty are very welcome to stay with my wife and me. I know my wife will be pleased to have the company," Jacob replied. "Please, don't worry about the time. We will take good care of them till you are able to return."

No service had been planned for that evening, but when people heard the Perry's were there, they began arriving at the church anyhow. They greeted the man and woman of God and although they didn't know who Chipo was, they were happy to meet her aunt.

Since so many people had come, a prayer time was in order. Rob had his guitar, so he and Lynn led the service.

"Let's begin by turning to Revelation 5:8," Rob began after they were all gathered in the front of the church.

"And when he had taken it," Rob began reading, "the four living creatures and the twenty–four elders fell down before the Lamb. Each one had a harp and they were holding golden bowls full of incense, which are the prayers of the saints." Laying his Bible aside, Rob began teaching. "I want to share a bit about intercession before we begin. The harp in this passage represents worship in song and the bowls were the prayers of the saints. When these two things are combined, worship in music and intercessory prayer, it becomes a very powerful tool for spiritual warfare. So as we begin today, I want us to start out singing praises to God, just worshiping and coming into His presence. Then we'll begin praying as the Lord leads. This 'harp and bowl' style of intercession might be new to some of us, but I believe it will be powerful."

Taking up his guitar, Rob began leading in worship. Soon the tangible presence of the Holy Spirit filled the room. After a while, as Rob continued to play his guitar, Lynn started praying. Sometimes the Spirit of the Lord would prompt Rob with what she was praying and he would start to sing the phrase she said, over and over in a song to the Lord. It didn't take long and other people started joining in on the singing and the praying. They had a great evening of prayer and when they were done, they felt rested and strengthened, ready to take on whatever the devil had planned for them.

The plans for the weekend included several services in a new area where a new church was being planted. Pastor Chinyoka had been visiting this area for three months now, teaching a Bible study and the time had come for a new church to be established. Beginning on Thursday, Rob, Lynn, and Jacob began teaching about God the Father and Jesus the Son, who they are and how we can be rightly related to them. Then they taught about the church and how the leadership should be set up. Lastly they taught about the Holy Spirit; who He is and what He does. They visited homes all around the area announcing that on Sunday they would have the first service at one of the local school classrooms.

On Friday afternoon during a much needed break, the Perry's and the Chinyoka's were at the pastor's house relaxing with their feet up, glad to be quiet in the heat of the day.

"How about you and I take a walk to see Alice and the baby," Lynn said to Precious Chinyoka. She was eager to see the baby again and make sure her guests were okay.

"Sure. Let me get some extra towels to take to them."

They walked the short distance from the main house to the hut where aunty Alice and the baby were staying. Finding the baby a bit fussy, Lynn decided to take her out for a walk and the other women joined them. Making a sling out of a Zambia cloth, Lynn placed the baby in it and hung it over her shoulder, supported on her hip. Seeing the curious look on the women's faces, Lynn explained.

"I saw the women in Mozambique carry their babies this way. It is much easier and puts less strain on my back than the way Zimbabwean ladies wrap their babies on their backs. So I always carry babies on my hip, Mozambique style." With the baby settled and secure, the three proceeded on their leisurely walk.

Arriving at the first village in the Sanyati area, Hans and the group of mercenaries came in quietly, guns up, ready to shoot. They were not only looking for the rebels, but also the foreigners that the rebels were meeting with. They quickly checked each home.

Arriving at Pastor Chinyoka's home, they thought they had struck the jackpot. Here was a foreigner. Roughly tying Rob to a chair, they started questioning him.

"Who are you?"

"My name is Rob Perry. What's this all about?" A violent smack across his mouth was the only reply Rob received to his question.

"We'll ask the questions. You just answer. What are you doing here?"

"I'm a missionary and we're starting a church here in this area on Sunday. The man you have in the other room is the pastor."

After some time, Keith realized his questioning was getting nowhere. He knew the headman was telling the truth about Jason Deke being in this area and he was sure that he would find the rebel meeting with foreigners, just as Mr. Shumba had said. Here was a foreigner, but he didn't fit the profile of any arms dealer or war broker Keith had ever met. This guy was too quiet and gentle to be what he had supposed he was. He had to get to the truth. Keith went outside the house.

"Where's Hans? I need him to get the truth out of this guy."

"He's still looking for the rebels. He wants to find Sam."

"Go get him! I need him here first. He can go looking for his revenge later."

The soldier obediently went and found Hans. He told him that Keith needed him to get the truth out of the American.

"I'll find out whatever he needs to know . . . and I'll find out where Sam is." Hans's reply was cold and calculating.

They had just brought Rob out to the front room when Hans came to the house. Ducking to get his huge frame through the small doorway, Hans entered the room. As soon as Rob saw him he knew who he was. He started to greet him, but Hans rushed forward and backhanded him. The blow was so hard it knocked Rob and his chair over into a heap on the floor.

"Okay, now I'm the one asking the questions. You tell the truth or I'll beat it out of you."

The man who had been guarding the front of the house had come in to watch Hans at work. Hans lifted Rob and the chair up and backhanded him again on the other side of the head, knocking him to the floor once more.

"I won't take any answer from you but the truth, so start talking. Who are you and what are you doing here?"

Lying on the floor, blood dripping from his mouth, Rob could only pray, trying to shake the feeling that he was about to die.

"My name is Rob Perry. I'm a missionary and we are here trying to start a church. It's the first time I have even been here . . . " At that Hans picked him up again and this time his huge fist struck a blow to Rob's face. Rob gave a groan and fell backward hitting his head on the floor. Quietly, almost in a whisper, Rob said, "Hans, I know who you are. I know your wife and child."

With a start Hans looked at the man on the floor at his feet.

"Wha–what are you talking about? How do you know my name?"

"I know who you are," Rob said in a whisper. "You were in an accident and you were thrown into the river. You thought that your wife and child had died, but they didn't. They were swept over into Zambia and are alive and . . . "

Rob didn't get to finish. Hans grabbed him by the shirt and lifted him up again. He held Rob's face close to his own and asked again, "What, what do you mean? How can they be alive?"

"I'm telling you, they are alive and doing well . . . at the Kufue settlement in Zambia." The words just tumbled out of Rob's mouth and he prayed he was making sense and his words would get through to the heart of this hardened man. "She told me she swam out of the car window with the baby and when she broke through the water a large tree branch hit her and knocked her unconscious. She was swept over to the other side of the river and was hidden from view by a large rock. She said that Nyasha climbed into her arms and went to sleep. When she woke up it was dark, she was confused and couldn't remember what had happened at first. Then she remembered about the explosion and found she was in Zambia. She called for you, but there was no answer. She thought you were dead, Hans. She thought you were . . . dead. She walked . . . and . . . finally she found a road that took her to the Kafue Settlement. My wife and I saw her just a few months ago. She is alive, Hans. Ingrid is alive."

At the mention of Ingrid's name, all Hans's resolve and bravado melted like butter in the sun. Again, Rob found himself in a heap on the floor as Hans's grip on the front of his shirt loosened and his arms went limp. Hans didn't know what to think. How could this man know his baby's name? How did he know that Ingrid swam out of the car through the window? This was too much. Just then the door opened and in walked Lynn carrying the baby just like Ingrid used to carry Nyasha; on her hip. Hans looked at the two of them. His eyes locked on the face of the little baby. It looked so much like little Nyasha. Hans was overcome with confusion. He didn't know what to do.

Lynn saw her husband lying on his side on the floor tied to a chair. He had a split lip and there was blood still oozing out of one side of his head spreading all through his hair. His eye was swollen and a giant of a man stood towering over him. Shock registered on her face. She hadn't seen anything going on outside. The guard was in the house with Hans and no other soldiers or strangers had been in sight. So, she had just walked right in, only to find her husband in a very bad situation.

"What's going on?" she blurted. The giant looked straight at her and she was surprised to see tears welling up in his eyes.

Rob looked from Hans to his wife and with a crooked grin said, "Honey, I'd like you to meet Hans, Ingrid's husband."

Slowly, the realization of what her husband just said flooded Lynn and her look of shock and surprise turned to one of understanding. For a brief moment no one moved or spoke. Then, motivated by shame, Hans carefully set Rob's chair right and began to loosen his bonds. Once he was free, Rob stood facing the giant man looking up into his face, shame and grief written all over it.

"Hans, I'd like you to meet Nyasha's little sister. She doesn't have a name yet. The girl who gave birth to Nyasha wanted you and Ingrid to have this baby also, if you want her."

Hans reached out a hand to touch the baby's cheek, but when he saw the blood drying on his fingers he quickly drew it away.

"I'm so sorry. What have I done?"

Vivid pictures of bloody faces and mutilated bodies inundated Hans's brain and the shame and guilt that came with them was more than he could bear. What did it matter now if his wife and baby were alive? How could anything ever be the same again? How could they ever forgive him, let alone love him and want him in their lives. The thoughts drove Hans from the house in a rush leaving those remaining puzzled and confused.

The guard had gone out when Hans first started looking so stunned. The situation in the room was just too weird for his liking. He immediately found Keith and told him all he had seen.

"Well, these are obviously not the people we are looking for," Keith said. "I guess we need to keep looking."

"Should I go get Hans?"

"No, leave him. I have the feeling his days of fighting are over."

Hans headed straight for the only place where he thought he could escape the horrible thoughts and overwhelming pain. The local beer–hall was just a short sprint away. Entering the dark room, Hans angrily ordered a bottle of cheap whiskey. Ignoring the glass, Hans began to down the strong drink as quickly as possible.

Lynn stood for a brief moment watching the giant man fleeing, but then her husband's swollen and bloody face spurred her into action. Handing the baby to aunty Alice who was just outside the door, Lynn quickly returned and began to tend to her husband trying to wipe the blood from his face with a handkerchief.

"Ow, that hurts. Stop!"

"Oh, sorry, but we need to clean you up," Lynn replied as the tears welled in her own eyes. Checking him over carefully, she was increasingly overwhelmed with her own pain at seeing her beloved husband with blood all over his face. She turned looking for someone to help and found Precious standing close by, ready to assist.

"How can I help?"

"Please, could you get some soap and water for me? Also, bandages if you have them."

Precious quickly left in search of the needed items.

In the solitude of the room, Lynn's tears flowed unchecked as her husband just held her in his arms.

"I'm okay, Lynn. The Lord was here. It was His hand that protected me."

"What happened, Rob? What was that all about?"

Rob began to relate the story as Lynn sat quietly, listening intently. When Precious returned with the water, soap, and a first aid kit, Lynn began to take care of her husband's wounds as he continued his story, pausing occasionally to complain when Lynn pressed too hard as she cleaned or when the first aid cream stung. Lynn interrupted once or twice with a question, but soon the story was completed and both husband and wife were amazed and relieved that Rob had only sustained superficial wounds. It could have been much worse.

Breathing a huge sigh, Rob continued. "Well, what do we do now?"

Before she had time to answer, Rob knew exactly what Lynn's next words were going to be.

"Let's pray," they both said together and then grinned at one another.

Asking Pastor Chinyoka and his wife to join them, the four bowed their heads together. At first the room was silent as the foursome collected their thoughts and emotions. Then utterances of praise and worship followed as well as declarations of thanksgiving for the Lord's hand of protection. As the presence of the Lord fell upon them, the four became silent again, this time overwhelmed with His awesome greatness. Rob and Lynn ended the prayer time with a collective sigh. As their eyes met they each knew the other had heard the Lord.

"You go first," Lynn remarked with a gentle nod and a twinkle in her eyes.

"Well, I think I know where our friend has gone," Rob said referring to Hans. "And I think we need to go find him."

"Mmmm, I agree," Lynn said but then her brows knit together. "Where do you think he has gone?"

"To the nearest bar."

"That makes sense. What I was seeing is that the man has lived such a horrible life since the accident he can't imagine how he can face his wife. I'm sure it will be even harder to face God." Lynn paused for a second then continued. "But . . . that's exactly what he needs to do. How do we get him to that point?"

"I'm not sure about the how, but I have a sense God has something amazing in store for that man and I can't wait to see what it is. Are you ready? Shall we go find him?"

"I'm with you, my darling."

Jacob and Precious promised to continue praying and offered to care for the baby. Lynn thought for a moment but then declined the offer.

"I have the feeling this baby may play a significant part in softening Hans's heart. I think I need to take her along with me." After getting directions, Rob and Lynn headed for the beer–hall with hearts full of expectation.

Hans had almost finished a whole bottle of whiskey when the Perry's came through the door with the baby on Lynn's hip. Hans saw them enter, but he was too wasted to concern himself with them or anything else. Rob approached him with boldness even though it was obvious to him the man was very drunk. Lynn followed in his wake, praying all the while. The couple seated themselves at the table with Hans. They remained quiet for just a few minutes, just waiting.

Soon Hans noticed them and his attention was drawn to the baby in Lynn's arms. As he gazed upon the baby's face the countenance on his own began to change. Tears began to fill his eyes and Rob detected the look of guilt and shame once again. Hans began to mutter, but his words were barely discernable, spoken through the fog of the whiskey.

Rob and Lynn continued to pray calling upon the Holy Spirit to bring a spirit of repentance. Ordinarily the couple would never try to counsel or pray with a man in Hans's condition but they continued, spurred on by the prompting of the Holy Spirit. They didn't know what to expect, but they both sensed the Lord was about to do something amazing.

Pretty soon Hans slipped from his chair to his knees. He began to cry out the first understandable words they had heard since they had come into the beer–hall.

"How can she ever forgive me?" Hans cried over and over again. "How can you ever forgive me?" he blurted looking straight at Rob.

"Hans, those questions may seem like good ones but the forgiveness you need to be seeking is firstly God's forgiveness."

Rob couldn't miss the look of doubt and disdain that crossed Hans's face in spite of his drunken condition.

"Hans I'm going to pray a prayer I've never prayed before. I'm going to ask the Lord to make you completely sober. If that happens, will you believe in the Lord? Will you accept His forgiveness?"

Hans sort of shrugged and murmured a reply. "Humph. I don't get sober easy," Hans said in his drunken slur.

Rob got down on his knees in front of Hans and laid his hand on Hans's shoulder.

"Father God, because of your love for this man and because I know it is your will to bring him to salvation through Jesus, I ask you to make him fully aware."

Rob took Hans's face and held it up with both hands so he could look straight into his eyes.

"Hans Grundey, in the name of Jesus Christ, BE SOBER!"

Instantly, Hans head went forward and then came all the way up and snapped backwards. When it came forward again so that Hans's eyes once again met Rob's gaze, he was totally lucid. His eyes were clear, his countenance was changed and he felt as though the heaviness of months of drinking was gone. Completely gone! Hans raised his hands and looked at them, steady and sure. He looked once again into the face of the man before him. This time with wonder and surprise.

In that moment, he knew that he needed the forgiveness of the God Rob spoke of and he wanted to know Him like this man seemed to know his God. The horror of the past months and the guilt and shame that came with it was overwhelming in the light of the goodness and rightness of a mighty

God that must really care for him, even the drunken disgusting man he had become. Once again, his head fell forward, this time in repentance, and now the words he cried were directed to the God he was longing to know.

"Oh, God, forgive me."

He remained there on his knees with his head bowed for what seemed a long time. Finally, Lynn reached over and touched Hans's face. Tears were streaming down his cheeks and she wiped them away. "Its okay, your struggle is finished now. God has forgiven you and we forgive you too."

Rob nodded his head. "I forgive you, Hans, you didn't know, and anger has been your master for a long time now."

Lynn had taken the baby off her hip and handed him toward Hans. Hans retreated a bit, not knowing if he should take the baby or not.

"Take her, it's okay." Lynn handed the baby to Hans who took her and sat down just staring at the baby's tiny face that looked so much like little Nyasha's. He kept saying over and over again, "They're alive? Are they really alive?"

"Why don't we go back to the house, Hans? I'm sure you will be welcome to stay with us. There's so much you need to hear, and not just about your family. Will you come?" Rob asked as he rose to his feet.

Hans nodded his agreement and followed the couple towards the door. He was surprised once again when the man of God took a detour to pay the bar keeper what was owed.

Once they were back at the Pastor's home, Rob and Hans spent most of the remainder of the day talking. They talked about life and Jesus. Hans had gone to church as a child but was kicked out of Sunday School class because of his unruly behavior, and from that point on he had decided that if they didn't want him then he surely didn't need them. But Rob Perry was different. Hans could see forgiveness and love in the man's eyes. The man's wife had even forgiven him. He couldn't understand that. Rob looked bad, all puffy around the lips and one eye was turning a shiny black already.

"How can you so easily forgive me?" Hans voiced his questions. "And how in the world can your wife forgive me? I know that when I thought Ingrid was dead I could never forgive the man who had done that to her. I was looking for him when they called me in to get answers from you. I would have killed him if I found him. But here you are with my fist print on your face and you forgive me."

"Hans, what you did hurt me physically, but it's nothing that won't heal. Oh, I'll have a shiner for a couple weeks, but that will fade. When I need to forgive someone, I first look at all that the Lord has forgiven in my life. What you did was no worse than some of those things. Jesus forgave me for what I did, and so there really isn't any reason for me not to forgive you."

Rob looked square at Hans, "We all sin, Hans, and we all need forgiveness. There is only one person who has lived a perfect life on this earth and that was Jesus Christ. But the religious authorities of the day decided he needed to die. They thought he was a troublemaker, stirring people up and causing unrest. So they figured if they killed him, all his disciples would run away and that would be the end of it. What they didn't know was that Jesus was the Son of God, come to pay the penalty for our sins in order that we can live. God is a just God, like a judge in a courtroom, and He demands that justice be served. But Jesus paid the penalty for us. Hans, Jesus died for you. You have already confessed to me how dirty you are, how low. You need to confess the same thing to Christ. If you do, and you accept him as your Lord, your boss, and as the Savior of your life, he will forgive you for all you have done. Ingrid has done this. She has accepted Jesus as her Lord and Savior and he has put his signature on her and he wants to put his signature on you."

"What do you mean he wants to put his signature on me?"

"He wants you to live your life for him and allow his Holy Spirit to dwell within you. The Holy Spirit is God's Spirit living in you, empowering you and changing you from the inside out. Do you want to accept him Hans? He loves you and wants to remove your sins far from you."

"I don't know . . . I've done . . . horrible things. If you knew the things I've done, you would be shocked. Can God forgive a murderer? Can he wash away all the blood on my hands?"

"Yes Hans, he specializes in forgiving people like you. Can I show you about a man in the Bible that he forgave, one that had killed others?"

"Sure, I would love to see that."

Rob picked up his Bible and turned to the book of Acts 9:1,2.

"Look at this man. His name was Saul. He had letters from the ruling religious authorities of the day to find and track down the Christians. Some, he had imprisoned, but others he had killed. Stephen was one of those men that he killed. We can find out about Stephen in Acts chapter seven. Stephen's only crime was doing good and healing the sick in the name of Jesus Christ. God sought after Saul, and when he got his attention he sent someone to him to tell him about Jesus. Saul accepted Jesus and then . . . God forgave him. Saul was not much different than you and God used him mightily. His name was changed to Paul and he wrote the majority of the New Testament. God did many wonders and miracles through the hand of Paul. God's signature was on Paul. What do you say to that?"

"Okay. I see it. I'm convinced. I am ready. I feel dirty for all the things I have done and I just want to be clean again. What do I have to do?"

"Let's pray." Rob got down on his knees in front of Hans and started praying. He led Hans in a prayer of repentance, asking for forgiveness. Lynn stood beside Rob as they witnessed this giant of a man humbly surrender his life to the Lord Jesus Christ.

After a while, Rob continued as the Holy Spirit prompted. "Hans, in the Jewish custom of the Bar Mitzvah of a boy, there is a point when the young man would sit in a chair and the uncles would lift him up carrying him around the room. The father would run in front yelling, 'This is my son, whom I love, in him I am well pleased.' I see father God, doing that to you. He is saying 'Hans, you are my son, I love you, and I am so pleased with you.' God loves you so much Hans, He wants you to know how proud He is of you."

Hans shook his head in wonder and awe. How could anyone love him? How could anyone be proud of him? But something in his heart of hearts knew it was true. The love of the Father was real, even for one like him. The next thought pushed its way in, unwelcome, unbidden. What about Ingrid? Could his wife ever really love him again? Those thoughts chased away the first ones, causing Hans to doubt the Father's love as quickly as it had come.

As if reading his thoughts Rob continued. "Hans, God wants you to know there is nothing you could ever do that would make Him not love you or want you to be His son."

How could this preacher know what he was thinking? He hadn't said anything to Rob at all. He had only thought those questions. The tears came unbidden, unchecked. Rob put his arm across Hans's shoulder and just held him.

After a good twenty minutes Hans spoke up and said, "I still don't feel very clean. All these things I have done are still in my memory. What can I do to get rid of them?"

"The things in your memory will always be with you. You won't forget what you have done, but you can know that you are forgiven." Rob paused for a moment and then continued. "Being baptized will help you to be rid of the unclean feeling. When the first sermon was preached at the first church service ever to be held, the apostle Peter told the people the man they had killed, Jesus, was the Son of God. It says the people were cut to the heart and asked, 'What must we do to be saved?' Peter told them to repent, or turn away from their wrong doing, in the name of Jesus and be baptized so that they could receive the gift of the Holy Spirit. When we are baptized, the old person is buried in a watery grave and then we are raised to a new life, like Jesus' death, burial and resurrection. Baptism is a testimony to our acceptance of what Jesus did for us."

Rob turned to scriptures as he continued to explain baptism and the plan of salvation to Hans.

"There's a river not far from here. Are you ready to be baptized?"

"Yes, yes, let's do it right now."

As they left the house heading for the river, others followed. The crowd watched while Hans was baptized and as he came up out of the water his outward countenance revealed an inner change.

Turning to Lynn, Rob commented, "Well, the Lord has done so much in one day, I guess we might as well finish it all up with the baptism of the Holy Spirit."

"I feel the same way."

Rob again opened the Bible and briefly explained Hans's need for the Holy Spirit.

"Might as well get it all done right here, right now. I'm ready," Hans responded.

Rob and Lynn placed their hands on Hans and prayed for the filling of the Holy Spirit and then stood back and watched as the Spirit came in with a rush. There stood before them a transformed man, filled with the Spirit and bursting with joy. Hans's salvation experience had been one of the most dramatic that Rob or Lynn had ever seen and they were excited to see what the Lord had in store for this precious man.

15

Reunion

"I've got to get to Zambia to see her. Does she know that I'm alive?" were the first words out of Hans's mouth once they were back at the house.

"We wrote to her and told her you were alive, but we have never received a reply. We don't know if she ever got that letter or not. Our next ministry stop is in Zambia in the area where she is living. We were going to leave the baby here because she doesn't have a passport to get across the border. Do you have a passport?"

Hans hung his head, "No I don't have one either, but I could sneak across the border. It really shouldn't be that hard." Hans looked over at the baby and then at Lynn and Rob. "No I can't do that, it would be wrong and what if the border patrol did happen to spot me, they might shoot first and ask questions later. I've got to live now. Before it didn't matter, but I want to see my wife and child."

"We still have a couple days here before we go. We'll go straight to Ingrid's house and tell her about you and bring her right back here. In the meantime, maybe you can go to the embassy here and work on getting a passport for yourself and your family so you can get on with your lives."

Hans wanted to go to Ingrid as soon as possible, but he knew it would be impossible without a passport. Rob's suggestion was a good plan and he would be able to stay with the baby and get to know her while they were gone. It would only be a few more days. He had waited over a year, so a few more days wouldn't matter. That's what he told himself, but the ache to see Ingrid was still very real.

With Corrie's visit at an end, Ingrid and Corrie made the return trip to Lusaka with Nyasha in the back seat chattering the whole way. The time together had been very special for both of the ladies, but now Ingrid was anxious to get back to a regular routine. While she was in Lusaka she went to the NGO offices to get some needed supplies. Mr. Hertzog heard her voice in the supply room and sought her out to talk to her.

"Hi Ingrid. How is the work at Kafue going?" He didn't wait for an answer. "Ingrid, I have a job I need you to do. We have a project in the Sanyanti settlement in Zimbabwe and the nurse there had to go to Harare because of an illness. She will be out for about two weeks. I need you to go there and take over for her."

"Back to Zimbabwe! Are you crazy? They're still fighting there aren't they? I won't go back to Zimbabwe until I hear that the fighting has finished."

"I knew you wouldn't go if the war was still going on, but I just heard, not a half hour ago, that Jason Deke was captured by some mercenaries and most of his band of rebels were either captured or killed. The fighting is over. They showed Deke being taken away in chains on television."

Ingrid was shocked to hear this news. It was good news, but it didn't help her. Hans was still dead and it was because of this man, Deke, that he was no longer with her. How could she go back to Zimbabwe?

Mr. Hertzog spoke very softly to Ingrid, "I know that this is a hard thing for you to do, but I really need someone to go there and you're the most logical person. You know the area, the people and some of the language. It's been over a year since the accident and I think a trip into Zimbabwe would help you. It would at least help to finalize Hans's death."

His gentleness and caring heart were more than Ingrid could resist. She heard herself saying, "Okay, I'll go. I don't have much in the way of clothes with me. What do I do about that?"

"We'll give you money to buy everything you need. I see Nyasha is with you. I figured you would take him with you when you go. We would like you to leave tomorrow. It's only a four–hour drive, plus the time at the border. If you leave in the morning you should get there by afternoon." He opened a little safe behind his desk and pulled out some money. "That should be enough to take care of everything." He handed her the money, laid his hand on her shoulder for a brief moment, then turned away and went into his office. Ingrid looked down at Nyasha, "Well my son, I guess we're going to go back to the land of your birth. Let's go and spend this money before he takes some of it back."

Two days later Ingrid found herself on the road heading back to Zimbabwe after more than a year of being away. It had been hard for her to make the drive from Lusaka to the Zimbabwe border. Fear and resentment bombarded her thoughts. Memories assailed her, but not even the good ones brought her much comfort. The Zambian roads were in very bad condition and made driving a chore. But even the bad roads couldn't keep her thoughts from straying. Crossing the border post brought the turmoil to a peak. But the further she got away from the border post, the easier things became. Zimbabwe roads were in good condition compared to the roads in Zambia and as driving became easier so did her mind. She was able to focus on the Lord and worship Him.

There were two routes to get to the Sanyati Settlement from the border. If she went the short way she would have to go by where the accident had happened. Although she couldn't remember exactly where the explosion took place she would know she was near the place when she got close. She decided to take the longer way around. It meant going almost to Karoi before she turned off the main road, and it would add at least an hour more onto her time. She didn't care; anything to avoid such horrible memories.

Ingrid arrived at the Sanyati settlement at about two o'clock that afternoon. She went to the clinic and let them know she was there and asked where she would be staying. The nurse on duty introduced herself as Kudzai Nyoni and told Ingrid she would be using the matron's house at the end of the road.

"It's open and you should find the keys on the kitchen table. I left tea things laid out for you and the kettle is full, ready to boil. Have a nice cup of tea and get settled in," she said with a gentle smile.

"Thanks, that sounds lovely," Ingrid replied with a sigh of relief. A cup of tea really did sound good after the long, difficult journey.

Ingrid went to the house and found things just as the nurse had described. She carried all the luggage in, with Nyasha toting the smaller pieces, of course.

"Look at what a big boy you are, son."

Nyasha grinned from ear to ear at the praise.

Once inside, Ingrid switched on the kettle and prepared tea for herself and Nyasha. Nyasha loved his "milky" tea and always had to be included whenever mommy had her cup. The tea was refreshing and gave the two the boosted energy they needed to do the unpacking, which took only a few minutes. The clinic was within walking distance, so taking Nyasha by the hand, they headed out the door and down the road. She found the same nurse, Kudzai, on duty.

"I think everything is under control here if you want to take the rest of the day off. I'm sure we can manage."

"I think I'd rather work just to keep busy. When my hands have nothing to do, then my brain finds too much to do," Ingrid tried to explain sensing that Kudzai was an understanding type of person. Being back in the area that was home before the accident was proving to be a challenge and she found herself falling back into her old survival mode.

"Our church is having special meetings this week in the evenings. It's only two kilometers away and there have been some amazing things happening at the services. In fact Chipoka has given his life to the Lord and people are amazed that such a man would ever accept Jesus."

"Who is Chipoka?" Ingrid had never heard this name before and didn't know anything about him.

"Haven't you heard? He was the man that was called the ghost during the war. He is a huge man, like a giant, but they say he can move like a ghost. He was with the mercenaries and killed many men. He was ruthless and extremely cruel. The story is that he killed to get revenge for the death of his wife and child. Just two days ago he gave his heart to the Lord. I even watched him be baptized."

"Who's preaching at these services?"

"It's a missionary couple from Gweru. Their names are Rob and Lynn . . ." Before she could finish Ingrid blurted out "Perry? Oh, I want to go then. They are the ones who led me to the Lord. Where is the church?"

After getting directions from her new found friend, Ingrid headed back to the house with Nyasha in tow. She was thrilled at the prospect of seeing the Perry's again. She hoped to get to the church early enough to speak to Rob and Lynn before the service began. Quickly packing lunch and a bag for Nyasha, she got in the car and headed for the church with great anticipation.

The drive was a short one and Ingrid found herself at the church with plenty of time to spare. The only people in sight were a man and woman cleaning the building for the evening service. Ingrid went in and sat down on the front bench. The man and woman came over and greeted her and after talking for a short while they went back to their work. Removing a blanket from the packed bag, Ingrid made a bed for Nyasha, thankful that he would get a short nap before the service began. Nyasha made no protest. Quietly laying his head on his special little travel pillow, he curled up and quickly fell asleep.

Ingrid pulled out her well worn Bible and started reading from it. After a few minutes, the man who had been cleaning came toward her. Ingrid looked up into his gentle, smiling face when he stopped right in front of her. She smiled up at him and sensing that he had something to say she patted the bench beside her, inviting him to sit.

Folding his tall frame onto the short bench he said, "I've been praying for you while I was sweeping and the Lord impressed some things on my heart that I would like to share if that's okay with you."

Tilting her head to one side, Ingrid measured the situation in her spirit before she replied. "Yes, I think that would be fine," she replied and the peace of God warmed her all over. She didn't even know this man, but his gentle spirit set her at ease.

"The Lord told me to tell you not to be afraid or uneasy. He is in control. He is giving you back that which you have lost. That's all He told me and I don't know exactly what it means. Do you?"

Ingrid stared at the man for a brief moment, trying to soak in what he had said. She knew that God was speaking to her through him and assumed it had something to do with the fear she had felt crossing into Zimbabwe again. She knew God was in control and didn't fully understand why He was telling her this. She puzzled over the words "He is giving you back that which you have lost." What had she lost? Her first thought was of Hans, but she knew he was gone, so what else could it be? Her peace of mind? Her joy in the Lord? Was there anything else?

Breathing a sigh, she thanked the man. "I believe I do understand what the Lord is saying. Thank you for being sensitive to the Spirit and willing to be used by Him."

Nodding his thanks, he went back to the work he was doing and Ingrid sat thinking about what he said.

After a long while Ingrid realized she was hungry. She had some *biltong*, dried meat similar to beef jerky, in the car so she went out and retrieved it from the sun baked Jeep. After locking the car and slamming the door shut, Ingrid turned and headed back toward the church. She noticed people walking on the road toward the church and after a closer look she realized that the older couple was Rob and Lynn. She smiled and waved, hurrying her steps to go and greet her friends. It was then that Ingrid noticed the man walking beside them and she stopped dead in her tracks. He looked so much like Hans. Her heart skipped a beat in her chest and her smile faded. Memories rushed to her mind bringing a bitter sweet feeling that always followed thoughts of her husband. Quickly Ingrid said a prayer and composed her feelings as she continued toward the threesome.

"Or rather the foursome," she thought to herself as she noticed her husband's look alike carrying a very small baby in his huge arms. The man had not yet seen her and Ingrid was thankful for the brief moments to compose herself as she stared at the giant man. The closer they got the more she was struck with the awareness of how very much he looked just like Hans. At that moment Lynn gently laid her hand on the big man's arm. When she had his attention she directed his gaze toward Ingrid, pointing at her with her outstretched hand.

"Look, Hans," was all she said. Ingrid heard the words but comprehension was slow in coming.

But not for Hans. As his eyes met hers, the rest of his body ceased to function or move. Lynn gently took the baby from his arms and with a gentle nudge, propelled him forward. He inched forward, slowly at first and then broke into a full run. He moved toward her like a huge stallion in full gallop, Ingrid stood motionless trying to grasp what was unfolding in front of her eyes. If this man had been with any other person, Ingrid would have refused to believe what she was seeing. But somehow being in the company of the couple she had come to know and trust so much, the idea of her husband being there . . . alive, returned from the dead . . . was not so hard to believe. As soon as he covered the distance between them, Hans scooped Ingrid up in his arms and began spinning her around in circles as though she were a small child. He finally set her back on her feet, but would not release his embrace until Ingrid pressed her hands against his chest in order to look at his face.

"Is it you, Hans? Is it really you?"

The only reply he was capable of making was a weak, throaty, "Yes, Ingrid," as tears streamed down his face.

Now it was Ingrid's turn. She threw her arms around his neck in an embrace that would have choked a smaller man. Hans grasped her again in a huge bear hug, lifting her from the ground once more. The couple only released their hold when they realized they were at the center of a circle of people which included Rob and Lynn. They shyly met the gaze of several of the on-lookers and were met with smiles and looks of understanding. Rob and Lynn approached the couple and Ingrid noticed tears streaming down their cheeks as well.

"Do you two know each other?" Rob said and then laughed at his own joke.

Ingrid felt a small tug on her skirt and looked down to find Nyasha at her side, having awakened from his nap. Hans's attention was drawn to the small boy at the same time and he let out a loud cry as he dropped to his knees in front of the child. Startled, Nyasha let out a cry of his own and clung to his mother's legs until she picked him up and held him close.

"Shhh, shh, it's ok, Nyasha. This . . . is your daddy."

No amount of reassurance could pry his grip off his mother's neck, so Hans had to be content to just look at his boy . . . for the moment.

Feeling very confused, Ingrid turned to the Perry's with her questions.

"How . . . What . . . ?" Ingrid couldn't even manage to put her thoughts together enough to voice the questions racing through her mind.

Lynn responded with a question of her own.

"Didn't you get the letter we sent you?"

"What letter?"

"I guess you didn't. When we left you a few months ago, we stopped by your house on our way through the area like we had promised. We obtained information while there that we forwarded on to you in a letter. Specifically, that your husband was not actually dead as you supposed. But it appears you never received that letter, obviously. So Ingrid, here is your husband."

Ingrid fixed her gaze on her husband's face once more.

"How, how can you really be here? You drowned in the accident. I don't understand." Then she remembered the word of the Lord that the church caretaker had given to her.

" . . . He's giving you back that which you lost."

Smiling to herself, Ingrid looked around to find the gentle janitor. He was standing at the corner of the building, leaning on his broom, looking on with a smile on his face. Ingrid smiled back.

At Rob's suggestion, the young couple decided to remain outside while the Perry's went into the building to start the evening service, taking the baby with them.

Ingrid retrieved Nyasha's blanket and other things and the two of them found a quiet spot to talk, Nyasha following close behind. Ingrid spread the blanket out and once seated, they both started talking at once.

"Okay, you go first," Hans said with a chuckle.

Ingrid proceeded to tell her story. Remembering the accident and the days that followed brought tears once again and then speaking of her new found faith and love in the Lord Jesus Christ brought tears of a different sort. When she finished, Hans breathed a deep sigh and lowered his head.

"Well, that's . . . that's amazing." He raised his head to meet her eyes, tears flowing from his own. "My story . . . my story is . . . quite different."

Ingrid grasped his hand and squeezed it, sensing his hesitancy and discomfort.

"It's okay, Hans. The Lord has brought us together again. It's his hand, his doing. I know it is. So tell me your story."

Hans began. It was one of the most difficult things he had ever done. But he knew in his heart that the whole story needed to be told, right now, right from the beginning. Relating the horrors of the past months to his beloved Ingrid, seeing it through the eyes of his precious wife, made the memory of them more disgusting than ever.

Ingrid interrupted to ask only one question. "Are you the one they call *Chipoko*?"

"I was that man. I'm not anymore."

Seeing the tears in her eyes, Hans forced himself to continue till he came to the events of the past few days. Pausing briefly, he continued, now with excitement in his voice, the emotion of it all causing the words to catch in his throat now and then. His eyes met his wife's when he began to speak of his deliverance and the surrender of his hate to the Lord. His heart was thrilled when he saw there in her eyes the same joy and understanding he had come to know in his new found faith. Overwhelmed with emotion, the two could do nothing more than embrace and cry in each other's arms. After a few moments, Hans led out in prayer, praising and thanking their new found Savior for his amazing love.

"Jesus . . . how can we ever thank you enough. We are together. And we are brand new. Only by your grace. Thank you Lord."

That was enough. The little family remained seated, embracing each other, happy to be alive.

The church service wound down and finally came to a close.

"Hans. Ingrid. Are you still out there?" Lynn's voice called from the doorway of the church.

"Yes, we're here," Ingrid replied.

"Why don't you come inside and we can talk."

Hans came into the building, a sleeping Nyasha in arms. Ingrid followed behind with the blanket and bags.

Warm hugs were exchanged amidst tears and laughter and then the small group circled some chairs in the corner of the building to spend some time catching up.

Once seated, Ingrid again noticed the small baby Lynn still held in her arms. Curious she peered closely at the small bundle.

A gasp escaped her lips as she looked into the baby's face. "That baby looks so much like Nyasha did when he was small. Who is this baby?"

"This is Nyasha's baby sister and she is yours if you want her." The reply came from Lynn as Ingrid watched Hans take the tiny baby, resting her on one arm while holding Nyasha in the other, a difficult maneuver for most men but not for this big "papa bear" of a man.

For the second time in the space of one evening Ingrid was shocked beyond words.

"What . . . how . . . ?" was all she managed to stammer.

Rob started out to fill in the details.

Nyasha's biological mother is the granddaughter of our good friend Alex Dube, a pastor in the *Silobela* area. We met the granddaughter, Chipo Sibanda several months ago."

"She's such a special young lady . . . " Lynn inserted.

"And beautiful," Rob continued. "Anyhow, after the birth of her first baby . . . Nyasha, Chipo disappeared. Her grandparents, Alex and Mary, were very concerned for her. We had been praying for this young lady for a long time asking the Lord to bring her home and back to Jesus. Then one day when we were in *Silobela* for a seminar, Chipo returned, out of the blue. It was a beautiful reunion," Rob said as the memory brought emotions to the surface and he paused to compose himself.

"It was . . . " Lynn stepped in where her husband left off. "Chipo gave her life to the Lord that same day. It was so much like the parable of the prodigal. It was so amazing to watch the beautiful transformation in her."

"Soon after that Chipo realized she was pregnant . . . again. What is so ironical is that the father of this baby is brother to Nyasha's father. Chipo struggled for a time to maintain her faith when she realized she was pregnant, but the Lord's grace and her grandparent's love and acceptance saw her through. When the baby was due, we were back in the area again and by then Chipo was totally convinced that the best thing for her baby would be to give it to the family who is raising her first child."

"We were so surprised when we found out that family was you!" Lynn exclaimed. "The plan was to bring the baby and her aunty this far and leave them here when we went on to Zambia tomorrow. We planned to find you there, assuming you and Hans would be there together by now, and make plans for the baby."

"But God had other plans. So this little girl is yours if you want her," Lynn finished with a smile.

Ingrid looked at the precious bundle sleeping in her husband's arms. "It appears my husband has already made that decision," Ingrid said with a twinkle in her eye. "How could I say no? Yes, I would love to adopt this baby also. Wow! I got my husband back and a new baby too. This is all too amazing."

Hans wanted to name the baby after Ingrid, but Ingrid didn't like that idea at all. They finally settled on Renee Rose Grundey. They didn't give her an official Shona name, but the villagers gave her the name *Kudzai*, which means "praise."

The next day the Perry's had to leave to go to Zambia. Hans and Ingrid had decided to stay in Zimbabwe for the time being. They felt it would be easier to get the new baby's birth certificate and passport in Zimbabwe rather than in Zambia. Ingrid gave instructions to the Perry's to tell Susan and the church the news.

"Please tell them we will come see them when we get a chance."

"We certainly will Ingrid," Lynn replied. "We plan to be gone for six months, but we will be sure to stop here to see you on our way back through."

"*Fambai Zvakanaka*, travel well," Hans said in the traditional Shona "good-bye."

"*Chisarai Zvakanaka*, stay well," came the response as the two couples parted company rejoicing.

16

Restoration

Pastor Joseph Mpofu had returned to the *Silobela* area for the third time to minister with his friends and mentors, Rob and Lynn Perry. After much prayer and discussion, Joseph was feeling very positive about the prospect of moving to the area to minister full time alongside Pastor Dube.

Rob Perry and Alex Dube had seen the need for added manpower for many months. The churches were growing and the workload was becoming more than Pastor Dube could handle. The plan was that Pastor Dube would work with the churches closer to his home area and Pastor Joseph would work with those further away.

When the Perry's had introduced him to Joseph, Alex liked him immediately. His youth and energy were balanced with a humble spirit and a teachable heart, a good combination for a young pastor to Alex's way of thinking. He saw in Joseph a genuine love for the people as well as love for the Lord. This final visit was the deciding factor toward a permanent move. They were all in agreement. Joseph Mpofu was to become a permanent addition to the churches in *Silobela*.

Joseph wasted no time. He moved out to the rural area just a day after the Perry's left. He started working with Mr. Dube right away and Alex soon was aware that along with his tender heart, God had given Joseph an amazing gift of healing.

On Joseph's second Sunday in the area, he was invited to minister at the church in Pastor Dube's home area. It so happened that this day was Chipo's first Sunday back to church after a long period of recuperation. As Joseph took his seat at the front of the church, his attention was immediately drawn to the lovely girl sitting with the children. She was absolutely the prettiest girl he'd ever seen, no doubt about it, but even more than that, he was attracted by the love of the Lord he saw on her countenance. He didn't know who she was or where she came from but he knew that he wanted to meet her. It was hard for him to concentrate on any part of the service that day. When it came time for him to preach he stumbled through his prepared sermon, unable to concentrate, losing his place more than once.

Chipo thought to herself, "Who is this man? I was only gone for a few weeks. Where did he come from?" She noticed that he glanced her way frequently and she averted her eyes so he wouldn't see her looking back.

He sure is a handsome man. I'm surprised no one told me there was another pastor in the area, Chipo pondered to herself.

When it was time for Chipo to go out with the children, she asked her younger brother to take them out in her place.

"I haven't heard a sermon in a long time," was the excuse she gave him.

When the pastor lost his place for the third time Chipo smiled to herself thinking he'd never make it as a preacher.

Maybe he has other gifts, she thought.

At the end of the service Joseph asked if there were any who wanted prayer, inviting them to come forward. Chipo wanted to go forward just so he would pray for her, but she knew she couldn't do that so she stayed in her seat and watched. When he started praying for people he seemed to be a different man. He didn't just say a prayer, he talked to God and she could see he was listening also. She was amazed at the words of knowledge he had for people. They were "right on" every time. There weren't any amazing miracles that Sunday. Even so, Chipo saw the depth of the Lord in Joseph Mpofu and she liked what she saw.

None of this was lost on Mary Dube. She immediately saw there was something happening between the two young people. There was a twinkle in Chipo's eye that she had never seen there before. And why is she sending her little brother out with the children? Chipo loves to teach the children. Mary's thoughts continued. Why does the preacher seem to be stumbling over his words? Mary smiled to herself. She knew exactly what was happening.

She remembered when she first met Alex. He was a handsome young preacher back then. She was just a school girl, but old enough to know when she was in love. Soon it was apparent that Alex felt the same way and it was only a short time until they were married.

I suppose this is not such a bad idea, Mary pondered. The two might make a very good match. I wonder if Joseph has plans for lunch today.

Both Chipo and Joseph were glad Mary had made the lunch invitation. It was a meal Chipo would remember always, although she couldn't even tell what she ate. Once the meal was finished, the older couple discretely excused themselves and the two younger people found themselves alone.

The conversation was light and easy as the two shared from their hearts. They found out they had a lot of things in common. Joseph loved to swim as did Chipo and they both loved to teach children.

"Teaching children is just . . . well, just more fun. They accept things so easily . . . the Bible, things of the Spirit . . . "

Joseph paused and Chipo jumped in. "They have no trouble just believing."

"Yes, that's it." The excitement in Joseph's eyes matched what he saw in Chipo's.

Joseph and Chipo started seeing each other and before long they became a couple. Their culture normally dictated that a young couple do their courting in secret until they were ready to marry, but both Joseph and Chipo felt the need to break tradition because of Joseph's position in the community. They also realized the need for Joseph to be very careful that he didn't neglect the rest of the church. But in reality the church people thought it was a good idea. They felt their new pastor needed a wife.

In the months that followed, the churches in the *Silobela* area grew rapidly. The church in the Siyezi township of *Silobela* offered Joseph some land right by the church building where he could build a house, grow crops, and even raise a few cattle. They liked this young man very much and wanted him to stay.

After only five months Joseph and Chipo decided that they would get married. Chipo's happiness was tainted by only one thing.

"My father says that I am dead and won't even greet me if he sees me. I wish things were different. I would love to see my father come to know Jesus like we do. He just doesn't trust anyone or anything. My heart is so sad for him," Chipo shared one evening under a starry sky.

"Chipo, I know we've already approached your grandfather in your father's stead, but I really feel that I need to talk to your father and ask his permission to marry you as well." Joseph thought for a moment then continued. "I am not going to send my uncle to your father. I will go myself. I think he needs to get to know me, and I need to share Jesus with him."

As Chipo's guardian, Alex had already given permission for them to marry. Joseph had approached the elderly gentleman in the traditional way, first using his uncle as a *Dombo*, a go–between, then later the two families met face to face.

Traditionally the two families would have met several times over a period of months to discuss *lobola*, the bride price, until a suitable agreement was made. Then the young man would begin making the payments and continue to do so until the full *lobola* price was paid.

Immediately after the first payment is made, the couple is allowed to move in together and are considered by tradition to be married. Sometimes years would pass while the young man worked to pay *lobola*. Only after the entire amount is paid would the couple plan their church wedding.

But because of Joseph's position in the community, the two families had decided to have an official church wedding right away. Although this was not the normal custom, they knew it was important for the whole community to witness their vows as soon as possible.

They wanted a simple wedding at the church and a nice but inexpensive reception at her grandfather's home. Alex had already started gathering some dirt from the anthills to make a walkway and dance floor for the wedding reception. When the anthill dirt was mixed with dung and water it could be used like cement to make a beautiful paved area for the reception celebrations. He drew on the ground with a stick mapping out the area to be paved. Mary was already busy cutting and sewing together long strips of cloth to be used as streamers to decorate the dance area and the walkways.

The couple had written to Pastor Rob asking him to perform the ceremony and they had already received his affirmative reply, and his heart felt congratulations. His P.S. read, "Lynn says she can't wait and requests the honor of baking the cakes for the reception." The Perry's scheduled return to Zimbabwe was two months away and the wedding was set to take place a month later.

Spurred on by the fast approaching wedding, Joseph pursued his plans to talk to Chipo's father. "Pastor Dube, I really want to talk to Chipo's father and get his blessing for our wedding. He is, after all, her father. I also want to talk to him about Jesus. Chipo would love it if he would accept Christ and become a Christian."

"Please Joseph you must call me Sekuru or grandfather. After all you're marrying my granddaughter and soon you will be family." Alex smiled at Joseph, "I haven't heard anything about Simon in many months now. With Chipo and the boys here I've had no opportunity to go that way. I think it would be good to visit with him. I can plan to go with you to his home on Tuesday next week if that works for you."

Joseph readily agreed to the plan. For some reason he had been feeling an urgency in his spirit about speaking to Chipo's father.

Four days prior to the anticipated visit, Joseph and Chipo had begun fasting and praying about the upcoming meeting with her father. When the day arrived, Alex and Joseph set out on foot for the area where Simon Sibanda lived with his two remaining wives and thirteen children. Chipo remained at home and spent the time praying. As Joseph and Alex walked to Simon's home, they prayed.

Joseph was a bit apprehensive about meeting Chipo's father. Most of the things Chipo had told him about her father weren't good and that really didn't help matters. As he had prayed for Simon Sibanda, Joseph had recognized a spirit of bitterness eating away at him. He was glad Alex was with him, but he knew that when it was time to talk about Chipo, Alex would leave the room so he could talk to him alone.

They arrived at the house just before eleven in the morning. It was a very nice home. The dirt was swept and the round huts were laid out nicely within the fenced in area. Joseph noticed a foundation in the corner of the enclosure where a hut had once been. He assumed it had been Chipo's house that had been left empty and allowed to deteriorate according to traditional beliefs, providing a place for the spirit of the dead to remain. The belief perpetuated fear that if anyone occupied that space the spirit of the deceased would be angry and somehow bring retaliation upon the family. Joseph hated that tradition and even more so in this case when he knew his beloved Chipo was very much alive.

As the two men approached the gate they were aware the place was very quiet, too quiet. There were several people in the yard, but something was obviously wrong.

"Joseph, you better wait by the gate until I see what is happening. Something isn't right here. Either someone has just died or is about to die."

After only a couple of minutes Alex returned.

"Chipo's father is very sick. He's dying. You won't be able to talk to him about marrying Chipo. His wives say he has not eaten in four days and they don't expect him to make it through the day."

Alex turned to go but then noticed that Joseph wasn't leaving with him. He watched as Joseph opened the gate and walked on into the yard.

"The Lord wants me to see him. I can feel the presence of the Lord right now. I've got to go in."

"Okay, I'll take you in and introduce you to Simon's wives. I know the oldest wife goes to church sometimes and I'm sure they won't mind if you pray for Simon."

They approached the two ladies and Alex made the introductions.

"Joseph, please meet Nora and Amanda Sibanda."

Joseph greeted the ladies and then Alex continued.

"We would like to pray with Simon before we go, if that is okay with you."

The ladies nodded their agreement and ushered the two men into the sick room. Alex was shocked to see Simon's appearance. He appeared to be already dead. The only indication that he was alive was the slight rise and fall of his skeletal chest as he took small shallow breaths. His eyes were open, staring blankly at the ceiling.

Joseph wasted no time but went right over to Simon's bed. Taking a bottle of oil from his pocket, Joseph poured a small amount into his hands and handed the bottle to Alex. As he rubbed the oil between his hands he began to share with the women about anointing the sick with oil.

"In James 5:14, 15 it says, 'Is any of you are sick? He should call the elders of the church to pray over him, and anoint him with oil in the name of the Lord. And the prayer offered in faith will make the sick person well; the Lord will raise him up. If he has sinned, he will be forgiven.' There is nothing magical in the oil. The oil represents the Holy Spirit and invites his presence to come."

He then laid his hands on Simon's head and chest and said, "In the name of Jesus Christ, the Son of God, I command this body to become strong again." At that Simon's breathing started becoming stronger, but the vacant look remained in his eyes. "In the name of my Savior and Lord, Jesus Christ, who died for our sins and heals all of our diseases, I command the spirit of bitterness to leave this man. Go now! I command you!"

Simon's back arched so high that only his head and feet were touching the mattress. He let out a scream and then fell back on his bed. Everyone thought he had died. His eyes were now closed and all was quiet.

"Simon Sibanda, get up!" Joseph commanded. Simon's eyes opened and he looked around at all the people in the room. His gaze rested on Joseph and he asked, "Who are you? What's going on here?" At that, bedlam broke loose in the room. The women and the children began screaming with joy, dancing, and jumping around the small room. Simon didn't know what was happening.

"I don't understand. What . . . what happened?"

"Simon, this is Joseph Mpofu. He is our new pastor," Alex began, not knowing quite how to explain it all. "He's been with us for about six months. He just prayed for you and commanded an evil spirit to come out of you. You were dying and through his prayers, Jesus Christ has healed you," Alex spoke loudly trying to make his voice heard over the excitement in the room as the two wives elatedly relayed the story at the same time.

Simon's response was to look at his much emancipated body and say, "I'm hungry. Would you two join me for something to eat?" Alex and Joseph just nodded their heads.

After the women left to prepare the food and the children were shooed out, Alex and Joseph were able to talk to Simon. Simon knew something had happened that had changed him. He felt different. It was like a heavy weight had been lifted off his shoulders. He was sitting up in bed and kept rotating his shoulders, first one way then the other.

"Mr. Sibanda," Joseph started, "I know you don't know me, but Jesus does and he wants you to know that he loves you and wants to be your friend." Although Joseph wanted to talk about Chipo he knew this man's salvation was the first thing that needed to be discussed. "I don't know what you know about Jesus, but I want to tell you about him."

Joseph went on to tell Simon all that Jesus had done for him, how he came as a baby, grew up, died on the cross and rose again. Simon listened to all Joseph had to say. Just as he was finishing up the Lord spoke to Joseph.

"I know during the war those white boys treated you wrong," Joseph said. "You didn't deserve it, but I want you to know Jesus was there with you and he was protecting you. It was Jesus who led you to leave the hospital when you did so you wouldn't be killed."

"How did you know about all that? Alex, have you told him about these things?"

"Mr. Sibanda, no one told me about these things. Chipo has told me you were beaten by some white men during the war, and you hated white people, but that's all. The Holy Spirit sometimes shows me things. He told me this about you. The most important part is not about what happened, but that he protected you from death because he has something for you to do."

Simon was at a loss as to what to say. He had heard a lot of this before from Martha. His dear Martha. How he missed her. The memory, on top of all that had just happened brought tears to his eyes. He didn't know why he was crying, but he couldn't stop.

"Mr. Sibanda, Jesus wants you to accept him and confess his name before men. Would you do that now?"

Simon heard himself answer, "Yes, I want to accept Jesus." Joseph and Alex were overjoyed. They held Simon's hands while they prayed with him. Simon accepted Jesus Christ as his own Lord and Savior in the same bed on which he was dying in his sins just a few minutes before. After he prayed he wanted his whole family to hear what had happened and what Jesus did for him. Nora came in right at that moment with some food for the three of them, but Simon said it could wait.

"Call everyone. I want them to come here because we have something very important to tell them."

When the family had gathered in the yard Simon, standing on the front porch, spoke first. "You saw what happened to me. I was healed and delivered right here not an hour ago. Mr. Dube and Mr. Mpofu have told me about Jesus Christ and I have accepted him as my Lord and Savior. Now I want you all to listen to what they have to say."

Joseph spoke to the family about Jesus and gave words of knowledge for some of them. One of the boys had cut his leg very badly a week ago and it was infected. Joseph prayed for him and right before their eyes the infection left and the cut was healed. After their discussion the entire family accepted the Lord and gave their hearts to Him.

"Well, I guess we need to start a new church in this area Joseph."

"Yes, we'll definitely need one here."

The men went back into the house and ate their lunch. They had a nice visit while they ate. After lunch, Alex excused himself and Joseph cleared his throat.

"Mr. Sibanda, I need to talk to you about something very important."

"What could be more important than what you have already talked to me about?"

"Chipo."

At the mention of her name Simon became very quiet. He looked down at the floor like he had lost something. When he looked up again he had tears in his eyes.

"What about Chipo?"

"Sir, I want your permission to marry her."

Simon only stared at the boy before him. He had no idea this young man had come to ask him permission to marry his daughter, the daughter he had pushed out of his house and life, the daughter he refused to admit was alive.

After a brief moment Simon smiled and said, "Boy, you may marry Chipo. But first I need to see her. I have made a very big mistake and I need to make amends." Joseph didn't know what to say, he was so overcome with joy.

Vigorously shaking Simon's hand he said, "I'll go get her. I'll go right now."

Joseph ran out of the house and found Alex. In his excitement he was barely understandable as he relayed the story to the old man. Alex stood there with a smile on his face as his imagination filled in the gaps. Joseph quickly ended his narrative saying, "We need to go now," and he turned on his heels, headed for the gate. Alex wondered to himself how long it would take Joseph to realize he had left the old man in the dust. All the while Simon stood in his doorway, watching with a huge smile of his own.

Joseph covered the distance in half the time it took him and Alex to walk it that morning. Everyone gathered around him as he told Chipo the news of her father, first of his salvation and then of his permission for them to marry.

Chipo's excitement and joy matched Joseph's. When Joseph told her that her father wanted to see her, she couldn't wait to get to his house. They walked briskly in that direction, but in a very short while Chipo was too tired to keep up the pace. Joseph realized that although he had eaten lunch, Chipo had not yet broken their fast. Leaving Chipo sitting by the road, he ran to a nearby shop and bought her something to drink, some bread and a candy bar. When he got back Joseph found Alex, who was just arriving from Simon's house, sitting there with her. After Joseph offered his humble apology for leaving him behind, Alex shared some news of his own with his granddaughter.

"After Joseph left, your father went over to your grave and kicked the gravestone over. He shouted, 'My daughter is alive and so is Jesus!' I think a new page in your life has just started and things will be a lot different from now on."

Chipo ate some food and then she and Joseph carried on to her father's house as Alex continued on toward home. It was a pleasant afternoon and the sun was warm on their backs.

"I just hope and pray my father is really serious about the Lord this time. My mother used to tell me there was a time when he went to church with her and he had accepted the Lord. That was before they were married. I never saw that part of my father. "

"I'm sure this time he has really accepted the Lord. The Lord worked really hard to get his attention and your father knows it."

When they were getting close to the house, Chipo's pace slowed. "I'm a bit scared. Are you sure it's all okay?"

"Yes, everything is all right now. Your father misses you and just wants to see you again. You heard what your grandfather said. He kicked over the tombstone."

Fear gripped Chipo's heart once again when they heard a shout and Simon came running out of the yard. But fear turned to overwhelming joy as her father's arms embraced her for the first time she could ever remember.

"Chipo, please forgive me. I have done you a great wrong. I am sorry for what I have put you through. I love you so much." Simon was holding her so tightly she couldn't even see his face. If she didn't recognize his voice, she wouldn't have believed it was her dad. She held on to her father tightly letting the tears flow freely down her face.

When they finally parted Simon led his daughter to the grave area. She saw that a gravestone had been knocked over and it appeared to have been smashed with a sledge hammer.

"Chipo, I knew all along you were alive. I pretended you were dead, but that was wrong," Simon confessed with head hung low.

Chipo could only nod her head in amazement and wonder at the man before her. Praise and thanksgiving filled her heart for the work of God's redemptive love in her father's heart.

Simon led Chipo from there to Martha's grave which was well kept with fresh flowers on it.

"Chipo, I loved your mother the best out of all my wives. She meant more to me than anyone. When you were born I almost divorced my other wives, but your mother wouldn't let me. She said that Jesus understood and I needed to continue to take care of them and the other children. I know that as I grew older, bitterness grew within me and it broke her heart. That's why I drank so much. Now things are different. I have a new life in Jesus. Did you know I accepted Christ . . . ? Of course you did. This young man of yours is quite a remarkable man. You know he asked my permission to marry you." Chipo only nodded her acknowledgement and smiled through the tears.

The threesome sat in the yard and visited for hours. Chipo could hardly contain her happiness.

Soon the discussion turned toward wedding plans. Throwing tradition to the wind Joseph plunged right in.

"Mr. Sibanda, about *lobola* . . . "

"Son, you have already given me more than I could ever imagine. Let's say that what you did for me is payment enough for my little girl." With that Joseph and Simon shook hands and Chipo stole away to make the announcement to her older mothers. The news was met with singing and dancing. A wedding was going to take place.

Chipo had told her father that they wanted an inexpensive wedding and her grandfather had already given the okay to use his home for the reception. Simon agreed, but when the time came he arrived with two cows that were to be butchered and enough vegetables to feed an army. The church family that now met at Simon's home accompanied him to the wedding, anxious to be a part of a celebration that was God centered.

Arriving the day before the wedding, Rob and Lynn warmly greeted the bride and groom. The news of Simon's transformation added to their excitement. Anticipation for the following day's event ran high.

The wedding day arrived. The bride was beautiful in her simple white dress and Joseph looked tall and handsome in his black suit. The wedding ceremony was conducted at the church and Rob did his best to keep it short and simple. But true to African tradition the service ended two hours later. The guests then made their way to Alex and Mary's home for the reception while the wedding party traveled by van to Simon's house for photos to be taken. Chipo's delight was evident when she arrived at her father's home and found that he had transformed the dirt yard into a beautiful flower garden in anticipation of his daughter's wedding photos.

Snacks and soft drinks were served while the guests waited for the arrival of the wedding party. Alex's place seemed transformed as well with decorations and flowers in place along the newly paved road leading from the gate and widening into the dance area at the back of the property.

The wedding van, carrying the entire wedding party, arrived amidst a flurry of singing and excitement. One by one they climbed from the van and formed two rows as if in military rank, guys on one side and the lovely bridesmaids on the other. The bride and groom were the last to disembark.

"It's amazing to me how many people can fit in one of those vans." Lynn commented quietly in her husband's ear. Rob only smiled and nodded his response.

With the music at full throttle on the sound system, the wedding party began dancing their way down the drive way toward the dance area with the bride and groom following in step, two steps forward, one step back, turn around, step, again . . .

The procession took a full twenty minutes to make its way to the dance area, amidst the excited cheering of the guests. Matronly ladies resplendent in their best dresses and lacy outdated hats added their own two step version to the dancing procession. Speeches and blessings were next on the program and then the wedding dinner followed by more dancing. It was a joyous occasion.

The wedding celebration was finished and all that remained to do was the clean up. Mary gathered the last of the dishes. Her hands were busy, but her thoughts were far away. She longed for her grandchildren, Chipo's babies. The loss was still heavy on the older woman's heart. Mary's thoughts turned to the young couple who had been whisked away to some unknown destination. Her granddaughter and new grandson–in–law would need a young one to keep them from being lonely. After all it was tradition. In most cases when a couple got married they would set up housekeeping with a younger sibling to care for, given to them by the parents. But in this case Chipo already had two young ones of her own. There was no need to provide a younger sibling. But how could this be brought about? Mary knew the place to start would be to talk to her husband and then with Rob and Lynn.

Mary found the three she sought seated together around the fire drinking the last of the soft drinks. Not wanting to waste a moment's time, Mary plunged right in.

"You know in our custom it's very important that the new couple not be alone. Usually if they don't already have children we would send one of their younger brothers or sisters to live with them. But Chipo has two children already. If we could get the children back, then they would have a family and could live their lives in peace."

Lynn and Rob looked at each other. They were startled at this suggestion but could see on Alex's face that his reaction was quite the opposite.

"Weeell, that might be hard to do." Rob said, "The couple who have the children love them very much and have legal custody of them. They have passports and birth certificates and . . . everything. Are you sure that's the best thing to do?"

"In our culture, that would be the best way to handle the situation. I know it would be hard for the couple, but the children really belong to Chipo. She's their mother." This response coming from Alex was an even greater shock to Rob and Lynn. Not knowing quite how to respond, Rob quickly tabled the discussion.

The next morning as the two couples made their way to church, the subject was brought up again, this time by Alex as he walked together with Rob. Once again Rob didn't know quite how to respond. He did his best to let the subject drop but he knew he had not heard the last of it. Sure enough, later in the day when the foursome sat around the evening fire, enjoying their tea, Alex brought the subject up once more. The discussion went round and round for several minutes.

"If it was your grandchildren, wouldn't you fight to be a part of their lives?" was Mary's final argument.

Rob and Lynn had to agree to that. "I'll tell you what; we'll talk to the Grundey's and see what they think. I won't promise anything, but I'll talk to them," Rob said knowing that was the only answer he could honestly give.

The next morning Rob and Lynn headed for home with the promise that they would drive out to where the children were the next week. Once on the road, Rob and Lynn discussed the situation. They weren't looking forward to their promised task at all and made the decision to go straight to Sanyati that day instead of having to make the trip later.

Lynn had to speak. "How can Alex ask such a thing? It's wrong to ask this of Hans and Ingrid. They shouldn't have to make a decision like this."

"I agree, it's not right, but I promised that I would talk to them and see what they said."

They arrived at the matron's house that afternoon, only to be told that the Grundey's had moved. After getting directions they made their way to the new place. Hans and Ingrid were overjoyed to see them.

Once the two couples were comfortably seated in the living room, Hans plunged in with exciting news.

"We have left the NGO and are now working for the Lord here in the village. We have started a church and have 85 members so far. The only problem is that we don't have a very in-depth knowledge of the Bible. I'm sure that will change as we study and grow, but in the meantime, we need your help. Can you help us?"

"Yes, we would be glad to help you. God is so good! We have some studies that we use for new Christians and they would be great for the work that you are doing here."

Hans and Ingrid invited the older couple to stay the night since it was getting late in the day. Rob and Lynn were happy to accept.

They talked into the evening about church related things and Bible questions until Rob knew they had to get down to what they had come for. Looking to his wife for added courage, Rob began.

"We've just come from a wedding."

Rob proceeded to tell them the whole story of what had happened in Chipo's life right up to her wedding the past weekend, with Lynn inserting details here and there. Hans and Ingrid thought it was a wonderful story and were excited to know the biological mother of their two young ones now knew the Lord. Then Rob dropped the bomb.

"That brings us to the main reason we are here. The grandparents, Alex and Mary Dube, have persuaded us to approach you about returning the two children to their biological mother and her new husband."

For a moment Ingrid was silent trying to understand if she had heard correctly. But the look on Lynn's face made her understand that she had heard all too well. Her silence was quickly replaced with questions and arguments and then broken hearted sobs as the reality settled upon her. She quickly stood to her feet and retreated to the bedroom where her two beautiful children slept peacefully in their beds. Hans just sat there dumbfounded.

Lynn followed Ingrid into the bedroom hoping to comfort her.

"How could they want them back? They gave them to us didn't they? We love them. They're ours." Lynn just listened as Ingrid vocalized her deep feelings.

"Lynn, please would you tell Hans to come here?"

Hesitantly, Lynn made her way back into the living room. The pain in Han's eyes matched that in Ingrid's.

"Hans, Ingrid needs you to come in there with her," Lynn said as she gently laid her hand on Han's shoulder. She was moved to tears of her own as she felt the silent sigh as Han's body deflated under her touch.

Hans stood up and walked into the bedroom in a daze. The couple stood holding one another with their eyes transfixed on Nyasha and Renee. Returning to the living room after a long while, they excused themselves for the night and made their way to their own bedroom where they quietly talked long into the night, to one another, and then to their loving Heavenly Father.

In the morning Rob and Lynn were surprised to find Ingrid up preparing breakfast seeming almost cheerful.

"Hans and I talked for hours last night and we prayed about it. You may take the children to Chipo. She's their real mother, and as a mother I know that I would want my own children. We will miss them, but somehow I just know this is the right thing to do and that God has a plan. I don't know what that is, but I have peace in my heart. I don't understand it. Before we prayed, I was ready to fight this with everything in me. But as we prayed I just knew . . . It's okay. It will be okay. Hans is okay too. He's with the kids right now, packing some things. God has given us both peace about this. We know it will all work out. God is not going to forsake us."

Rob and Lynn were so surprised.

"Are you sure? I mean . . . Are you really sure?" came Lynn's broken response.

"Honey, I think they're sure. This is not how we anticipated this to go, Ingrid," Rob said as he laid his arm across his wife's shoulders. "We expected to have to make apologies and arguments to the Dube's on your behalf and then let the whole thing drop. But . . . as you were talking I got a glimpse of the Father's heart myself, and . . . somehow . . . I think you're right."

At that moment Hans entered the room carrying a child in each arm. He too was smiling. "Ingrid told you the news, didn't she? I don't know why, but I feel . . . good. I know God is up to something. I just can't wait to see what it is."

Rob and Lynn stayed for two days while Ingrid carefully packed up the children's things in no rush to have to say goodbye. Finally everything was packed and loaded into the car. They had just enough room for the two car seats in the back. Hans and Ingrid kissed the kids trying to hold back the tears for Nyasha's sake. They stood clinging to one another as the car pulled away finally surrendering to the tears.

As Chipo walked through the gate at her grandparent's home she was consciously aware of a deep feeling of contentment. Her time away with her new husband had been good but coming home was even better. They had arrived at Joseph's home in the *Siyezi* Township the day before and the following morning got up early in order to make the long walk to *Makoronga*. Chipo was anxious to see her grandparents.

With Joseph at her side, Chipo made her way toward the main house and then noticed the Perry's vehicle parked under the shade of the *Msasa* tree. Curiosity and excitement filled her at the sight of the familiar car. Making their way into the small house, the couple was met with an excited welcome from a roomful of people. Chipo embraced her grandmother, and Lynn Perry and greeted the two men. As they took their seats Chipo directed her attention to the baby on her grandmother's lap and the small boy playing quietly on the floor.

"Who are the children?"

Chipo's question was met with an awkward silence.

"Well . . . they are actually your children," Rob Perry said breaking the silence.

Now it was Chipo's turn to feel awkward. "What do you mean they are my children? Where did they come from?"

Mary said nothing but simply rose to her feet and placed the baby in Chipo's arms.

"It is not good for the two of you to be alone," Mary said as she took her seat again. "They are your children, Chipo. It is better this way."

Chipo's thoughts and emotions tumbled round and round as she looked from one child to the other. Looking into the sweet face of the baby in her arms, she was struck by what a beautiful child she was. The small boy at their feet bore such a striking resemblance to Ethan that it startled her and brought old thoughts and feelings to the surface as though it had all happened yesterday.

Seeing Chipo's reactions and her obvious confusion spurred Rob Perry to speak.

"Your grandmother approached us the evening of your wedding with the idea of getting your children back," Rob began.

The story continued aided here and there by comments from Lynn.

When they finished, Mary and Alex shared their hearts as well.

"It isn't right that someone else should raise your children now that you are settled with a husband. Besides . . . I missed my grandchildren," Mary confessed.

"But what about the children?" Chipo looked pleadingly between the faces of her beloved grandparents. Her heart was torn between her previous resolve and the pleading look on her grandmother's face. Seeing the faces of the two babies she had given up caused pain and confusion where she had once had peace and assurance. A heavy silence hung in the room.

Joseph was the one to break the silence as he took hold of Chipo's hand.

"We need to pray."

"Amen," Rob said, breathing a long sigh.

The room became quiet again as the six adults bowed their heads. Prayer was slow in coming.

"Lord, we need Your wisdom," Lynn prayed sincerely.

After another long pause Rob spoke up. I feel like we just need to worship for a while, find the Lord's face. He's got the answer, but I think we are too far from hearing. We're too close to the situation and not close enough to Him. Let's just give thanks and praise for a while and seek His face.

With great earnest this time the group pressed in to the throne room of God, first with thanksgiving, then with open hearted praise and worship. Soon a silence of a different kind settled in the room bringing peace once again.

The silence was finally broken by a deep sigh coming from Joseph as though filling him with a firm but gentle resolve.

"I don't know what the rest of you heard from the Lord, but I for one feel like we have made a mistake taking these children from their adoptive parents."

Looking from face to face, Joseph could see that the others were in agreement with him, even Mary.

"But I think the final decision is Chipo's, and we need to support her either way."

Squeezing his young bride's hand he became quiet.

Taking courage from her husband's words, Chipo expressed her own thoughts.

"I must admit that before prayer I was very confused. Who wouldn't want to claim such beautiful children? But as we prayed I remembered what brought me to the decision to give up this baby in the first place. It was the Lord. And . . . I don't think He has changed His mind. He had a purpose in all that happened concerning these two babies and that purpose is not completed yet. *Gogo* . . . "

Mary spoke up even before her granddaughter could finish.

"I know Chipo and after praying I must say I can see what the Lord is saying to you. I can't help but miss my grandchildren, but in my spirit I know what you are saying is right. Your grandfather and I will support your decision, I promise."

In an instant, Chipo was kneeling at her grandmother's feet with the baby in her arms as Gogo embraced the two of them. There was not a dry eye in the room.

❖❖❖

Early the next morning the Perry's left for Sanyati once again. This time they were accompanied by Joseph and Chipo after making room for them in the packed car. It was their desire to make their apologies personally and to assure the adoptive parents that this would not ever happen again.

Upon arrival, they were met by the Grundey's before they had even managed to get out of the car.

"We were expecting you," Hans commented as he opened the car door for Lynn. "We've been praying ever since you left us yesterday and we felt the Lord assuring us that you would return . . . soon."

"That's amazing! Well, here we are," Lynn said.

"Mama!" Nyasha cried when he saw Ingrid.

Introductions were made all around and the Grundey's invited their guests into the house. Once inside, Chipo handed little Renee to Ingrid.

"We have come to return your children. We want to apologize for the misunderstanding and we want to assure you that it will never happen again."

The two women embraced until the baby squirmed her protest at being squashed in the middle.

The group settled in the comfortable living room chairs and Ingrid served ice cold lemonade all around.

Conversation amongst the men centered on ministry opportunities and ideas while the women quietly shared heart to heart. After some time Rob suggested that they pray for a while and the others whole heartedly agreed.

As they prayed, the presence of the Lord fell in their midst in a tangible way. Expressions of worship were followed by a song and then a word or a scripture passage as the group flowed by the leading of the Holy Spirit. At times they stood with hands held high and faces raised. Soon they found themselves pressed to the floor under the heavy weight of the hand of God. Time passed and when Rob looked at his watch he realized they had been praying for more than an hour and a half. As he looked around the room he was moved in his spirit, sensing that this gathering was appointed by God and that God had bigger purposes in mind than any of them had yet realized. As he shared his thoughts they were met with nods of understanding and agreement.

Since the afternoon was getting late, Ingrid invited the two couples to stay the night. Her invitation was gladly accepted and the three ladies made their way to the kitchen to prepare supper.

The men in the living room were soon into excited conversation once again.

"I just sense that our meeting was not a coincidence," Hans expressed his thoughts to Joseph.

"I'm feeling the same thing," Joseph responded. "Listen, Rob and I have made plans to do a seminar together here in Sanyati next month. How would you feel about joining us?"

I would love that! In fact I was thinking that we should network together. That sounds like a great place to start and we'll see where the Lord takes us from there. What do you think Rob?" Hans asked.

"Yes! Sounds great! Somehow I have the feeling we are standing at the brink of something big."

Epilogue

One Year Later

THE OUTREACH IN THE *Silobela* area had been a great success. God had moved in a mighty way and many people's lives had been touched and changed. Rob still marveled at what the Lord had put together. Joseph Mpofu and Hans Grundey had done many weekend outreaches together and were an amazing duo. Both men still worked in their separate church ministries, but often came together for special events such as the one just finished.

With the ministry part of the weekend behind them, the team was enjoying a quiet moment around the evening fire. Well, as quiet as could be expected with the two children running around. Mary was in her element watching the antics of her two grandchildren.

"*Gogo*, help me catch him," came Renee's happy cry.

Mary marveled again at how the Lord had given her the privilege of being a part of her "Grundey" grandchildren's lives. Her thanks went up one more time to the Lord of restoration for all He had done. With those thoughts, Mary spied Chipo waddling toward her, heavy with child. Smiling at her granddaughter Mary made room for her on the bench beside her.

"It won't be long now," Lynn commented with a smile.

The group talked the evening away and then headed for their beds planning an early start the next morning.

After breakfast, the team gathered for a final prayer time and then said their goodbyes. Hans, Ingrid, and the kids piled into the car with the Perry's and they headed out together. The two families enjoyed a quick lunch together upon arriving at the Grundey home in Sanyati.

Back in the car with his wife once again, Rob made good time, wanting to get home before dark. The couple enjoyed the journey, talking and praying intermittently with Lynn, dozing now and then.

Home was very welcoming. The pair made short work of the unloading and unpacking, having had much practice in that chore.

"I'm tired dear, I'm going to bed," Lynn said with a yawn.

"Okay, I just want to hook up to the internet and check our emails. I'm sure we have a lot."

"Alright, if we get any letters from the kids come in and read them to me."

"Okay. Night, babe."

Hooking up to email Rob found a lot of junk mail, but then he spied a letter from his son. He started to read it and then let out a big whoop. "Honey, come here, quick."

Lynn entered the room seconds later, wide awake with anticipation.

"We're going to be grandparents again!"